Jobina snu_____
head on hi_____
head to look at him, to memorize anew the lines of his
handsome profile. Several times her lips parted but no
sound came. Her heart fluttered. Her eyes were dazed,
dreamy, for she was a woman in love.

"I didn't want this evening to end, Jo," Mark said when
they had reached the door. "I really didn't."

"It doesn't have to end yet. Come in and have a
nightcap."

"No, I don't think so." Mark swept Jobina into his arms.
He kissed her hair, her eyes, her neck. He pressed his
mouth on hers, drawing her closer, ever closer. Moments
later, he released her, stepping back. "If I come in, I'll
stay," he said quietly. "And I'm not sure I should."

"I want you to stay, Mark."

"I know, because it's what I want. I want *you*, Jo. But
you're a woman for a lifetime, not a night. I return to
Washington the day after tomorrow. My life is there. Next
week, next month, it may be halfway around the world."

"I don't care."

"I do. I'm in love with you, Jo. I shouldn't be. I have no
right to be, but I am. I think it happened the first moment
we met . . . I heard a little voice telling me to run fast and
far. I didn't, of course. Tonight, when we were dancing,
when I held you in my arms . . ." Mark sighed. "I
should have listened to the little voice," he said.

"I have a little voice too." Jobina unlocked the door. She
turned, holding out her hand. "My little voice has been
calling your name. So has my heart . . ."

Barbara Harrison

Impulse

BANTAM BOOKS
TORONTO • NEW YORK • LONDON • SYDNEY • AUCKLAND

IMPULSE
A BANTAM BOOK 0 553 17268 9

First publication in Great Britain

PRINTING HISTORY
Bantam edition published 1987

Bantam Books are published by Transworld Publishers
Ltd., 61–63 Uxbridge Road, Ealing, London W5 5SA, in
Australia by Transworld Publishers (Aust.) Pty. Ltd.,
15–23 Helles Avenue, Moorebank, NSW 2170, and in New
Zealand by Transworld Publishers (N.Z.) Ltd., Cnr. Moselle
and Waipareira Avenues, Henderson, Auckland.

Printed and bound in Great Britain by
Cox & Wyman Ltd., Reading, Berks.

For Aunt Anna & Uncle Henry Harrison,
With love

Chapter One

Jobina Grant parted the silken draperies and moved closer to the window, gazing out at Gramercy Park. Snow had begun to fall, lacy little flakes whirling and leaping on the wind. The trees, under their covers of white, rustled gently, as if whispering to each other. The streets were hushed and nearly deserted. Now the night shadows deepened and in the darkness came the joyous pealing of church bells, for it was Christmas Eve.

When finally Jobina turned from the window, she was smiling. Her amber eyes swept across the drawing room to the forest of poinsettia plants dressing the mantel, to the splendid kissing ball of mistletoe and boxwood in the arched doorway, to the dozens and dozens of gaily wrapped presents filling an antique toy sleigh. Her glance fell last upon the Christmas tree, a tall and graceful spruce bedecked with white velvet doves, porcelain cherubs, and ruffled pomanders. How lovely it is, she thought, reaching her hand to the laden branches.

A clock was chiming in the hall as William Grant entered the drawing room. He stopped suddenly and

7

stood quite still, caught once again by his wife's radiant beauty. It was her beauty that had drawn him, her beauty that had held him, driven him; but on this snowy night in 1918 it seemed almost more than his despairing heart could bear. "Jobina," he called softly.

"William, you're home!" She ran to him, flinging her arms about his neck. "I was beginning to worry. You're naughty to be so late. And on Christmas Eve!"

"I'm sorry. It couldn't be helped."

Something in William's tone troubled Jobina. Her smile fled and a frown creased her smooth brow. "Darling, I was teasing," she said. "You know how I am about Christmas. Perhaps I make too much of it. Do you think so?"

William did not reply. He looked past his wife, silently regarding the festive decorations, the mountains of presents. He took no pleasure in the glad scene. Instead, he calculated the cost of such holiday extravagance, all the many bills yet to come, and his handsome mouth tightened. His head began to pound; his throat was dry, aching. What am I going to do, he wondered miserably. What am I going to do? "Are Caroline and Daisy asleep?" he asked when he was able to speak.

"Oh, they've been asleep for hours. Miss Pym told them Santa Claus wouldn't visit until they were alseep. Isn't Miss Pym clever! I'm convinced she's the best governess in New York. We're lucky to have her. But then we're lucky in everything, aren't we?" Jobina paused. She studied William's pale, closed face and was newly troubled. "What's wrong, darling? What is it? Poor thing, you've been working night and day ever since

8

the war ended. You need a rest. You need pampering. Come," she said, linking her arm in his, "come and sit down. I'll fix you a drink."

Gratefully, William settled his tall frame on the damask sofa. He sat back, staring at Jobina. She was exquisite in a long gown of crimson velvet, pearls encircling her slender throat. Her fine chestnut hair was brushed atop her head in shimmering waves. Her eyes were twin pools of polished amber and they glowed with a wondrous light. "You are more beautiful now than the night we met," he said with a sigh. "Do you remember that night?"

Indeed she remembered very well. She had been Jobina Winslow then, the sixteen-year-old daughter of California timber baron Jonas Winslow. She had been his only child and so she had been shamelessly indulged, her every wish and whim anticipated. An army of servants had hovered over her from birth—nursemaids and governesses and tutors hired to attend the needs of Miss Jobina. She had been Jonas's pet, his hope for the future, and on the night of her sixteenth birthday, he had hosted a gala ball in her honor. Amongst the five hundred guests had been William Grant, a young and unknown attorney visiting San Francisco on business. Within an hour of their meeting, William and Jobina had fallen in love; within the week, a justice of the peace had pronounced them man and wife.

There had been a great scandal, for the ecstatic couple had returned from their elopement to find the gates of the Winslow estate barred to them and Jobina's belongings packed and waiting in the carriage house.

Later, an enraged Jonas publicly announced his intention to disinherit his daughter and the man to whom he scornfully referred as "that penniless upstart lawyer."

Jobina had no regrets. She had loved William Grant in the winter of 1912 and she loved him still. He was her whole life, coming before family and friends and even her two little daughters. "Of course I remember," she replied, smiling. "It was love at first sight. I will always remember."

"And when you do, will you be sorry?"

Jobina's lips parted. "Sorry!" she cried. "How can you ask that, William? I have never been sorry. Never. *Never.*" With shaking hands she mixed a brandy and soda and carried it to her husband. "I don't understand," she said. "You're frightening me. Darling, I wish you would tell me what's wrong. Something has put you in this strange mood. What is it? Please tell me," she urged again.

If William heard her plea, he gave no sign. He sipped his drink, staring straight ahead. Once or twice he passed his hand across his pale face. "I've been remembering too," he said at last. "I've been thinking about that night. I can still see you walking toward me in the moonlight. Lord, you were the most beautiful creature I'd ever seen. You took my breath away."

"I intended to. I knew you were the man I was going to marry."

"You didn't know all you would have to sacrifice." William raised his glass and drank deeply. In the bright light of the chandelier he looked haggard, much older than his thirty years. "If you had known . . . ." he began, but the words died in his throat.

"It would have made no difference." Jobina sank down beside him, smoothing his fair hair. After a moment she covered his hands with her own as she gazed into his soft blue eyes. "I don't understand what this is all about," she said. "I told you long ago that Father's money meant nothing to me. He was wrong to do as he did. He was cruel, but it's in the past. Why do you bring it up now?"

William did not reply immediately. He could not, for he saw the confusion, the pain, in Jobina's face, and it was like a knife ripping at his heart. "Forgive me," he murmured. "Forgive me, dearest. It's just that . . . Oh God, I'm so afraid I've failed you."

"Failed me? Why, I can't imagine life without you."

"It would have been a better life."

"You must never say such a thing!" Jobina cried in alarm. "Never think it! You have given me perfect happiness. And as for my *sacrifice*, we are hardly paupers. Look around, William. Look at this house, at the treasures in it." She rose, walking to a small antique table upon which were several French porcelains. "Look at this lovely swan. I know it was dreadfully expensive because I peeked at the bill. You've showered me with treasures. Caroline and Daisy also. Their rooms are so filled with dolls and toys, it is hard to walk. Sometimes I wonder if you have a secret money tree."

No, thought William, merely an endless chain of creditors. But now they are demanding payment. They are making threats and I can do nothing about it. I will be ruined. We will all be ruined, my innocent Jobina. "Forgive me," he said again, very quietly.

11

Jobina's response was interrupted by the sudden appearance of the housekeeper, Mrs. Daltry. "Yes, what it is?" she asked the plump, white-haired woman.

"Excuse me, ma'am. It's the eggnog. Cook says the eggnog is ready. Will I bring it in now?"

A moment passed before Jobina remembered that this was Christmas Eve and guests were expected. She glanced quickly at William, then glanced away. "Not just yet. I'll ring, Mrs. Daltry."

"Yes, ma'am. But it's almost time for the party."

"I'll ring. Thank you, Mrs. Daltry. That's all."

"Yes, ma'am."

"Darling, I'm sorry," Jobina said when the house-keeper had gone. She returned to William's side, nestling her head on his broad shoulder. "I'm getting scatter-brained." She sighed. "I quite forgot about the party. It's too late to cancel it, but perhaps I can . . . encourage . . . our guests to leave early."

William's chaotic thoughts tumbled one on top of another. He wanted only to escape, to run to his room and lock his door against the world, but this he knew he could not do; he could not mar Jobina's Christmas. "Nonsense," he said. "I won't hear of it." He smiled, and in that instant he was himself again, handsome and carefree and young. "I've behaved badly tonight. Pay no attention to me." Tenderly, he caressed her shining chestnut hair, her milky cheek. "We'll have Christmas as usual," he announced with a heartiness he did not feel. "I'm not Scrooge, after all."

Jobina was relieved by the abrupt change in his mood, but she was not entirely persuaded. She knew something was wrong and she sensed it was serious, for never had he seemed so remote, so torn. "Is there anything you want to tell me?" she asked, fearing the answer even as she spoke. "You're . . . you're not ill, William?"

"I wouldn't dare be ill. You would smother me in quilts and mustard plasters." He put his arms around Jobina, holding her close. "You make such a fuss when I'm ill."

"Because I love you."

"I love you, my dearest. You and our girls are everything to me." William's eyes grew misty as he considered his sweet, trusting daughters and the ways in which their lives would soon be changed. He considered his failure, failure once grimly predicted by Jonas Winslow. Guilt assailed him. Without a word he left the sofa and walked across the room, stopping at the fireplace. He took up a bronze poker, stirring the flames into red and gold fury. After some moments, his troubled gaze came to rest on the mantel. There, amidst the profusion of holly and poinsettias, were Christmas envelopes for the servants, the postman, the milkman, the iceman, and the newsboy. "I hope you weren't too . . . generous," he said, forcing himself to smile.

"I tried to be sensible. Really I did, William. But I felt so sorry for Mr. Gentry. You know, our milkman? Poor thing, he lost his only son in the war. And then there was little Johnny Doyle. His brother was blinded in the war. His family has hardly any money and—"

"It's all right, Jobina. I understand."

"Do you, darling? I really *wanted* to be sensible. I *tried.*"

13

William could not help laughing at Jobina's youthful earnestness. He opened his arms wide and she flew into them, a vast smile lighting her lovely face. "You are the best husband in the world," she said. "You never scold me, not even when I spend all your money. George Thayer thinks you spoil me. I heard him grumbling to Irene when they were here for dinner."

"Never mind what George thinks. It's all right. Everything will be all right." William did not believe his brave words, but he wanted Jobina to believe them, if only for this night, this last Christmas in the house she cherished. "Mrs. Daltry must be getting anxious," he said softly. "Why don't you see to the party arrangements while I hurry upstairs and change. I promise I won't be long."

"You always say that," Jobina teased. "Then you stop to see Caroline and Daisy and you stay forever. Don't wake them, darling. Miss Pym will have an awful time putting them back to sleep."

"I'll be quiet as a mouse."

"Wait," she called, catching William at the door. "Have you forgotten the mistletoe? I haven't. I want my kiss." She stepped again into the warm circle of his arms, pressing her lips to his. A familiar thrill ran along her spine and she shivered in delight. "Yes, you must hurry," she murmured, "or I will never let you go."

Jobina watched William climb the few stairs to the hall. In her happiness she did not notice that his shoulders were hunched, his head bent. It was the walk of an old man, but she saw only her young and handsome husband, the great love of her life. She smiled, spinning around to ring for the housekeeper.

Mrs. Daltry, carrying a crystal punch bowl filled with eggnog, entered the drawing room an instant later. The kitchen maid, Bridget, followed close behind with a tray of twenty crystal cups. "Will we be serving from the sideboard, ma'am?" Bridget asked.

"Of course from the sideboard," Mrs. Daltry snapped before Jobina had a chance to reply. "Where else? Tend to your work, girlie. Company is coming any minute and we're just now setting out refreshments."

Jobina heard the implied rebuke in her housekeeper's voice. She colored, for this was not the first such rebuke. "I am sorry about the delay," she said coolly, "but there is no harm done."

"No, ma'am, no harm." Mrs. Daltry adjusted her glasses on the bridge of her nose. "Still, I like my parties to run on time."

"It is not really your party, is it?"

Mrs. Daltry opened her mouth to speak, then appeared to change her mind. She shook her head, turning her attention instead to Bridget. "The cups go *here*. That space over *there* is for Cook's Christmas log. Will you never learn? Are you an imbecile? And fetch the linen napkins from the cabinet. Be quick about it!"

Jobina had the mildest of tempers, but now she felt a sudden anger rising in her. William had hired Mrs. Daltry and so she had mutely endured the woman's stern glances, her churlish moods. But not tonight, she thought, moving to Bridget's side. "I will not have servants badgered in my house, Mrs. Daltry," she said. "You will please mind your tone."

15

"As you say, ma'am. But it was Mr. Grant who told me to bring some order to his household. His very words, ma'am. There's no order if you let servants go their way."

Jobina was astonished by the housekeeper's boldness. She took a deep breath, clasping her pretty hands behind her back. "I will be the judge of that," she replied. "I have dealt with servants all my life. I hope the matter is settled. You are being paid to respect my wishes."

"Paid, ma'am?" Mrs. Daltry's unsmiling gray eyes blinked behind their polished glasses. She regarded Jobina curiously, then looked away. "Well, as you say, ma'am. Bridget, have you found the napkins yet?"

Jobina, to her horror, realized that she had been dismissed. She saw Bridget watching and she imagined the petty kitchen gossip that would ensue. She turned, and her long skirts rushed up about her ankles as she walked swiftly to the other side of the room. It was a retreat, she admitted, a battle lost, but this bothered her less than Mrs. Daltry's attitude. The older woman seemed to know something that she herself did not. It occurred to her that Cook, too, had lately assumed a different, almost superior, attitude. How strange, she thought, her chestnut brows drawing together in a frown.

William returned to find Jobina sitting in pensive silence by the tree. The punch bowl and cups had been arranged on the gleaming sideboard, along with a tray of gingerbread men, a tray of miniature plum puddings, and Cook's special brandied Christmas log. The candles had been lighted and now the scent of bayberry mingled with the scents of holly and spruce. Bridget, wearing a

16

starched black uniform and lacy white cap, stood quietly off to the rear. "A penny for your thoughts," he said, taking his wife's hand.

Jobina gazed at William, a slim and elegant figure in his new dinner jacket, his onyx studs tracing his crisp shirtfront. "Darling, you look wonderful! Like a leading man in one of those very British plays!"

"Is that good?"

"Oh, you're fishing for compliments."

"What were you fishing for a moment ago? You were a million miles away when I came in."

Jobina's amber eyes darkened. "I'm not sure," she said. "It's a combination of things." She was about to explain the nagging bewilderment she felt, when the doorbell rang. "Our guests are here," she said as she smiled, shrugging. "Merry Christmas, darling."

"Merry Christmas, my dearest."

Hand in hand they crossed the room to the hall. Mrs. Daltry was already at the door, collecting hats and coats and mufflers from the jovial crowd. William and Jobina greeted their guests together. There were exuberant handshakes and kisses all around and soon the drawing room was thronged with revelers. Last to arrive were George and Irene Thayer, neighbors on Gramercy Park and the Grants' closest friends. "Well, they've done it again," George muttered, surveying the scene. "Another expensive party they can't afford. Not to mention that heap of presents they can't afford."

Irene, small and dark and pretty, frowned at her husband. "Then don't mention it. George, this isn't the right time."

"No? When is the right time? That's what I'd like to know. Just when is the right time?"

"Hush. Jobina is coming over. You wouldn't want to upset Jobina, would you?"

"Perish the thought." But George's determined bad humor was stilled by a glimpse of his radiant hostess. He watched her threading her way through the guests and his face softened. He saw the lights catch the gold in her hair, the vivid red of her gown, and he seemed to sigh. Irene, observing the change in her husband, laughed. "Jobina," he said, holding out his hands. "You are the finest decoration in the room. Merry Christmas."

"Thank you, George. You're looking awfully fine yourself," Jobina replied, her eyes twinkling. "There's eggnog, but I know you would prefer whiskey. All the men are drinking whiskey, much to Mrs. Daltry's displeasure. Poor William has to be bartender."

"Someone should tell that woman her place," Irene said.

"Are you volunteering?"

"Goodness no." Irene laughed again, tossing her black curls. "I'm volunteering George. He is always telling people their places. Aren't you, love?" she asked, kissing his cheek.

George was not listening. His dark eyes were thoughtful, fixed on a far corner of the room. "I think I'll find William," he said. "Excuse me, ladies."

William Thayer was a man of average height and average, pleasant appearance. He was a wealthy man—the inheritor of a large family trust—though no wealthier than many in the room tonight. There was nothing unusual about him, and yet wherever he was, his presence was immediately felt; businessmen older and wiser than he sought his advice, ill-tempered salesclerks fawned over him, space was made for him in crowded theaters, and paths cleared on crowded streets. Now a path cleared amongst the tangle of guests and he followed it, stopping a few times to call brief holiday greetings. "Double whiskey," he said when he reached William.

"Coming up."

He sipped his drink, his eyes fast on his beleaguered friend. "What's the matter with you?" he asked finally. "You look terrible."

"Thanks, George. And a very merry Christmas to you too."

"I'm serious. I saw how pale you were from across the room. What the hell's the matter?"

"Isn't it obvious? You know the problems I have. You're practically my banker. How much money have you lent me in the past months? I've lost count." William turned and glanced quickly around, worried that he had been overheard. "We can't talk here," he said. "I . . . I'm in trouble. It's bad."

"We'll go to your study."

"I'm bartender."

"Don't be an ass, William. Your guests can help themselves."

"No, I can't leave. I've been waiting all night for Chadway to arrive. He hasn't, and I'm afraid that may be a bad sign. I may be in more trouble than I know."

"What has Chadway to do with anything?"

William walked several steps away. He sat upon the

cushioned window seat, holding his aching head in his hands. "Oh God," he groaned.

"Tell me what Chadway has to do with this," George persisted.

"I don't know where to start." Martin Chadway was the most senior of the partners of the law firm of Chadway & Turnbull. He was a difficult man under any circumstances, and he had small affection for William. He had not bothered to disguise his feelings; it was well known around the firm that he considered his young associate to be imprudent and more than a little naive. Now William drew a great breath. He closed his eyes and, as he did so, he could see Martin Chadway, all pompous dignity and bristling white mustache. He felt sick. "It's very complicated," he said. "Chadway could ruin me."

"Why should he? He need only be patient and you will ruin yourself. This party, William. This ridiculous display. Have you lost your senses?"

"I wanted Jobina to have a happy Christmas. You can understand that."

"I understand that if you continue to treat her like a child, she will continue to act like a child." George paused. He turned his head, smiling at a group of men gathered by the bar. "You'll have to serve yourselves, fellows," he called. "The bartender's quit." After a moment, he turned back to William. "You're right about one thing." He nodded. "We certainly can't talk here. Come along to the study."

"Not now."

"Why not?"

William shrugged. He took a handkerchief from his

pocket and pressed it to his damp brow. "Because you'll lecture me," he replied in a ragged voice. "I can't listen to another lecture. Things have always come easily to you, George. You don't know how it is to fail. You don't know what it is to make a wrong step."

"I can help you, William."

"No, there is no help for me."

"What foolishness is that? You've had difficulties before. You've come through them. You will again. Every problem has its solution. Every . . ." George did not finish. His eyes narrowed as an alarming suspicion began forming in his mind. "You haven't done something stupid?" he asked. "William, you haven't dipped into the firm's trust accounts?"

"I needed money. It . . . it was to be a loan. Just a loan."

"Good Lord!" George stared at his stricken friend, shaking his head in disbelief. Embezzlement, he thought, shocked to his very soul. At the best it will mean disbarment; at the worst, prison. "Listen to me, William," he said, lowering his voice. "You must get hold of yourself. You must come with me to the study now. At once. We will discuss the matter and—"

"What is there to discuss? It's done."

"Listen to me. The books will not be audited until after the first of the year. The money can be replaced. There is time. We have a week yet."

A faint hope stirred in William. Slowly, he lifted his head. Across the room boisterous with voices, glittering with jewels and silks and candlelight, he saw Jobina. "She is an innocent," he said, sighing. "If I could spare her

21

this . . . But it is a lot of money, George. And it is dangerous for you to be involved. You've been a good friend to me. I can't ask it. I won't."

"You are in no position to argue. Come with me now or I will send all your guests home. I swear I will."

William struggled to his feet. He gulped the last of his drink and then followed meekly after George. "I meant only to borrow the money," he explained again, but in the noisy room his words were lost.

"Have you kept an accounting?" George asked when they had reached the hall. "An accurate accounting?"

"To the penny. I'm afraid it's quite a lot of money."

"Well, you never did do things halfway." George turned, looking into William's soft, sad blue eyes. "What I don't understand is how you could allow the situation to go so far. Did you never consider the consequences? How did you expect to make it right?"

"My investments were—"

"Investments! I warned you about your investments time and time over. You refused to listen."

William had no answer, for he knew his friend had spoken the truth. He had been warned, not once but dozens of times, and not only by George. His own broker had urged caution, to little avail. While other men of his age had been content to build their portfolios slowly, he had rushed headlong from stock to stock. He had eschewed sound investments, pouring his money instead into risky speculations. He had gambled and almost always he had lost. "I did very well early in the war," he said quietly, as if to himself. "I began to think my fortune was made. Funny, isn't it?" His reverie was interrupted by the sudden loud ringing of the doorbell. "Chadway," he said, exchanging glances with George. "No, it's all right, Mrs. Daltry. I will see to the door."

"Yes, sir."

"Go ahead, William," George said, putting a reassuring hand on his shoulder. "If it's Chadway, you don't want to keep him waiting."

"I suppose not."

"Then go ahead."

Pale and uneasy, William walked toward the door. He straightened his jacket, his tie. He stopped in front of the hall mirror and ran a hand through his fair hair. "Good evening, Martin," he said with a wan smile. "I'm glad you could come. Where is Sophie?"

"She is at home. This isn't a social call. I am here on business."

"Business?" William took the old man's hat and coat, carefully brushing snow from the rich wool. "The weather is so bad tonight. Perhaps you would like to stop in the drawing room for a drink."

"This isn't a social call," Martin Chadway repeated. "Let us find a quiet place where we can talk."

George had been watching the two men and now he stepped forward. "Hello, Martin," he said, extending his hand. "It's nice to see you again."

"Hello, George. Merry Christmas to you. I regret we won't have an opportunity to talk. I am here on business, you see."

"Business! But this is a party. Where's your holiday spirit? Surely business can wait until—"

"No, it cannot."

23

For one of the few times in his life, George did not know what to say. He felt the mounting tension; he saw William absolutely still and white, and his apprehension grew. "Very well, Martin, if you insist." He nodded. "But I insist the three of us have a drink together first. You may find it profitable. I heard some news about United Textiles today. I believe you will be interested."

"I'm sorry. As much as I value your opinion in such matters, I must decline." Martin Chadway opened the cover of a heavy gold pocket watch. "It is getting late," he said, snapping the cover shut. "William? I trust there is a quiet room somewhere."

"My study."

"Excellent. George, please make my apologies to Jobina."

"Don't alarm her, George," William said anxiously. "Don't spoil the party." He stared at his friend, a brief, tired smile edging his mouth. "I appreciate what you tried to do. Thank you."

"William—"

"It's no use. No use at all." He turned, striding away. He did not look back. "The second door to your left, Martin."

William's study was deep in shadows, with only a single lamp burning on the antique desk. There were framed English sporting prints on the walls and two leather wing chairs near the hearth. Books, largely unread, lined the mahogany shelves. "I could do with some light," Martin said.

"Certainly." William put his hand to a wall switch, then went to a side table that held a brandy decanter and several glasses. "A drink?" he asked.

"No." The old lawyer settled his ample girth in a chair. He took a thick, sealed envelope from his pocket, laying it across his lap. "Sit down," he said; it was an order.

"I would like to have this over with."

"Indeed." But Martin had waited years for this moment, this terrible reckoning, and now he was enjoying it. He stroked his white mustache. He plucked a cigar from a gold case and lighted it, exhaling great clouds of smoke. With his free hand he tapped the envelope. "Your fate, William," he said, raising the envelope aloft. "More to the point, your undoing."

A worried George returned to the party to find Jobina waiting for him. He saw questions in the amber of her eyes; he saw confusion, and he sighed. "Martin Chadway is here," he explained. "He and William are in the study. A business matter."

"On Christmas Eve!"

"It is rather an urgent matter. He sends his apologies."

"What's wrong, George? What is happening? William was behaving very strangely earlier this evening. *Everybody* seems to be behaving strangely. I thought I might be imagining it, but I'm not. I know I'm not." Jobina's voice was strained, breathless. Color flared in her cheeks and her mouth trembled. "Is something wrong with William? You must tell me."

"What have I missed?" Irene asked, joining them. She had been smiling, but her smile vanished as she looked from Jobina to George. She saw his warning glance and she took Jobina's arm. "It is midnight," she said softly. "Look, the servants are bringing in the champagne. You must have the first glass."

"I don't want champagne. I just want to know what is wrong. Irene, something is wrong with William, and George won't tell me."

"I'm sure nothing is wrong."

"Of course not," George agreed. "It is as I said, a business matter. Come now, Jobina, you are being fanciful. And you are neglecting your guests . . . Ah, here is Bridget with the champagne." He took two glasses from the silver tray, giving one to Jobina and the other to Irene. Absently, he took a glass for himself. "A fine vintage," he declared, anxious to steer the conversation into safer waters. "Was it ordered from Mr. Raynor's shop? I must telephone him. My own cellar is getting low."

"I don't know. William orders our wines. George, were you telling the truth about William? Do you swear there's nothing wrong?"

"He is discussing a business matter with Martin. The timing is unfortunate, but there it is. Let's hear no more about it. This is a party, after all. I see Tom Bolton at the piano. Are we to have Christmas carols?"

Jobina allowed herself to be led to the growing crowd around the spinet. She did not join in the singing, nor in the laughter when some amongst them sang the wrong notes. She glanced often over her shoulder toward the hall, but there was no sign of William. William, she thought; my darling William, what is wrong? She drank a second glass of champagne, and a third.

It was almost one o'clock when George slipped away from the crowd, motioning Irene to follow. "Thank heavens," she said, touching a lace handkerchief to her pretty face. "I have been on pins and needles wondering what the trouble is. Has something happened to our William?"

"I can't explain now, Irene. Take my word it is serious."

"Is there anything I can do?"

"Stay close to Jobina. I am going to see what is happening in the study. William's meeting is lasting too long. And I wish you would find a way to get these people out of here. Find a way to send them home. There's been quite enough party for one night."

"Yes, all right. I shall do my best."

George's dark eyes were thoughtful as he hurried from the room. He rushed through the hall, his mind on William's predicament. He had no doubt now that the embezzlement had been discovered. The question, he said to himself, is how to handle Martin Chadway. He knocked once at the door of the study; when no answer came, he went inside. He winced, for the air reeked of brandy and cigar smoke. "Gentlemen," he said, quickly crossing the room to open a window. "Ah, that's better."

"You weren't invited to this conference," Martin said. "It is Chadway & Turnbull business, and as much as I value—"

"Please, Martin. I am sorry to interrupt, but we need not mince words. I am here as William's friend. What concerns him concerns me also." George sat down. He looked at the desk strewn with papers and open ledgers.

He looked then at William, at his ashen face, at his eyes burning too brightly. "I am here to help," he said in a quiet voice. "There are ways out of this. Get hold of yourself, William."

Martin twirled his cigar in his fleshy fingers. "Perhaps you do not know the seriousness of the matter," he suggested.

"I know everything."

"Do you know your *friend* is a thief?"

"Bah! William is not the first lawyer to . . . borrow from trust accounts. I don't condone it, but he is neither the first nor the last. The money will be repaid with interest."

"That may be easier said than done," Martin replied, smiling slightly. A cold light danced in his rheumy blue eyes. He leaned his head against the back of the chair and stroked his mustache. "There are shortages totaling some eighty thousand dollars."

"Eighty thousand!" George was stunned. He looked from Martin to William and then back again. "Eighty thousand! It's not possible."

"That is what we have discovered so far. It may be, as they say, but the tip of the iceberg. Your friend William has refused to provide an accurate figure. There is something else, George. William is deeply in debt. We sit now in a mortgaged house, very probably on mortgaged furniture. There is an outstanding bill at Tiffany's in excess of five thousand dollars. There are other bills, many others. The new Pierce-Arrow is not paid for. I will wager the servants have not been paid in weeks."

George rose angrily from his chair. "How do you know

all this?" he demanded. "You've been snooping around in William's private affairs, haven't you?"

"You forget who is the injured party here. A crime has been committed. A most grievous crime indeed." Martin dropped his cigar into a pewter ashtray. He gathered his papers together and stood. "I will leave you now," he said. "Rest assured I do not blame you, George, for any of this. I have the highest regard for you and the Thayer family."

"Go to blazes," George snapped, his usual caution deserting him. "I see now that you came not to set things right but to torture William. That is despicable. You are a despicable man."

"A crime has been committed," Martin repeated evenly. "It is actionable."

"If you move against William, all Thayer business will be withdrawn from Chadway & Turnbull on the spot. Others will follow my lead. I will see to it."

"That is your privilege. Good evening, George. William."

Martin left and there was a profound silence in the room. George reached for a chair and sank into it, his face grim. He was the same age as William, but he looked at him now as a father might look at a troubled and innocent child; in his look was fear and pity and, finally, helplessness. "William," he said, sighing, "you can't sit there all night holding your head. We must discuss this."

"Everything Chadway said was true."

"Eighty thousand dollars, William?"

"Ninety-two thousand. Exactly ninety-two thousand." He finished his drink and poured another, turning feverish eyes to George. "It all started ... It all started ... A year ago I had a chance to get in on the Madden Copper deal ... but I was running behind in my bills. I had no money ... I took ten thousand from one of the trust accounts. That's how it started. When Madden Copper went under, I had to recoup my losses. I had to ... Then the Burton Oil deal came along. I took twenty thousand more. They drilled and drilled. They never did find the bloody oil." He laughed suddenly and it was a terrible sound, a harsh, broken cry of pain. "They are probably still drilling."

"All right, William, all right. I see how it is. Never mind the money. The money isn't even the important part here. It's something else. It's Chadway himself. He wants your hide and he may get it too. He is out to destroy you. Why?"

"Chadway." William put his glass to his mouth, drinking thirstily. "Chadway. Chadway offered me a choice tonight ... what is that old vaudeville joke? Your money or your life? Is that how it goes?"

George jumped up. He went to William, snatching the glass from his trembling hands. "You're not making sense," he said. "Tell me what Chadway offered. *What* choice?"

"My money or my life. Yes. Yes, that's how it goes."

"William! William, for God's sake!" But George could say no more, for Jobina was standing in the doorway.

Chapter Two

"What are you doing to my husband?" Jobina asked, her voice rising in accusation. She rushed to William and knelt beside him, cradling his head on her shoulder. The aroma of brandy was overpowering and she scowled. "Don't worry, darling," she said. "I am here now. You mustn't worry about anything. You know George. He is just being a bully again."

"I resent that, Jobina."

"I resent you shouting at my husband. Can't you see he's not well? I'm surprised at you, George Thayer. I thought you were William's friend. You should be ashamed of yourself."

"*I?*"

"Please," William murmured, pressing his hands to his throbbing temples, "that's enough. Please don't argue." He pulled away from Jobina and sat back, struggling to clear his mind. "You misunderstood," he said. "George was trying to help. Go back to your guests now. Go back to the party."

"But everyone has gone home. It is late, William. You

have been in here for hours."

"Late? Yes, I suppose it is. I'm sorry."

Jobina rose slowly to her feet. She paced in a circle around the hushed room, her eyes wary and downcast. I must remain calm, she thought; I must remain calm or I will never get to the bottom of this mystery. "There is something you're not telling me," she said. "It has to do with Martin Chadway. Did he bring bad news?"

William clutched at the arms of his chair, as if for strength. "It's true there is a . . . a slight business problem," he replied. "George will explain."

"George will lie."

"What! Lie! Now see here, Jobina," George sputtered. "I refuse to be insulted this way. In less than five minutes you have called me a bully and a liar. I tell you I won't have it!" Irene entered the study and he turned, flinging himself into a chair. "You're just in time to hear my character defamed. According to Jobina, I am a bully and a liar."

"Really?" Irene laughed. "Well, people do tend to get carried away at this hour of night. I've brought coffee. We will all feel better after we have some coffee."

"I doubt it. I very much doubt it."

"Don't be a spoilsport," Irene replied cheerfully, winking at her disgruntled husband. "Jobina, will you help me? The servants are busy tidying the drawing room and I could find only these heavy cups."

Jobina picked up her skirts and walked rapidly across the room. "Something is wrong," she whispered to Irene.

"I know. Be patient. Men prefer to tell their stories in little bits and pieces. It's their way. Be patient."

"I shall go mad if I have to wait much longer." Jobina shook her head, clasping her nervous hands behind her back. "William isn't himself at all. He's been drinking, Irene. The brandy decanter is almost empty. It isn't like him."

"No."

"I'm frightened. I was so looking forward to Christmas, but this has been the strangest Christmas of my life."

A sheltered life, thought Irene. Sheltered by that ogre, Jonas Winslow, and then by William, poor, sweet William, who keeps Jobina ignorant of his worries. She lives in a dreamworld and it's a shame, for all dreams end. "I confess men are often a puzzle to me," she said aloud. "Oh, I know it is difficult for them too. So much is expected of men. Success is expected. A man can be kind and sweet and wholly admirable, but if he isn't a success in business . . ." Irene shrugged. She poured coffee into rosy porcelain cups, adding sugar and cream. "The quest never ends," she said. "Soon enough men lose sight of what is truly important."

"William hasn't. I agree he works very hard, but it isn't in some silly quest. It's to provide for his family. It's only for the money."

Only, Irene said to herself, startled by Jobina's artless reply. She glanced at the checks and ledgers and crumpled scraps of paper covering William's desk from end to end. She glanced at William's exhausted face and her spirits fell. "We ought to serve this coffee before it gets cold."

William and George had their heads bent over a ledger

as the women approached. William hurriedly closed the leather-bound book, sweeping a pile of papers to one side. He looked up at Jobina and gently, almost timidly, touched her hand. "You needn't stay," he said. "It has been such a long night."

"I don't mind."

"Well, *I* do." George's voice was curt, impatient. "In case you haven't noticed, we are trying to discuss business."

"Are you asking me to leave a room in my own house?"

"All right, you two," Irene said, stepping between George and Jobina. "It's late and tempers are growing short. Business can certainly wait until tomorrow or the day after. No? Very well then. I will be blunt. This skulduggery is putting everyone on edge. We, Jobina and I, would like an explanation."

"Good Lord, Irene!"

"Don't take that tone with me, love. What is the deep, dark secret here? Are you and William plotting to overthrow the government? To run off and join the circus? We are all friends. Let's have it out in the open, whatever it is."

The Thayers had been married for eight years and George was accustomed to his wife's candor. It was a trait he admired, but there were times when he found such candor irksome, times when he wished for a woman more yielding and discreet. "Are you quite finished?" he asked.

"Yes." Irene nodded, her glossy black curls bobbing about her small face. "Quite. You have the floor."

"How nice." George paused to collect himself. From the corner of his eye he saw William's hands clench rigidly atop the desk. It was a gesture of pain, and in that moment he felt utterly defeated. I cannot speak freely, he thought, looking at Jobina; I dare not. I can only hint at the truth or else risk making an impossible situation worse. "As I understand it," he began carefully, "William has discovered several . . . errors in his trust accounts. By coincidence, Martin Chadway also discovered the errors. He came here tonight to . . . review the matter."

"Errors?"

"Put simply, the books are not in balance."

"Oh?" Jobina was quiet, considering George's explanation. She seemed relieved. The tension of this night left her face and in her amber eyes was a lovely light. "Is that what the fuss has been about? But that isn't serious at all!" And, indeed, to her it was not, for she had the greatest difficulty keeping her own personal accounts in balance. Each month a generous sum was deposited to her account and each month she found herself overdrawn. She had made a joke of it, a joke she laughingly shared with William. "It's only money. I mean it's *mathematical*."

There is that word again, thought Irene with a sigh: *only*. What a dangerous word it is. "Jobina," she said, "I'm sure you can see now why William is distressed. He is expected to keep proper records. Martin Chadway expects—"

"Oh, Martin Chadway is a slave driver." Jobina rushed around the side of the desk and wrapped her arms about

William. "My poor darling." She smiled, kissing the top of his head. "You are no better at figuring than I am. Don't worry. George will help you sort it out. Won't you, George? You are very good at money things."

"Money things," George muttered. He lighted a cigarette and walked to the sofa where Irene sat. He sat beside her, impatiently tapping his foot. "They are children," he said. "Both of them. They haven't the faintest idea of what life is about. They haven't a clue."

"I have. I listened to you picking your way through polite words and phrases. Has our William been up to no good?"

George shrugged. He stared into the distance, seeing nothing. "Jobina probably needed a solid gold bathtub, or something equally fantastic."

"You can't blame Jobina."

"I blame them both. Damned children, I tell you."

"Beautiful children. Look at them. They love each other so much."

"Good Lord, Irene, what has love to do with anything?" George flushed angrily. He threw his cigarette into an ashtray and turned to his wife. "You are Jobina's best friend. You tell me what good love will do her when William is in prison."

"Prison!" Irene gasped. Instantly she clapped her hand over her mouth. She glanced toward the desk, but when she saw she had not been overheard, she returned her attention to George. "You don't mean that."

"Martin Chadway means it. I gather he's offered William some kind of choice. Knowing that scoundrel Chadway, it's no choice at all. It's a trick, some foul trick.

Not that William doesn't deserve punishment. He's done a terrible thing. But he doesn't deserve *Chadway's* punishment. It will be vicious and . . . Why did we ever take up with the Grants in the first place? We must have been mad."

"We were bewitched. They are such sweet people, George. Nobody can resist them. I've never heard anyone say a bad word about William and Jobina. Have you?"

"If 'thief' is a bad word, yes. I heard Chadway say it several times tonight."

"He respects you. You can get around him."

"I doubt it. I have a bad feeling about this." George was tired. His orderly, untroubled life had been disrupted by events he had not foreseen and did not fully understand. He sensed there was another piece to the puzzle, but what piece he did not know. "Well," he said slowly, rising to his feet. "I suppose I had best find out about the choice William was offered. Can you tend to Jobina? Her presence hampers things."

"I shall try . . . George? Must you resolve matters tonight? It really is late. Ian will be bounding out of bed in just a few hours, looking for the presents Santa left."

"I know. Tend to Jobina and I will do the rest." Warily, he approached the desk. Jobina was leaning over William, murmuring to him and making him smile. A woman's touch, thought George, as much in irritation as in wonder. "I see you are feeling better, William. Good. We have a lot to discuss."

"Now?" Jobina cried. "No, I won't allow it. William needs rest. There will be no more foolishness about books and balances tonight." She shook her head back and forth, staring stubbornly at George. "No more."

"You are trying my patience, Jobina."

"Then it is mutual."

William had spoken very little in the last hour. Now he too looked at George, shrugging his apologies. "Perhaps Jobina is right," he said. "Perhaps another time . . ."

"Another time? Did you hear that, Irene?"

"I can't say I disagree."

George threw up his hands. "Fine. As Jobina has pointed out, it is only money. What do we care about money?" He grabbed two ledgers from the desk, pushing them under his arm. "I will take these with me anyway. Just for the fun of it, you understand. Come along, Irene."

William stood. He walked unsteadily around the desk, holding out his hand to George. "Thank you," he said, a woeful little smile lifting the corners of his mouth. "You're a good friend. I hope you aren't angry."

"I am, but it will pass. I will return your ledgers tomorrow, after we've done with Christmas. We can have a long talk then. Buck up, William. Things always look better in the morning."

"If you say so."

"Good night," Irene called, opening the door. "You needn't bother to walk us out." She laughed. "We know the way by now. Good night. Merry Christmas."

"Merry Christmas." Jobina watched them go. She waited until their footsteps faded in the hall and then spun around to William. "Darling," she said, smiling into his eyes, "I am glad this foolishness is over at last.

You must rest now. Come upstairs and I will tuck you in."

"Soon. I am not quite finished here, Jobina."

"Of course you are. Besides, George has taken your ledgers."

"Give me just a few minutes more. Please."

"All right," she reluctantly agreed. "But just a *few*. I am going to time you, darling. If you're late, I will come after you with a stick. Really I will."

"Fair enough."

Jobina kissed his cheek. She picked up her skirts and went quickly from the room. If she had any lingering doubts about the odd events of this evening, she put them out of her mind. Men, she thought, shaking her head in amusement as she climbed the stairs; they make mountains out of molehills!

She stopped at the top of the landing. Above her, on the third floor, she heard the servants moving around in their bedrooms. She heard whisperings and, now and again, muffled laughter. She listened for a moment, frowning. After a while she continued down the carpeted hall to her daughters' rooms. She opened Caroline's door and tiptoed inside. It was a charming room, all lace and ruffles and white wicker, much like the room she herself had had as a child. "My sweet," she murmured softly, bending over Caroline's bed. She smoothed the girl's long golden hair. Then she straightened the silken quilts, moving an immense teddy bear to a chair. "Sleep well, Caroline."

Daisy's room was nearly the duplicate of her sister's.

There were more dolls, shelves of them, but the furnishings, at Daisy's vehement insistence, were the same. Jobina was aware of the small jealousies that arose in her daughters and, though she denied it, she was aware that too often she sided with Daisy. She knew why, for while Caroline was inclined to William's gentle, brooding nature, it was Daisy who most resembled him. Now, gazing down at the sleeping child, she smiled. "Merry Christmas," she whispered. "Sleep well, my lovely." She tiptoed out of the room and closed the door. "Oh, Miss Pym," she said, surprised. "I am sorry if I awakened you."

"Not at all, madam. I thought I heard a noise and was coming to investigate." Miss Pym, a brisk and capable Englishwoman of thirty-five, pulled her robe close about her. "There is nothing wrong with the girls?"

"No, nothing. I just popped in to have a look. I am sorry I awakened you. Good night, Miss Pym."

"Good night, madam."

I am forever apologizing to the servants, thought Jobina, escaping into the sanctuary of her bedroom. The bed had been turned down and the lamps lighted. A fire burned in the hearth, its brilliant reds and blues and golds glittering behind the polished screen. Upon the rosewood tables sat fluted crystal bowls of *potpourri* blended especially for Jobina in Paris. This room, more than any other, meant home to her. Here was where she and William shared their private moments, their dreams and hopes; here was where they shared their love. She had always felt that in later years, when she looked back at her life, she would think first about this room.

Now Jobina went to the spacious, flower-sprigged dressing room. She removed her jewelry and took the pins from her hair, brushing it over her shoulders. Her crimson gown dropped to the floor, and then her silk underclothes. When she emerged, she was wearing a negligee of ivory satin with ivory lace billowing at the deep hem.

"How beautiful you are, Jobina."

She turned, smiling so radiantly that light actually seemed to fall from her. "Darling, you kept your promise! I'm glad. I was going to invade your study and throw all those silly papers into the fire."

"Yes, that is where they belong."

"Come, darling, you must hurry into your pajamas and then into bed. You are exhausted." Jobina caught William's hands in hers. "You need a good rest, and I intend to see you get it. I intend to pamper you. Like it or not!"

A lump came to William's throat and moisture filmed his eyes, for he could not remember a time when Jobina had not pampered him, when she had not placed his wants and needs above all else. He knew she did not see him as he saw himself. He knew the depths of her blind and uncompromising love and he felt ashamed. "I don't deserve you, my dearest," he said. "I wish . . . I wish . . ."

"There will be plenty of time for wishing once you've had your rest. Think how much better you will feel then, darling. Why, you will be a new man!"

"If only it were that simple."

Jobina laughed, giving William a playful push toward

the dressing room. She went to the window and opened the draperies, breathing the cool, fresh air. It had stopped snowing and the sky had begun to clear. She watched the scurrying clouds, clapping her hands together in delight as she glimpsed a crescent of silvery moon.

The lamps had been lowered when William returned to the bedroom. "Are you asleep?" he whispered into the shadows.

"Certainly not! Not before I get my good-night kiss!"

William slipped between the scented sheets of the big four-poster bed, reaching for Jobina. He felt her long hair brush his cheek. He felt the warmth of her lips, the quickened beating of her heart, and his embrace became more urgent. "I love you, I love you," he murmured over and over again, covering her face with kisses. He threw back the quilts, his hands seeking her swelling breasts. Now he was pulling at her gown, tearing it from her body. His own robe was thrown aside and he fell upon her, his hands, his feverish mouth, pressing her naked flesh.

Jobina cried out rapturously, for never had William been so passionate in his lovemaking. He was a man possessed, murmuring against her, moaning. His fiery touch was everywhere on her trembling body. "My darling . . . Oh, my darling," she cried, lost in an ecstasy that was as strange as it was sweet.

William awoke with a start. His heart was racing and perspiration stood on his brow, for he had had a terrifying nightmare. In his dream Martin Chadway had pursued him along a dark road overgrown with bramble and thorny brush. He had run as fast as he could, but finally the bramble had ensnared him, the spiked claws gripping his throat, forcing the air, the life, from his body. At that moment, out of the blackness, had appeared the towering figure of Jonas Winslow. *"Choose,"* Jonas had commanded. *"Choose before it is too late."*

Now William strained to catch his breath. He glanced at Jobina, sleeping peacefully beside him, and his hands began to shake. Quietly, he eased himself out of bed. He reached for his robe and staggered across the room. There is no escape, he thought, stumbling into the silent hall.

William's face was ashen as he crept downstairs to his study. He switched on the lights and went to the brandy decanter, pouring a large drink. He finished it in one great gulp and immediately poured another. Soon the decanter was empty. He opened the cellaret and withdrew a second bottle, carrying it to his desk. Each scrap of paper littering the desk was a reminder of the money he owed—to Chadway & Turnbull, to the bank, to his broker, to stores, to George Thayer and other friends. He stared at the papers, then swept them to the floor.

An ormolu clock on the mantel struck four, but William did not hear. He sat slumped in his chair, his chin drooping almost to his chest. Dark mists floated before his eyes, shifting and changing shape until he saw, once again, the faces of his enemies. "Oh God," he cried as if in supplication. He shivered. There was a fierce clanging in his head that grew louder with every breath he took. He reached his shaking hand to his glass and drank deeply. The mists seemed to recede. He stood and made his way across the study. He began to pace.

An hour passed, two, and still William paced, oblivious to the dying fire, to the first rays of dawn streaking the windows. His eyes were dark with misery and his hands clasped so tightly together that the knuckles sprang out beneath the skin. There is no answer, he thought, too tired and broken and ill to care. He lifted his tortured gaze to Jobina's portrait and the clanging in his head became thunderous. He staggered backward toward the desk. "Your money or your life," he murmured, his mouth twisting in a grotesque smile. "Your money or your life."

He sat down, staring off into space. After some moments he took pen in hand and scribbled a few words. Carefully he sealed the note, then propped it against the telephone. He opened the top drawer of his desk. The pistol was small, jet black. William put it to his temple.

Jobina was pulled from sleep by a loud pounding at the door. "Yes?" she called, drawing the quilts up about her chin. "Yes?"

"Mama," Daisy's excited voice came in reply. "It's Christmas!"

"Yes, Mama," Caroline added. "We waited and waited and now it's Christmas!"

Jobina laughed. "Just a minute, darlings. Mama is coming." She hurried out of bed, slipping into a lace-trimmed ivory robe. "William?" She glanced around and then went to the dressing room, poking her head inside. "William, are you ready for . . ." She saw that the room was empty. She shrugged. "I am the only slugabed today," she said to herself, shrugging again.

Caroline and Daisy were gesturing excitedly to each other when Jobina entered the hall. They were dressed in matching red robes and tiny red slippers with velvet bows. Their long golden hair, neatly parted and brushed, streamed down their backs. Caroline was five and Daisy four, but so alike were they in their mannerisms, they might have been twins. *"Mama,"* they chorused now, running into Jobina's arms. "Merry Christmas, Mama."

"Merry Christmas, my angels. Merry Christmas, Miss Pym."

"Thank you, madam. I did try to delay the celebration a bit. Your young ladies were most insistent. Straining at the leash, so to speak." Miss Pym, wearing a plain tweed suit and sensible low-heeled shoes, separated her charges from Jobina. "They are in high spirits this morning."

"Oh, I don't mind. It is a special day. Mr. Grant is already downstairs. Well," Jobina smiled at her daughters, "shall we see what Santa has brought you?"

"A tea set!" Caroline squealed. "I do hope he brought a tea set."

"He brought me a dollhouse," Daisy announced confidently, thumping her little chest. "With real windows and doors."

"We shall see." Jobina's smile was very bright as she led the happy procession downstairs. She loved the rituals of Christmas. There would be presents, endless presents. There would be cinnamon toast and thick, sweet cocoa heaped with whipped cream. Later, at church, there would be a choir singing ancient hymns. What a wonderful day it will be, she thought, her eyes twinkling.

Jobina was almost at the bottom of the stairs when she

heard the shot. Her hand froze on the rail, but only for a moment. In the next moment she was racing through the hall, her skirts thrown high about her ankles, her hair flying about her face. "William!" she cried, bursting into the study. "*William.*" A sudden dull horror possessed her. Sickness struck at her heart, at the pit of her stomach. "Oh God, oh God," she cried, for, on the floor, in a dark and widening pool of blood, lay William. She saw his white, still face, his staring eyes, his slack mouth. She screamed, falling to her knees. She hurled herself upon his prone body, crying out his name over and over again. Her husband's blood was on her robe now, on her hands and even in her hair. "*William. William,*" she cried, a terrible litany in the silent and shadowed room.

Miss Pym could offer no comfort, for all of her attention was centered on the children. She had pulled them from the doorway, blocking their view with her body, but not before Caroline had seen the ghastly sight. The child's eyes were huge in her pale face. Her mouth quivered, and dry, strangled sobs shook her shoulders. Daisy, too, began to cry. She clung to Miss Pym, tugging at her skirts. "There, there," the governess said. "You must be good girls and come along with me. You must . . ." Her voice trailed away as the servants rushed into the hall. "An accident," she said. "A most awful accident . . . Help me take the girls upstairs, Mrs. Daltry . . . Bridget, run next door and fetch the Thayers. Hurry, Bridget."

Mrs. Daltry stepped forward. She tried to get past Miss Pym, but the younger woman did not move. "What happened?" she asked. "Don't turn your nose up at me.

I've a right to know. The mistress is screaming like a banshee. We'll have half the neighborhood—"

"An accident," Miss Pym repeated firmly, evenly. "A most awful accident."

There were many things Jobina did not remember. She did not remember kneeling over William, screaming. She did not remember hands pulling at her, dragging her away. She did not remember the loud, frightened cries of her children. She did not want to remember these things, for they were a part of William's death.

Indeed, it was several hours before Jobina was able to comprehend her husband's death. She had been put to bed and there she had remained, staring blindly at the ceiling. She had not spoken. Irene had washed her, had changed her robe and combed her hair and bundled her in quilts, but these ministrations had elicited only silence. The servants had come with tea and brandy. The police had come with questions. Dr. Porterfield had come with vials of pills. If she had noticed her visitors, she made no sign.

Irene sat at Jobina's bedside. The windows had been closed and the draperies drawn against the late morning sun. Logs crackled in the hearth. A dainty porcelain clock ticked softly. "Jobina," she said now. "Jobina, won't you talk to me? I am here to help. Please let me help. Jobina, you must try. I know it is hard, but you must pull yourself together. Jobina?" Irene rose. She walked aimlessly around the room, her face etched with concern.

"William is dead."

"What?" Irene rushed back to the bed. "Did you say something? What did you say?"

"William is dead."

"I am so very sorry, Jobina. We are all very sorry."

"Yes."

"Dr. Porterfield is waiting outside. I will get him."

"Don't go. Don't leave me alone." Jobina sat up. The effort seemed to exhaust her and she rested her head on the pillows. Her eyes were empty, without spark or light. Her voice, when she spoke, was flat. "William is dead."

"I know. I'm sorry."

"He . . . There was a shot. I heard it. I went to the study. I ran, but it was too late. I don't understand. He . . . William . . . It was suicide."

"Jobina—"

"It was suicide. I saw the pistol. I saw the . . . wound. William held the pistol to his head and . . . pulled the trigger. I don't understand." She turned, staring intently at Irene. "Do you understand?" she asked. "Do you know why?"

"I think it may have had something to do with money."

"Money?"

Irene sat on the bed, patting Jobina's small, cold hand. She thought, The whole story will come out sooner or later. Sooner or later Jobina will have to know. But this is not the right time. No, Jobina cannot stand another shock. "There were some debts," she said carefully, hinting at the truth just as George had hinted at it hours before. "The debts, and then the . . . errors in the trust accounts. Perhaps it was too much. Too many worries preying on William's mind. Perhaps he felt there was no way out of it." She paused. She found her handkerchief and pressed it to her wet eyes. "Life can be so overwhelming. It is very sad."

"Debts? Why would there be debts?"

"Life can also be expensive, Jobina. William lived well. This house, the cars, the clothes, the trips. We live the same way, George and I. It is a costly way. And if investments should go wrong, that is another worry."

Jobina shook her head from side to side. "William is . . . He was clever about investments," she said. "Oh, Irene, why are we talking of investments and money? William is dead. My darling William. Oh God, my darling William." She collapsed in Irene's arms, sobbing as if her heart would break. "William. *William.*"

The door opened and George entered the room. He strode to the bed, peering down at Jobina. His unshaven face was haggard, his eyes puffy. Nervously, his hands clenched at his sides. "Irene?"

"Let her cry. It is good for her to cry. It is healthy."

"There are still some details. I'm afraid they won't wait. The police. Captain Ryan is still here, waiting."

"Really, George, you can see to all of that." Irene looked up at him. She frowned, inclining her head toward Jobina. "This is hardly a time for questions. Can't you deal with Captain Ryan? Can't you settle things?"

"There are formalities."

"Formalities be damned!"

"That is quite enough, Irene. We must do what we must do. Captain Ryan and I have made an arrangement. We've come to terms. But he still has to speak with

Jobina. It is a formality . . . I've done my best, Irene," he said, returning her impatient glare. "I don't *own* the police department. I've made an arrangement with them, but even arrangements have limits."

"Oh, very well. Jobina? Jobina, dear? Can you manage a few questions with Captain Ryan?" Irene took a cloth from the nightstand, touching it to Jobina's brow, to her streaming cheeks. "Just a few questions?"

"I'll try."

"Good girl! Now let me fix the pillows so you can sit up. That's it. That's much better. Here is your handkerchief." Irene draped a ruffled quilt about Jobina. She nodded. "All right, George. But there will be no bullying. I hope that is understood."

George did not bother to reply. He bent over the bed, looking into Jobina's reddened eyes. "I have arranged for the . . . matter . . . to be treated as an accident," he explained quietly. "Captain Ryan's report will say that William was cleaning his gun when it discharged. An accident. Such things happen all the time." It had cost George five thousand dollars to make his arrangement. Under the circumstances he considered it an excellent bargain, too trifling to mention. "You need only answer two or three questions and then we will be done. You have my word."

"I apologize, love." Irene smiled. "I underestimated you."

"Not the first time, is it? Jobina? Jobina, did you understand what I said?"

"Yes, I think so. It is very kind of you, George. I'm grateful. I wouldn't want the children to . . . The children!" Jobina cried, clutching Irene's hands. "Where are the children?"

"With Miss Pym. They are fine. Caroline was a little upset, but Dr. Porterfield gave her something. She is sleeping now. Miss Pym looks in on her every few minutes. Between looks, she plays games with Daisy. That woman is a marvel! I would steal her away from you if I could."

"Caroline and Daisy were behind me on the stairs," Jobina said, fresh tears welling in her eyes. "Did they . . . did they see?"

Irene glanced swiftly at George. "I think Caroline may have had a tiny peek," she replied. "I don't imagine she really saw very much. You mustn't worry, Jobina. Children are resilient. And their memories are so short."

Jobina had a sudden vision of William lying crumpled on the floor of the study. She saw his blood spreading in a darkening circle and she flung her hands up before her eyes, as if warding off a blow. "Oh God," she wailed. "I can't bear it. I *can't.*"

"You must be strong," Irene said. "You must think of Caroline and Daisy. They will need your strength. Pull yourself . . ." I am talking like a fool, thought Irene, who had scant patience for fools. I am mouthing platitudes and being ridiculous. "Never mind." She sighed. "I know you're not feeling very strong right now. I don't blame you. Just remember, George and I are here to help. That may be some comfort."

"It is. Thank you."

"Shall we see to Captain Ryan?"

Jobina dried her eyes. She took a breath, then another

and another. "Yes," she said, her voice catching. "I'll try."

George was relieved. He hurried to the door and threw it open. "Come in, Captain Ryan. Mrs. Grant will see you now."

"Thank you, sir." Captain Ryan was tall and florid and middle-aged. He wore a dark suit, shiny at the knees and in the seat, a cheap cotton shirt, and a dark necktie that was slightly frayed. These were his working clothes. At home he had many suits, none of them shiny, and many fine shirts and ties. Captain Ryan had been assigned to the Gramercy Park precinct for the last ten years. They had been lucrative years. The nature of his profession and his precinct had brought him into contact with wealthy people who often had secrets to hide; he willingly obliged. He made "arrangements" and offered what he considered to be fair prices. It was business, strictly business, and over the years it had given him a summer house in Breezy Point, a winter home in Florida, and a safe-deposit box bulging with cash. He was satisfied. He was careful to share the proceeds of his business with his men, and he was, in his view, never greedy. "Good morning to you, ma'am," he said, nodding first at Irene. "And you would be Mrs. Grant?"

"Yes."

"It's sorry I am for your loss, Mrs. Grant, ma'am. And I noticed you had a grand Christmas planned too. Ah, it's a shame. But you can never be telling about a gun. You'd be surprised how many accidents with guns I come across in my line of work."

"Yes," Jobina said again, looking away.

"Well, ma'am, I'll be getting to the point. I've a few questions. It won't take long at all." Captain Ryan removed a notebook from his pocket. "Would you be remembering the time of the accident, ma'am? It doesn't have to be exact, you understand. And would you be remembering your whereabouts?"

"It was after six," Jobina replied. She fixed her eyes on a spot of light far across the room. "I was on my way downstairs when I . . . heard the shot. It was very loud. I ran to the study . . . but it was too late."

"Ah, it's sorry I am, ma'am. One more thing and then I'll be taking my leave. It's about your husband's pistol. If I understand it right, your husband was planning to give the pistol to Mr. Thayer here for a Christmas present. Sure and that explains why he'd be cleaning a gun on Christmas morning. Wouldn't it, ma'am? Wouldn't that be your explanation of it?"

Captain Ryan's recitation had been so effortless that Jobina wondered for an instant if it might not be true. She turned her head to George. No, she thought, it is just a story they made up between them. "A Christmas present," she nodded obediently. "That is my understanding."

Captain Ryan closed his notebook. "Thank you, ma'am," he said. "I've seen many an accident like this in my line of work. You'll be glad to know I won't be troubling you again. My condolences to you, ma'am. Good-bye."

"Good-bye."

George walked Captain Ryan to the door. "You will see to the press?" he asked.

"It's all included in the arrangement, sir. I'll be giving the boyos a statement sharp at noon and I'll stand by it. You've no worries on that account."

George offered his hand. Captain Ryan accepted it, though he had only contempt for the wealthy and powerful men with whom he dealt. He took their money and he kept their secrets, but there was not one of these men he would have had for a friend, or even an acquaintance. No matter their origins, they were all the despised Sassenach. "Good day to you, sir," he said, striding into the hall.

"Well, it's done."

Jobina leaned back against the pillows. She felt cold and she gathered the quilts about her shoulders. "Did you pay Captain Ryan?" she asked. "Did you pay for his . . . cooperation?"

"Captain Ryan is a very *cooperative* fellow."

"Did you pay him?"

"What difference does it make? It isn't important."

"It is. You did it for William. To save his name. I'm grateful, George. It was a kind thing to do." Kindness was not a quality Jobina associated with George Thayer. She had always thought him too quick and harsh in his opinions, too ready to urge his opinions on others. She had thought him high-handed, especially where William was concerned, and this had bothered her. "William looked up to you," she said now. "He admired you."

"We were friends," George replied simply. He turned his back, for the strain of the morning was beginning to tell. He was not an emotional man, but he had been staggered by William's death. The appalling scene in the study had left him breathless and ill. He could still see the smudged, bloody impressions everywhere on the study floor and he winced. "I wish I could have done more," he said as if to himself. "I wish I had been in time." He took an envelope from his pocket. He stared at it. He thought about tossing it into the fire, then changed his mind. "I removed this from William's desk before the police arrived," he said to Jobina. "The seal is intact."

Trembling, Jobina broke the seal and withdrew a single, folded sheet of paper. She read the few scribbled words: "I have ruined your life, my dearest. Forgive me." Great tears splashed down her face unchecked. "I don't understand," she sobbed. "I don't understand at all."

Chapter Three

The funeral was in a beautiful old cemetery fifty miles north of New York City. Many people crowded the snowy grounds, black-clad friends and neighbors and all the one hundred employees of Chadway & Turnbull. Flowers stretched as far as the eye could see. There were opulent wreaths and sprays; there were huge bouquets and baskets skirted with long satin ribbons. A blanket of gardenias and white roses draped William's bronze casket.

Chairs had been assigned and Jobina sat in the first row, Irene on one side and William's only relative, his uncle, Ezra Grant, on the other. The minister was speaking, but Jobina did not hear. She stared at the casket, dry-eyed behind her heavy black veil, for she had no more tears to shed. She clutched a handkerchief in her hands, pulling at its lacy border. Every few minutes she seemed to sway, to tilt forward. When a sudden wind blew across the cemetery, she turned and clung to Irene's arm.

The eulogy was brief. George spoke of William's

gentleness, his deep love for his wife and children. He spoke of a "good man gone too soon from this world." Jobina heard the finality in George's words and a sob escaped her throat. It is true, she thought, burying her veiled face in her hands. William is gone. William, my darling William.

"William is with God," the minister said to Jobina when the service was over. "He is at peace."

"I want to believe that."

"You must believe it. Death is not an end but a beginning. It is promised in the Bible. It is God's promise to us, dear Jobina. You must take comfort in God's promise. You must believe."

"Yes . . . I will try. Thank you, Reverend Withers."

"Come, Jobina," Irene said briskly. "The car is waiting. Ezra, will you ride with us?"

Ezra Grant, thin and stooped and white haired, frowned. "I came in my carriage and I will leave in my carriage. It's good enough for me."

"Very well then. Please excuse us while we go on ahead. Come, Jobina. I am afraid you are getting a chill. It is so cold. Come," she said again as Jobina stumbled. "Here is my arm."

Ushers had been hired to escort the mourners to their cars. Now they escorted Irene and Jobina along the graveled path to a black Pierce-Arrow. George was standing at the open door. "Ladies," he said with a nod, helping them inside. He tapped the partition and the car glided away. "I have a flask of brandy," he said. "Jobina, I rather think you could do with a sip."

"No."

"I insist."

Jobina took the silver flask. The brandy burned, but it did not warm, and she returned the flask to George. "I hope the girls are all right," she said, pulling once more at her handkerchief. "They are so confused. Do you think they are all right?"

"I am certain of it," Irene replied. "They are very comfortable at our house and Ian is a very diverting playmate. He swore he would be on his best behavior today." She smiled. "And Miss Pym is there to make sure. Ian is a little cowed by Miss Pym."

"I hope they are all right." Jobina had tried to explain William's death to her daughters. She had faltered and in the end the task had fallen to Irene. She had stood off in a corner, mute, while Irene had talked about "accidents" and "going to Heaven." She had been ashamed of herself then; she was ashamed of herself now. "I failed them," she said. "When it came time to tell them about William, I couldn't find the words . . . Did I thank you, Irene? I don't remember. Everything is blurring together in my mind . . . But I know I failed them. I was cowardly."

"Nonsense. You were in shock. You cannot blame yourself. What does it matter who told the girls? They were given an explanation and they seemed to accept it."

"Caroline has been . . . moody."

"She will get over that."

Jobina sighed. She lifted her veil and pinned it back, touching her handkerchief to her red, swollen eyes. Her face was pale, the color of chalk. There were deep, shadowy hollows in her cheeks, for she had eaten very little during the past three days and she had not slept at all. The funeral arrangements had been left to George and the details of her household to Irene and the servants. She had remained in her room, crying, pacing, staring at photographs of William. "I'm sorry to have been such a burden," she sniffled. "I put everything on your shoulders. I'm sorry. You are right, Irene. I must pull myself together. I must try. I am determined to try."

"Good girl!"

George said nothing. He gazed through the car window and smoked a cigarette. Jobina's brave declaration gave him no comfort, for he knew the worst was yet to come. There would be his accountant's final audit of William's debts. There would be the reading of the will, a will made meaningless by those debts. He glanced at the unsuspecting Jobina. God help her, he thought.

A luncheon had been planned and now a dozen or so of the Grants' friends were gathered in the drawing room, sipping sherry. All the Christmas decorations had been removed, as had the masses of unopened presents. Faces were somber, befitting the occasion; voices were hushed. Condolences were offered to Jobina, though carefully, for in many minds questions remained about the true circumstances of William's death. The obituary notices had been identical, each listing an accidental gunshot wound as the cause of death. George had confirmed this explanation, but still questions and doubts persisted.

It was noon when Mrs. Daltry announced that luncheon was served. Jobina, leaning on George's arm, led her guests into the dining room. The table had been laid with crystal and silver and gleaming Haviland china. There were place cards and, at the center of the table, a deep silver bowl filled with roses. "Fancy," Ezra Grant commented, looking around. "William always did like the fancy life. You do too, I suppose."

Jobina was having trouble concentrating. She heard everything that was said, but dimly, as if the words came from a great distance. "I beg your paron, Uncle Ezra?"

The old man had no chance to reply, for George was rising to make a toast. "To William," he said. "We shall miss him. Godspeed."

Two maids in starched black uniforms served a clear soup, a roast of beef with Yorkshire pudding, and a salad of winter lettuce and cress. When those dishes had been cleared away, the maids served brandy tarts and mint wafers and cups of thick coffee with sweet cream.

"An excellent lunch, Jobina."

"Thank you, Uncle Ezra."

"But you eat like a bird. It is sinful to waste food. Don't you know that people are starving in Europe?"

"I beg your pardon?"

"It is sinful to waste food while others are starving. It is wrong."

Jobina put her hand to her head. Over the years she had grown accustomed to Ezra's pious pronouncements, but today she had neither the strength nor the patience to humor him. She dropped her napkin on the table and stood up, signaling the end of the luncheon. Her guests, as somber now as when they had arrived, were relieved.

"Good-bye. Thank you for coming," Jobina repeated again and again at the door. She offered her cheek to

61

Ezra, who was the last to leave. "Good-bye, Uncle. I hope you will come back soon to see the children," she said. "We will have a quiet dinner."

"Too much pomp and ceremony in this house for my tastes. I like a simple life."

"Yes, Ezra." Irene smiled, easing the old man toward the door. "You are an example to us all. A simple life, that's the ticket!"

"Eh? Ticket?"

"An expression. Good-bye, Ezra. Safe home." Irene closed the door, leaning against it. "He missed his calling. He should have been a minister. A Calvinist!"

"Oh, he means well."

"The man of *simple* tastes had two helpings of everything. I watched him. I know his type. He stints on food at home, but when he is invited out he eats like a teamster. Bless his miserly soul . . . George? Why are you pacing back and forth?"

"Eugene Marshall is waiting for me in the drawing room. We have business. I told you about it, Irene." George looked at his watch. "There is time yet before Chadway arrives with the will. You ladies run along upstairs and rest. It has been a difficult morning."

"The children," Jobina said.

"They are perfectly fine where they are. Run along upstairs. I can't conduct business with the two of you hovering about." George waited until the women had gone. He went down to the drawing room, closing the doors behind him. "Sit down," he said as his accountant rose. "I'm sorry to have been so long. Lunch dragged on and on and on. It seemed forever. People trying to make polite conversation but . . . Well, enough of that. Have you eaten?"

"Yes, sir."

George sank into a chair. He lighted a cigarette. "We needn't waste time with preliminaries. How bad is it?"

"Very bad, sir." The accountant, an eager, bespectacled man a few years younger than George, opened his briefcase. He removed a sheaf of papers, placing them on a gilded antique table. "I've gone through everything: bills, loans, mortgages, and, of course, the funds owed to Chadway & Turnbull. The final figure is slightly over two hundred thousand dollars. To be precise—"

"Two hundred thousand dollars? *Two hundred thousand?*"

"Yes, sir. That's correct. You see—"

"Two hundred thousand?"

"Yes, sir."

"It's not possible, Gene. You've made a mistake."

"No, sir. The precise figure—"

"Damn the precise figure." George leapt to his feet. He threw his cigarette into the hearth and rested his head on the mantel. "How?" he asked, his mouth a thin, taut line. *"How* is it possible?"

Eugene Marshall adjusted his glasses. He picked up a ledger sheet and glanced at it. "The figures are all here, sir," he said. "Mr. Grant's expenses had been running ahead of his income for some time. He was in debt before the war, though it was almost manageable. Given his salary, and the dividends he was then receiving, it was almost manageable. But it was still debt. If I had to guess, I'd guess that he saw the war as an opportunity to erase

all his debts and have something left over besides. A lot of
men thought that way during the war. It was a lure. But
to get back to Mr. Grant, that's where he made a critical
mistake. He sold his stocks to invest in speculations. He
also borrowed. He suffered heavy losses and he borrowed
again to cover those losses. But it didn't end there. The
losses continued, and the borrowing. The cycle continued. It's my opinion that Mr. Grant would have been
in trouble anyway. If I may say so, sir, he was living far
above his means."

"Yes," George admitted, sighing. "Yes, he was. I knew
that. I didn't know what to do about it. Talking was no
use . . . My God. Two hundred thousand dollars." It was
an enormous sum in the postwar America of 1918. At a
time when the average workingman was happy to earn
twenty dollars a week, it was incomprehensible. "Everything will have to be sold. I see no other way. Even at
that, I doubt it will be enough."

"Everything may be lost before it's sold, sir."

"What? What do you mean by lost?"

"Well," Eugene replied, warming to his subject,
"you're aware that creditors have first claim on an estate.
Mr. Grant hadn't paid a bill in six months. I have letters
threatening legal action. I have warning notices here
from several banks. Mr. Grant had two mortgages on this
house. The mortgages will certainly be foreclosed. This
house will be lost. So will everything else of value."

"I understand."

"There are a couple of other matters. Minor matters."

"How minor?"

"Mr. Grant recently paid the servants a month's

wages. I suppose because it was Christmas. But they are still owed five months' back wages. And Mrs. Grant's personal account is overdrawn."

George passed his hand across his mouth. "I want the servants paid today, Gene," he said. "Then telephone the bank and tell them I will be responsible for Mrs. Grant's account."

"Yes, sir."

"Pay the servants in cash. Five months' back wages? Perhaps they should each have a small bonus. I will trust your judgment."

"Thank you, sir."

George walked to a window and stared outside. He saw children building snowmen in Gramercy Park, their watchful governesses nearby. He saw butlers walking pedigreed dogs and chauffeurs polishing expensive cars. This is the world Jobina knows, he thought, a world of luxuries and servants. It is the only world she has ever known. Where will she go now? How will she manage? "Gene, Mr. Grant borrowed twenty thousand dollars from me some months ago. I assume you have that notation in your ledgers. Strike it. I intend to forgive the loan."

"Are you sure? It's a lot of money, sir."

"I'm quite sure."

"There's an excellent chance we can recover most of the money. An estate sale—"

"No. An estate sale cannot be avoided now, but I want no part of it. William Grant was my friend. He would have done the same for me were our situations reversed." George turned as a knock came at the door. "Yes, come in . . . Hello, Martin. You are right on time. Do you know my accountant, Eugene Marshall?"

"We have met. Good afternoon, Eugene."

"Good afternoon, sir." He collected his papers, folding them neatly and slipping them into his briefcase. He did not hurry, for he was fascinated by the dealings of rich men. Indeed he expected to be a rich man himself one day. "You may have more questions," he said, hoping to be asked to attend this meeting. "I don't mind waiting."

"That won't be necessary," George replied. "See to the matters we discussed. I will let you know if there is anything further. Good-bye, Gene."

"Good-bye, sir. Mr. Chadway."

"A nice young man," Martin said when the accountant had gone. "And a genius with figures, or so I hear."

"Do you?"

Martin sat down. He put his briefcase beside the chair and then crossed his hands over his bulging stomach. "I didn't mean to interrupt your business meeting, George. I offered to wait in the study, but Mrs. Daltry informed me it has been locked since the . . . unfortunate event."

"The unfortunate event? That is an interesting turn of phrase, Martin. Very tidy. Why don't you just say what is on your mind."

"Well, I'm not a fool. William's death was a tragedy, of course, but no accident. His theft was discovered and he took his own life. The last resort of a weak man."

"A *desperate* man."

"It is the same thing. I sense that you blame me, George. You are wrong. When your anger subsides, you will see the truth for what it is. Why, I've known you all your life. I knew your father. I was his friend."

"You were his attorney, never his friend."

"In my place," Martin sighed, "you would have acted as I did."

"Would I? Would I have given William a choice? A choice he apparently dared not make?" George drew his chair alongside Martin's. He leaned forward, staring hard into the old man's watery eyes. "I know you've been up to something vile," he said. "I don't expect to get the truth from you. You can take your dirty little scheme, whatever it was, to the grave with you, and the sooner the better . . . but I am giving you a warning. If you cause Jobina and her children any trouble, you will be sorry. Is that understood?"

"Trouble? I haven't the slightest idea what you are talking about. What trouble would I wish to cause Jobina, much less her children? Your hostility is misdirected. I am not the thief, the embezzler. I am certainly not the villain of the piece. Your good friend William stole from my firm."

"The money could have been returned."

"Never! William was drowning in a sea of debt. You must realize that by now. Each year his debts grew heavier, each month, in fact. The result was inevitable. I knew it was only a matter of time . . ." Martin fell silent, aware that he had said too much.

"You *knew?* How interesting, Martin. You knew. Perhaps you even helped him along to the *inevitable result.* Perhaps you set a trap. I would not put it past you." George rose. He paced about the room, his dark eyes narrowed in thought. "I have always been puzzled by your dislike of William. It was very strange. Nobody in the world disliked William; only you."

There is one other, thought Martin to himself. He shifted in his chair, reaching for his cigar case. "Dislike is too strong a word," he said blandly. "It is true we had our conflicts, but—"

"Why did you keep him on at Chadway & Turnbull?" George asked. "I have always been puzzled by that, too. Oh, I know why he stayed. You gave him several large trust accounts to manage. The fees were considerable and so he stayed. But *why* did you give him those accounts? Why did you keep him on at all?"

"I need not explain my business decisions to you. It is enough to say that our clients found William congenial."

"Gibberish, Martin. Lawyerly gibberish."

"I came here to day to read the will, not to argue. You must call Jobina downstairs."

"The will is meaningless now, and you know it. It is a charade."

"It is the law. The will must be read and filed for probate. After that," Martin shrugged, lighting a fat black cigar, "the matter rests between the court and legitimate creditors . . . including Chadway & Turnbull."

"No," George said with a chilly smile. "No, there you are wrong."

"I do not think so."

"You won't take this to court, Martin. You can't. The publicity would be ruinous. The very word embezzlement would be enough to start a panic among your clients. They would desert Chadway & Turnbull in droves, and who would blame them? No, Martin, you never intended to take this to court. You intended only to suggest the possibility to Jobina. Why? That is the question. You destroyed William's life. Now you want to destroy his memory. A memory is all Jobina has left, yet you want to destroy it. Why?"

"You have a vivid imagination, George. I must say it comes as a surprise. You are usually such a sensible chap. Can it be you have a personal interest in the lovely young widow?"

George stiffened. He was outraged by Martin's crude remark, and all the more outraged because it was untrue. "You will pay for that," he said. "I don't know exactly how. I must think about it. But take my word, you will pay."

"We have all been under a strain, George."

"You will pay."

"I have recently celebrated my sixtieth birthday. I have been threatened before in those years, many times."

"Not by me."

Martin realized that he had misjudged George Thayer. He had misjudged the younger man's commitment to a friendship and, worse, his commitment to the heirs of that friendship, Jobina and her daughters. "Well, I am sorry it has come to this," he said, sighing. "I have always had the highest regard—"

"That will do, Martin." George returned to his chair. He leaned his head against the rich leather and lighted a cigarette. "You are to say nothing about William's trust accounts to Jobina. You will take the loss in silence. It is a small price for a man's life. Read the will, if you must.

But I warn you again to say nothing untoward."

"Yesterday I learned that the shortages in William's accounts total ninety-two thousand dollars. You are asking me to cover those shortages from my own pocket."

"I am. I have no sympathy for you, Martin. You had a hand in William's tragedy. Probably both hands. I know how much you love money, but ninety-two thousand dollars is a small price for a man's life."

"You are upset. It is natural. We have all been under a strain." Martin regarded the smoldering tip of his cigar. "For Jobina's sake," he said slowly, "I will absorb the loss. You may consider the matter closed, although it is my obligation to point out that other people are aware of William's theft: the other partners, auditors, clerks. I can't promise there won't be talk."

"If I hear any talk, or more importantly, if *Jobina* hears any talk, I will make certain that your clients hear it as well."

"Such concern is admirable, George. I regret it will not be enough to save Jobina. The claims against the estate do not begin and end with Chadway & Turnbull after all. There are huge bills outstanding, and loans. Of course you could settle the claims on your own, but it would be a severe strain on your income." Martin stroked his bristling white mustache. He permitted himself a small smile. "There are rumors that you plan to start a magazine. Tricky business, publishing. It takes a great deal of money to get a proper start. Speaking as your attorney, I advise you to conserve your funds."

"You are no longer my attorney, Martin."

"I am still Jobina's attorney. I think it is time now to call her downstairs."

"If you are ready," Martin Chadway said, glancing from George to Jobina, "I shall begin."

"Yes, we are ready."

Martin cleared his throat. "'I, William Taylor Grant,'" he read, "'being of sound mind and body, do hereby declare this to be my last will and testament. First: If I am a resident of New York at the time of my demise, I appoint my dear friend, George Vannering Thayer, executor, to serve without bond. Second: To my beloved daughters, Caroline Taylor Grant and Daisy Winslow Grant, I give, devise, and bequeath the sum of twenty thousand dollars, to be held in irrevocable trust until they are of legal age. Third: To my beloved wife, Jobina Winslow Grant, I give, devise, and bequeath all the rest and remainder of my property as follows . . .'" Martin paused. He glanced once more at Jobina and then proceeded to read a list of William's property. It was a long list, including the house and all the furnishings within, artwork and cars and stocks and cash accounts.

Jobina listened as tears clouded her amber eyes. Her hands fidgeted in her lap and nervously she bit at her lip. It seemed to her that Martin had been speaking for hours. I want this to end, she thought; please let it end.

Martin continued, "'Fourth: It is my wish that my uncle, Ezra Taylor Grant, and my dear friend, George Vannering Thayer, select from my personal effects a keepsake of their choosing.'" Martin looked up. "That concludes the reading," he said quietly. "The will was drawn and witnessed on January 2, 1914. It is my obligation to inform you, Jobina, that there are now . . . encumbrances. George, as executor, may wish to explain. George?"

"Encumbrances?" Jobina asked.

"I will explain in just a moment," George replied. "Martin, we have kept you long enough. You needn't stay."

"You may find certain questions difficult to answer."

"Not at all. I haven't your facility with words, but I will manage somehow. I'm sure you are anxious to be going, Martin. Shall I ring for Mrs. Daltry, or will you find your own way out?"

Martin rose. "Again, my deepest sympathies," he said, bowing over Jobina's cold hand. "It is a great tragedy. A great tragedy."

"Thank you."

"If I can be of any help, you must not hesitate to call on me."

"Thank you."

"Good-bye, Martin," George said.

"Good-bye. Good-bye, Jobina."

The doors closed. George shook his head, sighing. "These ceremonies are barbaric! He was determined to read every word, every comma. I thought he would never finish."

"What did Martin mean by encumbrances?"

George took a chair opposite Jobina, looking into her pale and tired face. He had been dreading this moment for days. In his mind he had practiced a hundred different ways to break the news; hard as he had tried, he had not found a right way, an easy way. "There are problems," he said now. "There are debts. I must speak frankly, Jobina. The fact is that William was in debt. I'm afraid it is serious debt, almost a hundred thousand dollars."

Silence descended on the room. The handkerchief fell from Jobina's hands. She stared at George. She did not move; she hardly seemed to breathe. "What did you say?" she asked.

"It's true. My accountant has studied William's ledgers. There are many unpaid bills and loans. There are mortgages owed to the banks. The total is almost a hundred thousand dollars."

"I don't believe you. You are making it up."

"I wish I were."

"You are making up lies about William."

"No. You know better than that. You and I have never been the best of friends, Jobina. I admit it. But William and I *were* friends. We were not very much alike, and that is an understatement, but we were friends. Why would I lie about him?"

"Why would William be in debt? It's ridiculous."

"The war had a lot to do with it. There was a lot of wild speculating going on. Fly-by-night companies sprang up in great numbers, and they didn't lack for investors. I suppose William had hoped to make his fortune. A few men did, but only a few. Most were ruined. I tried to warn him. We argued, but nothing was solved. William had a . . . romantic nature. The idea of sudden, dramatic wealth appealed to him."

"We had everything. We didn't need *wealth*."

"Perhaps William saw it differently."

"If he did, it was my fault." Jobina looked away, her long black lashes shadowing her drawn face. "He was always buying me things. Always. He was always hiring more servants. We used to joke about . . . *Oh God,*" she cried, striking her small fists on her knees, "it's my fault."

George was uneasy around women's tears. He hesitated. Reluctantly he went to Jobina, touching her shoulder. "You must not blame yourself," he said. "You were not responsible."

"It is odd," she sniffed. "I was terrified all during the war. I was so afraid that William would be called to serve. I worried all the time. Then when he wasn't called . . . When the war ended I rushed to church and thanked God. But I was worrying about the wrong things, wasn't I? Instead of worrying about the dangers in France, I should have been worrying about what was right under my nose."

"You must not blame yourself," George said again, for he did not know what else to say.

"Well, I shall sell the house and make the debts good. I won't have a mark against William's name. I won't. I shall sell the house and get a flat somewhere. A flat is more economical. I would need only one or two servants in a flat. And there are other ways to economize. I will sell the cars. It is no hardship. There are plenty of taxicabs about. I will do without new clothes this year too. Of course Caroline must remain in Miss Beardsley's School. She should not be parted from her friends."

George listened to the innocent recital, a look of

amazement on his face. With sinking feeling, he realized that the enormity of the problem had completely escaped Jobina. *She believes it is a matter of selling a few things,* he thought in wonder; *she believes it is that simple.*

"You are staring at me," Jobina said. "I won't be dissuaded, George. I intend to make William's debts good."

"It is . . . complicated."

"I am not the ninny you imagine me to be."

"You don't have all the facts." George walked from one end of the room to the other. He sat down, but in the next moment he was on his feet again, pacing restlessly. A deep frown furrowed his brow. His eyes were so dark they were almost black. "Jobina," he said, sighing, "I see I cannot mince words. The fact is there is no house to sell. It is mortgaged. The bank is preparing to foreclose. The house will be lost. The cars also. The dealer will reclaim them for nonpayment. I am sorry, sincerely sorry, but that is the way it is. We must be adult about this. Settling William's debts is not a matter of choice; it is a matter of law. There will have to be an estate sale. All of this," he said, his arm sweeping in a wide arc across the antiques and porcelains and sculpted crystals, "will have to be sold. Even then, I am not certain there will be much left over for you and the girls. Their trust fund is beyond the reach of creditors. You will have the interest, about eight hundred dollars a year. That could be the only income you have. I am sorry, Jobina." He turned on his heel and walked to the door. "You may stop eavesdropping now, Irene," he said. "Come in."

"I was concerned."

"There is good reason. As you heard, I explained everything. It is done. Excuse me. I am going to find the whiskey."

Irene hurried to the sofa and sat beside her friend. "I am so sorry, Jobina. We kept it from you as long as we could."

"You knew? You knew all along?"

"George learned of the problems on Christmas Eve. He didn't know the full extent until his accountant came today."

"I see. You have been sparing my feelings. Everyone is always trying to spare my feelings." Jobina's voice was little more than a whisper. Her dazed eyes stared straight ahead. "I wonder why that is."

"You have led a sheltered life. We worry about you."

"Worry." Jobina sighed. "It was worry that put the pistol in William's hand. I understand now. His note . . . Do you remember his note, Irene? He said he had ruined my life. But that isn't true. William gave me the only happiness I ever had. He gave me *things* too. Gowns and furs and jewels. He gave me this house. But I would have lived with him in a cave." She slumped against the sofa cushions, absently twisting her wedding band around and around. "If he had told me about his problems . . . He should have told me."

"Yes."

"*I* should have seen what was right under my nose. William hadn't been himself. There were signs. Looking back, the signs were clear." Jobina recalled her last hours with William. She recalled the wild abandon of his lovemaking and she realized that he had been driven less by passion than by the stark and urgent need to escape his demons. "I must have been blind."

"Nonsense. Things seem clear now, in hindsight. They did not seem so clear then. You could not have been expected to read poor William's mind. Listen to me, Jobina. William was a dear man, but he was not strong. He was unable to confront his problems squarely. What is important is that you don't repeat his mistakes. Don't deny your problems. They are real and they must be faced."

"I will have to find a way to earn money. We can't live on eight hundred dollars a year. I will have to find a job." The thought of a job gave her pause, for she had no skills, no discernible talents. From her tutors she had learned history, literature, art, music, and a smattering of French. She had worked hard at mathematics, but to this day she could not add a row of numbers without using her fingers. She did not know how to cook, or even how to make a bed. "I am not really trained to do anything," she said. "My last governess taught me embroidery. That isn't a help, is it?"

"Embroidery is a pleasant hobby," Irene replied, smiling despite herself. "It will not earn your living. I'm sure we can come up with more practical solutions. George, for one. He hopes to start a magazine very soon. Perhaps you could work in the magazine office."

"What would I do there? I don't know typewriting or stenography. No, Irene, it would be charity. If I am to get off on the right foot, I must find an actual job. Besides, George and I are always having disagreements. We would be at loggerheads all the time."

"I have another idea. It is a sore subject with you, but your father—"

"*No.* No, that is quite impossible. Father humiliated William. He hurt him. I would rather starve than go to Father for help."

"You must think of Caroline and Daisy."

"I am. The girls are my responsibility now and I will take care of them somehow. But I will not expose them to Father's cruelty. Oh, he is all kindness and smiles as long as one does exactly as he says. Defy him, even in the smallest thing, and it is a different story. I will not expose Caroline and Daisy to that. All the luxuries in the world are not worth that."

"It is obvious you have made up your mind."

"A long time ago."

Irene showed no surprise, for she knew the rift between Jobina and the lordly Jonas Winslow was deep. Jonas had brought it on himself, she thought. Jobina could have forgiven anything, but not an affront to her beloved William. "There are other solutions," she said. "We shall find them."

"A job is the only solution."

"I admire your courage."

"Courage?" Jobina clasped her shaking hands together. "I am scared, Irene. Inside and out. But I must go on. It may sound strange, because I have never been very religious, . . . but I believe William is watching. He must see that my life is not ruined. Then he will be at peace."

"Jobina—"

"It is what I believe, Irene. I must make something of my life, for William."

Chapter Four

It was a cold, rainy afternoon in January when Jobina arrived at Ezra Grant's house on Washington Square. She had been summoned there, his terse note specifying both the date and the hour. No clue had been offered as to his purpose, nor had she been able to inquire, for Ezra considered the telephone a sinful waste of money and would not have one anywhere around.

Now Jobina closed her dripping umbrella and shook it over the stone steps. She rang the bell. She rang a second time and a third. "Oh, Mrs. Coyne," she said, smiling gratefully at Ezra's ancient housekeeper. "I was beginning to think I had the wrong day."

"Is it you, Mrs. Grant? Aye, you're expected. Come in, come in. The mister's expecting you. You'll find him in the front parlor. Scowling like the devil he is, too. You'll go easy with him if you know what's good."

"I appreciate the warning, Mrs. Coyne." Jobina put her umbrella in a tarnished brass stand. She struggled out of her heavy coat and proceeded to hang it in the closet. "I hope I am not late," she said. "Uncle Ezra values punctuality."

"Mrs. Grant . . . I wanted to say I'm terrible sorry about Mr. William. Aye, he was a good lad. I'm old now, but I can still remember the days when he lived here. There was a bit of life in this house then. Not like now. Mr. William always had a smile, a kind word. There was no sass in him neither. My own lads was all sass. Not Mr. William. I'm remembering him in my prayers."

"Thank you, Mrs. Coyne." Jobina hurried away. She turned into a long, dim hall and stumbled on the frayed edge of the carpet. She righted herself and then drew back sharply as she saw a cobweb dangling from the molded woodwork. "Uncle Ezra?" she called. "Uncle Ezra?"

The parlor door opened. "I am here, Jobina." He stepped aside to let her enter, gesturing toward a straight-backed chair. "Please be seated. There is tea and seed cake."

"Thank you, but I have already eaten."

"The cake is fresh. Mrs. Coyne baked it this morning."

"No, thank you."

"Tea?"

Jobina shook her head. "I don't mean to be rude, Uncle Ezra," she said. "It is just that I haven't much time. I really should be at home. There are appraisers going through all the rooms . . . It has to do with William's estate."

"Are you becoming a liar, Jobina? I know there is no estate. Have you forgotten that Martin Chadway is my lawyer also? He has been my lawyer for thirty years. It was at my suggestion that he hired William in the first place."

"Martin shouldn't be discussing William's private affairs."

"William was my nephew. He was my ward for five years. I took him in when his parents died. It was my duty. I gave him a home under my own roof from the time he was thirteen until he went off to university. And his education was paid for out of my own pocket. I have a right to know."

"There is nothing to know, Uncle."

"William died a pauper. Is that nothing?"

"It's not true!"

"His whole estate will be used to satisfy his debts. By my lights, that makes him a pauper."

"Not by mine. What does it matter anyway? If you brought me here to listen to such talk, you will be disappointed. I refuse to listen to another word of it. You are being heartless."

"Eh? Heartless? The world is a heartless place, child. That is why we must look beyond the world to God's grace." Ezra sat down. He stared at Jobina, pale and fragile in her black mourning clothes. "You are thinner," he said.

"Why did you call me here, Uncle? I don't understand."

"William's father was my younger brother. He, too, was a spendthrift. He squandered his inheritance, threw it away. I did not."

No, thought Jobina wearily. You hoarded every penny. You live in this drafty, dusty house and begrudge yourself even the simplest comforts. You are a rich man but *you* are the pauper. William had beauty in his life, and love. You have only sanctimony. "Please, Uncle Ezra." She sighed. "I have heard these family stories many times."

"There is a moral to them: Waste not, want not. All the years William lived under my roof, I tried to impress that on him. I tried to give him Christian values. But he went astray. It was the fancy life for him . . . Don't frown so, Jobina. I have a right to speak. It is my due."

"You have no right to speak harshly of William."

Ezra sipped his tea. He put the cup aside, touching a yellowed linen napkin to his dry lips. "False pride is dangerous," he said. "It is sinful. Remember, 'Pride goeth before a fall.'"

Jobina closed her eyes for a brief moment. Her hands were clenched in her lap. "I know you are an exemplary Christian, Uncle. You are a pillar of your church and you make generous contributions to the church's foreign missions. It is admirable. But I still don't understand why you called me here."

"We must discuss your future."

"My future?"

"George Thayer visited last week. He is careful with his words, too careful for my tastes. It was a long visit. In the end he confirmed what Martin Chadway said. Like Martin, he fears for your future."

Jobina's eyes flashed. She pressed her lips tightly together, and drew a deep breath. "I'm sorry George troubled you, Uncle," she replied. "He should not have interfered."

"On the contrary. You are a woman alone in a sinful

world. You have two children to support and only limited funds at your disposal. It is my duty to offer the protection of my home. You must come live with me."

"*Here?*" Jobina gasped.

"It's a large house. The upper floors were sealed years ago, but there is still more than enough room."

Jobina glanced about the parlor. She saw the faded draperies, the lumpy horsehair chairs, the threadbare carpet. She was appalled at the thought of living amidst such decay, yet her horror was tempered by a sudden surge of gratitude. Hospitality, she knew, was not in Ezra's nature. He was a reclusive man, a friendless and lifelong bachelor. He had few callers—his banker, his broker, the minister of his church—and even those few he rushed away in order to retreat once again into the solitude of his dingy parlor. She knew the sacrifice implicit in his invitation and she was moved. "It is very kind of you, Uncle Ezra," she said, brushing tears from her eyes. "Very kind. I . . . I'm afraid I cannot accept . . . It would be a great imposition."

"Eh?"

"I could not impose, Uncle."

"Do me the courtesy of listening, Jobina. Certainly you couldn't accept charity. You would not want to be beholden. I am proposing an arrangement of benefit to us both. My housekeeper, Mrs. Coyne, is too old to perform her chores. I care nothing for appearances, but cleanliness is another matter. Cleanliness is next to godliness. It is wrong to live in squalor." Ezra laced his bony fingers together, resting them on his knee. He nodded at Jobina. "You would agree with that?"

he asked.

"Yes."

"Then I will not keep you in suspense any longer. I propose you come to live here as my housekeeper. You will have your room and board. Within reason, I will pay your bills. I will also pay the cost of the children's schooling. Fortunately they are girls and will have no need of university. But a proper girls' school will do no harm. Reverend Barry has recommended an excellent school not far from here. He assures me they teach all the Christian—"

"You are asking me to be your servant?"

"My housekeeper, Jobina. Of course you will be free to hire an Irisher to do the heavy cleaning. They pour off the boats every day. And they don't put up an argument over wages. They can't. They have empty pockets, all of them." Ezra seemed pleased. A rare smile flickered about his mouth as he allowed himself a bite of seed cake. "Very tasty," he said. "Please remember to get Mrs. Coyne's recipe. I confess I enjoy an occasional sweet."

"You are asking me to be your *servant?*"

"I am offering to give you a home. You and your children. It will not be easy having children around. They are noisy creatures. I have noticed, however, that your girls mind their manners. That is in their favor."

"Is it? I'm so glad."

Jobina's tone was sharp and Ezra looked at her. "You are frowning again. I hope you are not a moody female. I hope I haven't misjudged you. Moody females are even more disruptive than children."

"Perhaps you are reconsidering your offer, Uncle."

"No. I thought it through carefully. It may be awkward at first. You are accustomed to having your own home. I am accustomed to my privacy. We will just have to make allowances."

"I think not."

"Eh?"

There was an angry glint in Jobina's eyes. She gripped the arms of her chair, fighting to maintain her composure. She had not expected assistance from Uncle Ezra Grant, but neither had she expected to be asked to live as a servant in his house. She felt demeaned. "I'm afraid you will have to look elsewhere for your housekeeper," she said after several moments had passed. "I am not interested."

"Why not? I set fair terms. More than fair."

"If there is nothing else, Uncle, I will be leaving. I have stayed too long as it is."

"What's wrong with you, child? You should be pleased. I offered you and your girls a place in my home."

"You offered me a position."

"A respectable position in my home. Work is good for the soul, if it's honest work. Or do you object to earning your keep?"

"I object to hypocrisy, Uncle."

"Meaning?"

"Meaning you do not practice what you preach. When did you ever earn your keep? You had a large inheritance. Brokers and bankers and a closed purse made it larger."

"Jobina!"

"I'm sorry, Uncle, but that is the truth. I dislike saying these things. Perhaps you are really trying to help. I don't know. It is hard to know what to think sometimes."

"How do you intend to support yourself?"

"I will find a way."

"And if you fail?"

Jobina had asked herself the same question during the last three weeks. Tossing and turning in her lonely bed, unable to sleep, she had wondered what was to become of her. At such times she had thought of Caroline and Daisy and her fears had increased. She had not confided her fears. When Irene had marveled at her serenity, she had quickly changed the subject. "I can't fail, Uncle," she said now.

"And if you do?"

Tears glittered on Jobina's lashes. She shook her head. "I don't know."

"*I* know," Ezra persisted, his scrawny hands forming into fists. "You will be pounding at my door, begging me to take you in. You and your starving children. Well, maybe I will and maybe I *won't*. Consider that before you throw this opportunity away."

Jobina dried her eyes. "You needn't worry, Uncle Ezra," she said stiffly. "I promise I will not be pounding at your door. I have not asked you for anything, nor do I intend to. I will manage. You have made me determined to succeed." She gathered up her purse and gloves. She rose. "I will be leaving now, Uncle. Good-bye."

"You are a disappointment to me, Jobina. You are like William after all."

"Good-bye, Uncle."

"'Pride goeth before a fall.'"

"So I have heard," Jobina replied, slamming the door

behind her.

In her anger, in her haste, Jobina forgot her brave promise to ride the streetcar home. She rushed from Ezra's and hailed a taxicab, flinging herself upon the cushioned seat. The driver tried to start a conversation, but she silenced him with a single glance. When finally the taxicab turned into Gramercy Park, she thrust a five-dollar bill forward and did not wait for change. She ran through the pouring rain, heedless of the water splashing her coat and her pale, angry face. Once inside the house, she tossed aside her purse and ran to the drawing room. "George? George, how *could* you?"

"Good Lord, Jobina! You are soaking wet!"

"Never mind that. How could you go behind my back to Uncle Ezra? It was an *awful* thing to do. How could you? *Ezra*, of all people. I am so angry I want to scream. I cannot remember being this angry in my *entire* life."

George was startled by Jobina's outburst, for it was unlike her. She had disagreed with him before, often, but rarely had she raised her voice and never had she glared at him with such fury. "Get hold of yourself, Jobina," he said. "Let me help you out of your wet things. You will catch pneumonia."

"Pneumonia would be nothing compared to what I have been through today. Saint Ezra of Washington Square had a *grand* time sermonizing. I was his captive audience and he made the most of it. I blame you, George. He is what he is. I don't think he can help it. But *you*. Surely you knew better."

"I . . . thought it was worth a try."

"You were *wrong*."

"Ezra has that big house all to himself. Why, there must be whole floors he hasn't seen in years. There is all that room. There are three separate entrances. You and the children could live there quite comfortably."

"Are you insane? There isn't a shred of comfort in that house. It's dark and drafty and *terrible*. There are *cobwebs*. I would sooner live in a dungeon! And what about Uncle Ezra? Do you suppose I could listen to his sermons day in and day out? Think of the effect on Caroline and Daisy. Their lives would be . . . warped."

"Come now, Jobina. It is not that bad."

"It is worse!"

"All right. All right, I made a mistake. I'm sorry. My intentions were good."

"Uncle Ezra would have something to say about *good intentions*. I can hear him. 'Remember, good intentions pave the way to hell.' He has a quotation at hand for all occasions."

George, chastened, looked away. He paced in a circle and then sat down. He looked back at Jobina. "I have not seen this side of you before," he said. "All this high spirit. I am not sure it is becoming . . . and incidentally, you are dripping on the carpet."

Jobina removed her coat. She threw it on a chair. "There. Are you happy now? Don't think you can distract me, George Thayer. You did an *awful* thing."

"In my defense, assuming I need a defense, let me remind you that I am your executor. It is my responsibility to look after your affairs. It occurred to me that Ezra might be a possible solution. At least it was worth a try. If I was wrong, I am sorry. But you must be realistic. The real world—"

"I am getting tired of hearing about the real world. Especially from you and Ezra, who have had very little to do with the *real* world. Neither one of you has worked a day in your lives. Both of you sit and clip coupons."

"Still, we are men. We understand the world. Women do not."

"Are you saying I need a man's protection?"

"You have always had a man's protection, Jobina."

George's blunt words seemed to quiet her anger. Her hands fluttered at her sides. She sank onto the sofa, bowing her head over her lap. "Yes." She nodded. "Yes, that is true. Perhaps that was the point Uncle Ezra was trying to make when he offered me his protection. He offered me a place in his house, George. All else aside, I didn't care for his terms. I am not prepared to be Uncle Ezra's housekeeper."

"His housekeeper!"

"Oh, you know Uncle Ezra. He tries to save his conscience and his bank account at the same time. It is his nature."

"The nerve of the man! I had no idea that was what he had in mind. I would have told him a thing or two. Good Lord, the nerve!"

"Do you think it is beneath me to be a housekeeper?" Jobina smiled slightly, brushing a strand of damp hair from her brow. "No, that is not what bothered me. If a stranger offered me such a position, I would not be offended. I would be surprised, because I haven't a housekeeper's skills. But I would not be offended. Uncle Ezra isn't a stranger though. He is family, and a rich man to boot. I admit I did not take his offer kindly. It was an insult to William. I know I shouldn't care what Ezra thinks about William. But I do. I care what everyone thinks. William's good name must be preserved. Promise me, George."

"I would like to promise. I cannot. Look around this room, Jobina. Do you see the little tags on the furniture? The appraisers have marked everything. The estate sale is scheduled for the first of the month. People draw only one conclusion from an estate sale. Word will get out. I'm sorry to say it already has."

"What do you mean?"

"Caroline and Daisy were supposed to attend Anna Raleigh's birthday party today."

"Yes."

"Mrs. Raleigh telephoned here moments after you left. She asked to speak with Miss Pym. She suggested to Miss Pym that the girls might not be comfortable at the party. She withdrew the invitation." George saw the sudden pain in Jobina's eyes. He reached across the sofa and patted her hand. "That is the real world," he said quietly. "I knew it would happen. I hoped it would not happen quite so soon."

"Caroline and Daisy will lose all their friends? Oh, why are people so *cruel?*"

"The girls will make new friends, Jobina. Children do."

"I must go to them."

"They are perfectly fine. Miss Pym took them to play

90

with Ian. Naturally Irene would not let Ian attend the party, once she heard. She has crossed the Raleighs off her list. A gesture," George said with a shrug. "The fact is, there will be more of these snubs."

"I don't care if I am excluded. But the children . . . It's *cruel* to exclude the children. The Raleighs were here on Christmas Eve, you know. They could not have been nicer. Eleanor asked me to join her hospital committee."

"That invitation will be withdrawn also."

"How did the Raleighs find out?"

"I suspect Mrs. Daltry. She is friendly with the other housekeepers in the neighborhood. They gossip."

"Mrs. Daltry! I have wanted to fire her for a long time. Now I'm going to do it. Today! This very minute!"

"Wait, Jobina. It will not be necessary to fire her. I have given all the servants notice. They will be paid through the end of the month. I did ask Miss Pym to stay on, at least temporarily."

"Can I afford Miss Pym?"

"Temporarily."

"Just a while ago I accused Uncle Ezra of hoarding every penny. Will I have to hoard every penny, George? Will I have to be a miser?"

"You will have to be extremely careful."

"It's the same thing, isn't it?" Jobina stood up. She walked around the room, touching the vases and bowls and figurines that were her treasures. All the objects had tags affixed to them, but she could not bear to look. "William bought this silver trinket box in London," she said. "It dates to the eighteenth century. And this plum-blossom vase he bought in France. There was a

91

flea market . . ."

"You are being sentimental, Jobina."

"I am remembering. It is a pity you can't put little tags on my memories. I have so many memories . . . I'm going upstairs now, George. My head is aching."

"Before you go, I would like you to sign some papers." George opened a leather folio. He removed six typewritten sheets and spread them on the table. "Here is my pen . . . don't you want to know what you are signing?"

"I suppose it has to do with your famous real world," she replied, a wry smile edging her mouth. "I know enough about it now."

"No, not yet."

"Think back over the past three weeks, George. I discovered William's . . . death. I cooperated in the bribery of a police officer. I endured the ravings of a sanctimonious old man who wanted to turn me into his servant. And I listened as you explained that my children are no longer welcome in the homes of their friends. Don't you see? I am not the same person I was three weeks ago. I will never be that person again."

"There is truth in what you say. But people do not change so quickly."

"Once a ninny always a ninny?" Jobina sighed, too tired to argue. "Well, you may be right. Time will tell. I'm going upstairs, George. Continue with your work, if you wish. Make yourself at home."

"I want you to know I am sincerely sorry for everything that has happened."

"Sorry don't feed the bulldog."

"I beg your pardon?"

Jobina paused in the doorway, looking at George. "When I was a child we had a wonderful Irish stableman. If anyone spoke of being sorry, he would grumble a little and say, 'Sorry don't feed the bulldog.' It's taken me until now to understand what he meant." She picked up her skirts and walked into the hall. Wearily, she climbed the stairs. Tags dangled from the paintings that lined the walls. There were other tags attached to the Sheraton mirror and console, and to the flock of delicate crystal birds perched atop the console. "Oh, William," she murmured. She fled into her room and fell upon the bed, burying her face in a pillow. "William, why did you leave me?"

Jobina displayed little emotion in the days that followed. She watched stoically as men from the auction house tramped through the hallways, moving her furniture here and there, draping it with muslin cloths. She watched as her furs were taken downstairs and hung on metal racks. She watched as the contents of her jewel boxes were sorted and tagged and arranged on velvet trays. Tears came often to her eyes, but she blinked them back. She answered her children's numerous questions, offering reassuring smiles and hugs. She was pleasant to the servants, and to the few people who telephoned. "I must remain calm," she told herself over and over again. "I must do it for William."

Jobina arose early on the day of the estate sale. She bathed and dressed and had breakfast with her children, making a special effort to be cheerful. She was smiling when she waved them out the door to play with Ian; she was still smiling an hour later when she left her house to meet Irene. "Good morning," she said, pulling on her gloves. "Miserable weather, isn't it? So gray and cold."

"You needn't pretend with me, Jobina. Your poise has been remarkable, but no one expects you to be the Rock of Gibraltar. It's quite all right to admit how you are really feeling. It's healthier."

"I am feeling cold. Must we stand in the street? I would much rather be in your nice warm car."

Irene nodded to her chauffeur. He opened the car door and helped the women inside. "We shall be heading uptown, Claus," she said. "I am not sure just where."

"*Ja*, madam," the chauffeur replied, his hand springing to his cap. He slid behind the wheel and turned the ignition key. "I will drive slow. When you think where you are going, you tell me stop."

"Thank you, Claus." Irene sat back, glancing sidelong at Jobina. "Have you an address in mind?" she asked.

"Several. I spent the last week scouring newspaper advertisements. There are lots of flats available. I marked the six that looked most promising."

"Oh?" Irene took the list. "Goodness!" she exclaimed. "These first two will not do at all. They are in Hell's Kitchen. Hell's Kitchen is a slum, Jobina. It is filled with young toughs. With gangs. They would eat you alive."

"But the rents are very low."

"Didn't you wonder why? Landlords are not philanthropists. They give nothing away. If rents are very low, you can be certain there is a reason. Nobody wants to live in Hell's Kitchen. It is all old tenement buildings."

"How do you know?"

"George and I have driven through that neighborhood once or twice. It is near the Opera House. Really, it is quite depressing."

"I cannot afford to be choosy, Irene."

"You cannot live in Hell's Kitchen. I will hear no more about it. I would not be able to sleep nights if you were in such a place. It's preposterous!"

A faint smile touched Jobina's lips. "Perhaps the Vanderbilt mansion is available," she said. "Would you approve of the Vanderbilt mansion?"

"Heartily," Irene laughed. "But I think we must look for something at least halfway between a mansion and a tenement. Here, these other addresses are not so bad. They are not what you are used to, of course, but we shall have a look anyway. There is no harm in that."

"I'm glad you are with me, Irene."

"Why, it will be fun! An adventure!"

Jobina was grateful for Irene's good humor, though not deceived. She had steeled herself to expect the worst and, as the morning grew later, her expectations were confirmed. At the first address, several blocks below Yorkville, she saw a fourth-floor railroad flat, water leaking from the rusted pipes, grease encrusting the battered kitchen stove. She saw years of soot embedded in rotting window frames; she saw walls so grimy and stained they could never be made clean again. The second address, a dank and airless basement flat, was no better. "We are certainly having an adventure," she said, climbing back into the car.

"Yes. The awful smells. I think I will be smelling

cabbage all day." Irene found her handkerchief and pressed the scented linen to her nose. "I wonder how people endure such mean places."

"They haven't a choice."

"Well, it has been interesting. You are very calm, everything considered."

"I knew what it would be like. Do you remember when Molly died? Molly, our downstairs maid? It was three years ago or more. William and I called on her family. I saw then what it was like to be poor. I tried to put it out of my thoughts. Now I am the one who is poor. It's odd. I don't feel poor. It is not real to me yet."

"Listen to me, Jobina. You must be sensible. I did not intend to raise the subject again, but your father—"

"*No*. That is a *closed* subject."

"It was. It is time to reopen it. George warned me what we would see today. Oh, I admit he can be stuffy and too proper about things, but he is usually correct in his observations. He is a man, after all. He knows the workings of the world. It is brave of you to want to manage on your own. It is foolish as well. You have responsibilities to Caroline and Daisy. I cannot imagine the grandchildren of Jonas Winslow living in a . . . a hovel."

"There are two more addresses on my list."

"What do you think we shall find at those addresses? Places not fit for mice, much less people! It simply won't work, Jobina. You deserve credit for trying, but it won't work. I have seen all I need to see. It is not in you to be a martyr."

"No, it isn't. Nor is it in you to give up so easily. I am

surprised, Irene. You were always the spunky one. And you always encouraged me to follow your lead. For weeks you have been telling me to face my problems. That is what I am doing."

Irene was silent, pondering Jobina's words. Like Jobina, she had been born into wealth, into a way of life that had shielded her from any possible hardship. During the course of her life she had given scant thought to people who were less fortunate; certainly she had given no thought at all to the stark truths of poverty. "It seems I owe you an apology," she said now. "Those flats had a distressing effect. They frightened me. I put myself in your shoes and I was frightened. I have never felt that way before. I suppose I lost my head. Of course you cannot go to your father. I understand, Jobina. But you cannot live in some dreadful tenement either. You must find the right sort of flat. I will help."

"That is the Irene Thayer I know."

"The spunky one?"

"Yes."

"There is no trick to being spunky when there is no importance to it. I am spunky in trivial matters. I run my household and I talk back to George and I have a say in our finances. All trivial matters, except perhaps for the last. I could not do what you are doing. I would be too scared."

"I *am* scared, Irene. My hands have not stopped shaking since William . . . since Christmas morning."

"But you are going on with your life. 'Onward and upward,' as Nanny used to say."

"I am not sure about the upward part."

97

Irene smiled. She looked thoughtfully at Jobina. "I suspect we have all underestimated you," she said. "It took courage to walk away from the Winslow millions, no matter how much you loved William. Heaven knows it takes courage to stay away now that you need help. In the same circumstances, I would forget my principles and board the first train home. I would go on bended knee if necessary. It's true. I value security too highly. I value my comforts. Well, you see what I am getting at. Beneath my fur-lined boots are feet of clay."

"You make yourself sound shallow. You're not. You are a good friend and the most generous woman I know."

"I can afford to be."

"I mean you have a generous spirit. You stood by me through these terrible times. That is more than I can say for my other friends." A frown crossed Jobina's brow. Something hard and sharp came into her expression. "The Boltons telephone every week." She sighed. "The Yorks also. They are the only ones. It is as if all the others, all my *dear, dear* friends, have dropped off the face of the earth. They were delighted to be my friends when times were good. Now I am an embarrassment to them. I passed Harriet Gorham on the street last week. She actually pretended not to see me . . . although if an enormous bag of money happened to fall down my chimney, Harriet would *fight* to be my friend again. The others too."

"You are learning."

"Oh, yes. Yes, I am learning. Money rules the world . . . Claus," Jobina called suddenly, tapping the partition, "please stop the car."

"What's wrong?" Irene asked.

"Something may be right. Look over there."

Irene followed Jobina's gaze to a trim brownstone building on the far side of Lexington Avenue. A hand-lettered sign in the window read "Flat To Let." She smiled, gathering up her skirts as the chauffeur opened the car door. "Perhaps our luck has turned," she said.

The two women waited impatiently for the traffic light to change. They hurried across the avenue to the brownstone. Jobina glanced about the small, neat vestibule and a smile came to her lips also. "Are you praying?"

"With all my heart."

The janitor, an amiable Polish immigrant named Stimick, showed them to a flat on the second floor. "This room is parlor," he said. "Is clean, missus. I keep nice."

Indeed the room seemed to sparkle. The walls were smooth and freshly painted, the wood floors burnished to a high shine. The fireplace grate was immaculate and light poured through the single bowed window. "It's charming! Isn't it charming, Irene?"

"After what we have seen today, it is a great relief. Come, let us have a look around." Just beyond the parlor was the kitchen. She paused, running her hand over a pristine white icebox. "Is it new?"

"All new, missus." Mr. Stimick beamed. "This building was private house once. Now all flats. All new. All clean."

"It certainly is." Irene laughed. "I wish you worked for me, Mr. Stimick. I am impressed."

Opposite the kitchen, a narrow hallway led to two

bedrooms. They were of modest size—half the size of the children's bedrooms on Gramercy Park—but they had lovely old woodwork and deep, scalloped window seats. "I think the girls would be comfortable here," Jobina said. She opened the closet door and peered inside. "There is almost enough space for their things. I could move their shelves from home, if George hasn't sold them. At least Caroline and Daisy would not have to share a room."

"But where would you sleep?"

"Oh, anywhere. The parlor. I could get a daybed. It doesn't matter where I sleep." Jobina went to the window, staring at the quiet, tree-shaded street below. She thought: It is a decent neighborhood and a decent flat. It is very small, but it is a thousand times better than what I expected. "Children are fussy," she said. "And I must admit that Caroline and Daisy are . . . a little spoiled." She turned, smiling into Irene's anxious eyes. "But I have made up my mind. I am going to take it."

"A moment, Jobina. Mr. Stimick? What is the rent?"

"Thirty-five dollar each month."

Irene hesitated briefly, then motioned Jobina to her side. "I am happy for you," she said. "It is a wise decision. The only decision. The alternative is too grim to consider. Still, I want you to be aware of a few things. The rent will come to more than four hundred dollars a year. At present, that is more than half your yearly income. Do you understand?"

"Of course I understand! I am not a complete fool, Irene! As you yourself said, the alternative is too grim to consider. The basement place had larger rooms and a much lower rent, but it was a black hole. This is clean and pretty. I have made up my mind. I shall just have to find a job right away. I have an incentive now. And there must be *something* I can do. In the meantime my girls will have a proper roof over their heads. Yes, I have made up my mind . . . Mr. Stimick?" she called. "I am ready to sign the lease!"

Jobina was pleased with her decision, not least because it was the first serious decision she had ever made by herself. She had lived her life as Jonas Winslow's daughter and then as William Grant's wife, and both men, different though they were, had insisted she must not "bother her pretty head." Her opinions had not been sought; her voice, in important matters, had not been heard. She had never questioned such treatment, but now, her first decision safely behind her, she felt a deep satisfaction. "I enjoyed today," she said to Irene. "I enjoyed signing *my* name to *my* lease."

"Shall we celebrate?"

"Can we? How?"

"How does lunch at the Brevoort sound?"

"Expensive. I can't afford it."

"Oh, I have an account there. It's all right, Jobina. We have earned a treat. Think what we've been through."

"Perhaps it is too soon after William."

"Nonsense. We are going to lunch, not to a party. I know you are in mourning, but you are allowed to eat. Besides, a respite will do you good. It is all settled. I won't take no for an answer. Claus, the Brevoort please."

The Brevoort, on Fifth Avenue in Greenwich Village, was something of an area landmark. Before the turn of the century, liveried coachmen had delivered bejeweled members of society to its doors; twenty years later, liveried chaufferus were still delivering the city's rich and famous. It was an elegant restaurant, luxurious in the French style.

"Lovely," Jobina sighed, settling into a wide velvet banquette. She glanced around at the crisp linens, the gilded mirrors, the elaborate floral arrangements. "You know," she said, "I am suddenly quite hungry."

It was past four when Irene and Jobina returned to Gramercy Park. They found George pacing the hall, his face stern and unsmiling. "Where the devil have you been?" he demanded.

"Looking at flats, as you well know," Irene replied. "Afterward we went to the Brevoort for lunch and then we went—"

"The Brevoort! While I was waiting here to discuss business? Bloody inconsiderate, if you ask me."

"I am sorry, George. It seemed like a good idea. Let us get out of our hats and coats and we will join you in the drawing room."

"Or what is left of it. I must warn you, Jobina. The sale was a success and that is excellent news. But it means that many of your things have already been taken away. The dining room is empty now. The drawing room very nearly so. I thought you should be warned, in case you are going to be sentimental."

Jobina removed her gloves and hat. She unbuttoned

her coat and hung it in the closet. "I am prepared," she said wearily. "Have the servants gone?"

"Yes, with the exception of Miss Pym. She and the girls are at our house . . . You understand that the contents of their bedrooms, and yours, were omitted from the sale?"

"I wish people would stop asking me if I understand. Of course I understand. Well? Shall we conclude our *business?*"

George took Jobina's arm, leading her to the drawing room. To his surprise, her expression did not change. "Bridget made tea before she left," he said. "It is still hot."

Jobina was silent. She walked about the room, stopping in the empty spaces where, just hours ago, chairs and tables and cabinets had stood. The floors were bare, and the walls. A lone porcelain vase adorned the polished mantle. The damask sofa remained, bracketed by two kitchen chairs. A large upturned carton, covered with papers and tea cups, was placed near the sofa. "You have had a busy day," she said, fumbling for her handkerchief. "But I suppose it is all right. The furniture wouldn't have fit into my new flat."

"Your new flat?"

"A very nice flat it is too," Irene said brightly. She recounted the events of the day to George, offering a glowing description of the flat on Lexington Avenue. "So you see," she finished, "our adventure had a happy ending after all."

"You should have let me read the lease before you signed it, Jobina. Jobina?"

"What?" She turned, drying her eyes. "The lease? I can *read*, George. I can and did read the lease. It is for three years at thirty-five dollars a month. That is high, I know, but it's done. The subject is closed." She sat on the sofa, brushing her long black skirts. "I wish you would stop treating me like a child." She sighed. "And please don't tell me that that is the way I have always been treated. Those days are in the past."

George looked at Irene. She shrugged and, muttering, he took a seat beside Jobina. "Shall I get straight to the point?" he asked. "Fine. The sale was a success. Our price was met on almost every item. My accountant was present for the sale. He has gone to make a final check of the figures." George reached his hand to the improvised table. He searched through the papers, picking up a thick folder. "These are duplicates," he explained. "You may wish to look them over. I believe, and Gene concurs, that the proceeds will bring enough to pay all of William's debts. The surplus will not exceed three thousand dollars. It may be less. Whatever it is, it will be carefully invested and you will have perhaps another hundred a year in interest income. Your total yearly income will be roughly nine hundred."

"I had hoped the sale would bring more, George," Irene said, disappointed. "Do your figures include everything?"

"Everything but the contents of the three bedrooms, and the few pieces of jewelry that Jobina asked to keep. I don't know why you are surprised. These sales never bring prices equal to the prices first paid. There is always a loss. A substantial loss. Even at that, we fared much better today than I had anticipated.''

''And I.'' Jobina was smiling. Color had returned to her face and light to her exquisite amber eyes. Impetuously, she leaned close to George and kissed his cheek. ''I'm sorry I snapped at you before,'' she said. ''You have worked very hard on William's behalf. And I am *very* grateful for the results. More grateful than you know.''

''The results?'' George frowned, concerned that Jobina had misunderstood. ''I am afraid the results do not alter your circumstances. You will still have difficult times ahead.''

''Oh, I don't care about that. I haven't been worried for myself, George. I will manage somehow . . . It was William's debts. But they can be paid now. There will be no mark against his name. That is what matters. Don't you see? William's name, his reputation, will be saved.'' Jobina rose. She ran to Irene and hugged her. ''Isn't it *wonderful* news? George has made it come out all right.''

''Jobina—''

''No, we have had enough business talk. I am going to change my dress and then I am going to collect Caroline and Daisy. Wait for me,'' she called. ''I will not be long.''

''Well,'' George said when she had gone. ''Irene? Irene, are you crying?''

''Of course I'm crying. Jobina is so poor now, but all she can think about is saving William's name. I always cry at love stories.''

George went to his wife, taking her head on his shoulder. ''She will need more than love stories to see her through,'' he said quietly. ''She will need a miracle.''

Chapter Five

"I want to go home, Mama." Caroline squirmed in her chair, impatiently kicking her little legs. "Take me home now."

"You *are* home, darling," Jobina replied. "I explained it to you yesterday and the day before and the day before that. This is our new home. This is where we live."

"I want to go *home*."

"You must not jump around so, Caroline. I am trying to braid your hair. Please, darling. Be Mama's good girl."

"I want to go *home*. Now." Caroline started to cry. Tears coursed down her flushed cheeks and she beat her fists on the kitchen table. "Mama, I want to go *home*," she sobbed.

Jobina was dismayed by her daughter's outburst, though not surprised, for it was the third such outburst in as many days. Each day had begun with tears and pleadings and anger; she knew that before the day was over there would also be sulks and pouts and dark looks sent her way.

Oddly, Jobina had had no trouble with Daisy. Her

younger daughter had explored the new flat, poking into closets and cupboards, and even into the icebox. Several times the child had walked back and forth between the two bedrooms, but once convinced that the rooms were exactly alike, she had relaxed. Her adjustment seemed effortless. She played with her dolls. She ate all her meals. She made a friend—young Annie Sisk, who lived next door.

I wish it were that simple for Caroline, thought Jobina now. "Just a moment more, darling." She sighed. "I have only to tie this ribbon and then . . . There! All finished!" She brought a cloth from the counter and dried Caroline's face. "How pretty you look today," she said. "You look like a princess in a picture book."

"Won't you take me home, Mama?"

"Caroline, we *are* home. Caroline!" Jobina cried as the child flung her cereal bowl away. "What a naughty thing to do! Here, stand up before you get oatmeal all over yourself."

"I don't care."

"That's enough, Caroline. You are behaving very badly."

"I don't care."

"If you continue to behave badly, you will be punished."

Caroline stared at her mother, petulance darkening the blue of her eyes. She took a step forward and jumped hard into a puddle of watery oatmeal.

Jobina's brows drew together in a frown, for at such moments she hardly recognized her daughter. She opened her mouth to speak, but just then the bell rang.

"That is Miss Pym," she said. "You will have some explaining to do, young lady." Still frowning, she left the kitchen and went to the door. "Good morning, Miss Pym. Please come in."

"Thank you, madam. I am sorry to be late. Traffic was heavy on the avenue."

"We are behind schedule also. Caroline has been having tantrums again. I've tried to do what you suggested, Miss Pym. Really I have. I've tried to make light of all this. It doesn't seem to help. Each day is worse. It is distressing."

"Yes. She is a sensitive child, but stubborn. Time is the only answer. Caroline will adjust, in time."

"Dr. Porterfield agrees with you. I wish I could be certain . . . Oh, be careful, Miss Pym. The floor is slippery. We had a slight accident, as you can see."

Miss Pym stared at the overturned bowl, at the spattered table and chairs. "Was it an accident, Caroline?" she asked.

"No."

"Did you make the mess on purpose?"

"Yes."

"Then you must clean it up. At once, Caroline."

"But—"

"At once. Fetch the dishrag from the sink." Miss Pym removed her gloves, folded them, and put them in her purse. She opened the top button of her coat. "We are waiting, Caroline," she said. "A lady does not keep people waiting. It is rude. Fetch the dishrag from the sink and get started."

"Yes, ma'am."

Jobina watched Caroline run to the sink. She smiled at Miss Pym, impressed once again by the woman's serene efficiency. "I don't know what I would do without you," she said. She spoke truthfully, for it was Miss Pym who had smoothed these first chaotic days in the new flat. It was Miss Pym who had taught her to sweep a floor and make a bed and cook simple meals. When Caroline's tantrums threatened to rage out of control, it was Miss Pym who appeared at the door. "I'm afraid I would be quite lost."

"It's kind of you to say, madam."

"Are you comfortable at the Thayers?"

"Indeed I am. My room is most comfortable. Master Ian feels put upon, with two governesses in the house. But he is coming 'round. I must say I enjoy the walk between here and Gramercy Park. A morning walk is bracing. At home, I walked five miles every day. Americans do not walk enough."

"We are lazy." Jobina smiled.

"Impatient, more likely. Everyone hurries in America. Perhaps that is the secret of America's success. Vitality, madam. Vitality is in the air."

"I must take deeper breaths. My own vitality is not what it used to be."

"If I may say so, madam, I think you are coping very well. It is a hard thing to change one's surroundings, especially when children are involved. Children dislike change. But then we are all creatures of habit . . . Caroline," Miss Pym said briskly, "you have missed a spot. There is a spot of oatmeal near the stove . . . that's it. Now rinse out the rag and hang it on the tap. Good job, Caroline. I hope you have learned your lesson."

"Yes, ma'am."

"In that case we are off to see the dinosaurs. We are going to the museum," Miss Pym explained to a startled Jobina. "Your young ladies have grown fond of the brontosaurus. It is a remarkable specimen. Remarkable! Have you seen it, madam?"

Jobina, who had small interest in museums, and no interest in old bones, shook her head. "I will get Daisy," she said, escaping to the hall. She knocked at Daisy's door and went inside. She laughed, for the child was almost hidden by masses of dolls and furry stuffed toys heaped atop the bed. "Darling, I spent hours putting all your things on the shelves. Why did you pull them down again?"

"Which one should I take, Mama? I don't know which one."

Jobina cleared a space on the bed and sat next to Daisy. "We go through this every morning," she said quietly. "You pull all your things on the bed. You fuss over them. In the end you always choose the same doll. This one. Isn't her name Elizabeth?"

"Yes, Mama. But I took Elizabeth yesterday."

"Darling, you always take Elizabeth. She is your favorite. Come along now, Daisy. Miss Pym is waiting. You are going to the museum to see the brontosaurus."

"Oh!" Daisy clapped her hands together. "Bronty is *so* big, Mama. He's up to the sky. I wanted to climb on his back, but Miss Pym said I couldn't. I said *please*, but she

111

said *no*."

"You are not supposed to touch things in museums, Daisy."

"I know. Miss Pym said."

Jobina bent and kissed Daisy's cheek. "Are you ready?" she asked, tugging playfully at her daughter's long golden braids. "Scoot."

"Miss Pym?" Daisy called. She ran into the kitchen, clutching her doll in her arms. "Miss Pym, Elizabeth is going too. She wants to see Bronty."

"Over here, young ladies. Don't dawdle." Miss Pym helped the children into their leggings. Sweaters came next, and then coats and mufflers and woolen hats with bright blue pom-poms. "Don't forget your mittens," she cautioned.

"'Bye, Mama," Daisy called at the door.

"Have a nice time, darling. Caroline, don't I get a kiss?" Jobina's smile vanished as she saw the cool, accusing look in Caroline's eyes. "It's all right, darling," she said. "Run along and have a nice time. Be good."

The door closed. Jobina started to return to the kitchen. She stopped in mid-stride and went instead to the parlor window, gazing outside until she glimpsed her girls. Daisy skipped happily through the street, long braids bobbing up and down, but Caroline's gait was listless. "Caroline," she murmured. "Poor darling, I wish I knew how to help you."

There was a last flash of blue before the girls disappeared around the corner with Miss Pym. Jobina sighed. She rolled up the sleeves of her dark shirtwaist and glanced about the parlor. The two ivory silk slipper chairs that had been in her Gramercy Park bedroom were here now. The dresser was here as well, and a small table. She had purchased a daybed; Irene had given her a fringed oval rug. Most of her clothing had been packed away and stored in Irene's attic. She had brought to the new flat several dresses, several skirts and waists, and these were hung on a plain metal rod that Mr. Stimick had installed. He had also installed a shelf and on it were her hats and shoes. Atop the mantel, in neat rows, were her lotions and creams and perfumes. On the narrow stand next to her bed were four pictures of William, each in a silver frame.

Memories, thought Jobina, rushing from the room. She had grown wary of her memories, for they brought no solace but pain. Night after night she had roamed the cluttered parlor, tears stinging her eyes. She had felt sorrow and anger and a crushing sense of regret. If outwardly she appeared to have accepted her fate, inwardly she felt bereft. She mourned, as much for herself as for William.

There was a numbing sameness to Jobina's new life. She rose early each morning to bathe and dress and fix the children's breakfast. She braided their hair and buttoned their jumpers and sent them off with Miss Pym. By nine o'clock each morning, the pampered daughter of Jonas Winslow was hard at her chores. The broom was still clumsy in her hands and sheets still bunched beneath the quilts, but such small lapses did not trouble her. "I am learning," she had explained to Irene, and it was true.

Now Jobina wiped her soapy hands on a towel and went

113

to the door. "Ellen," she said, smiling at her blond-haired neighbor, Ellen Sisk. "I was hoping you would come by. There is coffee on the stove, if you are brave enough to try my coffee again."

"I've had worse. Mine, when I first got married. Jack used to say I was poisoning him."

"Come into the kitchen, Ellen. I really am glad to see you. Mornings are so lonely . . . Where is Annie?"

"With her grandma. I have a day off when Grandma Sisk visits. She does the cooking and the cleaning, whether I want her to or not. The way she sees it, I don't do anything right. But she's good with Annie. And I don't mind the day off." Ellen sat at the kitchen table, watching as Jobina arranged cups and saucers. The two women had met earlier in the week, a meeting occasioned when Daisy had run into the hall and boldly opened the Sisks' door. Jobina had followed after her daughter, flustered and embarrassed. Later, over tea, they had all become acquainted. 'I saw Miss Pym taking your little ones outside," Ellen said now. "That's what I'd like to have, a governess."

"Oh, I won't have her much longer. I can't afford her. Try the cookies, Ellen. I didn't bake them." Jobina laughed. "My friends, the Thayers, brought them. They are always bringing me food. Irene has tasted my cooking, you see."

"You'll get the hang of it."

"I hope so. Caroline and Daisy are tiring of stew. Stew is my speciality, my *only* speciality."

"Chicken is easy. You can do a hundred different things with chicken. I'll show you, if you want."

"I would be grateful. We would *all* be grateful."

Ellen sipped her coffee. "Not bad," she said. "You're getting better."

"Thank you. I am trying."

"It's hard, at first." Ellen understood just how hard it was for her new neighbor. She was an avid reader of the society pages and over the years she had read quite a lot about Jobina Grant. Certainly she had been astonished to find that same Jobina Grant standing in her parlor. She too had been flustered, tearing off her stained apron and hiding it behind her back. But the awkwardness had passed; in almost the next moment she had warmed to her unexpected visitor. "I know what you're used to," she said. "It's hard getting used to something else."

"Well, life has twists and turns. I keep hoping one of those turns will lead me to a job. Irene suggested I register with an employment agency. I did. They had nothing for me. I applied at several department stores also. I thought I could be a sales clerk. They seemed to want people who have experience. They were awfully nice about it. But that doesn't pay the rent, does it?"

"I was waiting for you to bring up the subject, Jobina. In a way, it's why I'm here. I happened to mention to Jack that you were looking for work. Sometimes he hears about things. Anyhow, I mentioned it." Ellen paused, shaking her blond head back and forth. "I'm not one to mix in other people's business. Don't think I am. It's just that you're alone, and you have the kids to worry about."

"What are you trying to say, Ellen?"

"Tell me if it's none of my business, but I know where there's a job available. Jack was coming home from his

lodge meeting last night when he passed Greevy's
Pharmacy. There was a sign in the window, so he went
inside and asked some questions. Mr. Greevy is looking
for a woman to work behind the toiletries counter. He
told Jack the woman had to be a real lady. That's you,
Jobina. You have such fine manners, such a fine way of
talking. Anybody can see you're a real lady."

"Ellen, do you think he would hire me?"

"He'd be crazy not to. The question is, would you want
to work there? It's nothing fancy. A pharmacy with a
soda fountain in one part of the shop and a toiletries
counter in another." Again Ellen paused. Her own
parents had been shopkeepers, the owners of a small dry
goods, and she remembered the long hours she had spent
behind the counter. "I did that kind of work myself," she
explained. "Every day after school and all day Saturday.
I guess there are worse jobs, but for you . . . I mean, it's
not what you're used to. It's not fancy."

"My *fancy* days are in the past, Ellen. I must earn my
living now. Like it or not."

"Mr. Greevy will pay eighteen dollars a week. And you
get lunch too . . . But eighteen dollars. I mean, you
probably used to spend eighteen dollars on . . . on
handkerchiefs. It's not much, to you."

"It wasn't. It is now." A wry smile came to Jobina's
lips, for she knew that once upon a time eighteen dollars
had seemed a trifling sum, too trifling to consider. Indeed
she had spent hundreds of dollars each month at Madame
Yvette's dressmaking shop, and only slightly less at
Madame Claudine's millinery. "I led a charmed life," she
said, her voice low, faraway. "William . . . My husband

was a very generous man. He spoiled me. And I let him. Money was the farthest thing from my mind. Now it is all I can think of."

"Then you're not insulted? I mean about Greevy's?"

"Insulted! Ellen, if luck is with me and I get this job, I will be forever grateful. I don't dare get my hopes up. When Mr. Greevy learns I have no experience . . ."

"The way Jack told it, experience isn't important. He said Mr. Greevy's set on hiring a real lady. That's you. Born to the purple, like the expression goes."

Jobina laughed. Her amber eyes glowed, and in the bright morning sun her face shone with expectation. "I must hurry." She smiled. "Where is the pharmacy?"

"Madison Avenue near thirty-eighth street. It's walking distance. You'd save carfare."

"Keep your fingers crossed for me, will you? You may be my good luck."

"Want me to tag along? Grandma Sisk is looking after Annie."

"Thank you, Ellen. You are sweet to offer . . . I think I should do this by myself. But I will knock at your door the moment I return. I promise."

"Jobina, I hope you won't be disappointed. It's counter work in a pharmacy, that's all."

"But it *is* work. It's a chance. It means I will be able to pay the rent, and the food bills as well, if I'm careful. It means . . . Oh, Ellen, it means *everything*."

Theodore Greevy was sixty years old in this February of 1919. He was a husband, a father, a grandfather many

times over, but the one true love of his life was his
pharmacy. He opened the doors at precisely seven
o'clock every morning and did not close until seven at
night. He did not take vacations. On Sundays and
holidays, when businesses were closed by law, he retired
to a back room and studied his ledgers. Profits brought a
smile to his thin face. Losses, rare as they were, small as
they were, brought a frown.

He was a cautious man—the last of the neighborhood
merchants to have electric lights installed—and deeply
suspicious of anything "modern." Customer demand
forced him to stock all the new products of the age,
though amongst these items could also be found herbal
teas and mustard plasters and tonics and Greevy's
Arthritis Remedy. Children's scraped knees and cut
fingers were treated with his own first-aid salve; less
specific ailments with a spoonful of castor oil.

Mr. Greevy had only two employees, an adolescent boy
who made deliveries after school, and a young French
immigrant named Emile Lanteau who worked full-time.
From seven in the morning until closing, Emile was the
soda fountain attendant, the stock clerk, and the
inventory clerk; after closing, armed with mops and
brooms and disinfectants, he was the janitor. It was said,
correctly, that Greevy's Pharmacy was the cleanest shop
in Murray Hill. The proprietor did not disagree. Each day
he arrived to find all the glass and marble and wood
polished to mirror brightness. Each day he complimented
Emile, although a raise in salary was never suggested.

Now Mr. Greevy rushed forward as Jobina entered the
pharmacy. "Good morning, madam," he said, bowing

slightly. "May I help you?"

"Good morning. I wonder if I might see the owner?"

"I am the owner, madam. Theodore Greevy, registered pharmacist. How may I be of service?"

"Well, I understand you are looking for someone to work at your toiletries counter. I am applying for the job."

"You, madam?"

"Yes."

Mr. Greevy considered himself a keen judge of people and their stations in life. His judgments were based on small things—a gesture, a particular style of clothing, a particular manner of speech—and he considered them infallible. "It's a gift," he often told his wife, but gift or not, he was baffled by the woman who stood before him now. He saw a woman of breeding and wealth; he saw a lady. "You wish to work in my pharmacy?" he asked.

"Yes, Mr. Greevy. I do."

"Why?"

"I am a widow. I need to earn a living."

"Ah, a widow. And your circumstances are . . . strained?"

"To say the least."

"Ah, that would explain it then. You don't look like a clerk. I know people and you don't look like a clerk. Come with me. We will discuss the position. What's your name?"

"Jobina Grant."

"Come with me, Jobina Grant. We will see what we see. If you really want to work . . . ."

"Oh, I do, Mr. Greevy. Very much." She followed him

to a tiny office at the rear of the shop. There was a desk with a brass lamp atop it. There were two file cabinets and two straight-backed chairs. "I must tell you I haven't any experience," she said. "I have never worked."

"Ah, I knew that the moment you walked through the door. It is obvious you're not of the working class." Mr. Greevy removed his steel-rimmed glasses. He cleaned the lenses and then returned them to his nose. "Sit down, Jobina. That is an unusual name. A family name?"

"My great-grandfather's name was Joby."

"English?"

"Yes. He came to America in the early 1800's. According to family legend, he was a stowaway. It makes an amusing story, but it seems unlikely. It was such a long trip in those days."

"My people were English too. Sound English stock, the backbone of this country. I suppose you are a war widow? That is what we get for joining in Europe's wars—widows and orphans."

"William . . . My husband wasn't called to serve. He died after the war ended. There was an accident. I'm sorry, Mr. Greevy. It is still difficult to talk about."

"Of course. I wasn't prying, you understand. It's good business to know something of the people in my employ. I'm a businessman. It doesn't pay to be softhearted."

"I could provide personal references," Jobina said eagerly. "My friends would vouch for my character. And there is the minister, and Dr. Porterfield also."

Mr. Greevy's eyes blinked behind their sparkling lenses. He stared at Jobina, rubbing his fringe of white hair. "Dr. Andrew Porterfield?" he asked. "A fine man.

A credit to the medical profession. That is more than I can say for some of the new fellows, with their newfangled ideas. It's even worse since the war. Everything is changing. They call it progress. I call it humbug. Toiletries, for example. My competitors have begun to carry perfumes and face creams and hand creams in their shops. I am forced to follow suit or lose business. I, a registered pharmacist, have to worry about the latest thing in perfume! It's humbug. But what can I do?"

Jobina listened politely to Mr. Greevy's monologue. She nodded and smiled and tried not to fidget, though her fingers dug into the palms of her hands. It was an effort to remain in her chair, for now she sensed there was a chance she might be hired. There *is* a chance, she thought, if only I can keep him on the subject. "Mr. Greevy," she said, taking a breath, "I'm certain I could be helpful to you. I know a great deal about toiletries. I know all the French products and the American products as well. You would not have to be concerned. You could devote your time to more . . . serious matters. Women's tastes are fickle and—"

"Fickle, yes. That is the word. One day they want the scent of gardenias; the next the scent of roses. Salesmen come to my door every week, waving their new products at me. What's wrong with the old products? That's what I want to know. My wife has never used anything but rose water and glycerine on her hands. There is nothing wrong with it except that it's not modern. Modern!" Mr. Greevy exclaimed, wrinkling his nose. "I hope you aren't a suffragette, Jobina?"

"A suffragette? Why, no. I have no interest in such things."

"It is a relief to know there are still sensible women in the world. What would women do with their votes anyway? Cast them for the first handsome smile they see, that's what. The country would be ruined."

"You may rest assured I have no interest in politics, Mr. Greevy. I am interested only in finding work. I must earn my living."

"The position pays eighteen dollars a week. It's a generous wage for a woman. Especially for a woman with no experience. I allow my employees one meal a day. A sandwich, a beverage, and dessert. That is more than generous. You would be required to work six days a week, ten A.M. to seven P.M. Ladies do not begin their shopping until ten. I want no other kind of women in my pharmacy. I want no hussies. This is a respectable establishment."

Jobina clapped her hands together. "I am *hired*, Mr. Greevy?" she cried. "Oh, *thank you*. Thank you *very* much. You will not be sorry. I *swear* it." A vast smile lighted her lovely face. She was as radiant as a schoolgirl, for she knew she had been rescued. A terrible weight lifted from her shoulders and she felt giddy. She wanted to laugh, to cry, to shout the wonderful news. "I cannot tell you how much this means to me, Mr. Greevy. My children—"

"Children!"

"I have two little daughters, Caroline and Daisy."

"Children?" Mr. Greevy leaned back, tapping his fingers on the desk. He sighed. "That puts a different color on it," he said. "Children? You hardly look . . . You should have told me you had children, Jobina. I couldn't consider hiring a woman with children. It's out of the question. It's unfortunate. If I had known . . ."

Jobina was very still, very pale. Her throat burned and she swallowed. "Please, Mr. Greevy," she said when she was able to speak. "My children have nothing to do with this. I need work. I promise I will work very hard. I am asking for a chance, just a chance. I know I could be of help to you. I know . . ." She bowed her head, hiding her tears. "I apologize," she sniffled. "But I was so happy when I thought I was hired."

Mr. Greevy sighed again. He was of two minds now, for while he had always believed that tears were the weapons women turned against men, he was nevertheless susceptible to them. He studied the young and anguished widow. Frowning, he pulled at his tie. "Children need their mother," he said finally. "Your place is with your children."

"They need food also, Mr. Greevy," Jobina replied. "They need a roof over their heads and clothes to wear. I wouldn't be looking for work if I had the means to give them those things. It's not choice; it's necessity."

"You must see my side of it. Children are often sick. They have colds and upsets and fevers. They have whims. I'm a businessman. I expect my employees to be here every day on time, no matter their problems at home. It's the only way to run a business. I have four children of my own. They are grown now, but I remember how it was with them. Never a minute's peace, that's how it was."

"Please hear me out, Mr. Greevy. My children are

no trouble at all. They are very healthy."

"Children are children. If they're not falling down stairs, they're burning up with fever. It's a red throat one minute, measles the next. Pharmacists know children."

"I have already made arrangements for a woman to care for my girls," Jobina lied. "She is very reliable. She was a nurse, Mr. Greevy. She is retired, you see, and . . . and she lives in my building. She won't charge much . . . and she is reliable."

Mr. Greevy shook his head. Certainly he did not know all he claimed, but he knew a lie when he heard it. A brave lie it was too, he thought, his frown deepening. "I wish I could help you," he said. "But in business—"

"You are a businessman, Mr. Greevy, so I will put it in business terms. I will work here for a week at no salary. It will be a kind of test. If all goes well, then you can pay me sixteen dollars instead of eighteen. It's surely good business to save money, isn't it? And I would bring my own lunch from home. Another saving!"

Mr. Greevy took off his glasses. He wiped the lenses, looked through them, and wiped them again. "You are a determined young woman." He smiled. "More determined than you appear."

"I need this chance, Mr. Greevy. If it goes badly, you will lose nothing."

"All right. A chance. As you say, a test. I will agree to try you for a week. Then we will see. It's against my better judgment. But since you have found such a reliable woman to care for your children . . ." Mr. Greevy saw the color rush to Jobina's cheeks. He laughed. "Don't worry, I'm not so easily gulled. I'm not giving you the chance because I believed your story. I didn't, not a word of it. I'm giving you the chance because once somebody gave me a chance. I hope you find the woman you described, Jobina. You have until Monday. You start work Monday at ten A.M. sharp. And don't bring your lunch from home. Emile makes egg salad on Mondays."

"Emile?"

"My clerk. He's a foreigner, a Frenchy. But he is honest and hard working. I expect a day's work for a day's pay. Sentiment is one thing. It has its price. But it's money that moves the world. I don't give my money away. You will earn your salary."

"Mr. Greevy, I could hug you!"

"We will see. There are rules here, Jobina. You are to wear dark clothing. No jewelry besides a watch and wedding ring. No cosmetics at any time. The style of your hair is acceptable. Keep it that way; no combs or ribbons. Lastly, your friends are not to visit you here. My former clerk used my pharmacy as a social club. I will not permit that. Are we agreed?"

"Oh yes, Mr. Greevy. I understand."

"Do you have any questions?"

"Is there a cash register at the toiletries counter? I have never used one. I will have to learn."

"You will, come Monday. There are three registers. One at my counter, one at the fountain, and one at toiletries. I tally the receipts myself each evening at seven. We stay until all the receipts are tallied."

"Yes, I understand."

Mr. Greevy pushed his chair back. He stood. "I will see

you Monday. Sharp at ten."

Jobina stood too, offering her hand to Mr. Greevy. "I will be here," she said. "Thank you. Thank you so much."

The sun had disappeared, swallowed whole by thick gray clouds. Snow had begun to fall and the wind gathered strength, snatching hats from the heads of unwary pedestrians. Jobina almost lost her footing on the slippery pavement. She stumbled, but she quickly righted herself, juggling her packages in the crook of her arm while she tried to hold on to her hat. She laughed, for now everything seemed very funny. I have a job, she thought, her spirits soaring anew. I have an actual job.

Ellen Sisk was peering over the banister as Jobina hurried upstairs. "I saw you coming," she said. "My fingers are still crossed. How did it turn out?"

"Mr. Greevy hired me, bless him. I start work Monday morning."

"Congratulations, Jobina. I'm happy for you."

"It's all your doing. I will never be able to thank you enough. Come inside, Ellen. We will celebrate over tea and presents."

"Is that what those packages are? Presents?"

"Come." Jobina smiled, opening her door, "I will show you. I splurged a little. I know I shouldn't have, but I'm not sorry. It will be my last splurge for quite some time. Anyway, it's a special occasion. My first job!"

"I'll put the kettle on."

Jobina threw off her hat and coat and then followed Ellen into the kitchen. "You really did bring me luck," she said. "You and Jack. Things were looking awfully bleak. Now Mr. Greevy has given me my chance and I intend to make the most of it. I intend to be the best clerk he has ever had."

"Are you nervous about it? Your first job and all?"

"I was nervous about the interview. I was terrified. My heart was pounding so hard I thought it would burst. Poor Mr. Greevy. He didn't want to give me the job. He took pity on me."

"You got the job. That's all that counts."

"I can scarcely believe it, Ellen. If the streets had not been so snowy, I would have *danced* home." Jobina put cups and saucers on the table. She opened one of the packages and removed half a dozen cream buns, placing them on a plain white tray. "I told you I splurged," she said. "Though I am learning. I passed up the chocolate torte. Too expensive."

"It's good you can still smile. I'm used to counting my pennies and it's no fun. It must be worse for you, after what you're used to. Don't you get mad?"

"Sometimes. At night, when the children are asleep and I'm alone, I have terrible thoughts. It's foolish. I am old enough to know that life is unfair." Jobina sat down. She poured tea, warming her hands over the steam. "I always had servants, Ellen," she said quietly. "Of course I knew their lives were very different from mine, but I never questioned why that should be. Why should some people have everything while others have nothing? Life is unfair."

"Like I said before, some people are born to the purple."

"Well, my *purple* days are in the past. I shall have to see what I can do for myself now. Everybody is expecting me to fail. I cannot say I blame them. I have never been especially useful. Miss Pym had to show me how to make a shopping list. Dear Miss Pym. I bought a lovely silk scarf for her . . . These other packages are for you."

"Really?" Ellen's eyes widened. "For me?"

"Enjoy them."

Ellen opened the first package, a two-pound box of chocolates. The second package was a box of cigars for Jack, and the third, an assortment of satin hair ribbons for Annie. All these were things the Sisks' strict budget could not have provided; they were treats, small luxuries, and Ellen was delighted. "It's like Christmas." She smiled, her pretty blue eyes twinkling. "Wait till Annie sees the ribbons. And Jack! He buys one cigar every Saturday afternoon and makes it last till Sunday night. Now he'll have a whole box. Talk about splurging! I don't know what to say. Thank you, Jobina. I really mean it. It was really nice of you. I can imagine Annie's expression when she sees . . . But you shouldn't have spent your money."

"I wanted to. I wouldn't have a job, if not for you and Jack. It's a celebration. Oh, that reminds me. I stopped on my way home to telephone the Thayers. They are coming here tonight after dinner. I wish you and Jack would join us."

"I don't know, Jobina. The Thayers. They're kind of fancy. I mean you're fancy too, but . . . Well, you know what I mean. The Thayers are high up the ladder for Jack and me. We'd be out of place."

"Nonsense. I insist you come."

"I don't know. What would I wear? I've been saving to buy a new dress. I don't have enough yet. Don't get me wrong, Jobina," Ellen said quickly. "Jack gives us everything we need. It's the little extra things that are hard. His company promoted him to office manager, but he didn't get much of a raise. He's supporting his mother, and he helps support my mother too. It's hard. I was doing some sewing at home. The money came in handy. It made a big difference. Then I lost my customers, both of them in one week. So it's back to counting pennies."

"Sewing? I must have a word with Irene. She is unhappy with the woman she has now. Perhaps Irene could . . ." Jobina paused. Her gaze was dark and suddenly intent. She put her cup down, staring at Ellen. "I have an idea," she said. "There may be a way we can help each other, if you are willing. I do hope so. It would be too perfect to be true."

"What way?"

"Miss Pym is leaving at the end of February. She will be going to the Thayers. I shall have to find someone to look after Caroline and Daisy while I'm working. Irene suggested that I leave the girls at her house every day, but all that back and forth would be upsetting to them. Besides, they don't belong on Gramercy Park anymore. They must make new lives here. It's just that the timing is bad. In the fall the girls will be busy with school most of the day. Unfortunately, school is seven months off. In the meantime it is a problem."

"I see what you're getting at. *Me*. *I* could look after them."

"It would be extra money for you, Ellen. And it would be an enormous relief to me. Will you consider if? Daisy is no trouble. She's an easy child. Caroline has been . . . moody. Everyone says time will cure that."

Ellen was smiling broadly, shaking her blond head from side to side. "I don't have to consider it, Jobina," she said. "I'll *do* it. I'd have to ask Jack, but he won't mind. Any kind of work I can do at home is okay with him."

"You would have a long day. My hours at Greevy's are ten to seven."

"I'm home all day anyhow, except when I take Annie out or go to the market. One kid, three kids," Ellen shrugged, "what's the difference. *Sure* I'll do it. I can't take them fancy places, like Miss Pym, but I'll take good care of them. You can count on that."

"And Jack won't mind?"

"Why should he? He's always joking that I have things too soft. Now I'll be earning money again. Money is money. Did you happen to notice my sofa? The springs are popping out and one of the legs fell off. I stuck a book under there but you still have to be careful sitting down. We were going to wait till Jack's next promotion to buy another sofa. Now we won't have to. I can make time payments."

"Are you really sure, Ellen?"

"I can't wait to tell Jack. First I'll give him the cigars and then I'll tell him. Two surprises! Oh, he'll be smiling tonight. Looks like it's been a good day for both of us, Jobina."

"It's a start," she replied, glancing around at her clean and airy kitchen. I have a flat, she thought. I have a job and a new friend. Yes, it's a start.

Chapter Six

It was a little after nine when Jobina left the brownstone and plunged into the sharp cold of Monday morning. She was tired, for her sleep had been fitful, but the icy wind roaring along the avenue brought her quickly awake. The wind burned her face, her neck, the tips of her uncovered ears. She clutched at her hat, to no avail. It blew away, coming to rest beneath the wheels of a passing automobile. With a sigh, she drew her collar up about her chin and began the walk to Greevy's Pharmacy.

Jobina walked briskly, her eyes staring straight ahead, her gloved hands thrust into the pockets of her coat. She appeared confident, though in truth she was frightened. Perspiration misted her brow despite the bitter cold. She felt the thumping of her heart, the sudden weakness in her legs. She felt faint. She wanted to turn back, but she knew she could not. "Help me," she murmured. "Please help me to get through this."

Jobina had risen at dawn, trembling and sick to her stomach. She had been brusque with her children and, later, with Miss Pym. When the time had come to leave for work, she had had to force herself out the door. She had reminded herself that millions of people went to work every day, but such reminders had not stilled her fears. "What if I fail?" she had asked over and over again. "Please don't let me fail," she had prayed.

Now she huddled in her coat and stared at the pharmacy. *"Please,"* she implored, reaching her shaking hand to the doorknob. She saw Mr. Greevy approaching. She took a great breath. "Good morning," she said, trying to smile.

"You are early, Jobina."

"I was afraid I would be late."

"First day jitters." Mr. Greevy chuckled. "You look like a frightened deer facing the huntsmen."

"I'm sorry. I'm a little nervous this morning."

"There is time for a cup of tea before you begin work. Tea is soothing to the nerves."

"Thank you, Mr. Greevy, but I couldn't."

"I suppose your stomach is fluttering? I have a remedy for that. It's my own special elixir, very popular in the neighborhood. Come along, Jobina. I will show you where to leave your things and then we will see." Mr. Greevy led his new employee to a recessed storage area at the side of the shop. Deep shelves filled with boxes and bottles and jars lined the walls from floor to ceiling. There was a single chair, a single light fixture. "My stockroom," he explained. "The door to the left is the closet. You will share it with Emile. He's an honest young man. Your belongings will be safe. The facilities are to the right," he said, pointing to a second door. "And in the rear is the stairway to the basement. The basement is

Emile's domain. I permit him to keep a small workshop. He's always working at something or other. I didn't expect it of a foreigner." Mr. Greevy reached into his vest pocket and withdrew a round gold watch. "If you have no questions, I must get back to my counter."

Jobina glanced warily at the laden shelves. "I'm sure I will have questions," she replied. "I have a great deal to learn."

"I know you will do your best."

"Oh yes, Mr. Greevy. I promise I will."

"An honest effort is all I ask. A day's work for a day's pay. Don't wear yourself out with nerves. I'm strict, but not an ogre."

"Thank you, Mr. Greevy. I will remember that."

"Then we are agreed."

"Yes." Jobina smiled. "We are agreed."

Jobina was feeling stronger as she stepped behind the polished glass of the toiletries counter. She had washed her face and smoothed her windblown hair and dabbed cologne at her wrists. Obediently, she had swallowed Mr. Greevy's special elixir and the grumbling in her stomach had ceased. "I am ready, Mr. Greevy," she said now, excitement and apprehension mingling in her voice.

"I will show you the cash register first, Jobina. It's not hard. The drawer opens when you press a key, and all the keys are numbered. You must take your time in the beginning. If you hurry, you will press the wrong key. The figures will not tally. You will get used to the register after a week or so. Until then, you must take your time.

All right, we will pretend a customer has just made a five dollar purchase . . ."

Jobina listened carefully to Mr. Greevy's instructions, nodding when she understood, frowning when she did not. He repeated his instructions several times. He showed her how to write a sales receipt, how to strike the register keys and mark the inventory sheets. Twice he was called to the pharmacy counter and during these intervals she practiced. "Mr. Greevy," she smiled when he returned again, "the register does all the addition by itself!"

"Of course," he replied in surprise. "I couldn't have a woman here otherwise. Women can't be trusted with figures. Give a woman two and two and she will make it come out five. My own wife . . . Ah, Emile," he said, interrupting his thought to motion his clerk over. "Emile, this is Jobina. She will be working here. She has learned about the register. I will leave it to you to explain about the stock. The gift-wrapping too."

"Yes, sir."

"And take care of the first few customers yourself, Emile. Show Jobina the proper way."

"Yes, sir. I will do it."

"There is one more rule, Jobina. Anything you break will be deducted from your salary. I turn a blind eye to spills, but breakages will be deducted."

"That is fair."

"I will leave you to your work then. Good luck."

"Thank you, Mr. Greevy." A chair had not been provided behind the counter and so Jobina stood, smiling at Emile. "I am a little nervous about all this," she said.

"Thank you for helping me."

"I help you, I help me." Emile smiled back. "We are, how you say, all in the same boats. Mr. Greevy, he is the captain."

Jobina was charmed by Emile's accent, by his bright and cheerful manner. "I hope the boat doesn't sink," she replied. He laughed and it was clear that laughter was as natural to him, and as necessary, as breathing. "I think we are going to be friends, Emile. Yes, I am sure of it!"

Emile Lanteau was twenty-one years old, small and dark and slight of build. His black hair was parted in the center and brushed straight back. His eyes, not quite black, not quite brown, held a merry twinkle. All his features were narrow, though the upward tilt of his mouth saved them from severity. He was, as Jobina would later describe him, unquiet. His hands jumped about; his eyebrows shot up and down; his lips pursed and parted and smiled. He had two joys in life, his family and his small basement workshop. They were equal joys, for while his family gave him pleasure, he was convinced that his workshop would one day make him rich.

Emile had emigrated to America just before the war. He had earned his passage across the Atlantic, working as a cabin boy on a French liner. It had been an education, for he had observed at first hand the carefree ways of the rich. He had seen expensive clothing worn once and then tossed to the floor. He had seen huge amounts of money wagered on the turn of a card. He had seen fine old wines drunk like water, and enough food to feed his Provence village for a year. If he had been shocked by such extravagance, he had also been intrigued. It had occurred to him that life did not have to be a gray pattern of work and sleep and a Saturday visit to the café. It had occurred to him that there was more. He had made some promises to himself and it was said in Provence that Emile Lanteau always kept his promises.

Now he finished showing Jobina the last of the many toiletries at her counter. "The prices I mark each month," he explained. "Sometimes they go up, sometimes down. Not so often down. Profits for the cash box, yes? The more the merry."

"Emile, the perfumes are not displayed well. Look, they are almost hidden behind the hand lotions. Women buy perfume on impulse. If they cannot see it, they will not think to buy it. Could I . . . Would it be all right if I moved a few items around?"

"This impulse you say. It is important?"

"Very important, for things like perfume."

"Mr. Greevy, he gives the counter to you." Emile shrugged. "You can fix it how you want. I fixed the fountain how I want. It is good now. You can make the counter good. More profits, yes?"

"I do hope so."

"But you should not worry," Emile said. "When you worry, your face does not laugh. And such a pretty face you have. *Tres jolie.*"

"You are sweet, Emile . . . Oh, Emile, there is a customer coming."

"Watch and you will see," he replied with a wink. "It is easy."

Jobina stood quietly off to the side as Emile served their customer. He made a great fuss over the woman, and when she purchased a bottle of bath oil, he seemed pleased. *"Voilà!"* he said, snapping his fingers. "It is easy."

"Yes."

"Something is wrong?"

"Well, I was just thinking . . . Please don't misunderstand me, Emile. I think you are a charming salesman. But that woman would have bought more if she had been . . . encouraged to do so. She was looking at the night cream. A few words and she would have bought it. I'm sorry." Jobina shook her head. "I am new here. I should keep my opinions to myself."

"But no. I like to hear. In France, a woman knows what she wants and she buys. She buys only that. In America it is different, yes?"

"Not exactly. It's different with things like perfumes and creams. No one needs those things. They are . . . luxuries. They make a woman feel better. Pampered, if you see what I mean. Any woman, even if she is a careful shopper, will spend a little more for that feeling." Jobina glanced down at the counter, touching the dainty glass bottles and jars. "These luxuries are not expensive, Emile," she said. "A woman can afford to treat herself without spending too much money."

A bright light shone in Emile's eyes. He nodded vigorously, his hands jumping at his sides. "I see how you mean, Jobina. I see now. I will remember." He nodded again. "It is good to know for the future. You are a good teacher."

"I've *had* good teachers. I've spent a lot of time and money on the other side of the counter. I hate to admit it, but I've spent half my life shopping. And I am a woman. That helps."

"Here is another customer coming. Now is my turn to watch. I will learn, yes?"

Jobina clasped her shaking hands behind her back and stepped forward. "Good morning," she said. "May I help you?"

It was a busy morning. Customers streamed into the pharmacy, all the women amongst them stopping at the toiletries counter. "Just looking," they would announce, though few left without making a purchase. Jobina's nervousness deepened, for she was worried about mistakes on sales receipts, or worse, at the register. In her nervousness, she broke a bottle of cologne and almost broke a vial of French perfume, catching it only inches from the floor. "I'm afraid I am clumsy today," she said again and again to her customers. "I am new here."

Business surged during the noon hours. Often Jobina finished with one customer and looked up to find six others waiting. Politely, she answered their questions. She offered suggestions and gave advice when advice was requested. She wrapped packages, tying precise little bows. She smiled and smiled and smiled.

"Well, Jobina," Mr. Greevy said, "you have had quite a morning."

"I am sorry for the mess," she replied, quickly scooping up bits of wrapping paper and ribbon. "It's been bedlam. Is business always so . . . brisk?"

"There are good days and bad. This time of year is

usually good. Winter colds are going around. There is some strep too. That keeps the pharmacy busy. And women seem to buy more toiletries at this time of year. I suppose they are longing for spring, for flowery things. Women have their moods."

"They are certainly longing for bath oil. The shelf is almost empty. Are there replacements in the stock room?"

"Emile will see to the stock. You may take your lunch now."

"Is it time? I did not wear my watch."

"It's past two. Take your lunch while you can. I will mind the counter."

"Past two?" Jobina frowned. "But where has the time gone?"

"Into the register, I hope. I am going to check the receipts and then we will see."

"I don't think I made any mistakes, Mr. Greevy."

"We will see."

Jobina left the counter and walked across the shop to the fountain. "Am I supposed to eat here?" she asked Emile. "Or in the back?"

"Here. I have your sandwich ready. You would like tea? All the ladies, they drink tea. Sometimes cocoa, but not so often. Maybe you would like a soda? I have all kinds. Chocolate, vanilla, strawberry."

"Tea sounds lovely, Emile. Thank you." Jobina slid onto a stool, smoothing her long skirts. "It's wonderful to sit down." She sighed. "My legs are aching. My back is stiff. I have new respect for salesclerks. They earn their money."

"*We* earn." Emile laughed. "We are they, yes?"

Jobina looked at her hands, massaging the small paper cuts, the jagged scratches. She had caught her thumb in the register and now she noticed that the knuckle was red and swollen. "I have the scars to prove it," she replied. She turned as Mr. Greevy came up beside her. "Were there mistakes?" she asked anxiously.

"The register tallies. I am pleased with the receipts, Jobina. You did well. It was an excellent morning. Your inventory sheets, however, are incomplete. I expect you to complete them before you leave for the day."

"Yes, Mr. Greevy. I will."

"It's important."

"I understand. I'm sorry, Mr. Greevy. I wanted everything to be perfect. I tried."

"For your first morning, you did well. There is still a long afternoon ahead."

But the afternoon passed quickly. The hours between three and six were filled with customers, some of them amiable, others of them querulous and demanding. A very large, middle-aged woman examined all the six different brands of face cream, the five brands of hand lotion, and then bought nothing. A younger woman selected a costly bottle of perfume and then changed her mind as the package was being wrapped. Two women came to the counter together, arguing over the best brand of eye cream. When Jobina attempted to intervene, she was told, in the rudest terms, to mind her business. She smiled and let the argument continue, for at Greevy's Pharmacy the customer was always right.

Business slowed after six o'clock. Jobina completed

her inventory sheets, checked them, and checked them twice again. She swept the littered floor behind the counter. She straightened the shelves and wiped fingerprints from the glass display case. It was exactly seven when Mr. Greevy locked the doors. He pulled the shades, striding a moment later to Jobina's register. "I wondered if you would last through the day," he said.

"I wondered also."

Mr. Greevy studied Jobina's pale and weary face, the weary set of her shoulders. "I see the work was hard on you. Too hard?"

"Oh no, Mr. Greevy. No, you mustn't think that. I can do my job. I am stronger than I look. Really I am. I'm sorry about the inventory sheets. It won't happen again."

"Don't upset yourself, Jobina. I was merely asking. I would not want you collapsing in a heap. That was a joke," Mr. Greevy added, silencing her reply. "I enjoy a little joke from time to time. You shouldn't take every word wrong. If you do, you will wear yourself out with nerves."

"I'm sorry."

"And stop apologizing. You gave me an honest day's work." Mr. Greevy settled his glasses on his nose. He opened the register. "Excellent," he said after some moments. "You did two days' business in one. You may rest easy. All is well."

"I'm home," Jobina called, letting herself into the flat. The parlor lights had been dimmed and she walked to the kitchen. "Good evening, Miss Pym," she said. "Are the girls asleep?"

"Daisy slipped right off after dinner. Caroline is in her room drawing pictures. They had a nice day, madam. I took them to see the polar bears in Central Park Zoo. Later we stopped and watched the skaters. When we returned, your young ladies helped me fix a kidney pie. I saved some for your dinner. It's warming in the oven."

"I can't imagine how we are going to manage without you, Miss Pym."

"There is no cause to worry, madam. Mrs. Sisk and I have talked. She's a sensible woman. I believe she will be a good influence on Caroline and Daisy. Her own child is well behaved." Miss Pym took Jobina's coat and purse, laying them across a chair. "Do sit down, madam," she urged. "You look tired."

"I earned my keep today."

"The work was not strenuous, I hope."

Jobina smiled. She was exhausted and her body ached, but those were small matters, for she realized she was no longer afraid. She had survived her first day of work and she knew now she would survive all the others yet to come. "The truth is I am proud of myself," she replied. "Immodest as that may sound. I have a sense of accomplishment. The day went very quickly too. I was surprised."

"Shall I run a tub for you, madam?"

"Oh, I wouldn't think of it. Your day was busier than mine, and you have the walk to Gramercy Park besides. Thank you for making dinner, Miss Pym. That wasn't part of the bargain."

"I enjoy cooking. I haven't had much opportunity in recent years. One doesn't forget the old recipes though. And of course I had your young ladies to help me. Children can do simple kitchen tasks, madam. It's good for them to learn."

"I wish I'd learned."

Miss Pym got into her boots and muffler and coat. She tied a woolen scarf about her head and picked up her handbag. "I will be on my way now," she said. "A hot tub is the best thing for sore muscles. With a pinch of salts, madam."

"I may need the whole box. Good night, Miss Pym. Safe home."

"Good night, madam."

Jobina stretched her arms above her head. She yawned. After a moment she rose and crossed the hall to Caroline's room. "Hello, darling." She smiled, kissing the child's golden head. "I missed you today."

Caroline did not look up. She was tucked in bed, the quilts drawn close, a large tablet propped against her knees. "Hello, Mama," she said. "We went to the zoo."

"Yes, I heard. Did you have a nice time?"

"We saw the bears."

Jobina sat at the edge of the bed. Gently, she stroked her daughter's cheek. "Was it fun?" she asked. "Were the bears very ferocious? You are so quiet, Caroline. You never smile anymore." Jobina sighed, for she did not know which was worse—Caroline's tantrums, or the deep and somber silences that had replaced them. "You are a moody girl, my darling. Show me what you are drawing."

"Trees."

"What kind of trees? Let Mama see."

"No."

"Just a tiny peek?"

"No," Caroline repeated, wrenching the tablet from Jobina. "It's for Miss Pym. She's going away. She's going to be Ian's nanny."

"That's true, darling. But she will be here all this week, and next week you will have Mrs. Sisk."

"I don't want her."

"Oh, you will have lots of fun. You and Daisy and Mrs. Sisk. And there is Annie too. A new playmate!"

"I don't want her."

"Give Mama a good-night kiss, Caroline."

"No. You're making Miss Pym go away. You're mean."

"Caroline!"

The child moved suddenly. She threw the tablet down, turning her back to Jobina. "You're mean," she said again. *"Mean, mean, mean."*

Tears welled in Jobina's eyes. She fumbled for her handkerchief. She had explained Miss Pym's imminent departure to both her daughters, but only Caroline had seemed truly distressed. The tantrums had ended then; the silences had begun, broken on occasion by a harsh outburst, a mournful sigh. Jobina felt helpless. She felt as if she were losing Caroline, and the thought made her sick at heart. "I am sorry," she said now. "When you are older, you will understand."

"I *won't.*"

"Good night, Caroline."

Jobina did not expect a response and no response came. She stood, putting out the lights. Wearily, she walked to the door. She tiptoed into Daisy's room and bent over the bed. "Sleep well, darling," she whispered. "Sleep well."

It was almost ten when Jobina struggled into the parlor and fell upon her bed. She had eaten a few bits of kidney pie and drunk two cups of tea. She had washed the dishes, dried them, and stacked them in the cupboard. For thirty minutes she had soaked in the bathtub, massaging her throbbing legs, her swollen ankles. Now, nestling in the soft folds of her robe, she lay back and pulled the quilts to her chin. She closed her eyes and slept. Her dreams were chaotic, edgy, but for the first time since William's death, she slept through the night.

The sky was still dark when Jobina awoke Tuesday morning. She raised herself on one elbow and then collapsed against the pillows, feeling a searing pain across her shoulders. Cautiously, inch by inch, she raised herself again. The pain was fierce. It was in her back, her arms, her legs, and she gasped. She took a tiny step. She took another, and another. "Welcome to the real world," she muttered. "George, I wish you could see me now."

Pain did not keep Jobina from work. She allowed herself a half hour to walk the seven blocks to the pharmacy and, though she was breathless and slightly stooped, she arrived with time to spare. She voiced no complaints, offered no excuses. It was a work day. It was her job and she was determined to do her job.

If Tuesday was a struggle, Wednesday was much easier. Jobina realized that each day was easier than the day before and her confidence grew. By Saturday she felt as if she had been working all her life. She had mastered the register and the inventory sheets; she had learned the stock and the moods of her customers. She had made a discovery too, a discovery she shared with Emile. "I was wrong when I told you that women were treating themselves to little luxuries," she explained. "That's not it at all. They are treating themselves to fantasies. These perfumes and creams and lotions . . . They are fantasies, Emile. A woman applies a bit of perfume and she is changed. She isn't a housewife or a schoolteacher. For that moment at least, she is a temptress!"

"Temptress?"

"*Seducteur.*" Jobina smiled, wondering if she had the correct word.

"I see how you mean. I see. These are important things you are telling me, Jobina."

"Hardly important. Your work is here at the soda fountain. You don't have to worry about customers' fantasies."

"But I have other work. Different from here." Emile paused, shrugging. "Different and not so different," he amended. "Soon I will show you. You will see how I mean. Now is Mr. Greevy and our money. Payday," he said, a wide smile lighting his face.

"I cannot believe a whole week has passed . . . Oh, Mr. Greevy, I was just saying that I cannot believe a whole week has passed."

"A profitable week."

"Really?"

148

Mr. Greevy held out two small yellow envelopes. "Your salary, Emile. And yours, Jobina."

"I don't understand. Our agreement was for me to work this week at no salary. It was to be a test."

"I remember. I decided to alter our agreement. You earned your salary, Jobina. I'm an honest businessman. I don't cheat my employees. And since you are my employee I will give you a piece of advice: Never turn down money you have earned. Know what's coming to you and be sure to get it, every cent. Don't let people take advantage. You can't be a shrinking violet when it comes to money."

"Mr. Greevy, I could hug you!"

"You will notice your pay envelope is three dollars short. That is for breakage. A bottle of cologne and a bottle of bath crystals. I warned you I would deduct breakages. I try to be fair."

"You are, Mr. Greevy. More than fair."

"Good night, Jobina. Emile, there is a dripping faucet in the stockroom sink. See to it before you leave."

"Yes, sir. I will fix like new."

Jobina watched Mr. Greevy walk away. She smiled, spreading fifteen crisp dollar bills on the marble counter top. She touched each bill, pride and excitement shining in her eyes.

"Your first payday, yes?" Emile asked.

"It's a wonderful feeling." Indeed to Jobina it was an extraordinary feeling. The money meant a great deal, but the fact that she had earned it meant more. Her doubts were allayed at last, her fears put to rest. "I have proved something to myself, Emile," she said. "I think I have finally grown up."

Jobina's step was light as she left the pharmacy. She breathed deeply of the sharp, cold air and then turned toward the corner. She was engrossed in her thoughts, so engrossed that she jumped when a hand touched her shoulder. "Irene!" she cried. "Heavens, you scared me to death! What in the world are you doing here?"

"Waiting for you."

"For me? Why? Is anything wrong at home? The girls—"

"The girls are fine. It's nothing like that. George and I wanted to surprise you. We planned a celebration . . . I'm sorry if I startled you, Jobina. Didn't you see the car? It's right there."

"I wasn't paying attention."

"Come along," Irene said, tucking her hands into a sable muff. "This is no night to be standing outside. I am freezing. Aren't you freezing? I don't know how you manage the walk home in such weather. I would be an icicle."

"It isn't a long walk."

"But it's *freezing*. Come along, Jobina. I hope your flat is warm. I am chilled to the bone."

"Tell me what we are celebrating. Wait, I think I know. We are celebrating a milestone, my first week at Greevy's. You didn't expect I would last the week, did you?"

"Of course I did. George didn't but . . . Jobina, have

you forgotten that it's your birthday? How incredible! Of all the things to forget. I must buy you a calendar and mark the important dates."

"It seems silly, doesn't it? It's just that I had a lot on my mind. But I'm glad you remembered, Irene. We will have a nice little party. Miss Pym was going to fix lamb stew."

"Nonsense. I brought a hamper filled with food. There is squab and wild rice and turtle soup. It needs only to be heated. And Cook made a maple fudge cake with *heaps* of whipped cream. Really, it's quite sinful. I shall gain five pounds . . . In you go," Irene said as Claus opened the car door. "There, isn't that better?"

"Much. Hello, George. How are you?"

"The question is how are you? You look exhausted."

"Oh." Jobina laughed. "Wait until you see me in a strong light." She pulled off her gloves, her muffler, and settled back into the scented warmth of the upholstery. "Lovely." She sighed. "Like days of old."

"Jobina, your hands. What has happened to your hands?"

"Well," she laughed again, "let's see. This is where I jammed my thumb in the cash register. This is where I stabbed my palm with the scissors. All these others are paper cuts." She gazed at George, a mischievous light twinkling in her eyes. "Are you horrified?" she asked. "You shouldn't be. I wrap dozens of packages every day. I am always cutting myself. But I'm earning my keep in the *real* world, George. Surprising as that may be."

"I will admit I am surprised. I am pleased too, Jobina. You are to be congratulated."

"I know. I was paid today. Fifteen dollars!"

"Fifteen? Is that all?"

"There were deductions for things I broke. I don't claim to be a perfect salesclerk." Jobina shrugged, the light still twinkling in her eyes. "Not yet anyway. I have high hopes for the future."

"Your Mr. Greevy certainly gets his money's worth."

"With reason. I have learned how hard money is to come by. When I remember all the money I *threw* away . . . But no more. I am turning into a bit of a pinchpenny myself, George. Yes, it's true. I wrote a shopping list yesterday. An extremely *strict* shopping list. I am determined to live within my means. Caroline and Daisy will have what they need, and perhaps a few things they don't need. But there will be no more sprees. I will wear rags before I will go into debt."

"You are being dramatic, Jobina."

"Am I?"

"Yes, unless you plan to spend your entire life behind the toiletries counter of Greevy's Pharmacy. This is a temporary measure. Other . . . opportunities will present themselves. You won't be a salesclerk forever. You won't want to be."

Jobina gazed again at George and now the light fled from her eyes. "I know that tone of voice," she said. "You are humoring me. You think Greevy's is a passing fancy. It isn't, George. Other opportunities may present themselves, but not the opportunities you suppose."

"I am not supposing anything."

"You are, and I know what it is. You have it in your mind that I will get tired enough, discouraged enough, to run back to Father. Greevy's is a whim and I am a whimsical female. Isn't that it, George? Isn't it?"

"I wish you would face facts. You are working in that shop for the unprincely sum of eighteen dollars a week. Or fifteen, if you happen to break something. You are tired. You are thinner. Good Lord, look at your hands. Your hands tell the story."

"Hush, George," Irene said. "I have been listening to this conversation and it is pointless. Jobina has made her position clear. There is no sense in going on and on about it."

"Does that mean you disagree with me?"

"I think we must respect Jobina's position. And I hope we can change the subject now. Come, let's get out of the car and go upstairs. As I recall, we planned a celebration."

Jobina laughed suddenly, her spirits lifting. "Yes, George," she teased, "it's my birthday and you have to be very sweet to me. You can't nag or be a bully or tell me all the things I am doing wrong. Promise?"

"Have it your own way." George sighed. "You will in any case. You are developing a stubborn streak, Jobina. I cannot say it is becoming."

"Father used to say that women, like children, should be seen but not heard. Is that your opinion too, George?"

"Certainly not. Although I admit there are times when such an idea is appealing. Times when you and Irene gang up on me. You seem to enjoy it."

"Oh, we do!" Smiling, Jobina followed George and Irene from the car. She looked at the starry sky, linking arms with her friends. "I'm so glad we are together tonight," she said.

It was a nice night, the celebration brightened by champagne and presents and laughter. Jobina, her eyes misty, made a silent wish and blew out all the candles on the cake. Later, the three friends crowded around the hearth in the parlor and sipped George's prized brandy. There were recollections of other birthdays, other years. Jobina spoke tenderly of William, and when a toast was offered, she raised her glass to his picture. "My darling," she whispered as the fire rose and roared up the chimney. "My darling William."

It was midnight when Jobina said good-bye to the Thayers. She looked in on the children, straightening Daisy's covers, moving Caroline's enormous teddy bear aside. Quietly, she returned to the parlor. She sat upon the bed and opened her purse, holding out fifteen crisp dollar bills. "We are going to be all right, William," she said, staring again at his picture. "You must not worry, my darling. We are going to be fine."

Chapter Seven

Winter lingered in the city. A brief March thaw was followed by more snow, by bitter winds, and cold, soaking rains that pounded windows night and day. The sun disappeared, sulking behind ominous black clouds. It was said that winter would never end, but in April the skies cleared at last and the air became sweet. City gardeners tended their flower boxes, exclaiming over the first delicate buds of spring. Trees, blessed by so much rain, burst into bloom. Children were everywhere, high young voices rising as if in welcome to the new season.

"Window displays," Jobina said to Mr. Greevy one sparkling day in April. "The weather is lovely now and there are more people about. Window displays will draw their attention. Pretty displays with perfume bottles and colored jars, and perhaps a few flowers."

"Flowers! In my pharmacy!"

"It's a way of drawing attention. The streets are crowded with people. We must take advantage of that. Pretty displays will . . . lure them."

"Flowers in a pharmacy! I never heard of such a thing."

But Mr. Greevy heard quite a lot about it during the next weeks, for Jobina persisted. She selected a small, unused side window and asked to decorate it "as a test." She continued to ask until an exasperated Mr. Greevy, wearying of the argument, consented. With her own money she bought a bouquet of lilacs and two yards of satin ribbon; with her own hands she arranged jars and bottles and flowers and bows in a design she called Spring Dance.

To Mr. Greevy's amazement, business doubled. By June it had tripled and, with a sheepish grin, he put Jobina in charge of window displays. He offered a raise of two dollars a week. Gratefully, she accepted. It was a happy day; to the end of her life she would remember the day she got her first raise.

Emile had been paying close attention to events at the pharmacy. He had noticed that Jobina had many ideas, and that these ideas almost always resulted in profits. He was interested, for he had several ideas of his own. He began spending more time in his workshop. On a warm night near the end of June he decided he was ready. "Jobina," he called, walking into the stockroom. "You are in a hurry going home?"

"I try to have a few minutes with Caroline and Daisy before they fall asleep. If I can keep *my* eyes open, that is. I'm tired. The shop was so busy today."

"Because of you. You have a good head on your neck."

"What? Oh, Emile," Jobina laughed. "You mean I have a good head on my shoulders. Thank you. It's a charming compliment."

"I am still learning the English."

"You do very well. Much better than I do with French."

"My wife, she helps me. She was born here." Emile smiled, his dark brows wiggling up and down. "I study hard, but sometimes the words fly away."

"You mustn't worry. You really do very well. I can't imagine where you find the time to study. You work such long hours. And Mr. Greevy tells me that when you finish in the shop, you work in the basement."

"My workshop. You would like to see my workshop, Jobina?"

"I confess I am curious. Are you building something there?"

"Money. I don't build money," Emile corrected himself, shrugging. "But down there is my work to earn money. For in the future. In the future I will be rich. I know how."

"You are lucky. I wish I knew how."

"I will show you, Jobina. You would like to see?"

"Why, yes. I think I would."

Emile opened the door to the basement. He pulled a cord and sharp yellow light fell upon the stairs. "Be careful walking," he urged. "They are high steps."

"What is that aroma?" Jobina paused, sniffing the air. "No, it is a particular scent. It's . . . Emile, are you blending perfume down here?"

"Yes."

"*Yes?*"

"I learn from my uncles. They grow lavender on their farm in Provence. In Provence the name of

Lanteau is, how you say, famous for lavender. They sell to the perfume companies. The perfume companies, they get rich. But the Lanteaus, they stay poor. When I am coming here on the boat, I decide I can make perfume too. I can get rich."

Jobina reached the bottom step. She turned, her eyes widening as she saw an improvised laboratory. Six large wooden crates had been sanded and nailed into a single unit. Covering the unit from end to end were beakers and flower presses and tapered glass vials. There was a laboratory burner of the type she had seen pictured in books. Nearby shelves held gallon containers of alcohol and glycerine and witch hazel, and tins of paraffin. "Emile," she said, "did you put all this together yourself?"

"A little bit each week," he replied proudly. "I find where to buy cheap. I save from my salary and I buy cheap. Bargains, yes?"

Jobina was impressed, for she knew Emile's salary was only twenty-eight dollars a week. On his salary he supported a wife, two infant sons, and several inlaws. He worked twelve hours a day, six days a week in the shop; after closing time, he worked countless hours in his laboratory. As if that were not enough, thought Jobina, he studies English and hunts for bargains. "I admire you, Emile," she said. "Your ambition . . . your dreams."

"Not dreams, Jobina. I make it real. I work hard. In Provence I work hard too, but no money comes. It is different in America, yes?"

"Well, it's true there are opportunities here."

"Opportunities." Emile beamed. "That is what I find.

And maybe you find with me. You and me," he said, jabbing his chest. "We find together."

"Together?"

"In business," he added hastily, concerned that Jobina had misunderstood. "My perfume and your ideas. We could make together a business. I will show you my perfume now. I have been mixing, mixing. Now I have it right. I hope so. You will tell me." He went to his work table and took a vial from a wire rack. "My best sample."

Jobina uncorked the vial. She sniffed, then sniffed again. "It is an unusual scent," she said finally. "It's exotic, a nighttime scent."

"This exotic you say. It is good?"

"Would you object to a suggestion, Emile?"

"Please."

"It is a bit heavy. Just a bit. If you could lighten it, I think you might have something very special. Exotic perfumes are coming into fashion now. The timing is excellent. Women's tastes are changing. I have noticed that women's skirts are getting shorter, and many women are wearing lipstick. Perhaps it's the influence of motion pictures. Or perhaps it was the war. I don't know. Women seem to be feeling a little . . . naughty."

"Temptress, yes?"

Jobina smiled. "At least in their fantasies," she replied. She raised the vial and sniffed Emile's perfume once more. "It's naughty enough. If you could lighten it . . . Is there a way to do that?"

"I know how from my uncles. They have a little workshop like here. They try to make perfume, but they are too busy on the farm. It is a pip dream."

"Pipe dream, Emile."

"Pipe dream, yes," he laughed. "My uncles, they teach me perfume, but for their own they are too busy growing the lavender. It is different with me. I am young and I have my Greevy's job. I can make perfume in my other time."

"It takes a *long* time to build a business. Even in America. It takes money. You should find a patron, Emile. Someone to sponsor your efforts."

"I have figured it out. To start, a thousand dollars. It is very much, yes? My wife Inge, she says it is greenhorn talk, silly talk." Emile shrugged, his hands flying up in the air. "I am a greenhorn."

"You are ambitious. There is nothing wrong with ambition. America is a nation of greenhorns. I have heard that the first Astor in this country ate his peas off a knife and could barely read. Look how far they have come!"

"Soon I am becoming a citizen."

"That's wonderful, Emile."

"Then I am becoming rich. You and me together, Jobina. My perfume and your ideas. We are, how you say, partners."

Jobina was amused by Emile's enthusiasm. She met his dark, merry gaze and she smiled. "You are sweet to include me," she said. "And certainly I will be glad to help, if I can. But you don't need me. If you need a partner at all, it is a partner with money. I'm afraid my pockets are empty."

"We will find money somewhere. I am praying every day to St. Jude. In Provence I pray to him that I come to

160

America. My uncles, they laugh. They are still in Provence, yes? I am here."

"If there is any justice, your confidence will be rewarded. You must be patient, Emile. Great successes are not made overnight."

"I am young and you are young. The world is our oyster shell. This I know. But I don't know names. What is a good name for our perfume, Jobina?"

"Well, it's a nighttime scent, sort of mysterious . . . You could call it Midnight."

Emile was smiling as he lifted the perfume vial. *"Voilà,"* he said, staring at the amber liquid. "Midnight, the beginning of our riches."

Jobina devoted little thought to Emile's fledgling business in the weeks that followed. He came to her with questions and she answered them, though she was more amused than interested. Twice she pleaded Emile's cause to George, suggesting it might be a worthwhile investment; twice she was rebuffed and she deemed the subject closed. She had other concerns—her work, her chores, her children—and to these concerns she gave all her attention. Her life settled into a pattern, sometimes dreary, always lonely. She shed her severe black mourning clothes, but she could not shed her memories. In the small, quiet hours of night she stared at William's picture and longed for the comfort of his arms. "William," she whispered again and again, a litany of sorrow and love.

Time passed. The gentle spring turned to summer. A

161

heat wave gripped the city in August, the temperatures soaring so high that people gasped for breath. The sun was merciless, a yellow fire burning in a sky of unclouded blue. The air was heavy and moist and terrible. Each day rain was prophesied; each day the sun blazed, fatter, hotter than the day before. "When will it *end?*" Jobina moaned to Ellen Sisk one Sunday late in August. "Really, I want to scream."

"I can remember worse summers. It's always bad in the city."

"We used to go to Southampton every summer. William rented a cottage. Oh, it was lovely. Right on the beach. We had only to open the door and there was the ocean. The girls had such a good time. Of course they've had a wonderful time with you this summer, Ellen. Even Caroline smiles when she's setting off for Coney Island. It is a pleasure to see. She looks adorable with her little pail and shovel!"

"Coney Island isn't Southampton, but it's okay. They have rides and all. Here, the lemonade is ready. Take a rest, Jobina. It's no day to be ironing anyhow."

"I meant to do it last night. I was too tired. The shop was so busy, I had to help at the fountain. Then, when I got home, I had to hear all about the sand castle Caroline built." Jobina put her iron down. She smiled, brushing a lock of damp chestnut hair from her brow. "Caroline hasn't been that excited in a long time," she said. "It was nice while it lasted. It gave me hope."

"Caroline will be fine. Kids are moody at her age."

"She is too moody. I'm afraid a new school is going to complicate matters. Caroline was expecting to return to

Miss Beardsley's, where she went to kindergarten. I explained that it was impossible. She was quite upset. She's scarcely said a word to me since. I have bent over backward to make it up to her."

"You shouldn't let kids call the tune, Jobina. Tell me if it's none of my business, but I know about kids. There were six in my family. Five girls and one boy. The boy, my brother Tom, got all the attention. He called the tune all right. It was a mistake. He grew up selfish and spoiled. You wouldn't want that to happen to Caroline."

"I want her to be happy."

"Nobody is happy all the time. It's a lesson she'll have to learn sooner or later. Maybe it's best she learn now."

Jobina sipped her lemonade. She was quiet, staring out the window at the hot, steamy street below. "Caroline is perfectly happy to go off with you every morning. She was happy to go off with Irene today. But when she's here, she broods. It is as if she has *decided* to be unhappy here. I think she has decided to be unhappy at her new school too."

"She's not that stubborn."

"She is, Ellen. She's headstrong. Last week she threw her favorite doll in the trash basket. I asked her why and she said, 'Because.' I rescued the doll three times before I admitted it was no use. Caroline was determined to have her way."

"Well, this weather makes kids cranky."

"I wish it would rain."

Jobina's wish was granted the next week. Thunder crashed over the city and lightning flared; from the angry skies came great sheets of rain driven and tossed by the wind. It was still raining when Jobina bundled her daughters into their coats and took them to school. As arranged, she took Annie Sisk also, and tried to hold tightly to three small hands while the rain blew into her face and splashed down her neck. She was bedraggled when she returned to the flat. She was soaked through, her coat and hat streaming water, her hairpins askew. Muttering to herself, she slammed the kettle on the stove and then found a towel. She had no chance to dry her sodden hair, for at that moment the bell rang. "Coming," she called. "Yes, I'm coming!" She opened the door. Her lips parted and all the color drained from her face. "*Father!*" she gasped.

"May I come in, Jobina?"

"*Father.*"

"I'm glad you recognize me, Jobina. Now may I come in?" Jonas Winslow did not wait for a reply. He entered the flat and closed the door behind him. He removed his coat and draped it on a chair. His hard brown eyes roamed over the parlor, settling finally on Jobina. "I see you are surprised," he said.

"Yes."

"Pleasantly, I hope."

Jobina's walk was unsteady as she crossed the room. She sank down on the other chair, clasping her hands together. "I cannot say it is a pleasant surprise," she replied. Slowly, she raised her head and looked at her father. He was a large man, very tall and very broad. His hair was her own chestnut color, graying now at the temples. His face was suntanned, contrasting sharply with the severe brightness of his smile. She remembered that smile, for it had marked all his many victories over the men he had destroyed; in it was his power, his strength. "You have not changed, Father. You even managed to avoid the rain."

"I have a car downstairs, and a chauffeur with an umbrella. But I didn't come to discuss the weather."

"Why did you come?"

"That's a foolish question, everything considered. Look at this place. Look at what you have been reduced to. Jobina Winslow living in a tenement!"

"It isn't a tenement and my name isn't Winslow anymore. It's Grant. Or perhaps you have forgotten."

"Forgotten? My memory is long, Jobina. I forget nothing. Call yourself Grant, if you wish. A name can't erase the fact of your birth. You are *my* daughter and that makes you a Winslow." Jonas moved his coat aside. He sat down, stretching out his legs. "It is a name to be proud of. A family to be proud of. You are the one who has forgotten. And you are paying the price. Look at you, huddled in this miserable room like some urchin from the streets. Your hair is straggling. Your hands . . . Why, they are the hands of a common *hausfrau*."

"You must make up your mind, Father. Am I a street urchin or a common *hausfrau*?"

"I see you have developed a sharp tongue. Obviously it has done you no good. What is this foolishness, Jobina? Why are you living this way? Your hands were meant for jewels, not dirty dishwater. *You* were meant for parties and balls and travel. Instead you waste your life at Greevy's Pharmacy. Are you doing it to spite me? All right then. You have accomplished your goal. Now it's time to come home."

Jobina's amber eyes narrowed on Jonas. "How do you know about Greevy's?" she asked. "For that matter, how did you find out where I live? Has George Thayer been in contact with you?"

"Don't be ridiculous! I know everything about your life, Jobina. I have kept a close watch on things ever since you left San Francisco. My sources are far more thorough, and accommodating, than your friend, George Thayer. He has certain . . . loyalties."

"Of course you disapprove of loyalties, Father."

"If they get in the way."

"You mean if they get in *your* way."

"Especially if they get in my way," Jonas replied, his voice steely.

"So you have been watching me."

"Indirectly, yes. What's wrong with that? I am your father, Jobina. It's my place to look after your interests. You have no one else. You are alone now. A foolish young woman all alone, slaving in a shop for pennies. I warned you it would come to this."

"You certainly did. You also barred your doors to me. You gave statements to the newspapers, awful statements. You humiliated me, Father. But worse, much worse, you humiliated William."

"I am willing to forgive you. Why—"

"Forgive *me*? You are willing to forgive *me*?" Jobina's eyes flashed. She jumped up, her long skirts swirling about her ankles. "How dare you?" she cried. "You are the one who needs forgiving, not I. I married the man I loved, Father. That is neither a crime nor a sin. I had six wonderful years with William. Perfect years, despite what you would prefer to believe. Alone? I'm not alone. I have my daughters, William's daughters. And I have myself."

"You are penniless, Jobina."

"Not quite. Besides, I have my job. Oh, it doesn't offer a life of parties and balls and travel, but it's a job and I do it well. I am supporting my children. It seems incredible, even to me, but I am actually becoming a competent human being."

"Clerking in a shop is—"

"Clerking in a shop is the way I earn my living. I'm not ashamed of it, Father. On the contrary, I'm proud. There is satisfaction in earning one's own money. You wanted me to be some useless decoration—an adornment who knew her place and kept it. I lived in your house for sixteen years and not once did you ask my opinion. Not once did you consider my wishes. You promised me to John Grayson. *Promised* me, Father, as if I were a parcel of timber land to be bought and sold."

"It would have been an excellent marriage. John is a fine man."

"You didn't care about John's character. You cared only that the Graysons and the Winslows would be joined. It was another business deal! I dare you to deny it!"

"You will mind your tongue, Jobina. I am your father and you will show respect. Has your perfect marriage turned you into a shrew? Or is that the conduct of the new, modern woman? You were sweet and soft-spoken before you left San Francisco. What has happened to you?"

"Life has happened to me, Father. As George would call it, 'The real world.' I have been through a great deal in the last eight months. I have learned from my experiences."

"You have learned rudeness."

"No, it's not rude to speak up for myself. I didn't invite you here, Father. You came of your own accord. I'm sorry if you expected to find the silly, docile female I was years ago. I'm not silly anymore, and not very docile either. Tea parties and fashion magazines and girlish giggles are things of the past."

"It is a pity."

"You may choose to see it that way." Jobina sat down again. She looked at her watch, frowning. "I am due at Greevy's in an hour," she said. "I cannot be late."

"This conversation is far from over. I have bided my time, Jobina. I have been patient with you. But I am here for a purpose. Surely you realize I am not a man to be dismissed at will."

"What do you want, Father?"

"I came to take you and my grandchildren home to San Francisco."

"No. I'm sorry, the answer is no."

Jonas was silent. He studied Jobina, his eyes hard and suddenly cold. His mouth tightened, then relaxed. "Jobina," he said, his voice smooth, "I have no desire to quarrel. Nor do I want to make matters between us worse. You are my daughter and I care about you. I care about my grandchildren, grandchildren I have never even seen. I am not young, after all. I want to reclaim my family while there is still time."

"I don't believe a word of that. You haven't a sentimental bone in your body. And as for family, you *have* a family in San Francisco. I read of your remarriage, Father. It was in all the newspapers. You have a wife and a son."

"A milksop! A puny little thing with nervous ways and a game leg. He is his mother's son, not mine."

A stranger listening to Jonas would have been shocked by his callousness, by the offhand contempt he had voiced for his young son. Jobina was not shocked. She knew too well the sort of man he was; indeed she had always believed that his cruelties had driven her mother to an early grave. Yes, she thought, he is the one who needs forgiving, but he will have to look elsewhere. It's not in me to forgive him; not now, not ever. "There is nothing more to say, Father." She sighed. "If you wish to return later and meet your grandchildren, you are welcome to do so. Frankly, I see no point in it."

"You don't seem to understand. I am here to take you and my grandchildren home."

"We *are* home."

"You are trying my patience, Jobina. I won't have it. I didn't wait six years only to be turned away. You and Caroline and Daisy will come with me to San Francisco. You will be given anything you want, anything. The run of the estate; furs, jewels, trips, closets filled with Paris gowns."

Jobina smiled slightly. She shook her head. "Those things aren't the temptations you imagine," she said, "I have had those things, first from you and then from

William. The difference is that William—"

"Quiet! I have heard all I intend to hear about dear William. You really are a fool, Jobina. A romantic little fool." Jonas stood. He crossed the room in two long strides. He crossed back again and stared down at his daughter. "William would have been a pauper, if not for me. His career was ruined the day he eloped with you. Martin Chadway was ready to fire him. *I* ordered Martin to keep William on. *I* arranged to pay William's salary and bonuses. *I* saw to it that he was given lucrative trust accounts."

"Why would you? You despised William."

"Yes, I despised him. I despise all cowards and weaklings. But I knew that if I gave him enough rope, he would hang himself."

"What are you talking about?"

"In this case, enough rope meant enough money. William was given just enough money to make him want more. Men show their true colors at such times and William showed his. He embezzled funds, Jobina. He stole nearly a hundred thousand dollars from his trust accounts."

"You are lying. It's a vicious lie!"

"Your friend George Thayer knows all about it. Ask him. He will tell you that dear William was an embezzler, a thief."

"*No.*"

"Ask him."

"I won't listen to your lies, Father. You would say anything to get your way."

"Ask George Thayer if I am lying."

Jobina looked into Jonas's hard, implacable brown eyes. Her head began to ache and pain struck at her heart. She looked away, digging her fingers into the palms of her hands. "No," she said. "No. If it were true, Martin would have taken action against William."

"William was offered a choice. He could go to prison . . . or he could resign from Chadway & Turnbull, resign from the bar, and allow you to seek a divorce. No charges would have been brought, provided he renounced all claims and left the country."

Slowly, very slowly, Jobina lifted her aching head. "All claims?" she asked.

"To Chadway & Turnbull, to you and the children. Under the circumstances, it was a generous offer."

"It was *your* offer, wasn't it, Father? It was your plot. You plotted the whole thing."

"I gave William enough rope."

"Oh God. Oh God." Jobina held her hands before her eyes, as if shielding them from a cruel light only she could see. The last pieces of the tragic puzzle had fallen into place now. She understood. To her horror and revulsion, she understood. "You *murdered* William," she cried. "You are a *murderer.*"

"That's romantic nonsense, Jobina. Through Martin, I offered William a choice. A man would have fought back, but William was no man. He was a coward. He made the coward's choice."

"You *murdered* him."

"William put a gun to his head. That is suicide, not murder."

"*You* put the gun to his head. Oh God, it was you."

171

"I warn you," Jonas told her, sighing, "my patience has limits. I plan to restore you to my will. I plan to name you and the children as my principal heirs. Don't throw away millions over a spineless coward."

Jobina leapt up. She raised her hand and slapped Jonas's face. "Get out," she cried.

"Jobina!"

"Get out before I kill you."

"It's monstrous," George said. He paced the length of the parlor, his hands thrust into the pockets of his trousers, his eyes so dark they were almost black. "It's monstrous, Jobina. I knew there was some dirty dealing afoot. I didn't know *how* dirty. William kept repeating an old vaudeville line, 'Your money or your life.' It made no sense to me at the time. Now . . ."

"Now everything is clear."

"Drink your tea, Jobina," Irene urged quietly. "You look ready to collapse."

"I am stronger than I look."

"Yes, you must be. I can't believe you went to work today after . . . all that happened. I would have fallen on my bed and pulled the covers over my head."

"Oh, I thought about it. I thought about a lot of things. Why didn't you tell me the trouble William was in, George?"

"I didn't know myself until Christmas Eve. Afterward . . . well, there was little point afterward." George stared at Jobina. He saw a tired young woman, the innocence gone forever from her lovely eyes. "I don't

172

understand why Jonas told you. I certainly don't understand why he told you of his part in it."

"You would have to know him to understand. It's his fatal flaw. It has never been enough for him to ruin people. No, he must flaunt his triumphs too. He must show the world how clever he is, how deadly. I have heard him regaling dinner guests with such stories."

"I am very sorry, Jobina. I am sorry you had to find out."

"Am I the last? Who else knows?"

"I doubt anyone knows, beyond Martin and one or two of the other senior partners. They would not want word to get around. Bad for business."

"Why would Martin cooperate in Father's scheme?"

"Money, I suspect. He was probably paid a handsome sum. Martin has only two interests in life, Jobina. Money and his reputation. He takes a rather exalted view of his reputation."

"I see." She sat back, clasping and unclasping her hands. Her expression was thoughtful, though there was a determined set to her mouth, to the lift of her chin. "Then that is where I will start," she said.

"I beg your pardon?"

"George, how much money was left over from the estate sale? Three thousand dollars?"

"In round numbers."

"I want a thousand of it."

"Why?"

"I intend to invest in Emile's perfume company."

"What! Emile's perfume company! Did I hear you correctly?"

"You did."

George glanced swiftly at Irene, then walked the few steps to where Jobina sat. "Look here," he said. "Emile doesn't *have* a perfume company. He has some bits and pieces of things in a basement. He has dreams. All immigrants have dreams. Good Lord, Jobina, they come to America thinking they will find gold in the streets. Or in basement workshops. Thirty years later, they are still struggling, still hoping."

"Emile knows how to make perfume. I know how to sell it."

"Let's say I grant you that." George sighed, his scowl deepening. "What do you know about business?"

"I have learned from watching Mr. Greevy. It's true he is only a small businessman, but it seems to me the principles are the same."

"Mr. Greevy has a profession. He is a pharmacist."

"Emile is a perfume maker."

"He is a *clerk*, Jobina."

"He is also a perfume maker."

George threw up his hands. "You talk to her, Irene," he said. "Women understand each other."

"Jobina, isn't this awfully sudden? You would be risking your money on a speculation. You must consider the worst. What if you lost the thousand dollars? That money is your nest egg. It is safely invested now. If this perfume thing is so important to you, George will invest in it. He can afford a loss."

"I have decided, Irene."

"But why? You had a terrible shock today. I think perhaps you are not thinking clearly. Just months ago

174

you swore you were going to be careful with money. You were quite adamant."

"Yes, and I have kept my promise. I have been so thrifty, even Uncle Ezra would approve. That isn't going to change. But I *am* going to invest the thousand dollars."

"This has something to do with Jonas," Irene said.

"And with Martin Chadway also. There are scores to be settled."

George sat next to Jobina on the daybed. He lighted a cigarette, wearily shaking his head. "They are powerful men," he said. "I share your desire to strike at them. It's not possible. I withdrew all Thayer business from Martin's firm. I persuaded several friends to do the same. It was a severe blow, though hardly fatal. Martin has too much money, too much power. Such a combination makes him invulnerable. He cannot be hurt."

"I will find a way."

"And what of Jonas? There is no way in the world to hurt Jonas Winslow."

"Oh, he is easy," Jobina replied with a thin smile. "My misfortunes please him, you see. He pretends otherwise, but he is pleased. My misfortunes confirm that he was right all along. Father needs very much to be right. My success will break his heart. I intend to succeed at this, George. Scores will be settled. For William, and for me."

"You are being emotional. The reality of the situation—"

"I will make my own reality. Work doesn't frighten me anymore, George. Nor does life, for that matter. I have seen the worst of it now."

"I cannot let you risk your money. I will make a small investment in Emile's . . . enterprise. We shall see how things go. Perhaps later you can add to the investment."

"It isn't up to you to decide."

"I am your executor. Of course it is up to me. It is up to me to be sensible. It is assured that you will lose your money. Not only because Emile will fail . . . but because when Jonas learns of your plans, he will sabotage them."

"Father has never taken me seriously. He will consider this just another whim, another foolish mistake. Anyway, he has concluded that time is on his side, that I will tire of earning my living and return to San Francisco. He said as much before he left. He said I would come to my senses."

"He went to great lengths to assure your return, Jobina."

"The strange thing is that he has no real feelings for me. It is a question of control. He must always be in control, and he must always be right. That is Jonas Winslow."

"I don't envy you growing up with such a man," Irene said.

"I rarely saw him. Once a week the servants presented me for his approval. The horses and dogs had a similar schedule. We were all there to decorate his life . . . But I am getting off the subject. George, I would like the thousand dollars as soon as possible."

"I will think about it."

"I have already thought about it."

"A lot of people seek my advice, Jobina," George said. "They listen to my advice and they act upon it. To their

176

advantage, may I add. My advice to you is not to risk your money. I wouldn't have you invest in my new magazine, much less in Emile's perfume. All new businesses are gambles."

"Then I will gamble."

"George," Irene laughed, "you are going to give in eventually. You know you are. Why not make it easy on us all and give in now?"

"Yes. Yes, perhaps you have a point. One thousand dollars, Jobina." He sighed. "One thousand dollars *only*. That is the beginning and end of it. I will release no further esate funds. *Period*. I hope that is clear."

"You can really be very sweet, George. When you want to be!"

Chapter Eight

"I know a good name for our business," Emile cried happily. "We will call it Jobina Perfumes. High class name. It has, how you say, a chime to it."

"A ring, Emile."

"A ring, yes. It will look good on the labels. *Tres chic.* Women, they will like it."

"I am flattered, but shouldn't we have your name on the labels? It is your perfume, after all."

"My perfume we put in the bottles," Emile replied, smiling brightly. "Your name we put on the labels." He lifted a vial of amber liquid, holding it up to the light. *"Voilà!* Jobina Midnight. Soon we are becoming rich."

"Is he always so confident, Inge?"

"Always." Inge Lanteau had been married to Emile for three years. She was as fair as he was dark, a quiet young woman with soft blue eyes the color of cornflowers and thick, pale blond hair braided atop her head. She was the daughter of German immigrants, and from them she had inherited a certain caution, especially in matters of money. Now she gazed at the bottles and vials covering

Jobina's table and she shrugged. "I tell him we should have a savings account for rainy days. He says all our days will be sunny. He believes it."

"I have St. Jude."

Inge nodded, a smile flickering about her mouth. "If he isn't spending money on his perfume things, he's spending it on candles to St. Jude. What can I do?" She shrugged again, smoothing the collar of her neat shirtwaist. "He really believes."

"But Jobina believes too. All the money she puts in our business, Inge. That is believing, yes?"

"Mind you don't lose all her money."

"Lose? No, I make more. We make together. This is like gold here," Emile said proudly, his hand sweeping over the vials. "Midnight is the first, then come many more. But which Midnight? I bring with me five samples, Jobina. You will tell which you think is the best. I have my favorite. It is lighter, the way you say. Still it is temptress. Exotic, yes? You will tell me."

"Do you have a favorite, Inge?" Jobina asked. "A woman's opinion would be useful."

"They all smell nice. I'm no judge. I didn't even wear perfume until Emile started his workshop. Soap and water, that's my perfume. I guess I'm not cut out to be a temptress."

"It is the fantasy," Emile explained. "It is here," he added, tapping his head. "All here. That is right, Jobina?"

"Yes, though Inge is right also. Some women prefer cleaner scents. We must consider such a scent once Midnight is perfected."

Emile beamed, his eyes twinkling, his hands jumping about the table. "See, Inge?" he said. "Already we are having other scents."

Emile's enthusiasm did not lessen as weeks, and then months, passed. Jobina rejected sample after sample, but he remained blithely unconcerned. Each night he went to his basement laboratory, often working into the wee hours. He made no complaints and he never seemed to tire. Each morning he had new samples for Jobina; when these too were rejected, he smiled and promised to do better next time. When Inge nagged and his inlaws scoffed, he merely shrugged. "Soon we are becoming rich," he would say, turning his eyes to a small statue of St. Jude.

Jobina's enthusiasm was more measured, for there were dozens of perfumes on the market and women's tastes changed almost daily. She had observed her customers. She had questioned them, if subtly, and she understood that many factors influenced sales. Price was important, and packaging, and what she had begun to call the "language" of perfumes. "In olden times," she explained to Emile, "there was the language of the fan. A woman could express her moods simply by holding her fan in certain ways. I am convinced it is the same with perfumes. Every perfume should have its own language. Midnight should be romantic and a little naughty, though never . . . vulgar. Do you see what I mean?"

"*Now* I see," Emile replied, striking his forehead. "And now I will make Midnight the right language. Not shouting. Whispering, yes?"

"Yes, that is it exactly. I know I'm being hard on you,

Emile. But there is so much at stake."

"It is good you are hard. Our perfumes, they must be the best."

Jobina Inc. was founded in late November of 1919. Partnership papers drawn by George's lawyer were signed and notarized, and the company's assets recorded. For Emile it was a joyous occasion. He seemed to dance about the lawyer's office, lighting briefly and then jumping up again, all smiles and quick, exuberant gestures. Jobina's optimism, though no less real, was guarded. She sensed they had a worthy product in the reformulated Midnight, but she knew that only time would tell. We cannot count on luck, she thought; we must count on ourselves. "The serious work starts now," she cautioned Emile. "I hope we are up to it."

"We have St. Jude. We will make, how you say, a big sprinkle."

"Splash, Emile."

"Splash, yes. We will make very big splash. Soon we are becoming rich. It is our plan."

But the details of their plan—such details as bookkeeping and purchasing and packaging—Emile cheerfully left to Jobina. She dared not refuse. Each morning, after taking Caroline and Daisy to school, she went to the library. There she poured over books on business and accounting, filling two large yellow pads with her notes. By ten she was behind the toiletries counter at Greevy's. In the evening, after collecting the children from Ellen Sisk, she fixed dinner and cleaned the flat, and then settled down to a long night of study. It did not come easily to her. She struggled; she hurled her notes to the floor; she muttered to herself, sometimes using words that made her blush.

"I hate doing figures," she said to Ellen one Sunday morning in December. "There is no choice. Emile is the creative person. I have to be the business person. Imagine! When I told George, he practically fell off his chair laughing."

"I don't think it's so funny. Most women keep the family budget, you know. Family or business, it's not so different. It's figures either way. And at Jack's office all the bookkeepers are women. Ever since the war."

"Well," Jobina replied, smiling, "I started a company ledger last week. We shall see. I am always getting my decimal points mixed up. I have to work on that. It's important because there are going to be expenditures."

"The perfume bottles?"

Jobina's smile widened. She laughed. "We have perfume, but nothing to put the perfume *in*. That's why I'm off to Orchard Street today. Emile finds his bargains there. On my budget, I am certainly looking for bargains!"

"Orchard Street's the right place." Ellen nodded. "When I was a kid, we used to go to Paddy's Market on Ninth Avenue. Same thing, only Irish. Orchard Street is all Jews. And crowds and noise and pushing and shoving. You have to be quick, Jobina. If you see what you want, grab it or somebody else will. It's amazing what bargains do to people. At Paddy's I saw nice, respectable women almost in a fight over a yard of wool. You should take your umbrella."

"Why? Is rain expected?"

"An umbrella is good for poking."

"Poking!"

"Some women use their elbows, but some use umbrellas. At Paddy's, one woman was famous for using a hat pin. We all knew to stay away from her."

Jobina laughed again. She peered into the mirror above the sink, smoothing her upswept hair. "I am in for another adventure," she said. She turned, walking the few steps to the hall. "Caroline?" she called. "Daisy? Mama is leaving now."

Daisy appeared a moment later, and Caroline straggled behind. "Mama," Daisy said, "can we go too?"

"Oh, you wouldn't have a very pleasant time, darling. You and Caroline are going to Mrs. Sisk's for awhile. You can play with Annie until Aunt Irene comes. You can play jacks. I know that is your favorite game these days."

"But Annie always wins."

"Then you must try harder." Jobina bent down, gathering Daisy into her arms. "That's my sweet girl," she said. "Behave yourself, will you?"

"Yes, Mama."

"Caroline? Come give Mama a kiss." Reluctantly, Caroline stepped forward. She was quiet as she offered her cheek to Jobina. "Behave yourself, darling. Perhaps I will bring you a surprise. Would you like that?"

"Yes."

"Yes what?"

"Please."

"A surprise for me *too*," Daisy wailed, tugging at her

mother's sleeve. "For me *too*."

"For you too," Jobina replied, though her gaze remained on Caroline. Contrary to Dr. Porterfield's assurances, school had not eased the child's moods. She had made no friends, formed no attachments to her teachers. She was quiet most of the time now, unsmiling if not precisely sullen. She was, as her principal had described her, a very mournful six-year-old. "I won't be long, darling." Jobina sighed. "Later I will read to you. Any story you wish."

"Thank you, Mama."

Jobina watched the girls walk away to their rooms. She looked at Ellen, shrugging her slim shoulders. "Nothing seems to help," she said.

"Christmas is coming. That should cheer her up . . . Oh, I'm sorry, Jobina. I forgot. Gosh, I'm sorry."

"It's all right. Christmas doesn't stop just because I have terrible memories. There is no way to avoid the subject. I had to decorate the Christmas windows at Greevy's, and only a couple of days ago I helped the girls write notes to Santa Claus. You mustn't worry, Ellen. It really is all right. I even plan to have a small tree this year. I brought our ornaments from Gramercy Park."

"I hope you'll spend Christmas with us. Or are you going to the Thayers'?"

"I don't know. There is time yet. Heavens, look at the time! I'm off to Orchard Street."

The Orchard Street pushcart market dated to before the turn of the century and stretched for many blocks above and below Delancey Street. Its crowded carts offered foodstuffs and dry goods and hardware and any manner of notions. Prices were marked, but certain peddlers were willing to haggle; for some, haggling was traditional, part of the fun. There were shops also, tiny little shops nestled together in row after unbroken row. Standing in the doorways of these shops were men known as *schleppers*, and it was their responsibility to draw customers inside.

Jobina needed no special enticement. She was dazzled by the vast array of merchandise—clothing, linens, Victorian lamps and mantel clocks, porcelains, copper, glassware—displayed upon the packed shelves. She went from shop to shop, pushing back when she was pushed, dodging and ducking and fighting her way through the crowds. At Meyer's Fine Glassware she discovered the "closeout" bins. There, resting on beds of yellowed newspaper, she discovered boxes of small, square glass bottles with charming butterfly-shaped stoppers. The bottles were on sale for six cents apiece; she bought them all, paying an extra fifteen cents for five sturdy shopping bags. On her way home, she noticed Abe Green's print shop and immediately placed an order for labels. It's real now, she thought as she boarded the subway. Jobina Inc. is real!

"Is Santa Claus in the sky yet?" Daisy asked two days before Christmas. She ran around the side of the kitchen table, staring up at Jobina. "Where is he, Mama?"

"Oh, I imagine he's still at the North Pole."

"But that's far away. Shouldn't he be getting in his sleigh, Mama? Shouldn't he? He has far to go. Shouldn't he be starting?"

"Soon, darling."

"When is soon?"

"In two days."

"Two whole days?" Daisy's forehead wrinkled. The corners of her pretty little mouth turned downward. *"Two whole days?"* she asked again. "Are you sure, Mama?"

Jobina closed her ledger. She sighed. "Daisy," she said softly, "we have been having this conversation for a week now. You know Santa doesn't leave the North Pole until Christmas Eve. That is two days away. You must be patient, darling."

"I hope he won't forget my Raggedy Ann."

"We shall see. Don't you forget what I told you, young lady. Santa can't bring too many presents this year. There are lots of poor children since the war. We mustn't be greedy, must we?"

"Are we poor, Mama?"

"Certainly not! We are not rich, but we are not poor either. We have a nice place to live, and good food to eat . . . Why do you ask?"

"Caroline said we're poor. I told her I wanted Raggedy Ann and she said *we're* poor raggedymuffins."

Jobina's eyes darkened. She smiled very slightly, stroking Daisy's golden head. "Caroline was wrong, darling. We are not ragamuffins yet. We are just fine. Now scoot. Mama has work to do."

"Aunt Irene doesn't have work."

"I know."

"Why do you have work, Mama?"

Several different answers occurred to Jobina, easy, comforting answers that missed the point. She herself had received such answers as a child, but now, looking into Daisy's innocent blue eyes, she decided to reply truthfully. "I work to earn money," she said. "With the money I earn, I pay our bills. I pay the grocer, Mr. Lundy. I pay the landlord. I paid Mr. Dowd for your new middy blouse. Everything costs money, darling."

"You could ask Santa. He could bring money in his big sack."

"Perhaps years ago," Jobina laughed, "but not anymore. Now scoot! And not another word about Santa Claus! Christmas will be here soon enough."

"I hope there's snow."

"I hope not!"

Christmas Eve was cool and rainy, with the gray afternoon fading to a dim twilight and then to darkness. The weather, unpromising though it was, did not seem to deter last-minute shoppers. The toiletries counter at Greevy's was thronged with customers, many of them attracted by the festive holiday windows. Jobina worked until eight o'clock, when Mr. Greevy reluctantly closed his doors. Following long-standing custom, he gave each of his employees a ten-dollar bonus and a tin of herbal tea. The money was a blessing to Jobina, for she had spent a week's salary on Christmas presents. She was delighted, so delighted that she threw her arms about a startled Theodore Greevy and kissed his cheek.

Jobina had been determined to give her daughters a

happy Christmas. She had purchased a large Raggedy Ann doll for Daisy, and a smaller Raggedy Andy. For Caroline she had purchased an elaborate drawing set with myriad brushes and paints and colored pencils. She had purchased new dresses for both of them, their first new dresses in a year. She had filled their stockings with candy canes and china animals and bags of marbles. Now, gazing at the mountains of presents beneath the Thayers' tree, she felt her spirits lower. She frowned, turning away.

"What's wrong, Jobina?" Irene asked.

"Wrong? Oh, I suppose I am feeling sorry for myself. I tried very hard to please Caroline and Daisy this year. I spent weeks shopping, and much too much money. When I was wrapping the presents, I thought they were quite splendid. But looking at all your presents . . . It's really not the same, is it?"

"Nonsense. Of course the girls will be pleased."

"Perhaps it was a mistake to bring them here tonight, Irene. Their presents will seem paltry after all this. And their Christmas tree. It's a poor little thing, the runt of the litter."

"You don't sound like yourself, Jobina. Where is your optimism? You have been optimistic through the worst of times."

"When I see what the girls are missing . . ."

"What are they missing? More dolls and toys they will play with once and then cast aside? They are not missing important things, things that matter. And as for Christmas, it is fast becoming a merchants' festival."

Jobina glanced again at the Thayers' huge tree, at the

glittering decorations, the endless presents. "A festival in which you participated," she said dryly. "Were you dragged to the stores kicking and screaming?"

Irene laughed. "I went willingly," she replied. "That is the truth and I admit it. Now you must admit the truth. Your mood this evening has nothing to do with presents and Christmas silliness. It has to do with William. It's natural, Jobina. We are all sad this evening, remembering. But I am also remembering how far you have come since . . . then. Why, you are a different person! You have found your courage, your voice."

"A lot has happened in a year."

"There is a new year soon beginning. A new decade, Jobina. I believe it will be *your* decade. You may laugh if you wish, but that is what I believe."

"What does George believe?"

"George is of the old school. He believes women and business don't mix . . . Isn't that right, love?" She smiled as George joined them. "I was telling Jobina that you are a fuddy-duddy."

"I am onto your game," George replied with a smile. "It is part of a campaign, you see," he explained to Jobina. "Irene is campaigning to wear short skirts and cosmetics. She thinks she will goad me into acceptance. Naturally, she is wrong."

"Naturally."

"You will notice," George said to his wife, "that Jobina has not changed her style of dress."

"Heavens, all my clothes are a year old or more. And I can't afford cosmetics. My appearance is due to poverty, not choice!"

"So there," Irene laughed.

"As far as I'm concerned, the subject is closed. The subject now is dinner. Miss Pym is bringing the children downstairs and Cook is ready to serve. Shall we?"

Because it was Christmas, the children were allowed to join their elders in the formal dining room. They sat very straight and still, their young faces aglow in the light of the magnificent crystal chandelier. The first course was brought—a creamed mushroom soup—and they managed to eat it without spilling a single drop. They glanced occasionally at each other; if one of them giggled, all of them giggled, quickly ducking their heads.

It was a glorious meal. "A feast," Jobina declared happily. There was roast goose with chestnut dressing, cranberry sauce, spiced turnips, creamed onions, and potato soufflé. There was a salad of winter greens and there were three desserts—apple pie with cheddar cheese, chocolate pie, and glazed plum pudding. Miss Pym came to the dining room at nine o'clock. She led the children across the wide hall to the drawing room and the tree. Each child was permitted to open one present, identical presents it turned out, for Irene had bought them all bright red sleds. "Mama, a sled!" Daisy cried. "A sled!"

"It's beautiful, darling. But it's meant to be used *outside*. Be careful, Daisy. You mustn't ruin Aunt Irene's carpet."

"They can ruin the playroom floor," George said. "Come, children. We will take your sleds upstairs."

"Can I carry my own sled?" Caroline asked.

"If you let Ian help you."

191

"Yes, I'll help," Ian agreed. He was a handsome boy, all enormous brown eyes and thick, curly brown hair. He was Caroline's age, though he was shorter, his body narrower. "I'll take this end," he said. "It's the heavy end."

"Ian is quite the little gentleman," Jobina declared laughingly when the children had gone.

"Thanks to Miss Pym. He was quite the little rowdy before she arrived. Now George is worried that she is making him into a sissy. He says that is what English nannies do."

"Not Miss Pym. She is too sensible. I'm glad you hired her. It keeps her in the family, so to speak."

"Our family is your family. We wouldn't have it any other way. Merry Christmas, Jobina."

"Merry Christmas, Irene."

Despite Irene's urgings, Jobina chose to spend New Year's Eve alone. At midnight she looked in on Caroline and Daisy and then settled down with a cup of tea. The building was quiet, though laughter drifted up from the streets below. She heard party horns and firecrackers and, somewhere, the melodic tinkling of bells. She listened to these sounds, dropping her gaze to William's picture. By one o'clock the streets were silent again and she opened her ledger. "January 1, 1920," she wrote. The new decade, so eagerly anticipated, was here.

It was February, just after closing time, when Jobina

mustered her courage and approached Mr. Greevy. "There is something I have been wanting to speak to you about," she said. "Do you have a moment?"

"Certainly. What is it, Jobina?"

"Well, you might say it's a . . . business proposition." She turned her head to the fountain, motioning Emile over. "We have started a little business, Emile and I."

"A business!"

"I'm sure it seems foolish to you, Mr. Greevy, but we are serious about it. We have put time and money in. We hope to make a success."

"What sort of business?"

"Perfume." Jobina glanced at Emile, as if for reassurance. She took a breath and looked back at Mr. Greevy. "Emile has been blending perfume in his workshop," she explained. "Since last September he has given all his efforts to one particular scent. We call it Midnight." Slowly, she reached into her pocket and removed a small glass bottle with a butterfly stopper. "Perhaps it is immodest, but we think we have an excellent product."

Mr. Greevy was astonished. He gaped at the bottle in Jobina's outstretched hand, shaking his head from side to side. "The perfume business?" he asked. "You are going into the perfume business? You and Emile?"

"Yes, Mr. Greevy."

"You and Emile? But what do you know of business? It's complicated. It's hard work, and in the end most new businesses fail."

"We have considered the risks, Mr. Greevy," Jobina replied. "We are determined nevertheless."

193

"But what do you know of business? You are babes in the woods. And you, Jobina. You are a *woman*. Women are not meant for business. It is one thing to work, but business is another matter. Another matter altogether. Business is best left to men." Mr. Greevy plucked his glasses from his nose and began vigorously polishing the lenses. "I knew this would happen." He sighed. "Now that women are to have the vote, they are forgetting their proper role in life. The proper order of things has been disturbed. Mark my words, we will all be sorry."

"Mr. Greevy," Jobina tried again, "our little business has nothing to do with politics. We are hoping to make money. It is as simple as that."

"Everyone hopes to make money. Businesses are begun every day by people hoping to make money. But are they qualified? Do they know what they're doing? Do you, Jobina?"

"It's true I knew nothing of business when I came here, Mr. Greevy. I have learned from you. You have been my teacher. I watched you and I learned. And I have studied. The library has three shelves of business texts. I have read through them twice."

"That doesn't change your . . . gender. You are a woman, Jobina. A woman has no place in business."

"I will find a place."

"Well, it's none of my affair. If you are determined . . . Are you giving your notice?"

"Oh *no*, Mr. Greevy," Jobina cried, alarmed. "*No*, I need my salary. Both Emile and I need our salaries. We have no thought of leaving here."

"Business we do in our spare time," Emile added.

"After work and Sundays after church."

"In your spare time? Now I have heard everything!"

"Mr. Greevy, we are asking for a chance. You gave me a chance once before. I tried not to disappoint you. I don't think I did."

"What chance can I give you? If it's money—"

"No, it's not money," Jobina said quickly. "Not in the way you mean. We would like the chance to sell Midnight at your toiletries counter. Please, Mr. Greevy, hear me out before you decide. We know counter space is valuable, so we are asking for a two-week test. If at the end of two weeks, Midnight hasn't . . . earned its space, we will remove the bottles and say no more about it. And there is another thing. Jobina Inc. will offer you an additional twenty-five cents on each bottle sold. Twenty-five cents above your usual profit."

"Twenty-five cents?" Mr. Greevy's eyes narrowed behind his glasses. He was interested now, for while he was certain that Jobina Inc. would ultimately fail, he was not a man to throw quarters away. "Let me see what you have there," he said, taking the bottle in his hand. "It's attractive to the eye," he conceded. "The butterfly is a nice idea. Feminine. But that is only the outside. Let's see what is inside." He broke the seal and sniffed the amber liquid. "It is . . . provocative. I don't know. There are so many perfumes."

"But none like Midnight."

"Midnight I make special," Emile said, a proud smile lifting his mouth. "The language, it is exotic. But whispering."

"What? Whispering? I don't pretend to know about

perfume. Why a registered pharmacist should know about perfume is beyond me. Still, I suppose a Frenchy would know." Mr. Greevy sniffed the liquid again. "It is . . . provocative. Too provocative, in my opinion. My wife would not wear such a scent. I am thankful she is not one of those *modern* women I read about in the newspapers."

"Times are changing, Mr. Greevy."

"We will all be sorry. When it is too late, we will be sorry . . . How many bottles do you have?"

"Emile has one hundred bottles sealed and labeled. There is enough perfume for a hundred more."

"At what price?"

"We plan to charge four dollars a bottle. I admit the price is high. We want it high. These are prosperous times and we had in mind a luxury scent."

"Perfume is cheap to make," Mr. Greevy remarked thoughtfully. "You could turn a pretty profit at that price. Yes, a very pretty profit."

"We are becoming rich," Emile said.

"Don't count your chickens. You could charge a thousand dollars, but if you have no customers, what good is it? Remember, first and foremost you have to please the customers."

"We intend to, Mr. Greevy. We certainly intend to try."

"All right. I will allow you counter space for six bottles and a tester. You may put them out in the morning. Then we will see. Jobina, I am trusting you not to favor Midnight over our other brands. Are we agreed?"

"I wouldn't think of taking advantage, Mr. Greevy.

This test is important to us also. I hope to be able to sample the customers' reactions, to learn from them. Emile and I believe Midnight is a special scent. Time will tell."

"It will indeed." Mr. Greevy chuckled, striding away.

"What is this counting chickens?" Emile asked.

"The expression is, 'Don't count your chickens before they're hatched.' It means we mustn't take anything for granted. We mustn't . . . count our money before it is actually in our hands."

"Soon we are counting lots of money, yes?"

"I hope so, Emile."

"I am sure of it. See, my face is laughing!"

Jobina considered herself fortunate to have a partner like Emile Lanteau, for his enthusiasm, his good humor, never waned. When Tuesday passed and no sales of Midnight were recorded, he merely shrugged, asserting that "tomorrow is the day." He repeated his assertions on Wednesday and Thursday and Friday; on Saturday, when the first bottle of Midnight was finally sold, he clasped his hands above his head in the classic gesture of victory.

Four more bottles were sold during the next week. It was a respectable beginning, if not spectacular, and Mr. Greevy allowed the young entrepreneurs to continue. Jobina designed a Midnight window display with paper fans and swirls of black lace and two champagne glasses. The implications of her display were not lost on Mr. Greevy, though his criticism was muted by dramatically increased sales.

It was April when Jobina decided that the time had

come to expand their horizons. She began visiting other stores, samples of Midnight tucked in a neat leather case. She dreaded these visits, for often she was turned away. She was the object of derisive laughter, of rude comments, of boorish and leering advances. She was teased and she was lectured. Doors were closed in her face, but still she persisted. It was June when her efforts were rewarded. Proudly, she marked two new clients in her ledger—a small women's shop on Madison Avenue and the dignified, elegant Lord & Taylor department store. "We did it!" she cried to Emile. "We are on our way! But we must leave nothing to chance."

"Chance?"

"Well, we can't wait for success to happen. We must . . . encourage it. Advertising is very important. I think we should plan an advertisement."

"It is expensive, yes?"

"My friend George Thayer has started a magazine called *Gotham*. It is just the right magazine for us. And because it's new, the advertising rates are quite low. I know we are on a tight budget, but I believe this is something we should do. We will create an interest in Midnight. If enough customers are interested, the stores will have to place orders. Altman's is already interested. An advertisement might make the difference. It would be a feather in our caps to get Altman's."

"Then we must do it, Jobina. Soon we are having many feathers in our caps, yes? Soon we are looking like birds."

"I hope so."

"I am sure."

"But you are always sure, Emile."

"And always I am right. We have our business and our customers. Soon we will have our feathers!"

The Midnight advertisement took weeks of planning. *Gotham*'s tiny art department presented dozens of sketches; much to George's consternation, Jobina rejected them all. He argued and he cajoled, though in vain. He ordered her out of the office, but she returned a day later, bringing her own sketch. "This is what I want," she said.

George studied the sketch. It showed two champagne glasses filled with bottles of Midnight. In the background were swirls of ruffled black lace and to the side was a single orchid. "*This* is what you want?" he asked, dismayed. "Jobina, it is more than a little suggestive. Surely you don't mean—"

"But I do. These are suggestive times, George. You have only to look around to see how things are changing. The newspapers write of the new woman and they are correct. There *is* a new woman. Her mood is lighter. I would say a bit naughty. My sketch is a bit naughty also."

"A bit?"

"Everything is in the eye of the beholder, George."

"Am I to assume that you are one of the *new* women?"

"Perhaps, in a way."

"God help us."

"You must stop being such a bluenose." Jobina laughed, shaking her head at George. "We aren't in the dark ages anymore. It's 1920!"

Chapter Nine

Indeed Jobina was optimistic as the decade of the 1920's progressed. It was an optimistic time, for prosperity had returned and the mood of the nation was jaunty. There was a wonderful new invention called radio. There were new dances and new clubs where Le Jazz Hot was played. There were new voices, the magical new voices of F. Scott Fitzgerald and Ernest Hemingway. In New York, the Barrymores were together on Broadway, not far from where Mr. Ziegfeld's follies' girls. pranced the stage in sumptuous costumes and towering, plumed headdresses. Americans, their minds and attitudes broadened by the war, were ready to enjoy themselves at last.

Prohibition had become law in July of 1920, but it was a law doomed to failure, for bootleggers and speakeasies were everywhere. The Anti-Saloon League urged people to "Shake hands with Uncle Sam and board the water wagon;" this slogan, too, was doomed to failure, drowned out by the more popular passwords, "Joe sent me."

The popular song of the day was a saucy little tune

entitled "I'll Say She Does." Newspaper editorials maligned the lyrics, for they seemed to describe the modern woman. This modern woman shortened her skirts a full six inches, displaying long-hidden legs in sheer stockings often rolled below the knee. She bobbed her hair and plucked her brows. She rouged her cheeks and lips and lined her eyes with kohl. She smoked cigarettes. She danced—not the sedate waltz, but the tango and the Charleston and the Black Bottom. If one's interest in the modern woman of the 1920's was parental, it was a worrisome time.

Jobina's interest was financial. She continued to observe her customers, to question them. She observed women in other stores, and on streetcars and subways. She noted the widespread popularity of cosmetics and, in 1924, contrary to almost everybody's advice, she decided once again to expand.

It was a difficult decision, for company funds were low. Midnight had been a modest success, the line having grown to include perfume, cologne, and hand lotion, but along with success had come greatly increased expenses. The distinctive butterfly bottles Jobina had found on Orchard Street now had to be duplicated at a glass factory in Brooklyn; boxes had to be imprinted with the butterfly motif. An exhausted Emile, worn down by twenty-hour days, had been forced to hire two assistants, college students who worked at his side in the basement laboratory. There were delivery costs, advertising costs. There was rent on the laboratory itself—five dollars a week paid to Mr. Greevy.

Night after night Jobina had poured over her ledgers,

seeking ways to cut expenses. She had discussed the problems with Emile, though to little avail. Reluctantly, she decided that a bolder approach was necessary. "It's time to take another gamble," she said, glancing from Emile to Inge. "It *is* a gamble. I see no other choice."

"You have a new idea, yes?" Emile asked.

"Cosmetics. I think we should start with lipstick. A bright, vivid red lipstick. Scarlet, like these scarlet times."

"Jobina Scarlet!" Emile cried. "We will call it Jobina Scarlet!"

"Wait a minute." Inge sighed. "I don't mean to be a wet blanket . . . but the way I look at it, things are getting out of hand. I've been quiet up to now. I can't be quiet anymore. The way I look at it, we can't afford another gamble. Speaking for me and Emile, that is. Emile's worked his heart out. I know you have too, Jobina. What do you have to show for it? At least in the beginning there were profits. Now all I hear is expenses, expenses. It doesn't make sense."

"Inge, what you say is not nice."

"Nice or not, it's true. You know it's true, Emile. You're killing yourself for a few dollars in profits. And some months there are no profits at all. Coming home at two, three o'clock in the morning. Leaving again at six. If you put all that extra time into another job, you'd be making another salary. There'd be some sense to it. Where's the sense now?"

"You must be patience, Inge. Patient, I mean to say. Soon we are becoming—"

"I don't want to hear that anymore. It's a pipe dream.

You've been selling Midnight for four years, Emile. Are we rich? If we are, the butcher and the grocer will be glad. We owe them money, and every other storekeeper in Yorkville too. I'm sorry, but we can't afford to throw good money after bad."

Jobina rose. She brought the coffeepot to the table and filled their cups. "I understand how you feel," she said. "Perhaps we were overly optimistic in the beginning. That was my fault. I failed to anticipate rising expenses. It seems the more successful Midnight is, the higher our expenses."

"It's not your fault, Jobina. It's not anybody's fault. You and Emile worked very hard. And you turned Midnight into a success. I see it in the stores and I'm real proud. But pride's no help paying bills. We need money. I don't want Emile to stay at Greevy's the rest of his life. He could get a better job now. Only he won't, because of the perfume business. He has to have Mr. Greevy's basement."

"Inge," Emile said quietly, "you make me ashamed. Jobina, she is our friend. All her money she puts in our company."

"Jobina got her money back from the first profits. Will you get your time back, Emile? You have three little boys you never see. If it was building for the future, I could understand. It's not. It's a pipe dream. The years are going by real fast, but nothing's changing. We're still living in a tenement. We still owe money. Ma's still taking in washing."

"Inge! It is enough you have said now." Emile's face was flushed, the smile gone from his eyes. He stared at his wife and his mouth became a harsh line. "Enough," he repeated. "We are invited here by Jobina. We are guests."

"Well, I'm sorry if I spoke out of turn. It's best to clear the air. It's always best."

"We mustn't argue," Jobina said lightly. "We all want the same thing, don't we? We went into business to earn money. Pride is wonderful, but it doesn't pay the bills. Inge is quite right about that. And so now we must decide what to do. We could limit our business to the Midnight line and see what happens. Or we could take one more chance. May I explain what I have in mind, Inge?"

"Sure . . . What I said, it was nothing against you, Jobina. Sure we all want the same thing. It's how to get it. That's where we have different ideas."

"My idea, as I mentioned, is a new lipstick. A lipstick meant to appeal especially to younger women. Flappers, they are called. You see, compared to perfume, lipstick is an inexpensive product. We would have a much wider market. The way to solve the problem of expenses is through volume. Companies that sell in volume diminish their expenses. Oh, there are expenses at first, but over a period of time they diminish. Our situation has been just the opposite. That is why we need to reach a wider market. Of course it would be hard for you, Emile. You would have to learn—"

"I learn already! I am in front of you this time, Jobina!" Emile cried, his good humor restored. "Ahead of you, I mean to say. Lipstick is not so different to perfume. Some different ingredients, yes? But it is all in the blending. For blending, I am the expert."

"Then you would be willing to try?"

"In my workshop I have already three samples. Rouges for lips or cheeks. I thought maybe someday . . . But someday is now, yes?"

"It could be. Inge, what do you think?"

"You know what I think. I'm not saying your idea doesn't sound good. They all sound good. I'm just trying to be practical, Jobina. How can you make anything, like you say, in volume? Emile did a lot with Mr. Greevy's basement, but it's still a basement. The way you talk, he'd need a factory."

"Yes." Jobina rose again. She walked a circle around the kitchen, nervously twisting her fingers together. "You spoke of my getting my money back, Inge," she said after several moments had passed. "That's true. The thousand dollars was returned from our first profits. I didn't return it to my personal account, however. I put it in a special company account. It's available to us. I propose we use it now. There is a small factory for rent on Hudson Street. They made witch hazel there once, and most of the equipment would suit our purposes as well."

"*Mon Dieu!*" Emile exclaimed, jumping to his feet. "Our own factory! It is possible, Jobina?"

"I have given a deposit to the owner. We have a week to decide. It's a big decision. I want to be honest, Emile, Inge. The owner insists on a five-year lease. If we fail, we will be paying off the lease forever. It will take all our Midnight profits and more besides." Jobina paused. She stopped at the window and stared outside. "George Thayer thinks I am insane," she said softly. "Perhaps I am. We all have children to worry about. Caroline and Daisy have outgrown their winter coats. They will need coats and new shoes also. Children are always outgrowing their shoes . . . I don't know. Perhaps George is right . . . But I have this *feeling*. I *feel* we should go ahead and rent the factory." She turned, looking uneasily at Emile. "We would be risking a great deal of money." She sighed.

"*Emile*," Inge said. "Tell Jobina no."

"My mind is decided. It is business, Inge, and in business we must take the opportunities. It is, how you say, opportunity knocking down the door."

"Oh, Emile."

"This is the right thing to do. Jobina has the feeling, but I have the knowing. This is the right thing to do."

Jobina Inc. moved to its new headquarters in January of 1924. Emile recreated his laboratory on the factory's first floor, for they could not afford to heat and light the other three. Each night, after finishing at Greevy's, he packed a sandwich and rode the subway to Hudson Street. There he joined his assistants, often working with them until morning. Jobina had provided a color swatch cut from one of her old gowns; it was a true scarlet, and although he came close several times, it was months before he was able to duplicate the bright, impudent tint. When he finally did, he was ecstatic. "*Voilà,*" he cried to Jobina. "Scarlet, yes?"

"It's perfect, Emile. Absolutely perfect. Why, you are a genius!"

"My assistants, they are studying chemistry in their college. But for blending, I am the expert. A little bit of this, a little bit of that." Emile shrugged. His dark eyes twinkled and his smile seemed to stretch from ear to ear. "That is the secret of good cooking, but maybe of good cosmetics too," he said. "You think so?"

"I wouldn't be surprised. There is an art to both, a special touch. I'm sure it helps to be French." Jobina laughed.

"American. I am a citizen now. All the time I am counting up my blessings. My wife, my sons, my friend Jobina, and the business we are building. America gives me all these blessings."

"But not much money."

"Soon."

"Yes, I know, Emile. Soon we are becoming rich."

Jobina Scarlet was introduced in the spring. Eighteen stores and shops had placed orders, Greevy's Pharmacy amongst them. Jobina risked the last of her thousand dollars to have display cards printed. The design—bold scarlet butterflies on a background of stark white—was repeated in window displays and in carefully timed magazine advertisements. "We have done all we can," she said to Emile. "Now we must wait and see."

The waiting was a torture for Jobina. She realized too well how much was at stake, and as the first disappointing sales figures were recorded, her anxiety deepened. Her nights were sleepless. She ate little and there were times when she ate nothing at all. She was tense, preoccupied; at least twice during the long spring she fled her ledgers in tears.

"You must stop this, Jobina," Irene said sharply. "You are ruining your health. I want you to come out to Long Island with me. I promised Caroline and Daisy I would try to bring you out. Now that I have seen you, I am determined."

"I can't leave. I'm glad the girls are enjoying their vacation, but I can't leave. I would feel like the rat deserting the sinking ship."

"Nonsense! It is a question of your health, Jobina. You are very pale, and thinner than you have been in years. Besides, it is early yet to declare the ship sunk."

"Early? It's August."

"Oh, I know it's August. The city is like an oven. And this flat also. It is stifling! Come to Long Island, if only for a few days. It will do you a world of good, Jobina. You have *earned* a vacation."

"Hardly. I have failed, Irene. What is worse, I have dragged Emile into my failure. Poor Emile. He has worked so hard. He's *tried* so hard. What is his reward?"

"You are jumping to conclusions. I am no business-woman, Jobina, but even I know that new products take time to succeed. You cannot expect miracles."

"I stopped hoping for miracles long ago."

"Then what is all this talk of failure and sinking ships? You are being precipitous."

"I can read a ledger. And so can my clients." Jobina stood, walking to the sink. She splashed cold water on her face, her neck. She returned to the table, fixing her tired amber eyes on Irene. "We began with eighteen clients," she said. "In May the figure rose to twenty. We have seven clients left, including Mr. Greevy. Counter space is valuable, Irene. Only a certain amount of time is *allowed* a new product to succeed. Our time has come and gone. We have a lease on the factory, new equipment, repair bills on the old equipment . . . and seven clients. I haven't had the courage to tell George."

"Never mind George. He will go to his grave believing a woman's place is in the home. He is right about a great many things, but in this case, his belief clouds his judgment."

"Oh? There is something you don't know, Irene. I asked you to take the girls for the summer because I couldn't afford to have them here. I couldn't afford to pay Ellen Sisk to look after them. That's how bad; how desperate, the situation is . . . I am putting every cent into the factory. Sometimes I think I have lost my senses. I have certainly lost everything else."

"Do you want me to speak to George?"

"No, please don't. I realize now I am not a very gracious loser. I am not ready to face George."

"I want to understand, Jobina," Irene said, leaning forward. "What exactly is lost?"

"Everything. Our business, the money *in* our business."

"But how is it lost? You still have your factory. You have products and clients."

"*Seven* clients." Tears sprang to Jobina's eyes. She fumbled for her handkerchief, quickly turning her head. "I'm sorry." She sighed. "I don't seem to be myself these days."

"You are working too hard and worrying too much."

"Is that surprising, under the circumstances?"

"But what, really, are the circumstances? Tell me why Jobina Scarlet was created in the first place."

"Why? To make money, of course. Preferably *lots*

of money."

"But why Jobina Scarlet? Why not another perfume or cologne? Why not an eye pencil or some such? Why a lipstick?"

"That was my brilliant idea. I wanted a cheaper product, one we could sell in volume. A cosmetic. Lipstick is the cosmetic women are using most. Perhaps not older women, but all younger women appear to be using lipstick now. It made sense to me. I knew we had to have just the right color, a Twenties color. There is nothing like our Scarlet on the market. It's perfect, Irene. It is today's color. Or so I thought."

"Why have you changed your mind?"

"It was changed for me. Nobody is *buying* it, Irene. If things continue this way, we will be bankrupt in a month."

"You said 'if.' That means you still have hopes."

"I try not to." Jobina turned, looking back at Irene. "You see," she said quietly, "I have this feeling. I can't explain it, least of all to myself. It's quite a . . . strong . . . feeling. Our Scarlet is the right product at the right time; that's what it says. All the evidence is to the contrary, yet the feeling persists. Silly, isn't it?"

"I have learned to trust your intuition," Irene replied. "Your instincts. They are sound. And now I have heard your reasoning. It is sound also. I believe you are worried only because there is such a great sum of money involved. Think a moment before you answer. If there were not such a great sum involved, would you be doubting yourself?"

"I don't know . . . but it is something to consider. It's

true we have the product we set out to create. We have the right product at the right time. I wonder . . ." Jobina's eyes flashed suddenly. She jumped up, striding back and forth across the small kitchen, her head bent in thought. "I wonder," she said again.

"What do you wonder?"

"Irene, I wonder if we have it in the right *stores*. My God, I think I understand the problem now. It's the right product but the wrong *stores*. We are reaching the wrong market."

"I can see your mind whirling and spinning, Jobina."

"Oh, you certainly can! Because I know what to do now. I have a month before we run out of money. I can do a lot in a month. If I start now, this minute . . . Keep your fingers crossed, Irene. I think I am onto something here. Yes, I am sure of it!"

Jobina's plan was simply to reach the right market—a market of young workingwomen and housewives on limited budgets. She lowered the price of Jobina Scarlet to thirty cents and, in a rush of frenzied activity, visited all the 5 & 10's, all the chain stores and variety stores she had excluded the first time around. She offered special discounts and incentive bonuses. She offered to style counter displays. She bargained; she persuaded; she talked until her jaw ached. By the end of August she had covered all the five boroughs and had personally overseen the delivery of Emile's entire inventory. "Now we will know one way or the other," she said to the Lanteaus. "It shouldn't be long."

Indeed success seemed to come almost immediately. There was a trickle of reorders and then a stream and then a deluge. In the middle of September an order clerk was hired to work at the Hudson Street factory; in late September a second order clerk was hired and a shipping department was formed. Jobina packed the reorder files in her leather case and went off to the Manhattan Fidelity Bank. There she negotiated a loan of five thousand dollars—working capital to take them through the end of the year. She put George's accountant, Eugene Marshall, on retainer and happily turned her ledgers over to him. She retained a lawyer, Philip Claymore, Jr. "We are in business, Emile," she declared, a vast smile wreathing her face. "Soon we are becoming rich!"

Jobina gave notice to Mr. Greevy in February of 1925. She did so with mixed emotions, for she was genuinely sorry to be leaving. She stayed until a replacement was hired and trained, but on the last day behind the counter she had long regarded as her own, she found herself in tears. "I will never forget you, Mr. Greevy," she said, sniffling. "I will never stop being grateful. I owe everything to you. Sometimes I think you saved my life."

"Now, now, Jobina."

"You don't know how desperate I was when I first came here. How frightened. You made everything all right, Mr. Greevy. You even listened to my crazy ideas."

"I disapproved of your ideas, but they brought business to my pharmacy. The credit is yours. Unlike most women, you have a flair for business." Mr. Greevy looked down at the counter. Prominently displayed was the Jobina Scarlet line—lipstick, rouge, and the newest product in the line, nail polish. "It's a far cry from the days of rose water and glycerine." He sighed. "Still, there is no quarreling with success. You can be proud of your success, Jobina."

"It hardly seems real. We are introducing a new mascara next month. And Emile is working on eye shadows also. He says we shouldn't put all our eggs 'in one bushel.'"

"I have missed Emile." Mr. Greevy chuckled. "He was an excellent worker, for a foreigner. He has ambition."

"He has more than that. He has faith. Our company suffered through some dark moments, but Emile never lost faith."

"Well, look who his partner is. You make believers of us all."

"Thank you, Mr. Greevy." Jobina felt a lump in her throat. She glanced around the pharmacy and tears rushed again to her eyes. "I hate to leave," she said softly. "This has been my second home."

"You are moving up in the world now, Jobina. You and Emile both. I see big things ahead. As Emile would say, the world is your oyster shell. I hope you enjoy it."

"Yes, Mr. Greevy. I hope so too."

The Jobina Ebony line, introduced in April, was a spectacular success. Orders and then reorders were huge, for the mascaras, eye pencils, and eye shadows were instantly snatched from shelves by eager customers. Emile put the factory on two shifts, tripling his already large staff. Additional salesmen were hired, some of them servicing accounts as far west as Chicago. "I would say you've struck gold," Eugene Marshall commented, and neither Emile nor Jobina disagreed.

"Are we rich, Mama?" Caroline asked one winter day in 1926. "Are we?"

"Not exactly, darling. We're not poor, but we're not rich either. We are . . . comfortable."

"Annie says we're rich. Ian says we have *pots* of money."

Jobina smiled, studying her daughter. Caroline was thirteen now, a beautiful young girl with deep blue eyes and masses of long golden hair. She was tall for her age, and sturdy, though her manner was so quiet, so grave, she seemed almost fragile. "I'm afraid Ian exaggerates, darling. Of course the company is doing very well. The company is rich. Company money is not necessarily my money."

"Some of it is."

"Yes, some. What is this all about, Caroline? There can't be anything you want. Your closet is bursting with new dresses, and your shelves with books and games. I bought you a new bicycle—"

"Why do we have to live here, Mama? It's an awful old place. I hate it here. Emile has such a big apartment. It's pretty. It even has an elevator. Why can't we have a big apartment too, Mama? It's not *fair*."

Jobina was silent, considering her reply. Certainly she had been urged to move, not only by Emile, but by Irene and George, and by Eugene Marshall. Once or twice she had been tempted; always at the last moment she had changed her mind. She thought: It isn't sentiment. It's the money. After years of scrimping and saving, I am afraid to spend money. I leave it in the bank, in investments, and like a miser I watch it grow. "You may have a point, Caroline." She sighed. "Is a new apartment really important to you?"

"I hate it here, Mama."

"And how does Daisy feel?"

"Oh, *Daisy*," Caroline moaned. "She doesn't care. She's so *good*. That's why she's teacher's pet. She stays after school to clap the erasers and everything. Everybody knows she's teacher's pet."

"Daisy is a good student. She brings home wonderful report cards."

"She's your pet too."

"That's not true, Caroline," Jobina said sharply. "I love you both. I have no favorites."

"Daisy is *everybody's* favorite."

"Well, you would be everybody's favorite also, if you were more . . . friendly. You must make an effort, darling. You must give people a chance. We've discussed this before, haven't we? You should be out every afternoon, playing. Instead you hide yourself away with books and sketch pads."

Caroline finished her milk. She stared at Jobina, slowly pulling a lock of golden hair through her fingers. "Can we have a nice apartment, Mama?" she asked again.

"Perhaps. We shall see."

"I want to see *now*, Mama."

"Perhaps we can make a bargain. I will think about moving, if you will think about what I said. I want you to have friends, darling. Friends are far more important than fancy apartments or new dresses or anything else. And you, miss," Jobina teased, "are far too young to be a hermit."

"I would have friends at Miss Beardsley's School."

"Miss Beardsley's! Caroline, I am astonished that you remember Miss Beardsley's. It was so long ago."

"I remember the olden days, Mama."

Yes, thought Jobina, and that is the problem; you remember things best forgotten. "Looking back to the olden days can be interesting," she said. "But it's much more fun to look ahead. Why, when I was a child, I was always wondering about the future. It was fun to dream, to pretend. That's what childhood is for, darling. It should be a happy time."

"I would be happy if we had a nice apartment, Mama. Like Emile's. Just like Emile's."

"Would you *smile* occasionally?"

"I promise," Caroline replied in her serious, somber way.

"Well then," Jobina laughed, "it might be worth it. We shall see. This might be the time to make some changes after all. Run along now, darling. Daisy and Annie are waiting downstairs. You mustn't waste such a pretty Sunday. Take your hat and your mittens . . . and button all your buttons," she called as the door closed. She cleared the dishes from the table, leaving them to soak. She was about to walk away when she noticed her reflection in the mirror. It had been years since she had given any thought to her appearance, but now, studying her unfashionable hairstyle, her unfashionable shirtwaist, she frowned. "Heavens," she cried, "*I* look like the olden days. It really is time to make some changes!"

In March Jobina and her daughters moved to the Stockard, a gracious, twenty-two story apartment building overlooking Beekman Place. Their apartment was composed of ten rooms, large, airy rooms with gleaming parquet floors and high ceilings. All the bedrooms had fireplaces and marble mantels; all the bathrooms had sunken marble tubs. Jobina spent the better part of a year decorating the new apartment and she was proud of it. With its pale walls, its silken couches, its slender and polished tables, it was her refuge, her serene retreat. It was home, not in the way Gramercy Park had been home, nor even in the way the Lexington Avenue flat had been home, but home nevertheless.

If the circumstances of Jobina's life had changed greatly, so had Jobina herself. Irene often remarked that she had come into her own, and it was true. At thirty-one, she was a confident woman, a comfortable woman without pretensions of any sort. Her doubts had been allayed, and most of her fears. She was able to laugh at her foibles, at the world's foibles, and she encouraged her daughters to do the same. She tried to teach them that love was important, love and kindness and loyalty. Indeed when people spoke of Jobina Grant, loyalty was amongst the first words they used.

Jobina's loyalty was especially fierce in matters concerning her friends and family. Nine years after William's death, the pain of his loss had been muted, though not the anger. Cruelties had been inflicted on

William, and his widow had not forgotten. She felt strongly that there was a score to be settled and that the time had come at last. "Please sit down, Captain Ryan," she said now, her hand sweeping toward the chairs in her cozy study. "Would you care for tea or coffee? Perhaps a drink?"

"No, ma'am, thank you."

"You are probably wondering why I asked you here. Do you remember me, Captain?"

"I do. Policemen are trained to remember, ma'am. I'm not saying I didn't go back to my files after you called. But only to refresh the details, if you see what I mean. We had occasion to meet on Christmas day, 1918. Ah, a tragic occasion it was too." Captain Ryan paused, staring at Jobina. He saw a beautiful and stylish woman, her shining chestnut hair bobbed in the current fashion. Her amber eyes, enhanced by mascara, glowed with golden light. Her lips and cheeks were delicately, perfectly rouged. She wore an elegant dress of jade silk, its hem just grazing her shapely calves. He noticed that she still wore her wedding ring. "My heart went out to you, ma'am. Sure and it was a terrible accident."

"Yes. I appreciated your . . . assistance."

"It was nothing, ma'am."

"I find myself needing your assistance again." Jobina went to her desk and sat down. She took a breath, then lifted her gaze to Captain Ryan. "I need information about a certain individual," she said. "I want to know if there are any skeletons in his closet, so to speak."

"And could you be telling me why, ma'am?"

"My reasons are personal, Captain."

"As you say, but I like to have the idea of things before I make an arrangement. I don't like getting in over my head, ma'am. I've been a long time on the force. I'm nearing retirement and I want it smooth."

"Of course. I can assure you I am not planning anything illegal. There is a certain individual who once humiliated somebody I loved. Simply put, I wish now to reciprocate."

"To show up this individual? Would that be about the size of it, ma'am?"

"Exactly the size, Captain. But I need the right information."

"And have you reason to believe there is such information, ma'am?"

"No, no reason. It is a feeling. Everyone has little secrets, harmless secrets. I have observed that wealthy and powerful people very often have nasty secrets. Wouldn't you agree?"

Captain Ryan smiled. "I'm thinking we understand each other, ma'am," he said. "I'm thinking we can make an arrangement."

Jobina's expression did not change, though she was relieved. She gazed at William's framed photograph and then opened the top drawer of her desk. She removed an envelope, placing it before the police officer. "You will have expenses, Captain," she said quietly. "I hope five thousand dollars is sufficient. When our business is concluded, there will be another five thousand dollars for your time."

"And the name of the individual, ma'am?"

"Martin Chadway."

Captain Ryan looked up. "I see," he said. "Yes, ma'am, I see."

It was half an hour later when Jobina took Captain Ryan to the door. Their parting was brief and formal. After the elevator came, she sank into a chair, bowing her head over her lap. Her hands had begun to shake; her head throbbed. She reached for her handkerchief and pressed it to her damp brow.

"Mrs. Grant, are you sick?"

"I'm fine, Rose," Jobina replied, smiling wanly at her young housekeeper. "Perhaps a bit tired. I didn't sleep well last night."

"You're working too hard. That's the reason, mum."

No, thought Jobina to herself, that's not the reason. The reason is my conscience. I am doing what I must, but still my conscience nags me. Perhaps justice is only revenge after all, and revenge is a bitter thing. "Speaking of work," she said, sighing and glancing at her watch, "I should be going. It's almost nine."

"Tea's on. A cup would do you good. I have sugar buns hot from the oven too."

"Thank you, Rose. I haven't time."

"You eat like a bird, you do, mum. I guess it's how you keep your figure."

"I promise I will eat a big dinner." Jobina stood. She turned to the hall table, idly sorting through the morning mail. A cream-colored vellum envelope caught her eye and she opened it. She frowned as she read the enclosed invitation: "The partners and associates of Chadway & Turnbull request the honor of your presence at a testimonial dinner celebrating the seventieth birthday of

Martin Chadway, Esquire." She threw the invitation down, then picked it up again. A moment passed. She began to laugh. She laughed until her shoulders shook and tears streaked her cheeks.

"Mrs. Grant, what is it?"

"Oh, it's very funny, Rose. It is hilarious!"

Chapter Ten

"George tells me you have bought up most of Hudson Street. Is that true?"

"Certainly not, Irene!" Jobina laughed as she sat down at the dressing table in her bedroom. It was a lovely room, all soft blues and greens with here and there a touch of ivory, a splash of yellow. The bed was antique brass, and ruffled sheets and quilts covered the feather mattress. Two silk slipper chairs bracketed the fireplace; near the terrace doors was a long silk chaise. Silver-framed photographs of Caroline and Daisy adorned the table-tops. Flowers were everywhere, in vases and bowls and little wicker baskets. "I bought the building next to our factory," she explained. "I didn't want to. I had to. The factory is operating on three shifts and still we are having trouble filling orders. The new Primrose line alone is keeping us on overtime . . . I notice you are wearing Primrose tonight."

"George much prefers it to your Scarlet, and even to your Burgundy. He says it is ladylike."

"Not too ladylike, I hope. It is supposed to have a *saucy*

kind of innocence. At least that is the effect Emile tried to create."

"How is Emile? We've seen very little of him lately."

"He has a real laboratory now and he loves it. I am putting in rather long hours myself, but they are nothing compared to Emile's hours. I'm afraid it is causing problems with Inge."

"Serious problems?"

"More serious than Emile realizes. I've tried to talk to him." Jobina shrugged, turning to face Irene. "He always sees the best in a situation, never the worst. He is always so optimistic. He is . . . chirpy. Some of our employees call him the cricket. Fondly, of course."

"Of course."

"I invited Emile and Inge to join us tonight. Emile insisted he had to work."

"Perhaps it is for the best."

"Irene, you always said you liked Emile."

"I do. It is impossible *not* to like Emile. But lately we haven't seen much of you either. You have been busy, or George has been busy at the magazine. We hoped to have you to ourselves this evening."

"I'm yours," Jobina replied, smiling. She left her dressing table and stepped behind a graceful silk screen. When she emerged moments later, she was wearing a short black dress fringed at the hem and shimmering with tiny jet beads. "What do you think?" she asked, spinning aorund. "Do you approve?"

"It's marvelous! Simply marvelous, Jobina! Wherever did you find it?"

"There is a new shop in the Village, near our factory as

a matter of fact. I happened to be passing by."

"I am jealous."

"Don't be. Because they had the same dress in white . . . and I bought it for you." Jobina darted behind the screen again, reappearing with a shiny, beribboned box. "Enjoy it, Irene. No, don't say a word. You have been such a thoughtful friend. It's my turn now. And I'm having a grand time."

"In that case, I won't spoil your fun. Shall we be on our way?"

"I want to look in on the girls first. Have a drink with George while you're waiting. The bar is well stocked. I found a new bootlegger. His name is Shrimp Malone."

"Shrimp?"

"I think he is a gangster. They all have strange names." Jobina picked up her beaded black purse and hurried into the hall. Caroline's door was closed, as always. She knocked. "May I come in, darling?"

"Yes, Mummy. Come in."

"Caroline," Jobina said, entering the room. "I have asked you not to call me that. It is an affectation . . . one of many you have acquired recently. You are not a royal princess, no matter how hard you try to act the part."

"It isn't acting. It's . . . refinement. Miss Beardsley says young ladies must be refined."

"Does she?"

"You wouldn't understand."

"Why wouldn't I? Because I'm in trade? I suppose it's *déclassé* to be in trade. Yes, darling," Jobina laughed, "I know a word or two of French myself." She turned, glancing about Caroline's room. All the chairs and coverlets and draperies were white. The rug was white also, and the ruffled skirt of the little Victorian dressing table. Caroline's hundreds of books were neatly arranged on their shelves. She had no toys or games, though her enormous teddy bear, the last remnant of her childhood, sat upon a white wicker rocker. "You could do with a bit of color in here," Jobina commented, not for the first time. "A bit of warmth."

"I like my room, Mummy. *Mama.*"

"Thank you. Have you finished your homework?"

"We didn't have any. Miss Beardsley gives us one night a week just to think about things."

"And what things have you been thinking about?"

Caroline put her sketch pad aside. Slowly, she raised her blue eyes to Jobina. "I've been planning my dress," she replied. "My dress for Suzanne's party. It's next month. I want a white dress with full sleeves and a big sash. Dark blue satin, I think."

"We shall see."

"But there's no time to see, Mama. The party is next month. We still have to buy the fabric and the trimmings and—"

"Caroline, I agreed to buy you a new dress. I didn't agree to have the dress made. It is ridiculous at your age to even consider such a thing. We will go to Lord & Taylor or to Best's. They have lovely party dresses."

"Suzanne is having her dress made. She has already had a fitting. She told me all about it, Mama. She's having a matching stole and matching shoes."

"That is her mother's concern. *Your* mother will buy your dress and shoes at a department store. The subject is closed, Caroline."

"Oh, you don't understand anything. You wanted me to have friends, Mama. You said so a million times. How can I have friends if my clothes are . . . are raggedy old sacks?"

"Raggedy old sacks!" Jobina sat down, shaking her head. She knew that fifteen was a difficult age, but it was being made even more difficult by Caroline's choice of friends. She thought them a snobbish group, too worldly by far. She thought them mean spirited and she was concerned. "You are right, Caroline," she said now. "I wanted you to have friends, but true friends. True friends don't care about your clothes or your apartment or your allowance. They care about you."

"I won't go to the party if I can't have my dress made."

"Then you won't go to the party. I suggest you think about it, Caroline. I suggest you think about your behavior recently. I sent you to Miss Beardsley's School to round out your education, *not* to learn airs and graces."

"Miss Beardsley is a lady."

"In my opinion, Agatha Beardsley is silly and pretentious. If you continue to copy her, you will find yourself back in public school. Look at me when I am speaking to you, Caroline . . . Now I will have no more of this nonsense. There will be no *grande dames* in this house. I'm serious."

"Yes, Mama."

Jobina rose. She went to Caroline, kissing her golden head. "I don't like to be harsh with you," she said. "It's for your own good."

227

"Yes, Mama."

"Don't stay up too late, darling."

"No, Mama."

"Can I have one smile before I go? One teeny, tiny smile?" Jobina waited, but Caroline turned away, reaching for her sketch pad. "Caroline?"

"Good night, Mama."

Jobina left, her shoulders rising and falling in a great sigh. She crossed the hall to Daisy's room. Carefully, she stepped over discarded comic books and magazines, over dirty knee socks and rumpled gym bloomers. Through the shadows, she saw stuffed animals heaped on the chairs, schoolbooks spilled on the desk. She saw Daisy's robe hanging from a doorknob, its belt curled like a snake on the littered floor. How can two girls be so different? she wondered, gazing down at her sleeping daughter. "Sweet dreams," she whispered. "Sweet dreams, darling."

George was pouring a second whiskey as Jobina entered the living room. "We were beginning to think you had deserted us," he said. "Jobina, that is quite a costume you are wearing."

"It's a dress, George."

"What there is of it. If it were any shorter . . . I know, I know. You are going to tell me it's the fashion now. Please don't. I hear enough of that from Irene."

"If you read the fashion column in your own magazine, we wouldn't need to tell you. At least *Gotham* keeps up with the times."

"We have an enlightened editorial policy," George replied. "Perhaps you have noticed. Why, there are some who call us liberals."

"Liberals!" Jobina laughed. "Watch your language, George. Remember you are in mixed company."

"I'm not really the dinosaur you think I am."

"No?"

"It's true," Irene said. "He is getting better. Well, a little better anyway. He's trying. How are the girls, Jobina?"

"The chaotic one is sound asleep. Caroline . . . Caroline is sketching dress designs. She's rather a good artist."

"Soon you will be able to use her in your advertising department."

"I have an idea she plans to marry a rich man and live happily ever after. Like you, Irene. She approves of your way of life. She even approves of you, George. Though I believe she has her sights set on Ian. We may be relatives one day. Imagine!"

George smiled. He finished his drink and put down the glass. "Shall we be off?" he asked. "It's impossible to make reservations at speakeasies. We will have to take our chances."

"Are we going to the 21 Club?"

"Club Harley."

"Harley Kilburne is a friend of yours, isn't he?"

"He used to be my stockbroker. If you want to imagine something, Jobina, imagine that. He left Rutherford & Day to open a speakeasy. Just kicked over the traces and started a new life. The world's gone mad."

"The world's having fun," Irene replied. "New York is certainly having fun. We are in the midst of one vast party. Blame it on Prohibition."

"Stupid law," George muttered. "Stupid, stupid law."

There were some twenty thousand speakeasies dotting New York in the spring of 1928. Many of them were little more than dingy basements and back rooms, but others were popular night spots offering food and entertainment and the chance to rub shoulders with the city's elite. Jack and Charlie's 21 Club was favored by writers and show people. Texas Guinan's Club Intime, while a mecca for tourists, was also favored by reporters and the sporting crowd. Club Harley was favored by publishers and Wall Street brokers and younger members of society.

None of these clubs was inexpensive. Scotch and champagne sold for twenty dollars a bottle, rye for fifteen. People who chose to bring their own liquor paid two dollars for a pitcher of water, two dollars for a bowl of ice. The newly invented *couvert* charge was ten dollars. No one complained. It was the glorious 1920's, and money rained from a rich and bountiful stock market; it was indeed a party.

"I hope we get a table downstairs," Jobina said as the Thayers' car approached Club Harley. "I love the noise and the crowding together. Can you use your influence, George?"

"Perhaps after dinner. I thought we would have dinner upstairs first . . . I've asked a friend of mine to join us. His name is David Amory. The Amorys are a fine old family, Jobina. David is a very successful broker."

Jobina's smile faded. "Are you playing matchmaker

again, George?" She sighed. "I don't like having dates arranged for me. We've discussed this before, too many times. The last time, you promised to stay out of my personal affairs."

"It's my fault," Irene admitted sheepishly. "It was my idea. I suggested to George that he—"

"Irene, how could you!"

"There is no harm in a simple dinner date. I worry about you, Jobina. You can't give your whole life to work and children. If you were old, it would be different. It's all well and good to sit by the fire when one is old. But you are young. Young and beautiful and . . . unencumbered. You should be out dancing every night. I would be, in your place."

"That is beside the point, Irene."

"It's precisely the point. We have introduced you to a dozen nice men. You turned them all away. I get quite discouraged sometimes. What is wrong with a little fun?"

"I have fun."

"You don't socialize, Jobina. You haven't been out socially in months. Going out with us or the Sisks or Emile doesn't count. You should be meeting new people. I don't know this David Amory fellow, but George assures me he is charming. And it is only a dinner date. A foursome at that. George and I will chaperone."

"I don't want a chaperone and I don't want a date."

"It is too late now," Irene replied, smiling. "The deed is done. Come now, you are not facing a firing squad. It's just dinner."

"With a stranger."

"A charming stranger."

"A stranger nevertheless. I would rather have the firing squad." Jobina's remark was not entirely in jest, for her few previous dinner dates had been awkward. She shuddered to remember the uncomfortable silences, the forced and clumsy small talk, the fumbling hesitations at night's end. "The first question," she said, "will be, 'Where are you from?' Then there will be some general comments. And then there will be pauses that seem to stretch for hours. When your David Amory sees me home, he will wonder if he should take my hand or kiss my cheek. I will wonder also. We will both feel sixteen years old. We will both be terribly embarrassed, and terribly relieved when the evening is over. That's dating, Irene. I *hate* dating."

"Everyone hates dating," Irene laughed. "At least in the beginning. Why, I was a bundle of nerves during my first few dates with George. Wasn't I, love? Didn't I spill the wine at Alice Webster's dinner dance?"

"The soup."

"The soup!" Irene laughed again. "That's even worse! But it proves my point, Jobina. We are all nervous in the beginning. Those feelings pass. By my third date with George I was poised and utterly captivating. Half the girls I knew were after George. By our third date he was mine."

"So you had your cap set for me, Irene?" George asked.

"Of course. Are you surprised?"

"Surprised to hear you admit it. I've heard the other version of this story, the one in which I relentlessly pursued *you*." George smiled, touching Irene's bare shoulder. "You may have two versions of the story," he said. "I have only one. I fell in love with you when you spilled the soup. That was the moment. A certain moment, a certain gesture. Sometimes it happens that way."

Irene snuggled closer to George. She clasped his hand, lifting it to her lips. She did not speak, though her expression became gentle, infinitely soft.

Jobina watched, startled by the sudden change of mood. But that is marriage, she thought to herself, the shared memories, the little intimacies. That is what I miss. That and so many other things. "We . . . We're here," she said quietly.

"Yes." George leaned forward, peering through the car window. "There is David. He is standing near the canopy. He's brought you a corsage, Jobina."

"How sweet of him."

"You will like David."

Claus opened the car door and the three friends stepped onto the sidewalk. Club Harley was located in a lovely three-story brownstone building. Neither the building nor the canopy was marked, though a small metal grille built into the door identified it as a speakeasy. "Do you know the password?" Jobina asked.

"It's 'roly-poly,'" George replied. "Not that passwords are necessary. The clubs use them to amuse their customers."

"I thought they were meant to keep the police out."

"Bah! All these clubs are well known to the police and Federal agents. They make raids from time to time. Miss Guinan seems to get the worst of it. But the next week, the next month, it is business as usual . . . David, hello. Have you been waiting long?"

"I arrived early. I don't blame you for taking your time, George. I would do the same, if I had two beautiful women on my arm. Which beautiful woman is Irene?"

"I am. And I'm delighted to meet you. Jobina, this is David. David, Jobina."

"How do you do, Jobina? It is a pleasure."

"Thank you." Warily, Jobina turned her gaze to David Amory. He was an attractive man, slender and fair haired. In the light of the street lamp she could see that his eyes were gray, deep gray flecked with blue. She liked his smile, for it was confident, very sure. "George has been telling me nice things about you, David."

"They're all true. You can trust George to tell the truth."

"Oh, everybody trusts George."

"I was counting on that." David's smile widened. He held out clear flower boxes to Irene and Jobina, bowing slightly. "With my compliments," he said.

"White orchids. How sweet."

"If the formalities are over," George said, "let's go inside."

David took Jobina's arm, guiding her through the crowded foyer to a narrow elevator at the rear of the club. He greeted several people along the way, but in the crush, in the loud and merry uproar, conversation was impossible. "I am always tempted to bring earplugs to these places," he said as the elevator doors closed.

"You would be missing half the fun."

"Fun? Yes, I suppose so. My work has kept me quite

busy. I haven't had time for fun."

"That is something you and Jobina have in common," Irene said.

It was not the only thing, for David, like Jobina, had come from great wealth. The Amorys had made their money in the coal fields of Pennsylvania, controlling nearly a quarter of that state's most profitable mines. They worked their miners to death, housing them in miserable shanties, forcing them to spend their meager wages in company stores. Men who dared to complain were threatened, even beaten. The old, the sick, were evicted. It was business, and the Amorys allowed nothing to interfere with business. David himself had never visited a mine, had never spoken to any of the miners. He referred to them as Irishers and Hunkies, seeing small distinction between the two. "They are all foreigners," he had remarked once, and if it had occurred to him that these foreigners had made him rich, he did not say.

Now the elevator doors slid open and again he took Jobina's arm. "Have you eaten here before?" he asked. "The food is excellent. The surroundings are pleasant too."

Jobina turned, glancing about the large dining room. The walls were paneled, elaborately carved. Snowy linen dressed the tables, which were set with china and crystal and tall white candles. The chair cushions were pale rose velvet. "It's pretty," she said. "I confess I prefer the hustle and bustle downstairs."

"Then we will stop downstairs after dinner. A beautiful woman must have her way."

It was a nice compliment, lightly and smoothly

uttered. Jobina looked at David and she knew that he was different from the other men she had met. Although the circumstances were awkward, there was nothing awkward about him. He had spoken only a few words, but they had been the right words, as right, as perfect, as his manners. She found herself savoring the prospect of this evening. To her surprise, she found herself blushing. "I am not used to compliments," she said. "My work has kept me busy also."

"Perhaps you will allow me to distract you."

"Perhaps."

Irene, watching the brief exchange, smiled. "See," she whispered, poking George. "I told you Jobina was ready to come out of her shell. I told you."

"Give David some credit. He seems to have caught her fancy."

"Did you coach him?"

"I warned him to go easy," George replied. "The last fellow we introduced to Jobina was so intimidated by her looks, her success . . . why, he practically fell all over himself. It was a disaster, if you remember. But of course David isn't intimidated by anything. He is a true Amory."

"Is that good?"

"The Amorys are worth millions. Jobina wouldn't have to be concerned with lipsticks and face powders. She could be a lady of leisure again. And about time too. Come along, Irene. They have our table."

Champagne was brought, a fine French champagne smuggled across the border from Canada. Jobina mentioned her bootlegger and soon David was entertaining the group with tales of his bootlegger, Big Jake Ginzler. "The punch line is even better," he laughed, "because *then* Big Jake said, 'Well, yeah, but I got my principles.'"

"That's marvelous, David," Irene said, wiping her eyes. "Tell us more."

"I hoard my Big Jake stories. I may write a book one day. If Harley Kilburne can open a speakeasy, I can write a book. Harley has given us notions . . . Can you imagine a man leaving the Street to open a club?"

"I can," Jobina said. "It's . . . romantic."

"In a foolish sort of way. Harley was always different. His wife is in business, you know. The Kilburne Baking Company is hers."

"Really?"

"Harley doesn't appear to mind."

"Mind?" Jobina asked. "I should think he would be proud."

David's wide gray eyes flickered. They settled softly on Jobina, lingering. "There is that," he agreed. "It's twice as hard for a woman to make a success in business. It's something to be proud of. I'm sure you are proud of Jobina Inc. A worthy company, Jobina Inc. It has great potential. Having met you, I understand why. Every successful company needs a guiding spirit. In this case, yours."

"And my partner's."

"Ah, you are modest too. Spirit and modesty. What a beguiling combination."

Jobina felt the color rush again to her cheeks. "Two compliments in one night," she said with a smile. "I am overwhelmed."

"The night is young," David replied. He took the menu from the waiter and glanced at it. "Shall I order for you, Jobina? The veal is quite good here. You will like it. Yes," he said to the waiter. "The veal in mushroom sauce. And tell the chef it's for my party."

Irene frowned. "I was thinking of trying the chicken," she said.

"The veal is much better."

"But—"

"Come now, Irene." George sighed. "It makes no difference. If David's judgment in food is half as good as his judgment in stocks, we will be feasting tonight."

David smiled. "My judgment is excellent, Irene," he said.

It was midnight when David and Jobina and the Thayers left the dining room. Once downstairs, they pushed through the crowd to a showroom complete with musicians and a tiny stage. Tables were packed tightly around the stage, though front tables were particularly desired by male patrons, for there there were only scant inches away from long-legged chorus girls wearing feathers and spangles and little else. George was amongst those seeking a front table, but David, in his smooth and charming way, selected a table off to the side. "We will be more comfortable," he explained, and the matter was settled. He ordered a bottle of brandy, and that matter, too, was settled.

"I don't like him," Irene said to George as they rode

home. "I just don't like him."

"Good Lord, Irene! A few hours ago you were telling him he was *marvelous*."

"Well, he's charming and funny and he has beautiful manners."

"He is also filthy rich. What more do you want?"

"I don't like his attitude. He asks questions, but he doesn't really wait for the answers. He dominates things, George. He is very polite about it, but still . . . You must have noticed that he took over the entire conversation. We ate what he wanted us to eat. We sat where he wanted us to sit. We even drank the brandy *he* ordered."

"You neglected to mention that he paid the check. That's one for his side."

"George, I'm serious."

"All right. I will admit David tends to be . . . to be sure of himself."

"Arrogant is the word you are searching for, love."

"No. I wouldn't go that far. He has fixed opinions. We all have fixed opinions, Irene. David is sure of his." George sighed. He lighted a cigarette and leaned his head back, watching the smoke. "It isn't easy finding someone for Jobina," he said after a while. "The Jobina we used to know, yes. Not the Jobina we know now."

"Why not?"

"She is successful in her own right, Irene. It is difficult for men to deal with that. Men are competitive by nature. They want to have all the success. David, on the other hand, is confident enough—"

"Arrogant enough."

"I refuse to quibble over words. Despite your qualms,

it was obvious that Jobina found David most congenial. You were there. You saw her."

"I saw something else, George. Something was nagging me all evening. I finally figured out what. David bears a certain resemblance to William. His coloring is the same, the soft look in his eyes. He is nothing *like* William, but there is a certain physical resemblance."

"Yes."

"Yes? Is that your only comment?"

"I was aware of the resemblance. I thought about it, Irene. In the end I decided it wasn't such a bad thing. You must admit Jobina was at ease with David. Perhaps she noticed the resemblance; perhaps she didn't. I happen to believe it smoothed the way."

"But that's terrible."

"Finding a suitor for Jobina was your idea. I am doing my best to cooperate. I am also running out of eligible men. Good Lord, I can't go to a store and *buy* one."

"David is wrong for her."

"I don't know that. Nor do you, Irene. Jobina is a grown woman. She will make her choices as she sees fit."

"She's vulnerable. She has been alone a long time."

"By *choice*. Perhaps it is time now for different choices." George sighed again. He dropped his cigarette into the ashtray, then slid his arm around Irene's shoulder. "Either way," he said quietly, "Jobina will manage. She always does. She is . . . Jobina."

"I hope you plan to invite me in for a drink," David

said, leaning lightly against the door. "I have a sudden thirst."

"It's late."

"If I promise not to stay too long?"

"Well . . . if you promise."

David took the keys from Jobina's hand. He unlocked the door, then stepped aside to let her enter. His eyes followed the shapely curves of her legs, the sway of her figure beneath her beaded black dress. All night he had imagined himself tearing her dress away; he had imagined her standing naked before him and his senses had throbbed with desire. Tonight, he thought now; I must have her tonight. "Your keys," he said, and as he returned them, his fingers brushed her breast. He did not apologize. He strode into the living room, going directly to the bar. "Brandy?" he asked.

"No, I don't—"

"A small brandy then."

"David," Jobina laughed, "I've really had quite enough to drink. My head will be pounding tomorrow. And tomorrow is a work day."

"But I insist. Brandy is good for the soul."

"Oh?"

"You mustn't doubt me, beautiful lady," David replied, smiling. "I know about such things. Brandy is one of life's pleasures. You haven't allowed yourself many pleasures, have you? You're devoted to your work. We are alike in that, Jobina. I would say we've earned our pleasures."

Jobina was silent, her gaze averted, as she wondered

what to make of David Amory. She had been drawn to him from the very beginning—to the look in his eyes, to his smile, to his presence. She knew he had had an unsettling effect on her. Several times he had touched her hand and at his touch her pulse had quickened. Several times she had imagined his arms about her. She had blushed bright red, but she had not denied the stirrings she felt. I am behaving like a schoolgirl, she chided herself now, her heart soaring even as she did so.

"Were you the decorator?"

David's voice seemed to come from a great distance. Jobina blinked, turning around. "What? I beg your pardon, David. What did you say?"

"I was talking about your apartment, beautiful lady. Did you decorate the apartment yourself?"

"Oh yes. Yes, I did. It took forever."

"I approve of the results. You have excellent taste."

"Thank you . . . David, it really is late."

"Allow me another moment or two. Shall we step onto the terrace? I would like to see the view."

"The view?"

"You know," David laughed, "tall buildings, the river, the sky."

"Perhaps . . . another time."

"Come," David said, catching Jobina's hand in his. "We'll step outside and count the stars."

"Do you always get your way?"

"I try, Jobina. I try not to let opportunities slip away."

"Opportunities?"

"To count the stars. To look at a beautiful woman by moonlight. Those are very special opportunities."

"But it's late. And tomorrow is a work day."

"Tomorrow is tomorrow, Jobina. We have tonight. A soft spring night," David added, leading her onto the terrace. "Look at all the stars. They are putting on a show just for us."

"You have a romantic turn of mind, for a stock-broker."

David did not disagree, though in truth he had an entirely practical turn of mind. He enjoyed women and he studied them, much as he studied the financial pages. He had learned how to charm, how to flatter, how and when to speak the right words. It was a practical matter, for he had found that it was easier to win a woman's body if first he won her heart. "You make me feel romantic," he said now. "You've cast a spell on me, Jobina. I am bewitched."

"Please don't say anymore."

"Why?"

"Oh, because I'm gullible. I'm likely to believe you." Jobina walked to the terrace ledge to stare up at the endless, starry sky. There was a moon, a crescent of silver shining upon the river, upon the silent and darkened apartment buildings. There was a gentle breeze, fragrant with spring. "I think you should leave, David," she said with a sigh.

"You don't want me to leave."

"I think it's best."

"Best?" David went to Jobina. He tilted her face to him, tracing the line of her mouth. "What's best is this," he said, kissing her. "And this," he added, taking her into his arms. He pressed close to her and soon his hands were

243

caressing her breasts. "I want you, Jobina," he murmured hoarsely. "My God, I want you."

"No, David, don't . . . Don't."

He slipped the straps from her shoulders, pulling at her dress until it fell to her waist. "Jobina," he murmured as the moonlight struck her bare shoulders, her bare breasts. "Jobina." Now his mouth was on her, his hands persuading, urging, demanding. "Jobina."

She felt the frenzied beating of her heart. She felt dizzy, unable to catch her breath. "No, David," she gasped. "*No.*"

"Are you shy? Don't be shy. There's no one to see us. Only the man in the moon."

"David . . . David, *stop,*" Jobina cried, grabbing at her dress. "We can't do this. The girls . . . my girls are just down the hall."

"I want you. I want you so much."

Jobina steadied herself against David, for she was shaking. "God help me," she whispered, "I want you too."

David drew the shades and closed the doors. He held out his hand to Jobina, taking her to a long white chaise. He stripped away her dress, her satin panties, her garters and stockings. With a low cry, he sank down beside her. "Jobina," he murmured. They murmured to each other, mindless, incoherent sounds carried off by the breeze. In the shadowy night the lovers knew the depths of their turbulent passion, and it was, for them, the only truth.

Jobina did not sleep. She remained on the terrace long

after David had gone, stealing into her bedroom at dawn. She bathed and dressed and brushed her hair until her arms ached. She paced, first to the left, then to the right, and then in a circle that led her finally to William's photograph. She studied his handsome face and tears misted her eyes. Slowly, very slowly, she picked up the photograph and placed it in a drawer. She took her wedding ring from her finger, placing it atop the photograph. She closed the drawer. "William," she whispered, then sighed, as much in resignation as in sorrow.

Chapter Eleven

"Please sit down, Captain Ryan," Jobina said, gesturing to a chair near her desk. "It's good of you to come so early."

"I'm an early riser myself, ma'am. A habit from the old country. When you're the only boyo on a farm . . . But I'm not here to tell you my memories, am I now? You'd be wondering about Mr. Martin Chadway. And it seems your suspicions were right. There's information you can use."

"The nature of the information?"

"Well, ma'am, you might say it's of a delicate nature. Until about eight years ago, it was the usual. Chorus girls and floozies, if you see what I mean. All very quiet like. Then, eight years ago, Mr. Chadway took a bad turn. His women started getting younger and younger. He went looking for new excitements. That would be my sense of it, ma'am . . . I'm sorry to say Mr. Chadway went looking for little girls. There have been incidents. Little girls twelve, thirteen years old. When he was found out, he paid through the nose. To the girls' families, you see. He paid them to keep quiet. Ah, but he can afford to pay, so he's still on the loose."

"Little girls?" Jobina asked weakly. "Are you certain?"

"It's all here, ma'am. It's all in my report. Mr. Chadway was arrested twice. Of course it was hushed up. The families were paid and they dropped the charges. A lot of people were paid. The records were lost. In the confusion, you understand, ma'am."

"You found the records, Captain?"

"I did. And I went past the records, ma'am. I did some careful checking of my own. Ah, it's an ugly story, but I'll stand behind every word."

"You are absolutely certain? There is no mistake?"

"No mistake, ma'am."

"Then why wasn't anything *done?*"

Captain Ryan shrugged. "Money," he replied. "When a poor man touches a child, he's carted off to prison, if the child's da doesn't get him first. A rich man opens his purse and goes on to the next. It's the way of the world, ma'am. A sorry way it is too."

Jobina felt sick. She had heard of such things, read of them; as a child she had been warned time and time again never to speak to strangers. But Martin Chadway, she thought, revulsion washing over her. Martin Chadway! "I don't know what to say, Captain. I hadn't expected . . ."

"Sure and you already said it, ma'am. Some secrets are nastier than others."

"Yes."

"I'll be leaving you my report, ma'am. Two copies,

248

typewritten. If you don't mind my saying so, it's not fit reading for a lady."

"I don't intend to read it. I don't intend to look at it. Only one person will see your report, the person most directly concerned."

"Ah, that's as it should be." Captain Ryan stood. He took the thick envelope from Jobina's desk, putting it in in his jacket pocket. "Sometimes I think there's a justice to things after all," he remarked. "Not often, ma'am, but sometimes. I don't mind telling you it does my heart good."

Jobina stood also. She walked with Captain Ryan into the hall. "Do you ever wonder if justice is merely another name for revenge?"

"Well, ma'am, I wouldn't know about that. What did Mr. Shakespeare write? 'A rose by any other name'? It's a question of getting things to come out even. It's the best we can hope for, in this world. That's how I see it, ma'am. That's the truth of it."

It was noon when Jobina arrived at the offices of Chadway & Turnbull. She rode Martin Chadway's private elevator to the top floor, then passed through a formal reception area and two large, paneled outer offices before reaching her destination. "I am Mrs. Grant," she said to the gnarled old man who guarded Martin's door. "I am expected."

"Certainly, Mrs. Grant. You may go right in."

"Thank you." Jobina paused on the threshold. She took a breath and then entered the office. It was huge, with dark oak wainscoting and tufted leather chairs and signed English hunting prints. The lamps were polished brass. The many books were bound in leather and tooled in gold. Martin's desk was a magnificent Hepplewhite, adorned by an antique pen stand and a single marble figure—the blindfolded figure of justice. Now Martin rose behind his desk, extending his hand to Jobina. "Hello, Martin," she said. "Thank you for seeing me at such short notice."

"I am always happy to see you, Jobina. You grow more beautiful as the years pass. Please sit down, my dear. May I offer you sherry? Or perhaps you would prefer tea?"

"No, thank you. I'm afraid this isn't a social call, Martin. I am here . . . on William's behalf."

"William!"

"Then you remember my husband, William?"

Martin frowned, staring at his visitor. "Of course I remember William," he replied. "Jobina, what is the matter? You look . . . strained. Are you well?"

"Quite well, Martin. But I see I have startled you."

"I confess you have roused my curiosity. When you telephoned, I supposed it had something to do with my testimonial dinner. Everyone is calling about it. We are in a dither of plans and preparations. Mayor Walker will be attending, you know. We are hoping to have the governor also. It is a great honor. To be honored by one's peers . . ." Martin fell silent, for alarm had begun to stir in him. He continued to stare at Jobina and his alarm deepened. There is something wrong here, he thought, his spine prickling. "Forgive me for sounding immodest," he said. "You must tell me what is on your mind."

"William is on my mind."

"I don't understand, my dear. It is a long time since William's tragic death. Why, it is ten years at least."

"Come Christmas."

"Yes. The timing was so . . . unfortunate." Martin reached his hand to a humidor. He removed a fat black cigar and began rolling it between his fleshy fingers. He dropped the cigar after a moment, then picked it up again. He shifted around in his chair. "Well, Jobina," he said with a calmness he did not feel, "what exactly about William is on your mind?"

"You seem nervous, Martin."

"As I mentioned, we have been in a dither here. The guest lists. The dinner plans."

"There isn't going to be a dinner."

"I beg your pardon?"

"There isn't going to be a dinner, Martin. Not for you." Jobina drew another breath. She had waited for this moment, longed for it, but now she felt no pleasure. She looked at Martin, at the venal, corrupt old man he was. She looked at the envelope she held in her hand. "Ten years," she murmured and, as she did so, she saw William lying in a pool of blood, his jaw slack, the life gone from his eyes. I must do this, she thought. I must. "Ten years ago," she said, "you did a despicable thing to William. You schemed . . . For money, you joined my father's plot against him. For money, though you had more money than you could use in five lifetimes. You

251

offered William a choice, I believe. I'm here today to offer *you* a choice, Martin. It's simple enough. You will resign from Chadway & Turnbull, from the bar. You will leave New York and move to your house on the Cape. You will do these things immediately, or I will ruin you."

"Ruin me? *Ruin me?* You must be mad, Jobina."

"No."

"You are under a strain," Martin said. "Your company is too much for you. Women were not meant for business, Jobina. You are feeling the strain."

"Believe what you wish. But I warn you, I am serious."

"Serious? You are . . . you are absurd," Martin sputtered. "You dare to come in here and make threats? To threaten *me?*"

"As you once threatened William."

"William was a thief, an embezzler."

Jobina broke the seal on the envelope. She withdrew Captain Ryan's report and placed it before Martin. "And what are you?" she asked quietly.

Martin fumbled for his glasses. As he peered at the report, all the color drained from his face. His eyes were hollow with fear, with dread. Shaking, he reached across the desk and poured a whiskey. "Lies," he said, his voice a strangled cry.

"No."

"Damned lies," Martin insisted, though his mouth trembled and his head slumped on his chest.

Don't let him die, thought Jobina, rising. Please don't let him die. "Martin? Shall I call a doctor?"

"What?"

"Do you want a doctor?"

Martin poured another whiskey. He drank it, slowly lifting his stricken gaze to Jobina. "A doctor? I have no need of a doctor. I am not a weakling like . . . Where did you get this information?"

"It will be destroyed, providing you resign and go away."

"If I refuse?"

Jobina hesitated. She turned her head to Martin, but again she saw William, still and white in death. "If you refuse," she replied finally, "the information will be sent to the newspapers. Some will disregard it, of course. Others will not."

"You are your father's daughter after all, Jobina."

"You were his accomplice."

Martin peered once more at Captain Ryan's report. His shoulders sagged. His clenched hands fell upon the desk. "The dinner is next week," he said in a quavering voice. "I will announce my resignation then."

"No, Martin. Today. And you will cancel the dinner."

"I am an old man. You would not be so cruel to an old man."

"Cruel? That is an odd word, coming from you. William was a young man, with a young wife and two young children. At least you have lived your life, Martin. Your life was not taken from you."

"William took his own life."

"You and Father put the gun in his hand."

"There were reasons. Jobina, you must try to understand. Jonas had important plans for you. When those plans were ruined, he blamed William. He was

253

determined that William be made to suffer the consequences. I was merely his . . . instrument."

"Instrument or accomplice, it is the same thing. I hope
you are not expecting sympathy, Martin. I have as much
sympathy for you as you had for William."

"But he was a *thief*."

"You force me to repeat my question," Jobina said,
glancing pointedly at the four typewritten pages of
Captain Ryan's report. "What are you? There is a name
for it. Don't force me to use the name."

Color flared in Martin's ashen face. He snatched the
pages from his desk and ripped them apart, hurling the
pieces at Jobina. *"Lies,"* he cried.

"The truth, Martin."

"What do you know of the truth? It is necessary to
examine a man's whole life before passing judgment. My
life is filled with achievements. I am admired. I am
respected."

"Wealth is always respected."

"And rightly so. It is the symbol of achievement, of
strength. Only weak men are poor. They lead their
miserable, sniveling little lives and contribute nothing to
the world. They have no character. Your precious
William was such a man. He had no strength. God knows
he had no character. He would have led his whole life one
step ahead of the bankruptcy courts. He was a spineless
fool."

"Are you quite finished?"

Martin saw the loathing in Jobina's eyes. He saw the
icy anger too, and he shrank away. "I . . . If you . . . You
must forgive me," he stammered, trying to still his

254

shaking hands. "This has been most difficult for me. To be faced with such accusations . . . I am an old man, Jobina. Forgive me."

"There is no way out of this, Martin. I have given you my terms."

"I was acting for your *father*. Have you given *Jonas* your terms?"

"Oh, I haven't forgotten about Father. When the time is right, I will deal with him. He is harder than you are, Martin. He doesn't care about his reputation, you see. If his depraved secrets got out, he would laugh. No, he cares only about money and power. That requires a different approach."

"Jobina—"

"I won't take any more of your time. You have a lot to do. There is a resignation to prepare, a dinner to cancel."

"You can't ask me to cancel the dinner, Jobina. It is a tribute . . . the culmination of my career, of my *life*. I am to be honored by the city's finest people. People are coming from Washington also. It is supposed to be a surprise, but President Hoover is sending an aide to represent him. He is sending a personal letter of congratulations."

"The President will have to congratulate someone else."

"Where is your kindness, Jobina?"

"What kindness did you show William that night in the study? I admit he made a terrible mistake. But then he was meant to, wasn't he? It was all part of the plan you and Father devised. A plan to destroy him. Well, you succeeded. Do you really expect me to sit by and allow a *tribute?*"

"I didn't know he would take his life."

"Nor did you care. You may speak candidly, Martin. There are no more secrets to keep. You didn't care and you weren't sorry. Is that about the size of it?"

Martin passed his hand across his face. Despite his great bulk, he appeared diminished, almost frail. "I have been looking forward to the dinner for so long," he murmured.

"Yes, it's a shame."

A strange smile touched Martin's white lips. He raised his head slightly and tears filled the sunken hollows of his eyes. "I don't know what I will do in retirement. My work has been my life. Without it . . ."

"I wouldn't worry. The Martin Chadways of the world seem to live forever. Perhaps that is your true punishment. You will have years and years to remember all your cruelties. Years and years and years."

While Martin Chadway's sudden resignation surprised everybody, the sudden cancellation of his testimonial dinner caused talk. Rumors of ill health abounded. Later, when he moved from New York to his isolated Cape Cod estate, there were rumors of mental problems, of "second childhood"—the polite term for senility. Martin himself refused all comment. His wife chose not to leave the city, and he acceded to a formal separation agreement. His children insisted that his assets be placed in trust, and because he feared a court battle, he acceded to their demand also.

Jobina was aware of the gossip, and the glee with which it was passed along. Privately she took the blame for her role in Martin's downfall, but publicly she said nothing. "I'm too busy to think about such things," she replied to George's suspicious questions. "The company keeps me busy day and night."

It was only a slight exaggeration, for Jobina Inc. was now a national company, its perfumes and cosmetics and beauty creams in stores from coast to coast. The trademark butterfly was seen everywhere, recognized everywhere. To Jobina and Emile, the butterfly had become the symbol of soaring profits. Eugene Marshall spoke of a gold mine, Emile of a money tree, and they were both correct; the company that had begun in Mr. Greevy's basement was a phenomenal success. "Keeping up with our success," Jobina said one brisk November afternoon, "that's the worry."

"I pray for worries like that," Eugene Marshall said with a laugh. "Though I see what you mean. There's no question about it. We need the Chicago factory to service our western accounts. We have to make the investment."

"Emile? You are very quiet."

"We need another factory. I don't disagree. But Chicago, it is so far." Emile left the conference table to pace Jobina's large ivory and green office. "My lab is here," he said. "Here I can watch everything. Control, yes? Here the colors come out right. The textures are right, the scents. Because I am watching. How can I watch in Chicago?"

"You won't have to," Jobina replied. "Your formulas

will be followed exactly. There will be chemists to supervise, but the formula will be yours. We're in mass production now, Emile. I see no other way. Do you?"

"I wish there could be two of me, one for here and one for Chicago. It is not so easy to give my formulas to strangers. With my formulas, I am the miser." Emile shrugged. He returned to the table and sat down. "But we do what is best for the company," he said, smiling at Jobina. "Always the company comes first, yes?"

"If we want to stay in business. We just can't fill West Coast orders from a New York factory. It takes too long."

"Then it is settled. Chicago is the answer. Maybe I can go to Chicago once in a while?"

"Of course, Emile. You can go as often as you wish. I think it may be a good idea. You will keep them on their toes. You are the boss, after all."

Emile laughed merrily, shaking his dark head. "We know who is the boss, Jobina," he said. "But I will try. In Chicago I will wear my serious face."

"Can I proceed with the paper work?" Eugene asked.

"You can begin. Before we sign anything, I would like you to go out there and have one more look at the factory. It's a costly investment, Gene. I don't want unpleasant surprises."

"Yes, Jobina. I understand."

"And take Jack Sisk along. He can begin interviewing personnel. If we buy the factory, it should be in full operation by the first of the year. That's our target date. Jack will need the extra time."

Eugene adjusted his glasses as he flipped through a thick manila folder. "I don't have the projected figures on personnel. Did Jack prepare a budget?"

"Last week." Jobina smiled, a mischievous light twinkling in her lovely amber eyes. "I think he is hesitant to show it to you," she said. "He knows you will lecture him. Really, Gene, you are becoming famous for your lectures."

"It's my job to see that company money isn't wasted. If Jack is hesitating, it means he's prepared a budget for a union shop. We disagree about unions."

"So I have heard."

"Do you want some union telling you how you can run Jobina Inc.? Let the unions in and they will make all the rules. They're agitators. Nothing is ever good enough for them. We will be plagued by grievances and strikes."

"I doubt that. We are paying wages higher than union scale."

"We *choose* to, Jobina. Or you choose to. Let the unions in and you won't have any choice in the matter. You won't have any say. There is something else you ought to consider. We pay more, but our hours are longer. Unions have a rule they call overtime. Workers on overtime earn bonus wages. That increases the budget right away. I'm not surprised Jack is hesitating. He's wasting company money."

"He must deal with realities, Gene." Jobina sighed. "One of the realities is that unions are gathering strength. It isn't a passing fancy. People want them."

"Do you want them?"

"I told Jack to keep an eye on the situation. Should a majority of our employees decide to organize, I wouldn't want to stand in their way. But if it's any consolation,

Emile agrees with you. Don't you, Emile?"

"Unions, they interfere. It is our company, yes? Not the unions. Was there the union for us when we worked at Greevy's Pharmacy? I worked twelve hours a day, Gene," Emile explained, turning to the accountant. "Six days a week. Because Mr. Greevy said so. It was his pharmacy, yes? He said the hours and the wages. From Greevy's Pharmacy we build this whole company. So who is right?"

"Emile makes a strong point, Jobina."

"Granted. I don't pretend to know who is right and who is wrong. I do know that we will soon be expanding into a new city. Distance alone is bound to create problems. I'm trying to *limit* our problems. We may be asked to accept a union in Chicago. Jack thinks we may. It is best to be prepared."

"If you took a position—"

"My position is that we must be practical. I don't want to be at war with our employees. It's bad for them and bad for us. They aren't the enemy, for heaven's sake. Nor are we."

"They will be cutting into our profits."

"Well"—Jobina sighed again—"I don't object to a modest cut. I'm not a fool, Gene. I have no intention of handing over the company to outsiders. But we can afford to be fair. Emile has told you about our years at Greevy's. Our long hours and tiny wages. It was the way then. It wasn't necessarily the right way. Mr. Greevy was fair, by the standards of his day. Times change. All I am saying is that we should be fair, by today's standards."

"See who is the boss?" Emile laughed. "It is no use

to argue."

"You don't mind if I take a close look at Jack's budget?"

"Certainly not. Thrash it out between yourselves. There is room for compromise, providing you don't make it a philosophic battle. Your philosophies are too far apart."

"Jack's philosophy," Eugene sniffed, "is spend, spend, spend. He's allowing our employees *forty-five* minutes for lunch. Do you know what that extra time costs us?"

"How long do you take for lunch, Gene?" Jobina asked.

"But that's different."

"Oh."

Eugene stood, gathering his folders together. "I'm not a factory worker. I don't compare myself to factory workers. They have their place and I have mine. That's what's wrong. The lines are being blurred." He glanced at his watch as he moved to the door. "I'll have another talk with Jack," he said.

"As you wish." Jobina waited until the door closed and then turned to Emile. "Eugene Marshall has no sense of humor. Have you noticed? And he is becoming pompous to boot. I suppose it's all the money he's made in the stock market. It's gone to his head."

"Money changes people. That I have noticed."

"You are the same, Emile."

"Because I am French. The French, they do not change."

"How are your investments doing?"

"Every day my stocks go up more. Every morning first thing I look in the newspaper. *Voilà!* More profits. I can't believe it. Always I am looking for, how you say, the catch?"

"You aren't alone. David is convinced the market is rising too fast."

"He told me. He told me the stocks to sell. But to lose such profits . . . I can ask you a personal question, Jobina?"

"Of course."

"You and David, it is serious?"

"Oh, I don't know. Sometimes it seems to be. Other times I'm not so sure. I don't know." Jobina stretched her hand to a vase of yellow roses. The roses were from David, one of several bouquets he sent each week. The bouquets arrived with romantic little cards, as did the books of poetry, the antique music boxes, and the Swiss chocolates in ruffled pink packages. There was no end to his presents. On Easter he had given her a huge plush bunny, an exquisite strand of pearls draped about its neck; on the Fourth of July he had given her a dozen sparklers tied with a diamond chain; and on Halloween, a gold Cartier brooch in the shape of a pumpkin. Jobina had been touched by his thoughtfulness, yet a certain ambivalence remained. Some eight months after the date of their first meeting, she still did not know what to make of David Amory. "Do you like David?" she asked now.

"He is a good broker. Very smart," Emile replied, tapping his forehead.

"Do you like him as a person?"

"I am your friend, Jobina. If you like him, I like him.

He puts the stars in your eyes, yes? Since David comes along, your face is laughing more. Such a pretty face you have. It should be laughing all the time. I tell Inge maybe David is the one for you."

"Does she approve?"

"She says David is *charming*. It is her new word. Money in the bank gives her new words. My sons also. They complain about my English. I think they are ashamed."

"Ashamed? Of you?"

Emile shrugged. His hands rested briefly on the table, then began to jump around. "I remember when we were poor," he said. "We were all six of us crowding together in our little flat. And everywhere you looked was laundry lines, because the grandmother was taking in washing. But we were happy. Sometimes we had fights. They started, and then they were over just like that," he added, snapping his fingers. "Now we are having fights every day. The Lanteaus are not so happy anymore. Money, it changes people."

"I'm sorry, Emile. Why don't you and Inge go away for awhile? You both need a vacation, a second honeymoon."

"Inge is too busy. She has her clubs and her lunches. Luncheons, she calls them. She has shopping. *Mon Dieu*, she loves shopping."

Jobina studied Emile's small, dark face. He looked much as he had ten years ago, though in his eyes she glimpsed a shadowy sadness. His smile could not hide it, nor could the exuberance of his gestures. It was part of him now, mute testimony to hopes and plans gone wrong.

"If you will forgive me for speaking in cliches," she said quietly, "all married couples have ups and downs. Try to be patient with Inge. She isn't used to having money. Once the novelty wears off, she will be herself again."

"No, the money is everything. She is making my sons to be snobs. They have their fancy schools. And such fancy ways! Ooh la la, such fancy ways! We give the boys American names, yes? But Johnny isn't Johnny anymore. He is calling himself Jacques. Pete is Pierre. They are, how you say, fancy-pants."

"Children go through phases." Jobina laughed. "What about Billy?"

"He is still Billy. For how long, I do not know."

"You mustn't worry, Emile. Caroline is older than your boys, but she is going through a snooty phase too. Children can be difficult at any age."

"In Provence, my uncles use the strap on my *derriere*. No more difficult. I tell Inge about my uncles. She says the strap is old-fashioned. Instead I talk to my sons. They talk back."

"Poor Emile."

"Rich Emile. Maybe that is the problem, yes? I think you have a different problem, Jobina," he said, lightly touching her arm. "It is David?"

"Oh, I suppose I am confused. There seem to be two Davids. In his own world, our world, he is very sweet and polite and . . . dear."

"Charming?"

"Yes," Jobina agreed with a quick smile. "Then I see the other David. When he's out of his world . . . when he's talking to waiters or taxi drivers or salesclerks, he's not the same."

"I know how you mean. He talks down his nose."

"Looks down his nose, Emile. He is very brusque, almost disdainful. It's worse when he's talking to the servants. It bothers me. I have an idea that's the real David."

"A fancy-pants?"

"Well," Jobina replied, smiling again, "in a way. Not fancy so much as . . . lordly. At times David is quite the lord of the manor. He tries to keep that side of himself from me. I can see him making the effort to be what *I* want him to be."

"If he's trying, that is what counts."

"Oh, we all try, in the beginning. And sooner or later we all stop trying. That's just human nature, Emile. Sooner or later we feel comfortable enough, secure enough, to be ourselves. Our true selves. I'm not sure I would like David's true self."

"You don't like him, but maybe you love him."

"I'm . . . I'm not sure. You see," Jobina explained with a sigh. "I'm confused."

"It is what I said. David puts the stars in your eyes. Romance, yes? Moonlight and roses. A long time ago you tell me about fantasies. Your David, maybe he is your fantasy."

Jobina moved the crystal vase away. She sat back, staring off into the distance. "I hate to think I am that foolish, Emile."

"Foolish? But romance is foolish. The giddy head, the shaking knees, that is the fun of it. Sometimes it is also love. You will know, Jobina. In your mind will be a voice.

And in your heart. If the voices are the same, *voilà!*"

"My voices argue with each other."

"Then you must wait."

"Yes. Yes, I suppose so." The intercome rang and Jobina picked up the telephone. "Five minutes," she said, replacing the receiver. "Speaking of waiting, David is here."

Chapter Twelve

"Are you certain Mrs. Grant knows I'm here?" David asked Jobina's secretary. "It's been more than five minutes."

"Yes, sir. She knows."

"Ring her again."

"But—"

"Do as I say. Ring Mrs. Grant again."

"Yes, sir." Jobina's secretary was a shy and pretty young woman named Amy Reed. She had come to New York to be an actress, though that idea had been abandoned when she found herself too tongue-tied to audition. She had gone to secretarial school and then from office to office, seeking employment. There had been less than a dollar in her pocket on the day Jobina had hired her; she was grateful, utterly loyal, and she disliked David Amory. Now she ended her conversation and looked up into his restive gray eyes. "Mrs. Grant is just finishing with Mr. Lanteau, sir," she explained. "If you would be patient for another—"

"Oh, very well," David snapped. "Business comes

first, doesn't it?" He paced the carpeted floor, his hands clasped behind his back. Once or twice he stopped to glance idly at the large silk butterflies decorating the walls, but in the next moment his pacing would resume. He could not help himself, for the waiting seemed interminable. It always did, when the person he awaited was Jobina. The mere thought of her stirred his blood, his senses. The thought of her body, all yielding soft curves, was more than he could bear. He remembered a starry spring night eight months before. He had set out to seduce Jobina Grant that night. He had succeeded, but somehow he had fallen into his own trap. I will never have enough of her, he silently admitted, and again the hated word "marriage" crossed his mind. He chased it away, as he had chased it from the minds of dozens of women. "Now the shoe is on the other foot," he muttered.

"Did you say something, sir?" Amy asked.

"What? No, nothing. What time do you have?"

"Twenty minutes past five."

David looked at his watch. He sighed. He was about to hurl himself into a chair when the door opened. "Ah, Emile," he said, holding out his hand. "It's nice to see you. I hope I didn't interrupt your meeting."

"We are finished, David. We had much to discuss. The new factory—"

"Yes, of course. Excuse me, Emile, but I think I'd best hurry Jobina out of here while I can. Call me about those stocks, will you?"

"I am still considering."

"Don't wait too long."

"Maybe if I . . ." Emile began, but David had already closed the door.

"Jobina?"

"There you are, David. I seem to be running a little late today. Are you angry?"

"It's impossible to be angry with you. Besides, I know business comes first."

Jobina left her desk and walked toward David. She was radiant in a dress of scarlet wool, gold clips at her ears, gold bracelets encircling her slim wrists. Her hair, short and loose about her face, had a lovely shine; her amber eyes glowed. "I rely on your understanding," she laughed as David pulled her to him.

"Three days," he murmured. "God, I missed you."

Jobina felt his arms tighten around her. She felt his lips on hers, his hands sliding over her body. "Not here, David," she managed to say.

"I missed you so much."

"I missed you. I always miss you," Jobina whispered, returning his passionate kiss. After a moment she drew away, dropping her head to his shoulder. "David, I want to believe there's more to us than . . . this."

"*This* is awfully good," he replied, cupping her breasts through the scarlet wool. "You know it is."

"David, please."

"All right. All right, beautiful lady." He sighed. "I won't insist. We have the whole evening ahead. Perhaps I can interest you in dinner? And then the Follies? I happen to have two tickets. Excellent seats."

"Let me fix my face."

"I like your face the way it is. But if you must . . ."

"I must."

"What kept you so busy today?" David asked as Jobina walked back to her desk. "Emile mentioned the new factory. Is it settled?"

"There are a few details remaining. Gene is worried about budgets. Jack Sisk is worried about unions."

"Unions!" David's smile fled. His eyes narrowed on Jobina. "I hope you made your position quite clear," he said. "The gall of these people! Unions! You might just as well *give* them your company, lock, stock, and barrel."

Jobina closed her compact. She glanced at David and a small frown wrinkled her brow. "It's nothing to get excited about," she said quietly.

"Altogether too many people take that attitude, Jobina. It certainly *is* something to get excited about. Something unsavory is creeping into American business. The guise is the labor movement. The labor movement! I have another name for it. I call it communism."

"David, you can't be serious."

"American business is being turned inside out. It's a very clever campaign, filled with high-flown phrases. We're asked to look kindly on the 'rights of the poor workingman.' That's a high-flown phrase, and a popular one these days. You built this business, Jobina. What of your rights?"

"Really, you are making mountains out of molehills."

"I'm sorry, but I disagree. It's a matter of principle. Beyond that, it's a matter of dollars and cents. I won't allow you to jeopardize—"

"Allow me?"

A quick smile lighted David's face. He took a step

toward Jobina, reaching for her hands. "We're wasting time on an absurd subject," he said lightly. "We have better things to talk about, beautiful lady. Better things to do," he added, once again pulling her to him.

"No, don't. All our little arguments have been settled in the bedroom, in bedroom ways. Not this time, David."

"But we have no argument."

"Now it is my turn to disagree. I know you have a low opinion of working people. Perhaps you can't help it, David. You were raised to believe certain things, and you continue to hold to those beliefs. That's fine. What you believe is up to you. I never intended to . . . change your views. But you are trying to change mine. You are interfering."

"I'm only trying to protect your interests."

Jobina shook off David's hand. "My interests," she replied, "have nothing to do with silly harangues about communism."

"Of course not. I apologize. I was wrong. I admit I was carried away. It isn't hard to understand, Jobina. My family has been suffering labor problems for a hundred years. Literally a hundred years. Generations of miners owe everything to my family. The food in their mouths, the clothes on their miserable backs . . . And what is my family's reward? Turmoil and violence and—"

"Don't say any more, David. I'm well aware of the history of Amory Coal. Not the history you learned at your grandfather's knee, but the true history. It parallels the history of Winslow Timber. They are both blood-stained."

"Jobina!"

"It's a sore subject between us, David. Perhaps just one of many."

"You don't mean that. You're upset."

"I think I've been upset, in one way or another, ever since I met you. You make me *pretend* to myself."

"Pretend?"

"That there is more to us than . . . than bedrooms." Jobina walked to the far side of the office, sinking down on a long chintz couch. "I was attracted to you," she sighed, "drawn to you. I still am. It's a kind of love, I suppose. An empty kind, because I don't really like you."

"Jobina—"

"It's all right, David. You don't really like me either, do you? No. We are too different. The only thing we share is desire. Oh, we have that. But it isn't enough. Not for me."

David went swiftly to Jobina and sat beside her. "You don't mean any of this," he insisted, his eyes darkening. "You know what we have together. You know how I make you feel. Or do you need a reminder?" He caught her in his arms, crushing his mouth on hers. He fell on top of her, his hands pressing her body, tearing at her dress. He was murmuring, moaning, his breath coming in short, hot bursts.

"David, stop," she gasped. She tried to push him away. She struggled. With her last strength she pushed him again, thrusting him from her to the couch. She staggered to her feet and slowly made her way back to the desk. "David," she said, her voice ragged, "is this what we've become?"

"I . . . I don't know what to say. I'm sorry, Jobina. I'm

terribly sorry. I just don't want to lose you." David searched his pockets for his handkerchief. He touched the snowy linen to his damp brow, his pale and shaking mouth. "I realize it's the wrong time to ask," he said with a sigh, "but I am asking anyway. Please reconsider. We have so much together."

"I tried to believe that, David. I'm tired of pretending. We have what we have. After a while, it's not enough. It's cheap. I've felt cheap these past few months. Sneaking around . . . Leaving your apartment in the dead of night and sneaking back to mine. Hoping the doorman wouldn't give me a funny look. Hoping the girls wouldn't hear me come in. I don't like living that way."

"I was thoughtless, Jobina. I'm sorry."

"It wasn't your fault. I chose to be with you. I don't deny we have a strong . . . feeling . . . for each other. I want more, David. I want *all* the feelings. That's not possible with us. If I could, I would change almost everything about you. You would change almost everything about me. That doesn't leave us much, does it?"

"You are always on my mind. Not twenty minutes ago, my mind was on marriage. What would you say if I asked you to marry me?"

"I would say no. I would be very flattered, but I would say no. And you would be relieved. You aren't the marrying kind, David. I've known that all along. You prefer your pleasures without strings attached. Perhaps you will marry someday. Oh, years from now. Years from now when you are old and the chase has lost its allure."

"Do you think so little of me?"

"I think we see things differently. You're a charming man. You're a wonderful lover. You were my fantasy, David, at a time when I badly needed a fantasy."

"You were lonely."

"Yes."

"You will be lonely again."

"Loneliness is the human condition," Jobina replied, a faint smile edging her mouth. "Somehow we survive."

"Why do you have to take so many suitcases?" Daisy asked her sister, Caroline. "We're only going for the weekend."

"There may be parties."

"Parties!" Daisy hooted. "Way out in the country? Aunt Irene and Uncle George never have parties in the country. It's not Gramercy Park, you know. They have all their parties at Gramercy Park." She flopped down on Caroline's pristine white bed, kicking off her shoes. "Ian won't even be there," she added, lacing her fingers behind her head. "He won't be home from school till Thanksgiving."

"Oh, who cares about Ian?"

"You cared a lot, till you met Teddy Hamilton. It's all over school that you're sweet on Teddy Hamilton, who's *practically* old enough to be your *father*."

"He is not."

"Is too." Daisy sat up. She was, at fourteen, a hearty girl, spirited and sunny by nature. Her hair was long and straight and very blond; her eyes a gentle blue. She knew that Caroline was considered the beautiful one; she did not mind, for the jealousies of childhood had long since passed. "You better hope Ma doesn't hear," she said now. "Ma will have your head."

"There's nothing to hear, Daisy."

"Hah! What about the Halloween Cotillion? You danced with Teddy Hamilton the *whole* night. He wasn't even supposed to be there. He came with Suzanne's brother. Her *older* brother."

"A few dances, that's all."

"You and Teddy Hamilton disappeared for ten minutes. The chaperones were so mad. They were running around like chickens. They were looking everywhere."

"I told you I broke the heel on my shoe," Caroline replied, color rising in her ivory cheeks. "Teddy was helping me."

"I bet you were *kissing*."

"We were not! I broke the heel on my shoe."

"It's a good story, but Ma won't believe it."

"Never mind her. I'm almost sixteen, Daisy. I can choose my own dancing partners. All the boys at the Cotillion were . . . boys. Silly boys. Teddy is a man."

"He's old. Rosemary St. John says he's nearly *thirty*."

"He's twenty-eight."

"See? Rosemary was right."

"Right about what?" Jobina asked, entering Caroline's room. "Am I interrupting a private meeting?" She laughed, amused by her daughters' startled expressions. "I knocked. Really I did."

"We were just talking, Mama," Caroline said. "Why aren't you out with Mr. Amory? It's Friday."

"Mr. Amory and I have decided to . . . go our separate ways. We had a nice talk and we decided."

Daisy frowned. She was an avid, if secret, reader of romance magazines, and the idea of a broken romance touched her sympathetic young heart. Quite suddenly she saw her mother as the forlorn heroine, the shattered heroine alone in a cruel world. She left the bed, going to Jobina's side. "Poor Ma." She sighed dramatically. "Are you very sad?"

"No, darling, not very. We had some lovely times together. And we are still friends, after all."

"But now you'll *never* get married."

Jobina laughed again. She hugged Daisy, then held her away. "Listen here, miss," she said lightly, "you must stop trying to marry me off. I had a wonderful marriage, to your father. I have a wonderful life now. I am content."

"But you'll be *alone*."

"Alone?"

"Caroline and I are growing up, Ma. What will happen to you when we get married and go away? You'll be all alone."

"We have a few years to worry about that, darling. It will be a few years at least before you walk down the aisle. Don't rush things. Heavens, Daisy, where do you get your ideas?"

"She reads *True Romance Tales*," Caroline said, lifting her pretty little nose in the air. "She's such a child."

Daisy spun around, angered and hurt by her sister's words. "It's better than mooning over Teddy Hamilton,"

276

she cried. "It's better than being the talk of the *whole* school."

"What's this?" Jobina asked. "The talk of the whole school?"

Caroline slammed her suitcase shut. "It's nothing, Mama," she replied. "Uncle George's car will be here soon. We should go downstairs."

"Daisy, run along to your room and collect your things. I want a moment with Caroline."

"Don't blame Caroline, Ma. I was making it up. What I just said, about Teddy Hamilton and school. I was making it up."

Jobina studied Daisy's contrite face. "I don't think so. I don't like tattling, young lady, but I don't like lying either. When you return from your weekend, we will discuss it. Now run along."

"Ma—"

"Scoot." Jobina waited until the door closed. She sat down, looking at Caroline. "All right, darling." She sighed. "Who is Teddy Hamilton?"

"Just someone I danced with. You remember the Halloween Cotillion, Mama. He was one of my dancing partners. I broke the heel on my shoe and he helped me. He's very handsome. The other girls were jealous. That's why they're talking about me behind my back. It's not the whole school; only the girls from the Cotillion."

"And what are they saying?"

"Oh, silly things. They're silly girls, Mama. They were *green* with jealousy. You can ask Suzanne, if you don't believe me."

"I'm not at all certain I would believe Suzanne. She has been known to stretch the truth."

"She's my best friend."

"I'm keeping that in mind, Caroline. Tell me about Teddy Hamilton. Is he a nice boy? He didn't try to take . . . liberties?"

"No, Mama. He's very nice. He's one of the *Philadelphia* Hamiltons. They are in society. And they have scads of money. Just scads. Teddy is the most perfect dancer. He could go on the stage."

"Really? Boys of his age tend to be awkward."

"Teddy isn't awkward, Mama. He was the hit of the Cotillion."

"I see."

"May I leave now, Mama? It's getting late and we should be downstairs. Claus expects us to be downstairs."

Jobina hesitated, for she sensed there was more to the Teddy Hamilton story than Caroline had revealed. But that was like Caroline; it was typical. Daisy's small lies, her elaborations and omissions, had always been easy to detect. The same could not be said about her older sister. My sphinx, thought Jobina, unsure how to proceed. "Do you remember what I told you about pretty young girls and their reputations?" she asked. "Pretty girls must take extra care."

"Yes, Mama, I remember."

"People are quicker to make assumptions about pretty girls. It is unfortunate but true. I don't want your reputation hurt. Talk is hard to stop, once it starts."

"Nothing is starting, Mama."

"Good." Jobina rose. She walked to where Caroline stood and gently stroked her thick golden hair. "Perhaps it would be best to avoid Teddy Hamilton for now. There are always other dancing partners. In your case, there must be hundreds of them. You can have your pick. Not all girls are so lucky."

"Mama, I wish you wouldn't talk to me like a child. I'll be sixteen soon. You were married when you were sixteen. You should understand. I want to choose my own friends. I can't help it if there's silly talk. It doesn't matter. It's gossip. You told us never to listen to gossip. Have you changed your mind?"

"I would prefer you weren't the *subject* of gossip, Caroline. You are too young to have a cloud over your head. As for your friends, of course the choice is yours. Suzanne is an example of your choice. I happen to think she is involving you with a fast crowd. And that is where I draw the line."

"I don't know what you mean."

"You know exactly what I mean. I am asking you to avoid this Teddy Hamilton for now. Since he is only a casual acquaintance, it shouldn't be difficult . . . I'm serious, Caroline. Call it gossip or silly talk . . . Call it anything you wish, but it ends here."

"All right, Mama. May I leave now?"

Jobina realized she would get no further response from Caroline. A veil had dropped over her deep blue eyes; her face was closed and impassive. "It would be nice if you confided in me more, darling. Adolescence is a confusing time. It helps to talk things out."

"I talk to Suzanne."

"Well, I have no answer to that . . . Perhaps you will let me help you with your suitcases?"

"Thank you, Mama."

"I do like to feel useful." Jobina lifted the largest of Caroline's bags and carried it into the hall. "Daisy?" she called. "Time to go."

"I'm ready, Ma."

"Are you sure you have everything? Your satchel is awfully small. Did you pack your heavy sweater? And your boots?"

"I left my boots at Aunt Irene's. It's easier to keep them there. I don't like to pack."

"What about your sweater?"

"I'm wearing it, Ma," Daisy replied, opening her coat. "Besides, Aunt Irene has a million sweaters. She has enough sweaters for the North Pole."

"Be a good girl and listen to Aunt Irene," Jobina laughed as they walked to the door. "You too, Caroline."

"Yes, Mama."

"Don't go off by yourselves in the woods."

"No, Mama."

Jobina pressed the elevator button. "Have a wonderful time," she said, kissing her daughters. "If you find any pinecones—"

"We'll bring them back, Ma," Daisy promised. "You won't be sad here, will you?"

"I'll be fine, darling . . . Enjoy yourselves."

Jobina spent the weekend alone, her first solitary weekend in eight months. She was restless, unable to concentrate. Several times she picked up her needle-point, only to toss it aside moments later. She tried to read, but she could read no more than a page or two before losing interest. She declined the large meals Rose prepared, settling for little snacks of biscuits and tea. She thought often about David, and at such times her eyes filled with regret. I did the right thing, she told herself, though as the long weekend dragged on, she was not comforted.

It was Sunday when David telephoned. Jobina refused the call, and the two others that followed. Flowers arrived—huge autumn bouquets of chrysanthemums and yellow roses—but she sent them back, the card unopened. By noon on Sunday she had forced herself to her desk and the stack of papers awaiting her signature. As always, work proved a great tonic. She felt refreshed, somehow lighter in spirit. That evening, when Caroline and Daisy returned, she was smiling.

"Good morning, Amy," Jobina said bright and early on Monday. "You are always the first one in the office. I am beginning to think you sleep here. You don't, do you?"

Amy smiled, blushing. "I like to get a head start on the day, Mrs. Grant," she replied. "I'm used to it. At home I was up with the birds."

"There aren't many birds in Manhattan."

"I have a canary. A friend gave him to me. He sings . . . The canary, not my friend," Amy added, her blush deepening.

"He seems to have an excellent effect on you," Jobina

said, for she had never before heard shy Amy Reed speak more than a few words at a time. "Your canary or your friend, or both."

"Thank you, Mrs. Grant."

"Well, I think I'll try to get a head start myself. Bring the mail right in when it comes. I'm expecting some papers from Chicago."

"I will. Mrs. Grant? Mr. Lanteau is in your office. He was the first one here this morning."

"Really. How strange. He usually goes straight to the lab." Jobina entered her office. She saw Emile seated behind the desk. Even at a distance she saw that his eyes were puffy, red-rimmed. "Emile? What is it? What's wrong?"

Emile looked up. He shrugged. "I have bad news, Jobina. Mr. Greevy, he is dead."

"No!"

"Sunday it happened. They say it was his heart. One minute he is reading the newspaper; the next minute he is dead. Like that." Emile sighed, snapping his fingers. "He was old, over seventy, but it is a shame."

Jobina dropped her coat and purse and briefcase on a chair. She crossed the room, perching at the edge of her desk. "It is a shame," she agreed softly. "He was a sweet man, for all his bluster. I don't know what I would have done without him."

"And I. I had no family when I came to America. I had nobody. Mr. Greevy, he was my family. The stern uncle, yes? Stern, but also fair. When they call to tell me, the tears start. Look, my face is still crying."

"I'm so sorry, Emile. When did they call?"

"Last night. It was after dinner. Inge says to call you, but I decide it can wait. It was your time with David."

"David and I have . . . parted ways."

"Parted ways?" Emile frowned. "You and David are *finis?*"

"Are you surprised?"

"Only a little bit. I say to myself it is coming. The stars are in your eyes, but the doubts too. Doubts, they are like seeds. Tiny in the beginning, then getting bigger and bigger. You are unhappy, Jobina? About these parted ways?"

"It was the right thing to do."

"Maybe you change your mind, yes?"

A wry smiled played at the corners of Jobina's mouth. "How often do I change my mind, Emile?" she asked. "Rose says I'm as stubborn as Paddy's pig. It's an expression. In this case it means I won't be seeing David again . . . You didn't like him, did you?"

"He is a good broker. Very smart."

"*You* are a diplomat."

"Sometimes." Emile sat back, removing a sheet of paper from the pocket of his white lab coat. "David I will not miss," he admitted. "It is not diplomat to say, but it is true. Mr. Greevy I will miss very much. The funeral is tomorrow, Jobina. I wrote down the information they tell me. The directions. We can go?"

"Certainly, Emile." Jobina took the paper. She glanced at it, nodding. "We will have to hire a car. I'll just give this to Amy. She can hire a car for us, and send a wreath. I hope Mrs. Greevy is all right. They were so close."

"The Greevys, they are a big family. She will have her family."

"Yes, that helps." Jobina glanced once more at the paper, reading the carefully written directions. Tears sprang to her eyes and she brushed them away. "I'll give this to Amy now," she sniffled, going to the door. She stopped in the doorway, seeing Amy's blond head bent over an enormous basket of roses and carnations. "Please have those flowers returned," she said. "As soon as possible."

"Returned, Mrs. Grant?"

"And any other flowers that Mr. Amory may send."

"I'm sorry, Mrs. Grant, but the flowers . . . Well, they aren't from Mr. Amory. They . . . they were sent to me."

"Oh, Amy," Jobina laughed, "then of course you must keep them. Forgive me. I am getting conceited. I see flowers and assume they're mine. Isn't that terrible? I'm ashamed of myself . . . They're lovely flowers too," she said, sniffing the mingled scents. Her eye fell upon the card. She frowned, for while she was not close enough to read it, she was close enough to recognize the handwriting; the handwriting, unmistakably, was George Thayer's. It isn't possible, she thought, but when she saw Amy trying to hide the card she knew it was indeed possible, indeed true. "Your . . . friend is very generous, Amy," she said. "Such a large basket. It's charming."

"Thank you, Mrs. Grant." Amy's discomfort was obvious. She was flushed, fidgeting in her chair. Her gaze, usually so clear and blue, was troubled. "I'll move the basket out of your way," she offered, almost toppling it in her haste. "There, that's better."

"Amy, I have a few notes," Jobina said, quickly dictating a list of instructions. She did not linger long at the desk, for she feared her young secretary was on the verge of tears. And with good reason, she mused, returning to her office.

"Something is wrong, Jobina?" Emile asked.

"Nothing. Amy will make all the arrangements for tomorrow."

"A sad day, yes? Another chapter closed in the book. I am feeling old."

"I know what you mean."

"But it will pass."

"I hope so," Jobina replied, glancing toward the door. "I do hope so."

Emile stood. "Now I give you back your chair," he said, smiling. "Your office too. It is already nine o'clock. They will be waiting for me in the lab. If we are lucky, we will finish the new Corals line today. Five different shades of coral, all pretty shades. Later I will bring the samples."

"I was telling Mr. Greevy about our new line just the other day. He was in a perky mood. He even made a little joke. I remember he said to be careful or we would soon run out of colors. Then he said it was all right, because you would invent colors of your own. He was proud of you. So am I."

Emile lifted Jobina's hand to his lips. "Very French, yes?" He laughed. "I learn from the movies."

"Mr. Greevy always said you were a fast learner."

"For a foreigner." Emile laughed again. "Mr. Greevy, he was, how you say, a pep?"

"Pip."

"He was a pip."

Theodore Greevy was laid to rest in a pleasant old cemetery near Yonkers. Some forty members of his family were present, as were many neighbors and several generations of customers who had traded at his pharmacy. The brief service was followed by an informal buffet lunch—an occasion for reminiscing, for affectionate laughter and misty-eyed toasts. Emile was the last to speak. He concluded his toast with the announcement of a Theodore Greevy scholarship. "It is our thank you," he said, "to our friend."

The sky was dark when Emile and Jobina left the Greevy apartment. They had been away from the factory since eleven, but now neither of them felt like returning. "We can catch up on work tomorrow," Jobina suggested.

"Tomorrow," Emile readily agreed. "Tonight we will treat ourselves. There is a new café, Armand's. Every morning on my way to work, I pass by. Tonight we go in, yes?"

"Wouldn't you rather go home?"

"It's Tuesday," Emile replied, shrugging. "My sons, they have their German Club on Tuesday. Inge, she has her bridge game. Only the servants are home. Fancy-pants servants. If I make a mistake and use the wrong spoon, they are offended. They look at me with daggers."

"Why don't you hire different servants?"

Emile turned to Jobina, his eyes twinkling. "And start a war?" he asked. "They are Inge's servants. I pay the bills, but she says who is hired. She likes fancy-pants ways. She can show off to her friends. They show off to each other. It is a game."

Jobina did not respond, though she was concerned. She wondered at Inge's childish behavior, at the effect on Emile. Poor Emile, she thought. Inge is taking advantage of his good nature, but even he has his limits. "Oh, here we are," she said, stopping in front of a small café. "Armand's."

"We will go in?"

"Why not?"

Armand's, two blocks north of the factory, was new to the area. It had perhaps twenty tables, each with striped cloths and candles in fluted glass bowls. There was a stone fireplace with scented logs crackling on the grate. The lighting was dim, very soft; music murmured in the background. "It's a real café," Emile declared happily, looking around. "It has, how you say, atmosphere."

"What little I can see of it. I'm afraid I will need a candle to light my way."

"But it's cozy. A real café!" Emile beamed. "Already I can taste the pastries and *demitasse*. I hope they have chocolate tarts. I will eat all the chocolate tarts and get fat like a pig."

"So you have a secret vice." Jobina laughed. "A sweet tooth."

"For chocolate tarts, my whole mouth is sweet. You stay here, yes? I will get a table."

Jobina unbuttoned her coat. Slowly, her eyes became accustomed to the darkness. She saw an enormous tray of pastries and smaller trays of sandwiches; nearby she saw a beautiful silver coffee urn. Her glance strayed across the room to the tables. She saw couples, most of them young, and all of them holding hands. Atmosphere, she said to herself, smiling. She had begun to turn away when she realized that one of the couples was familiar. She peered through the smoky darkness. Her smile vanished, for the couple was George Thayer and Amy Reed. To her horror, she saw George look up. There was nothing to do, no place to hide. His eyes met hers and, as they did so, his face seemed to freeze. The two old friends stared at each other. It was a terrible moment. When finally Jobina was able to turn away, she found that her hands were shaking—whether in anger or embarrassment, she did not know.

"Something is wrong, Jobina?" Emile asked.

"We . . . I'm sorry, but we must leave. Right now. We must leave right now, Emile. Please. I can't explain."

"Don't be upset, Jobina. We will leave." He took her arm and walked her to the door. "You are feeling sick?" he asked when they were outside.

"I'm not sure what I'm feeling. I'm sorry, Emile. I didn't mean to ruin your evening. I just saw a friend of mine holding hands with a woman who isn't his wife. I suppose I was . . . surprised. His wife is a friend of mine too, you see. It is a difficult situation."

"Sometimes these things, they are whims. They begin and then *poof*, they are over."

"I wish it were that simple," Jobina replied quietly. She pulled up her collar and dropped her gaze to the pavement. "Someone is bound to be hurt." She sighed. "Someone always is . . . Perhaps you could find me a taxi, Emile? I want to go home."

"You will be all right?"

"Yes, fine. Emile? I know your mouth was set for chocolate tarts, but I'd rather you didn't go back inside. Tomorrow I will bring you boxes and boxes of tarts. I promise."

Emile glanced toward Armand's. His eyes widened, as if in recognition. *"Mon Dieu,"* he exclaimed. "The woman you saw, she is our Amy? No, you don't have to say. Two times *I* saw Amy when George was around. Her face, it was so happy. It was shining like a Christmas tree. And George's face also. I say to myself it is only flirting. George comes often to your office and Amy is always there. Men and women, they flirt, yes? I say to myself it is harmless. I forget about it. Now I remember."

"We must keep this between us, Emile."

"It is nobody's business. You know the three monkeys? See no evil, hear no evil, speak no evil? I am the three monkeys."

Chapter Thirteen

"Mrs. Grant?" Rose called softly. "Mrs. Grant, are you awake, mum? There's a caller. Mr. Thayer is here."

Jobina put her book aside. She threw the quilts back and hurried out of bed, reaching for her robe as she went to the door. "Come in, Rose," she said. "We mustn't wake the girls."

"No, mum. I had a look and they're sleeping sound. You're the one I'm worried about. Mr. Thayer is here. He's awful jumpy, he is. Nothing will do but that he has a word with you. A few thousand words, more likely. If you ask me, he's in a mood to go on and on."

"I don't doubt it."

"Excuse me, mum?"

"Never mind, Rose. I will see to Mr. Thayer. I wasn't sleeping anyway. But you were, so it's off to bed."

"I thought I'd fix tea."

"Tea!" Jobina smiled. "This isn't a tea sort of night," she said. "Go to bed, Rose. You know you get grumpy when you don't have enough sleep."

"It's my worst fault, mum."

"Good night then."

"Good night, mum. If you need me—"

"I won't, Rose. Mr. Thayer and I have some business to discuss. Go on to bed and don't worry." Jobina buttoned her robe and tied the belt. She thrust her hands in her pockets and strode down the long hall to the living room. George was at the bar, an open whiskey bottle before him. A cigarette dangled from his pale lips; another cigarette burned in the ahstray. He looked sad, uncharacteristically vulnerable, and her expression softened. "George?" she said, closing the door.

"I apologize for the late hour."

"It isn't that late. I was reading the new Agatha Christie novel. Miss Christie has a tricky mind, very interesting . . . Well?" Jobina sighed. "Shall I continue to make polite conversation, or shall we get to the point of this visit?"

"Did you telephone Irene? Did you see her?"

"Of course not, George. Irene is my best friend. Do you really suppose I would hurt her? I won't be the one to break her heart."

"Meaning that *I* will?"

"I saw what I saw." Jobina walked to the couch and sat down. She plumped the flowered silk cushions and leaned back against them. "All night I have tried to find an explanation," she said. "An explanation beyond the obvious. There isn't any."

"No."

"Then there's nothing to say, is there?"

"It is complicated."

"Complicated? You are a fool, George Thayer. It's no

more complicated than that."

"All right. I admit it. I have been a fool. Are you satisfied?" George poured a drink. He brought the glass to his lips and drank. When he finished, he poured another. He left the bar, taking a chair opposite Jobina. "I don't know how it started," he said. "It was all quite innocent, in the beginning."

"You don't owe me the details," Jobina replied. "I happened to be in the wrong place at the wrong time. I'm sorry about that, sorrier than you know. The rest of it is none of my business."

"I want you to understand. It's important, for Irene's sake, if not for mine. I never intended Irene to be hurt. I love her. I always have and I always will . . . strange as that may sound now." George sipped his drink. After a while he put the glass down and passed his hand across his haggard face. "Strange as it may sound, this . . . situation . . . has very little to do with Irene. Unless you consider the matter of contrasts." He raised his eyes and looked imploringly at Jobina. "Perhaps . . . Perhaps you have noticed how different Irene and Amy are."

"They are night and day. What of it?"

"Irene is a spirited woman," George replied quietly. "It is her way to joke and tease and poke fun. We have been married almost twenty years, Jobina, and she has always been a . . . challenge. I often wondered what life would be like with a woman who was more yielding. A woman who was . . . softer in nature. Many men must wonder about such things. Usually it begins and ends there. But I met Amy. It really was quite innocent. She delivered your advertising layouts to my office and we sometimes exchanged a few words. Once or twice we had coffee. Then, one night, we were leaving the office at the same time and . . . well, Irene was in the country and I suggested we have dinner together."

"You were intrigued."

"Yes." George sighed. "It is difficult for me to admit, but I was flattered also. This sweet, pretty young woman was deferring to me, hanging on my every word. She agreed with my opinions. She laughed at my jokes. Good Lord, Jobina, I knew that in *her* eyes, I could do no wrong. I was immensely flattered."

"I see."

"That was the beginning. I found myself thinking a great deal about Amy. I wanted to be with her. It was a . . . need. We were happy together. We had a different kind of happiness, different from any I had known before. Until tonight at Armand's, I thought we were the two happiest people in the world."

"I can't believe I'm hearing this. I can't believe I'm hearing this from *you*, of all people. Your whole life has been sensible and orderly and . . . perfect. Never a false step, that's George Thayer."

"It was. Everything has always come easily to me, Jobina. Money, success. I was warned time and time again that I would lose my shirt in the magazine business. I went ahead anyway. Needless to say, *Gotham* is coining money. It is the publishing success of the decade. Marriage came easily to me, and fatherhood. The fact is, I had everything I could possibly want. Then I met Amy and she was what I wanted. I'm not proud of myself, but there it is."

"Do you love her?"

George did not answer immediately. He sipped his drink. He lighted a cigarette. He stared at the floor, kicking at the edge of the antique carpet. "Would you believe me if I said I love both Irene and Amy?"

Jobina threw up her hands. "Oh, I'd believe it," she snapped. "The more I see of men, the more willing I am to believe *anything*." She rose and walked to the bar, fixing a brandy and soda. "I don't know whether to laugh or cry," she said, returning to the couch. "Has it occurred to you that one of your loves is going to be hurt? And perhaps both?"

"Amy has already been hurt. When she saw you tonight she was extremely upset. As was I. You were the cold dash of reality we have been denying for months. The reality is cold indeed. Neither of us is cut out to lead a double life. Amy is a sweet, decent woman. An innocent. I can't bear to hurt her. I can't bear to hurt Irene . . . yet decisions must be made."

A curt reply sprang to Jobina's lips. It died there, for George's face was suddenly gray and crumpled. She went to him, resting her hand on his shoulder. "I'm sorry," she said. "I've been hard on you, George. It's just so unexpected. You are the last person I ever expected to find in such a situation. I mean that as a compliment. You're the steadiest person I know."

"And the dullest. No, don't bother to disagree. Perhaps that was part of it. Perhaps I got tired of being good old reliable George. When a man turns forty, he starts to wonder about the things he has missed. I certainly did. And then I met Amy."

"I'm very fond of Amy," Jobina said. "But Irene is my dear friend. My loyalties, and my sympathies, are with her."

"I know. Your loyalties are deep. It is an admirable trait. Still, I ask you to understand that Amy is not to blame for any of this. I am responsible. I alone . . . What a bloody mess! Either way I turn is the wrong way."

"That's not true, George. Even if it were, you *do* have to turn one way or the other. You can't allow matters to continue unresolved. It would be terribly unfair to Irene, and a strain on Amy. I'm sure she has enough to handle as it is."

"Yes. She was in a state when we left Armand's. I've never seen her so upset. I managed to calm her . . . But you are right, Jobina. The situation cannot continue." George stood. He wandered to the terrace doors and lifted one of the long, pale silk shades. He clasped his hands behind his back, sighing. "I realize we've put you in an awkward position," he said. "I'm sorry."

"It's awkward all the way around. Irene comes to my office from time to time. She's coming by this Friday. We have a lunch date. Under the circumstances, it's a bad idea for Irene and Amy to cross paths."

"Amy would be the first to agree. She plans to resign. After tonight, there is no choice . . . She feels very bad, Jobina. You have been kind to her and she feels she's disappointed you."

"Well, that's beside the point, isn't it?"

"She's a sensitive creature."

"And Irene? What is she?"

"Strong." George wandered back to his chair. He

started to sit down, then changed his mind. "I've taken enough of your time, Jobina," he said. "Thank you for listening."

"I wasn't much help."

"Talking about things puts them into perspective. It was good of you to listen. There is nobody else I would trust with my sad tale. We've been through a lot together after all . . . and now our roles have reversed. I am the one in need of guidance."

"No, George. You're in need of a little clear thought. Amy won't always look at you with big cow eyes. She won't always laugh at your jokes or run to fetch your pipe and slippers. She's young. As you say, an innocent. In time, her awe will fade. But Irene will always love you."

"There is more to Amy and me than what you describe."

"Of course there is. But is there so much more that you would throw over your marriage, your family? Look ahead ten years, George. How do you see yourself ten years from now? It's not an idle question."

"You push to the heart of the matter," George replied with a slight smile. "You have come a long way, Jobina."

"Step by painful step." She laughed. "Life plays tricks."

"Caroline has been talking to me about her graduation party," Irene said to Jobina early in 1929. "She wants it to be a coming-out party. A formal debut. How do you feel about that?"

"Oh, I'm willing to give her a small dinner dance. I'm not willing to make it an extravaganza. Which is why she talked to you first. My Caroline is a clever girl. She's lining up supporters to plead her case." Jobina paused, smiling at Irene. It was teatime and they were seated in the Palm Court of the Plaza. Gloved waiters passed amongst the tables, serving tiny sandwiches and tiny whipped cream pastries. Conversation was low, sprinkled now and then with laughter; from behind the tall palms came the sound of violins. "Isn't that why you invited me here?" she asked. "Tell the truth, Irene."

"Caroline does have a point. I know these society rituals are foolish, not to mention costly. But they are *expected*, Jobina. You want her to snare a rich husband, don't you?"

"I want her to be happy."

"It's the same thing. Well, it is. Can you imagine Caroline being happy with a man who has to work for a living? She is hardly the type to scrimp and save."

"Caroline has some very grand ideas," Jobina replied, "all of them revolving around money. Last fall she seemed smitten with a boy she met at the Cotillion. Her main reason seemed to be that he was one of *the* Philadelphia Hamiltons."

"Greg Hamilton? He's a lovely boy."

"No, that wasn't the name. Let me see . . . It was Teddy, Teddy Hamilton."

Irene's dark brows drew together. She shook her head. "Teddy Hamilton is thirty if he's a day," she said. "You must be mistaken."

"Not about Teddy. He's sort of the black sheep of that family. The Hamiltons are serious, upright people. All the men devote themselves to the family business,

Hamilton Steel. All the women devote themselves to charitable causes. It's their tradition. Why, there has never been a frivolous Hamilton . . . until Teddy came along. He simply refused to toe the line. He refused to take his place in the company, in any company. He simply refused to work."

"What does he do?"

"He plays tennis and squash. I hear he's quite good."

"Is that all?"

"He traveled around Europe for awhile," Irene continued. "Then he was ordered home. Where he proceeded to fill his days with tennis and squash, and his nights with parties. I suppose the Hamiltons just gave up. They cut him off. Oh, they didn't exactly cut him off without a cent. He has a small allowance. If the rumors are correct, he has other sources of income as well."

"Rumors?"

"Teddy is a handsome devil. His lady friends tend to be older, married, and rich. They give him . . . presents. Or so rumor has it. I don't understand why he would have been at the Cotillion, Jobina. Those girls couldn't possibly interest him. But I would have a talk with Caroline anyway, if I were you."

"We had our talk last fall. I sensed there was something odd about the situation. I don't know why. Caroline was the same. She is always secretive and indirect. Yet I had a feeling." Jobina sighed, raising her cup to her lips. "Thank heavens that's all behind us now," she said.

"You don't sound convinced."

"I keep a close eye on Caroline's schedule, Irene.

There has been nothing unusual. Though I can only guess at what goes on in her mind. I don't like to press her. When I do, she becomes even more distant. Daisy is an open book. Caroline has her secrets. It bothers me that she would have been drawn to a Teddy Hamilton in the first place. Boys flock to her, nice boys. She can have her pick."

"Caroline is at an age," Irene replied. "Teddy must seem awfully glamorous. I'm sure she hasn't heard the rumors. They are being kept quiet, out of respect for the Hamiltons. I wouldn't worry. She will have a great many crushes in the next year or two."

"Yes, and there are a great many Teddy Hamiltons around. Lounge lizards!"

Irene smiled. She sat back, rearranging her furs on the chair. "Lounge lizards carry high price tags," she said. "Caroline isn't very likely to play that game. If I know our Caroline, she will ask for bank references before she gives her heart. She is stubborn, but no fool."

"I think she's bound for an early marriage. She refuses to consider college. And she is forever reminding me that *I* was already married at her age. She has an answer for everything. It drives me wild. I'm going to name my first gray hairs Caroline."

"Mine are named George," Irene replied quietly.

Jobina looked up. She had not seen George since Christmas, though even then the strain in the Thayer household had been apparent. She had made light of it, as had Irene. Now, studying Irene's dwindling smile, she realized that matters remained unresolved. "Is George being difficult?" she asked. "He didn't seem himself at Christmas."

"He's moved to his club."

"What?"

"Three nights ago. George came home and packed a bag and announced he was moving to his club. No explanation. Not that an explanation was really necessary. Things haven't been right between us for months."

"Irene, I'm sorry. Why didn't you call me?"

"I didn't know what to say. George and I have been at odds, but I . . . I never expected it would come to this. I still don't know what to say, Jobina. There is a problem, but I don't know what it is. It started last summer. George was somehow different. Restless, edgy. I tried to talk to him. Each time he hurried away. There is something *guilty* in his behavior," Irene declared suddenly, staring at Jobina. "That much is clear. I can think of only one reason . . . another woman."

Jobina had been dreading this moment and, now that it was here, she knew she had to be careful, to say as little as possible. "Another woman?" she asked with a pale smile. "George?"

"Stranger things have happened. Men are susceptible. Their eyes roam. Their imaginations roam. And the grass is always greener on the other side of the fence."

"Not always."

"I cried the night George left. I cried the whole night and all of the next day. Then I sat myself down and tried to make sense of things. I intend to fight for my husband, Jobina, but I must know what I'm fighting. Whatever it is, I *must* know. I'm asking you to help me. Will you?"

"Of course. You and George are my dearest friends in

301

the world. Of course I'll help. If you want me to talk to him—"

"I think you already have," Irene said. "One night several months ago George came home quite late, quite upset. He wouldn't talk about it, but the following morning I found one of your butterfly matchbooks, the matchbooks you keep at home. It was in his coat pocket. I knew he had been to see you, Jobina. I think he confided in you that night. You have been trying to spare my feelings ever since."

"Irene, those matches could have been in George's pocket for weeks."

"No, the coat was new. Brand new. I know he was at your apartment. The fact that neither of you mentioned the visit . . . Well, you see what I mean."

"I'm not sure I do."

Irene's face was watchful. Her eyes were intent, steady, on Jobina. "Don't worry about my feelings," she said. "The truth is what I need now. If I am to save my marriage, you must tell me what I'm up against. Is George seeing another woman?"

Jobina glanced away, her amber gaze surveying the crowded tables. "We can't talk here, Irene," she said after several moments had passed. "It's too public. Come home with me and—"

"No, I want to stay. I trust myself here. I know I won't fall apart in a public place. Besides, there isn't very much to talk about. I don't plan to ask embarrassing questions. Only one question concerns me. Is George seeing another woman?"

"He was." Jobina reached across the table, clasping

Irene's small hand. "But that was back in November," she said. "I learned about it by accident. Then George came to see me and we talked. He told me he loved you, Irene. I had the impression he just needed time to work this . . . other thing out. For a man like George to find himself in such a situation . . . I'm not excusing him. Not at all. I'm saying that the situation was deeply painful to him."

"I understand." Irene withdrew her hand. She dabbed lightly at her eyes, trying to smile. "Men will be men." She sighed. "And men like George are apt to take flirtations seriously. What begins as a harmless diversion ends as something else."

"It may already have ended, Irene. It was three months ago. I honestly don't know what's happened since then."

"George has moved to his club. That's what's happened. Score one point for the . . . competition."

"George loves you. He said he always would. I think the competition, if there is such a thing, is no more than a passing fancy."

"He was unhappy about turning forty. That was the first warning sign. I should have paid closer attention. But we've been married a long time." Irene sighed again. "One grows complacent. Or in my case, smug. I've learned a lesson, haven't I?"

"What are you going to do?"

"Well, I'm *not* going to fall apart. I need my wits about me. I need a plan, a battle plan . . . There is one thing more I must know, Jobina. Is the woman younger than I?"

"Irene—"

"Don't worry about my feelings. A younger woman requires a different plan. Forewarned is forearmed."

"Yes, she's younger."

Irene's dark eyes flashed. She gathered up her purse and gloves, then reached for her furs. "This is one battle I am going to win, Jobina," she said. "Or die trying."

"Mrs. Grant, you're home early," Rose said, opening the door. "Here, I'll take your things. Would you like tea, mum?"

"Perhaps later. Were there any calls, Rose? Did Mr. Thayer call by any chance?"

"No calls, mum. But Miss Caroline's been hanging on the telephone all the afternoon."

"Oh?"

"Jabbering away with Miss Suzanne, I'll wager. I don't know for sure. She·talks low, so I can't hear. Miss Caroline likes her secrets, she does. There's locks on her drawers, locks on her diary. I asked her was she a spy. A little joke, mum."

"Don't waste your time." Jobina laughed. "Caroline has no sense of humor."

"It's the truth. She's a quiet lass."

"Is she home?"

"In her room, mum."

Jobina walked through the silent living room to the hall. She heard the radio blaring in Daisy's room and she smiled. She turned to Caroline's room, knocking on the door. "May I come in, darling?" she called.

"Yes, Mama."

"I got away early today, Caroline. I thought we could talk. I saw Aunt Irene. You will be glad to know she agrees with you about your coming-out party . . . Heavens, is that a smile? Yes, a real smile!"

"I was hoping she would convince you, Mama."

"Let's say I'm willing to compromise," Jobina replied. She crossed the room to sit in a white wicker chair near the immaculate hearth. "Wouldn't you like a fire?" she asked. "A fire is so nice on a cold day. It's cozy."

"The ashes make an awful mess. I prefer the radiator. We're not living in the olden days, Mama."

"No, we're all very modern now . . . Well, about your party, darling. What would you say to a small dinner dance at the St. Regis?"

"How small?"

"Perhaps fifty people."

Caroline looked at Jobina, tossing her mane of golden hair. "Mama, Suzanne is having a *hundred* and fifty. She's having a society orchestra and orchids on all the tables. And her gown is coming from *Paris*. She's going to wear her mother's diamond tiara too."

"My! A diamond tiara!"

"You always do that, Mama. You always tease me."

"I'm sorry, darling. Really I am. It's not you I'm teasing; it's Suzanne's vanity. Orchids and diamond tiaras and such. You must see the humor. Anyway, the sixteen-year-olds in this house don't wear diamond tiaras. *I* don't even wear diamond tiaras, and I'm twice sixteen."

"Why can't I have orchids?"

"Must you copy everything Suzanne does? Show some originality, Caroline. You're a talented artist. Why, you could design charming floral arrangements for your party. They would be special because they would be *your* design. Roses, camellias, peonies. Gardenias are lovely. At least think about it, darling. I will have to make most of the plans in advance, but you have a full three months to plan the flowers."

"Can I have Eddie Worthington's orchestra? He's all the rage."

"If it's that important to you." Jobina sighed.

Caroline brightened. "Thank you, Mama," she said. "Can I wear your pearls? The double strand with the sapphire clasp?"

"They will look beautiful on you."

"Do you think so?" Caroline was smiling, spinning around in a rare and telling gesture of delight. "I want to look *very* beautiful, Mama," she cried. "I want to be the belle of the ball."

Jobina watched, dazzled by her daughter's sudden radiance. She went to Caroline, holding out her arms. "This may be a good time to get a hug," she said. "Yes?"

"Yes, Mama."

Tears came to Jobina's eyes. It was silly, she knew, but she could not help herself. "Perhaps this is a new beginning for us, Caroline," she sniffled. "Let's make it a new beginning, shall we?"

"I'd like that. Oh, but you're crushing the ruffles on my blouse."

"Sorry." Jobina stepped back. She stroked Caroline's hair, staring into the deep blue of her eyes. "You're growing up, darling. I will have to remember you're not my little girl anymore. It's hard. You won't understand how hard until you have children of your own. In the meantime, try to be patient with me."

"You can give me advice. About my children, I mean."

Jobina laughed. "I'd rather not think of myself as a grandmother just yet. Let's talk some more about your party. I suppose it's too soon to choose an escort. Or do you have a boy in mind?"

"Maybe."

"Well, I won't pry. I know he will be wonderful, whoever he is."

"He'll be rich," Caroline replied, spinning away from Jobina. "Rich, rich, rich. I have to think of my future, Mama."

"Money isn't everything. There's love."

"Did you love David?"

"I was fond of him. I loved your father with all my heart. I wouldn't trade that love, Caroline. Not for all the money in the world."

"I want both."

"You were very keen on Ian, once upon a time."

"Ian is nice."

"And then there was . . . What was his name? Teddy Hamilton?" Jobina's tone was casual, for she was wary of spoiling Caroline's good mood. She shrugged; wary or not, she had to be certain that Teddy Hamilton was no longer in Caroline's thoughts. "Do I have the right name?" she asked.

"Yes, Mama."

"What is he up to these days?"

"Oh, Teddy isn't in our group, Mama. He's a friend of Suzanne's brother. They play squash together. Suzanne says golf is a more civilized game. Her father plays golf. Did Papa play golf?"

"No, he wasn't a sportsman. Unless you count billiards."

"Suzanne's father is the club champion. He has lots of trophies, Mama. Suzanne's uncles play too."

Jobina listened as Caroline went on about Suzanne and the various members of Suzanne's family. It was a lengthy recitation, filled with details, with descriptions. Teddy Hamilton was not mentioned again. Jobina noticed the omission, though she said nothing. Later, troubled by a feeling she could not explain, she wondered if the omission had been deliberate. She almost returned to Caroline's room but stopped herself at the door. I'm being too suspicious, she thought. Caroline is secretive but hardly a schemer!

Another winter passed, the gray February giving way to a brisk and sparkling March, a gentle April. In May, Caroline was graduated from Miss Beardsley's School For Young Ladies. Jobina savored every moment of the long ceremony, crying when her daughter ascended the stage to receive a special art award; she was still crying when Caroline hurried off to the first round of parties marking the occasion.

Caroline's own party had been scheduled and then rescheduled several times before she settled finally on the date of October 1—a date chosen to coincide with the beginning of the New York social season. "Everything has to be *perfect*, Mama," she insisted, repeating those words until Jobina wanted to scream. For weeks the Beekman Place apartment was in chaos, littered with fabric samples and menus and guest lists. The dressmaker, trailed by a seamstress and a fitter, took over the living room; the hairdresser came and went at will, bringing sketches and ribbons and plumes. There was a constant stream of deliveries, and an even more constant stream of telephone calls. Jobina's many protests were to no avail. Conceding defeat, she retreated to her study and closed the door.

"How do I look, Mama?" Caroline asked early on the night of her party. Gracefully, she twirled around. She smiled. "Was it worth all the fuss?"

"Why, you're beautiful," Jobina gasped. And indeed Caroline was a vision in a bare-shouldered gown of white silk and organza, a slender blue sash at her waist. Her shimmering golden hair was brushed atop her head, the small, perfect curls threaded with blue ribbons. She wore long white kid gloves and Jobina's pearl necklace and earrings. "You have your wish, darling. You will be the belle of the ball."

"Do you think so, Mama?"

"I guarantee it. But first we must get there. You don't want to be late for your own party, do you? Or do you plan to make a grand entrance?" Jobina glanced at her watch. "Heavens, we really will be late. Where is your beau?"

"We're meeting at the St. Regis."

"At the St. Regis? I thought he was going to call for

you here, Caroline. Your escort is supposed to call for you at home."

"I want to make my grand entrance all alone. It was my idea."

"An odd idea. At least tell me his name. You've been quite mysterious about him. I confess I'm curious."

Caroline kissed Jobina's cheek. "It's my night, Mama," she said lightly. "Let me have my mystery a little longer. Please?"

"All right." Jobina sighed. "We haven't time to argue anyway. Daisy?" she called. "Hurry, Daisy, we're late . . . Daisy? Oh, there you are, darling." She reached out, catching Daisy's gloved hand. "Don't you look pretty! That pink is very becoming. And your hair is lovely. Now I know what it looks like when it's combed."

"Oh, Ma."

"Get your coat, Daisy. Caroline, let me help you with your cape. I hope you will be warm enough."

"I'll be fine, Mama."

Jobina glanced again at her watch. "Come, girls. We mustn't be the last to arrive. Not tonight, of all nights." She watched Caroline sweep majestically into the hall, Daisy following close behind. My girls are growing up, she thought. Soon the birds will be leaving the nest.

"Here's the elevator, Ma."

"Yes, I'm coming."

The St. Regis was an elegant turn-of-the-century hotel, the frequent site of charity balls and debutante parties. Jobina had selected the hotel, but she had allowed Caroline to arrange the menu and decor; the results, everyone agreed, were charming. Circular tables ringed the glittering ballroom, the tables dressed with pale blue cloths, blue china, candles, and scalloped vases of white roses and lily of the valley. Rose petals floated in scalloped finger bowls. The place cards were edged in silver, and near each place was a remembrance of the evening, a small silver trinket box from Tiffanys.

Jobina's table was off to the side and filled with her friends—the Sisks, the Claymores, the Lanteaus. There were chairs for the Thayers, though those chairs were empty, for Irene was away and George was still estranged from his family and friends. "You are hoping they will come, yes?" Emile asked. "George and Irene?"

"I'm afraid it's a faint hope. Irene is probably enjoying a moonlight stroll on the beach right now. She's in Bermuda. No one knows where George is. I've been calling his office for days. I miss them, Emile."

"But look what they are missing." He turned, gazing across the dance floor at the sea of young couples. "Caroline, she is beautiful like a movie star. Like Mary Pickford. Which boy is her date, Jobina? Always she is dancing with different boys."

"I have yet to meet Caroline's date. I think she's afraid I'll embarrass her by saying something *parental*. We parents are such nuisances to our children. Do you have that problem, Inge?"

"Never. My sons are angels."

"On the outside they are angels," Emile said, glancing sharply at his wife. "On the inside, I'm not sure."

Inge was about to reply when Jack Sisk asked her to dance. "Thank you," she said. "It's nice *someone* is a gentleman."

They left the table, followed soon by the Claymores. Emile looked from Ellen to Jobina. He shrugged, a cool twinkle in his dark eyes. "Mrs. Fancy-Pants thinks I have bad manners," he explained with a laugh. "I am the peasant, yes? She tries to teach me which fork to use, which thing to say. I tell her it is enough that I pay the bills." Emile laughed once more, leaning back in his chair. "Big speech I make. It shuts up her mouth, but then she opens it again."

Jobina felt a sudden swift anger. She watched Inge spinning on the dance floor, watched the blaze of her diamond earrings and necklace and bracelets. "You spoil her," she said.

"It is better than hearing complaints. Easier. The money I don't care about. You remember in the beginning, Jobina? Always I am wishing to become rich. I am praying to St. Jude. But there is an old saying: Be careful what you wish for. It is a wise saying, yes?"

"Would you do anything differently?"

"Maybe. Not with our business. That is a happy thing. Other things, they are not so happy. This gentleman stuff . . . I am the same Emile Lanteau, the farm boy from Provence. It's good enough for me."

"It's quite a lot, Emile."

"Sure it is," Ellen agreed. "Some people don't know when they're lucky. Not mentioning any names, but some people need a kick right in the fancy-pants."

Emile smiled, swinging his foot out. "That idea I like," he said. "Jobina, look who is coming. Our little movie star, she is coming to say hello to us . . . and she is bringing her date. Is he her date? They are holding hands."

"Her date?" Ellen asked. "He's pretty old to be her date."

Jobina's head snapped up. She saw Caroline approaching the table, a tall, handsome man at her side. She started to rise but found she could not. "Caroline," she murmured, gripping the edge of the table.

Caroline was radiant. Her smile was vast, her face shining; her eyes were pools of brilliant blue light. "Mama," she said, "Mrs. Sisk, Mr. Lanteau . . . this is Teddy Hamilton."

"How do you do, Mr. Hamilton?" Jobina replied.

"But you mustn't be so formal, Mama." Caroline laughed. She stretched her hand to Jobina, displaying an antique diamond ring encircled with sapphires. "Teddy and I are engaged!"

Chapter Fourteen

It was the next morning and Jobina paced her office, trying to calm her frenzied thoughts. She had not slept, nor had she said very much to Caroline, lest she say the wrong thing. For hours she had listened silently to her daughter's romantic exclamations. She had listened to a history of the Hamilton family, a history of wealth and power from the first generation to the present. When finally she had returned to her room, she had wept. "What am I going to do, Emile?" she asked now. "I feel helpless, utterly helpless."

"Caroline, she is so young. She has the puppy love. Next week, next month, *poof*, it will be over. There will be somebody else."

"No, it's more complicated than that. I told you what the Hamilton fellow is. Adventurer is the kindest word for him. He has something up his sleeve. I'm certain of it. But what? *Why* did he go after Caroline?"

"She is beautiful and young. Those are good reasons, yes?"

"New York is filled with beautiful young women. He's

turned a blind eye to them all. He's gone after the old ones. He's made his *living* that way, for heaven's sake. Caroline has no idea, of course. She thinks he's rich. According to her, he has *scads* of money. But according to Phil Claymore, he hasn't a cent." Jobina sank into a chair, putting her throbbing head in her hands. "I don't know what I'm going to do."

"You must, how you say, lay the law out to Caroline."

"I don't want her running off, Emile. I'm terrified that she will. History repeating itself." Jobina sighed. "When I was sixteen I ran off. William and I eloped. Oh, I don't regret it. I would do it again. But William was kind and decent. We loved each other. Teddy Hamilton is . . . No, I must be very careful."

"Maybe you should talk to him, Jobina. Ask him what is his game. He will not tell the truth. It's all right. Your instincts, they are good. You will know."

"Will I? He's been at his game, whatever it is, for some time. I don't doubt he is expert. I would be at a disadvantage. And I've learned how dangerous it is to be at a disadvantage."

"Let me call around, Jobina. Maybe I can find George. They could talk man to man, yes?"

"Man to *skunk*. Besides, George is nowhere to be found. I telephoned Irene in Bermuda. I couldn't reach her. I left a message. I hope she returns my call soon. Sometime before I go mad . . . I never thought I would feel this helpless again, Emile. Money was my shield. It was—" Jobina looked up as a knock came at the door. "Yes? Come in . . . Yes, Muriel. What is it?"

"There's a gentleman to see you, Mrs. Grant. I told

him you were busy. He insists."

"I'm sorry. I can't see anyone now. What does he want?"

"He wouldn't say, Mrs. Grant. His name is Teddy Hamilton, if that means anything. He gave me his calling card. He insists you'll want to see him."

Jobina glanced at Emile. "What do you suppose he's up to?" she asked. "Trouble?"

"In his business, there is always trouble. See him, Jobina. Make the air clear. This way, no more worrying."

"Perhaps you are right. I don't know."

"See him, Jobina. You will have it in the open, yes?"

"Perhaps . . . Very well, Muriel." She sighed. "Tell Mr. Hamilton . . . Tell him I can spare five minutes."

"Yes, Mrs. Grant."

Jobina turned back to Emile. "I hope I'm not making a terrible mistake," she said.

"Not you. You are smart."

"He may be smarter."

There was another knock and Teddy Hamilton entered the office. He was indeed handsome, with light brown hair and classic, clean-cut features. His tailoring was perfect, as was his grooming. He had an athletic build, though a certain softness had begun to blur the line of his waist. "Thank you for seeing me, Mrs. Grant," he said. "Good morning, Mr. Lanteau."

A lounge lizard, thought Jobina, gesturing to a chair at the other side of her desk. "I wasn't expecting you, Mr. Hamilton. Or shall I call you Teddy?"

"Please."

"Well then, Teddy, what can I do for you?"

317

"It's a delicate matter, Mrs. Grant. Perhaps it would be better if we talked alone."

"Oh, I have no secrets from Emile. He's family, so to speak."

"The matter concerns Caroline."

"I rather imagined it did." Jobina smiled, folding her hands atop the desk. "Emile has watched Caroline grow up. He used to help her with her French compositions. It seems a long time ago, but of course it wasn't. Only last spring she was worrying about exams and grades and such. Now she is planning her trousseau . . . Forgive me, Teddy. I'm running on and on. You were saying?"

"The thing is, there's been a slight misunderstanding."

"Oh?"

"Do you mind if I smoke?"

"Not at all."

Teddy removed a gold case from the inside pocket of his jacket. Politely, he offered cigarettes to Jobina and Emile; when they were refused, he lighted one for himself. "The thing is," he continued, "I didn't actually propose to Caroline. We were talking about the future. Marriage was mentioned, in a way. But I didn't actually propose."

"Oh?"

Teddy met Jobina's level amber gaze and he realized that he had underestimated her. She was not the distraught mother he had expected to encounter today; she was composed, her thoughts well hidden. "I wouldn't like to play poker with you, Mrs. Grant," he said, smiling his boyish smile. "I would lose."

318

"Let's pretend we're playing poker, Teddy. I think you ought to put your cards on the table, face up. You want something. What?"

"You're very direct."

"I'm very busy."

"All right, I will come to the point. Caroline is young. She should have time to enjoy her youth. I'm sure you agree with me that marriage, now, would be a mistake. At the least it would be unfair. There are so many experiences she would miss." Teddy paused, measuring Jobina's reaction. Once again he was disappointed in his expectations, for he saw no relief, no gratitude. "You *do* agree, Mrs. Grant?" he asked.

"Caroline is wearing your engagement ring."

"It's a family heirloom, one of several left to me in my grandmother's will. I wanted Caroline to have it, but not as an engagement ring. We are friends, good friends. Caroline misunderstood."

"This is not making sense," Emile said. "You talk to Caroline about marriage. You give her a ring. To me it is clear. To you it is a misunderstanding. How can that be?"

"We discussed marriage in an . . . abstract sort of way," Teddy replied. "The ring was a gift, no more, no less. I never *proposed* marriage, Mr. Lanteau. It never even occurred to me."

"He is lying, Jobina."

"Yes, but why?" She turned, drumming her fingers on the desk as she regarded Teddy Hamilton. "Obviously you have been seeing Caroline for months," she said. "You've been seeing her behind my back and against my wishes. You must have had some reason. It's true

319

Caroline is beautiful. That seems to me a poor reason."

"She's a charming girl, Mrs. Grant."

Jobina's brows lifted. "Charming?" she asked. "By what definition? I love Caroline. I also know her limitations. She talks only of clothes and parties and herself. And her dear friend Suzanne, of course. She's serious about silly things. In short, she is a sixteen-year-old. She would hold no interest for a man of the world like yourself."

"If I'm not mistaken, you were a sixteen-year-old when you married Mr. Grant."

"Ah, but there was a difference. My husband was almost as innocent as I. We were children together. You, Teddy, are no innocent, no child. Your reputation speaks for itself."

"My reputation! May I remind you I am a Hamilton?"

"An *exiled* Hamilton. Your family allows you to live in one of their apartments here. They send you a small monthly allowance. That is the extent of your income, yet you manage to live very well. Shall we discuss how?"

"*How* is none of your business," Teddy snapped, flinging his cigarette into an ashtray. He stood, striding past the desk, past Emile, to the windows. "We make choices," he said after a while. "I don't choose to spend my life in an office, running steel mills. There is more to life than that. I intend to have it."

"Everybody wants more, Teddy," Jobina said with a sigh.

"I'm *entitled* to more. Entitled by birth. I was born into one of the richest families in America. Do they enjoy their money? They do *not*. They run steel mills and go to church and contribute to worthy causes. That's their life. It's always been their life. They're *good,* good, dried-up old sticks. My brothers were old at twelve . . . but I was different. You're right, Mrs. Grant. When I insisted on enjoying the family fortune, I was exiled. There's nothing I can do about it. My trust fund doesn't come due until I'm forty, ten years from now. In the meantime, I'm stony broke."

"If you're bidding for sympathy, don't."

"I don't want sympathy," Teddy replied, gazing across the office at Jobina. "I want money. I intend to leave New York. The pickings are getting slim anyway," he added with a bitter smile. "Hollywood may be the place for me. I still have my looks. I did a little acting in college. Why not? I'm willing to work, as long as it's fun. But I intend to arrive in style. To make a great splash. And that's where you come in."

"Really?"

"Caroline knows nothing of my . . . reputation. She knows, however, the rather *strict* nature of my family. If I tell her they oppose our marriage because of her age . . . If I tell her they will cut me off without a penny . . . You see what I mean, Mrs. Grant, don't you? Caroline will then end the engagement herself. She'll have a wonderful tale to tell her friends, a tale filled with adolescent tragedy and romance. All will be well."

"Or?"

"Or I can tell her the truth. That I was using her to get to your money. You're very calm and collected, but you're Caroline's mother. You won't allow her to be humiliated that way. You won't allow her feelings to

321

be hurt."

"Swine!" Emile shouted, rising from his chair. "You are swine!"

"Emile," Jobina said quietly, "it's all right. Teddy knows what he is."

"Was that meant to hurt me, Mrs. Grant? I'm beyond hurt. Is Caroline?"

"She believes she's in love with you."

"She's in love with the idea of wealth and position. She wants to be a Hamilton. God knows she's not the first. The funny thing is, she wouldn't fit into my family any better than I do. You might say I'm doing her a favor."

"And what is your price for this favor?" Jobina asked.

"I'm not greedy. I expect to do well in Hollywood."

"Your price?"

"Twenty thousand."

"Emile," Jobina said, for he had again started to rise. "It's all right."

"You are going to pay the swine?"

Jobina looked away. She wished she knew the workings of Caroline's mind, the hidden feelings, the thoughts. But I can only guess, she admitted to herself. I can only guess that Caroline is not up to the truth. It's too sudden, too cruel. "Yes, Emile," she replied. "I am going to pay the swine. *Once*," she added pointedly.

"You needn't worry, Mrs. Grant. I'm not all bad. There's a small streak of Hamilton in me. Small, but enough to guarantee I won't be back."

Jobina finished writing the check. She tossed it across the desk. "I want a few things understood," she said. "First of all, you're not dealing with a fool. Don't suppose you can make more trouble. If you try, you will be sorry. And that *I* guarantee."

"It's understood."

"You must be very gentle with Caroline. You've been in this sort of situation before. She hasn't. She must see this as your *family's* decision, based solely on her age. She is *not* to feel unwanted."

"I know what to say."

"I'm sure you do. Practice makes perfect."

Teddy picked up the check and slipped it into his pocket. "Whatever you believe," he said, "I'm fond of Caroline. In some ways we are alike."

"That's insulting."

"Is it? I didn't pursue Caroline, you know. We met at a cotillion. We danced. I noticed how beautiful she was, but adolescents aren't really in my repertoire. No, Mrs. Grant. Caroline found out I was a Hamilton, one of *the* Hamiltons, and she pursued me. Suzanne was in on it. I was amused, nothing more. Then I found out *she* was the daughter of Jobina Inc. I saw my chance. I took it."

"You took advantage."

Teddy smiled. "I could have," he replied. "As I said, adolescents aren't in my repertoire. Your daughter and I read poetry to each other. We held hands. We shared a few chaste kisses . . . I concede my motive was money, but so was hers. She wouldn't have been interested in me if my name were Jones."

"Get out."

"I hope there are no hard feelings, Mrs. Grant. Good day. Good day, Mr. Lanteau."

"Here is my answer to you, Mr. Teddy Hamilton,"

Emile said, spitting into Teddy's outstretched hand. "You understand?"

"Oh yes. I understand."

"Swine!" Emile cried as the door closed. "Why did you pay the swine, Jobina?"

"Caroline isn't ready to hear the truth."

"But she could learn a lesson from it."

"Perhaps, Emile. Perhaps not. I don't want her to become a cynic at such a young age. She will learn her lessons, in time. We all do. There's no hurry."

"She has only the puppy love."

"I'm trying to put myself in Caroline's place. Imagine being sixteen and being courted by a handsome, sophisticated older man, a man who supposedly offers great wealth and position. That's heady stuff, Emile. Caroline is caught up in it. To what degree, I don't know. Nor will she tell me. She keeps everything to herself. She kept Teddy Hamilton a secret all these months."

"The swine! It makes me mad that you have to pay him money."

"If I hadn't, he might have been very cruel to Caroline. I couldn't take the risk. This way her pride will be saved, her illusions."

"They are expensive illusions."

"Well, what else could I do?" Jobina sighed. "Caroline has no perspective. I don't want her viewing all men with suspicion. Someday the *right* man will come along."

"I hope it is soon. This is too much worry, yes?"

"Yes," Jobina agreed quietly. "Too much."

*   *   *

Jobina was tense as the week drew to an end. She spent more time at home, watching in helpless dismay while Caroline planned her engagement party. Once again there was chaos, though it was short lived; the following Monday Jobina arrived home to find the apartment hushed and Caroline in tears. "Darling, what's wrong?" she asked, knowing the answer even before she spoke.

"My life is ruined, Mama."

"Ruined? Why, your life has hardly begun."

"I can't marry Teddy," Caroline sobbed, dropping her head on Jobina's shoulder. "It's all over. He's going away."

"What happened, darling?"

"The Hamiltons . . . The Hamiltons are so mean. They won't allow us to marry. They say I'm too young. It wouldn't matter, except for the money. They threatened to cut Teddy off. To *disown* him, Mama. He said he didn't care. But *I* care. We would be *poor*."

"Perhaps the Hamiltons will change their minds."

"No, they won't. Teddy's been in Philadelphia almost all week. He was trying to convince them. It's no use." Caroline pulled a crumpled sheet of paper out of her pocket. "Teddy brought this letter back," she explained between sobs. "It's from his mother. She says her decision is final."

A nice touch, thought Jobina, taking the letter. And indeed is was a skillful deception, for the phrasing was formal yet firm, the handwriting properly old-fashioned. "I'm very sorry, darling," she said. "I suppose Mrs. Hamilton is used to having the last word."

"She's mean. They're all mean. Teddy begged me to

marry him anyway. He said it's only money."

"Did he? What did you say?"

"Oh, Mama, I don't want to be *poor* . . . I was miserable when we were poor. I hated it. I was scared."

"Scared?" Jobina frowned. "But why? We had everything we needed."

"I don't know. I just was. I'm not like you and Daisy. I'm not brave." Caroline wiped her eyes. She looked at Jobina. "I was scared something would happen to you, the way it happened to Papa. Then I wouldn't have anybody, not Papa or you or Miss Pym or anybody. I was scared all the time."

"I never realized . . . Why didn't you tell me, darling? We could have talked—"

"There was nothing to talk about, Mama. My life was ruined. Now it's ruined again. Oh, it's so *unfair*."

"Sometimes things have a way of working out for the best. The Hamiltons sound awfully stuffy to me, Caroline. You wouldn't be happy among such people. I've heard they disapprove of parties, of all extravagance."

"Teddy doesn't disapprove."

"That puts him at odds with his family. I think you and Teddy would have had your problems, darling. So perhaps it really is for the best. You will find someone else. You will find just the right boy, and then all this will be forgotten. In the meantime you have wonderful, romantic memories. Why, Teddy offered to give up his fortune for you! Not every girl can say as much."

Caroline's eyes softened. A faint smile touched her lovely mouth. "I hadn't thought of that, Mama," she said. "It is romantic, isn't it?"

"Suzanne will be jealous."

"And I still have Teddy's ring," Caroline remarked, holding out her hand. "He insisted I keep it. That's romantic too, don't you think?"

"I certainly do. You have quite a story to tell, darling . . . when you're feeling better."

"But all my plans, Mama. They're ruined."

"There are always new plans. That's the advantage to being young. Tomorrow is always a new day; and there are always new plans, new boys waiting in the wings."

"They won't be like Teddy."

"No," Jobina replied more quickly than she had intended. "No, they won't. Differences are what make people interesting."

"Teddy was perfect. He was my dream, Mama. For years and years and years I dreamed of someone exactly like Teddy Hamilton. The dream almost came true," Caroline sniffled, tears starting again in her eyes. "It's so unfair."

Jobina listened sympathetically to Caroline's sad laments. She dried her tears, stroked her pale cheek, but she said little. What *can* I say, she thought. It's done and I'm glad it's done. "Are you feeling better, darling?" she asked when at last Caroline was still. "It helps to cry."

"I'll be very lonely, Mama."

"Not for long. There will be Christmas parties and New Year's parties. Ian will be home from school in a few months. He always has a big party."

"Iam may go away this Christmas. It's because of Aunt Irene and Uncle George. Are they doing to be divorced, Mama?"

"I don't know," Jobina replied truthfully. "They have some problems. We're all hoping they will work their problems out."

"Oh, why do people have to be so silly? Aunt Irene and Uncle George have been married a million years. Why can't they just be happy? Ian thinks Uncle George has a girlfriend. At his age! It's embarrassing. Why can't he just be happy with Aunt Irene?"

"Sometimes people need to be apart from each other for awhile. Especially if they've been married a *million* years," Jobina added, smiling. "And Uncle George isn't ancient, by the way."

"He shouldn't have a girlfriend."

"I don't know that he does. Neither do you, Caroline. Poor Ian is upset and searching for answers. All the rest is gossip. I don't want to hear you repeating gossip."

"Will there be gossip about Teddy and me?"

"Perhaps a little. Teddy *is* a Hamilton, after all. You are a pretty young woman. That's an inviting combination. But I wouldn't worry, darling. There are no scandalous details to keep tongues wagging. Though you must remember that gossips often make up their own details. You may hear . . . odd things about Teddy, or yourself. Pay no attention."

"I'll miss him, Mama."

"You will find someone else."

Caroline looked at her ring, then reached out to touch the diamond and each of the sapphires. "Someone rich," she said. "Don't frown, Mama. I want a certain kind of life and I admit it. Teddy understood."

"Everybody wants to be rich, darling."

"Well, everybody *should* be rich. That's what I think!"

A great many people would have agreed with Caroline in this autumn of 1929. The economy was strong, the stock market booming. General Electric had soared to 396 dollars a share, compared to 128 the year before; American Telephone and Telegraph to 304, against 179 the year before; Westinghouse to 289, against 91. No one knew how many investors were in the market, though some estimates ran as high as twenty-five million. Wall Street, long the exclusive province of the mighty, had been joined by the not-so-mighty: clerks and shopkeepers and farmers. There was good reason, for success stories abounded, most of them true.

But true or not, there were occasional setbacks—a sudden flurry of selling early in October and then an avalanche of selling two weeks later. "Warning signs," Jobina said to Eugene Marshall one cold October Monday. "I'm glad I got out of the market when I did."

"Nonsense. I refuse to listen to the doomsayers. That's what they are, Jobina. A bunch of doomsaying economists who have been predicting trouble for months, *years*. They were wrong then and they're wrong now. I believe President Hoover. The American economy is sound. Look at our profits this year. You can't quarrel with profits."

"These are prosperous times and we happen to make an inexpensive product. I'm not complaining, Gene. I'm concerned. The market is under pressure. If it starts to slip—"

"It won't."

"Nevertheless, I want a factory-by-factory audit. It's best to know where we stand, just in case. Three factories are operating practically around the clock. If there's trouble, we could wind up with an enormous inventory."

"That isn't at all likely."

"Do the audit, Gene. Put your whole department on it, if necessary."

"We'll need ten days."

"Fine, ten days," Jobina replied, marking her calendar. She was sorting through another file when the door opened. She smiled, for there stood Irene, slim and suntanned and swathed in mink. "Is it really you?" she cried, jumping to her feet.

"I hope you don't mind my barging in," Irene said with a laugh. "Muriel was away from her desk and I couldn't wait a moment longer. Well? Are you glad to see me?"

Jobina rushed across the office to her friend. "I'm delighted," she said. "And look at you. You look wonderful!"

"I should. I've had the loveliest holiday . . . Hello, Gene."

"It's nice to see you again, Mrs. Thayer. I'll be going now, Jobina. We can continue our meeting later."

"Thank you, Gene."

"I'm interrupting," Irene said.

"Certainly not. Come and sit down. I want to hear all about your holiday. It must be quite a story, Irene. I was beginning to think you were *never* coming back. Didn't you get my messages? I called a dozen times."

"First let me catch my breath. We got back last night and it's been bedlam ever since."

"We?"

"George and I."

"George? George was with you in Bermuda?"

"I went by myself," Irene explained, draping her furs on the couch. "George followed. It was part of my plan. My last, desperate plan. All the others had failed. I knew I had to get George alone somewhere. I had to get him out of New York, if only for a little while. That's what I did."

"But how?" Jobina asked.

"Before I sailed, I withdrew a lot of money from our personal account. A *lot* of money. I also emptied our checking account and two safe deposit boxes. It was a terrible trick, but I had to get George's attention. I would have done anything, Jobina. To make a long story short, it worked. Once he discovered that the mcney was missing, he began calling and sending cables. I refused his calls. I just ignored the cables. A week later, he arrived in Bermuda."

"Poor George. He must have been furious."

"He was breathing fire. I had never seen him so angry. But at least he was *there*. It was the first step."

"And then?"

"Oh, he ranted and raved. I managed to convince him that I hadn't thrown all his money into the ocean . . . or given it to some beach boy. He started feeling better. He finally figured out what I was up to. He was surprised. I think, secretly, he was pleased."

"And then?"

"And then I seduced my husband," Irene replied

with a radiant smile. "Bermuda is a very romantic place. The scene was set: A balcony overlooking the Atlantic; Champagne on ice; A new black lace negligee. We fell in love all over again."

"Irene, I'm so happy for you."

"I felt like a bride. We took long walks. We went swimming in the moonlight. George chartered a yacht and we sailed around the islands. We talked, Jobina, really talked . . . We still have problems to resolve, but we understand them now. I don't think we'll repeat our mistakes. Of course there are always new mistakes. That's life."

"That's marriage," Jobina said. "Loving each other despite mistakes and faults and problems. You and George love each other."

"We needed reminding. Perhaps I'm putting it too simply, but you see what I mean. When people live together a long time, there are no more surprises. Romantic gestures become fewer and fewer. It's called being in a rut." Irene laughed. "It's deadly!"

"You lived to tell the tale."

"I *fought*. And I wasn't above using feminine wiles, Jobina. All's fair in love and war. If I had let George continue on his way, we would have found ourselves divorced. It was reaching that point. It was the most awful strain. I was concerned about Ian also. He's seventeen now, old enough to read between the lines. I was concerned about the effect on him."

"Ian is a sensible young man."

"Thank heavens! He's had to learn that his parents aren't perfect after all. Far from it. Years ago, when I made the same discovery, *I* was shocked."

"Well, children seem more knowing these days."

"Yes," Irene replied, "and they get ideas. George was setting the wrong example for Ian. We both were. We were both so involved with our own problems, we almost forgot about Ian."

"Have you told him the good news?"

"We called from Bermuda. We're planning a much longer talk at Christmas time. Ian will be home then. Things will be back to normal, I hope."

"You hope?" Jobina smiled. "Judging by your glow, I would say it's a foregone conclusion."

"There are odds and ends. George went to see Amy last night . . . I can actually say her name without choking. Aren't you proud of me? It's very Noel Coward!"

"You haven't lost your sense of humor, Irene."

"It's my protection against the cruel, cruel world . . . But I was talking about Amy. I gather she plans to leave the city. I hope it's soon. The danger has passed. Unfortunately, the situation is still awkward. I wouldn't want to run into her somewhere. That's too Noel Coward for me."

"Shall I give her a little push? She will probably need a job, Irene. I can send her to our offices in Chicago or Los Angeles."

"Would you?"

"Of course." Jobina went to her desk and scribbled a note. "I'll have Jack telephone Amy this afternoon," she said. "Consider it done."

A twinkle came into Irene's dark eyes. She tilted her head, staring thoughtfully at Jobina. "I keep forgetting you are a tycoon. I can't imagine why. Your butterflies are everywhere. Even in Bermuda. How does it feel to be Madame Jobina Inc.?"

"You're teasing me."

"I'm not. I want to know."

"It's fun, most of the time. I enjoy the challenge, the work. And I have no money worries."

"But it's lonely."

Jobina turned suddenly, shaking her finger at Irene. "I know what's coming," she declared. "You have romance on the brain and you want to try matchmaking again. Don't. I'm quite happy with things the way they are. My life isn't all work. I go out. I have my share of dates. Simple, uncomplicated dates. I will gladly leave the moonlight and roses to you."

"I happened to meet a man in Bermuda—"

"No."

"Really, Jobina, you can at least let me finish. "This man isn't a moonlight and roses sort. He isn't a David Amory, not at all. He's wonderful! His name is Mark—"

"I don't care if his name is Rudolph Valentino. The answer is *no*. You are wasting your time."

"Won't you let me finish?"

"There is nothing to finish, Irene. I'm simply not interested. Believe me, I'm not. I intend to stay close to home for awhile. You will understand why when I tell you about Caroline's recent adventures. They include a brief engagement to none other than Teddy Hamilton."

"*What?*"

"It's a long and ugly story. Come," Jobina said, looking at her watch. "I'll take you to lunch. I'm free until one o'clock. After that, I have a full schedule."

"Caroline was engaged to Teddy?"

"Briefly."

"Engaged?"

"Get your coat." Jobina laughed, taking her own coat and hat from the closet. "I promise to keep you spellbound."

"Teddy Hamilton is certainly a busy fellow. I'm amazed that somebody hasn't shot him by now."

"He is quick on his feet."

"Yes, he must be."

Jobina opened the door, then followed Irene outside. She saw Emile bent over the radio console behind her secretary's desk. He was frowning, his face grim. "What's wrong?" she asked. "Emile? What's wrong?"

"It is the market, Jobina. All morning my broker is calling. Wait . . . Here it comes on the radio. The market is, how you say, making a tumble."

Chapter Fifteen

Jobina had little chance to reassure Emile, for the panic had begun. Thirteen million shares of stock were sold on Monday, with market losses exceeding ten billion dollars. The next day, a day that would forever be known as Black Tuesday, the market crashed.

There was bedlam on the trading floor as desperate men shouted and cursed and wept. According to a Stock Exchange guard, "They roared like a lot of lions and tigers. They howled and screamed. They clawed at one another's collars. They were like a bunch of crazy men. Every once in a while, when Radio or Steel or Auburn would take another tumble, you'd see some poor devil collapse and fall to the floor."

It was a disaster, the toll stupendous. The selling off of twenty-three million shares let loose a panic that would destroy thirty billion dollars in market values. Great investment trusts were suddenly bankrupt. Great corporations, the very backbone of American business, were struck a mortal blow. And now the market's big men went down with the clerks and shopkeepers and farmers who had put their last pennies into the golden dreams of Wall Street.

Emile lost half a million dollars. "I blame myself," he said to Jobina the morning after, "because it was my greed. Now I must start over." But such calm and measured acceptance was unusual. Eugene Marshall, wiped out in the crash, strode to his bedroom window and jumped eighteen stories to his death. He left no note, nor was a note necessary, for there were many suicides as the true enormity of the crash became clear.

Ezra Grant understood at once. He suffered a stroke and died several days later. His funeral, austere as it was, mirrored the austerity of the life he had led. There were no fond remembrances, no tearful words of farewell. There was only one floral arrangement, a sheaf of lilies from Jobina. There were only two mourners, Jobina and an attorney who drowsed throughout the service.

If Ezra's funeral mirrored his life, his will was the final confirmation. He left nothing to his housekeeper, nor to the carriage driver who had served him for more than thirty years. To Caroline and Daisy he left one hundred dollars each; to Jobina he left the family Bible. The remainder of his estate—despite market losses, an astonishing two million dollars—he left to the church's foreign missions. "You may want to contest the will on behalf of your children," the attorney explained to Jobina. "There are sufficient grounds." Without regret, without even a second thought, she declined.

It was early evening when Jobina returned home. She found the living room darkened and a shadowy figure curled up in a chair near the terrace doors. "Caroline, is that you?" she asked.

"Yes, Mama."

"Why are you sitting in the dark?"

"I don't know."

Jobina switched on the lamps, glancing curiously at her daughter. "Have you been deserted?" She smiled. "Where is everyone?"

"Daisy went to the movies with Annie Sisk. Rose went to Confession. It's Saturday, Mama."

"So it is. But that doesn't explain why you were sitting here in the dark. What's wrong, darling?"

"Suzanne is moving away. Her father lost all his money. The Dunstons are flat broke."

"I'm sorry, Caroline. Really I am. Is there anything I can do to help?" Jobina sat down, her amber eyes thoughtful. "A lot of people are in the same boat now, you know. And it's going to get worse before it gets better. I'm afraid there are hard times ahead . . . We are luckier than most. Poor Emile lost his money too, almost all."

Caroline shrugged. "Suzanne said terrible things about her father. Bad things, Mama. I was surprised. Mr. Dunston didn't lose his money on purpose. It was the stock market. I didn't like Suzanne today."

"You're growing up, darling."

"But Suzanne is my best friend. She was. I didn't understand why she was being so mean. Why do people have to be mean?"

"I think, deep down, you always knew Suzanne wasn't very nice."

"She was nice to *me*, Mama. She was my best friend."

"Did you argue?" Jobina asked, taking Caroline's hand. "All friends argue once in a while, even best friends."

"No, this was different."

"Perhaps you saw Suzanne as she really is. It's just as well. People aren't always what they seem. If you have learned that lesson, I'm glad, because now you will look beneath the surface. You will find *true* friends."

"I want to go to art school, Mama. I decided."

"Caroline, that's wonderful!"

"College isn't for me, but art school . . . I want something to do, Mama. Teddy is gone, and half the deb parties have been canceled. I don't want to sit in my room day after day. It's boring. It's . . . lonely."

"I'm proud of you. A little reward wouldn't hurt, would it?" Jobina laughed. "Uncle Ezra left you a hundred dollars. You may spend it any way you wish."

"Give it to Daisy. She has her eye on a new Italian bicycle. It has speeds and things."

"You are turning down money?" Jobina asked in surprise.

"I don't need it. What's the use of buying new dresses? Where would I wear them? Everything's changed, Mama. *Everything*."

Indeed an era had ended, for the Great Crash ushered in the Great Depression—as grim a time as the nation had ever seen. Unemployment was the immediate consequence, and it worsened from year to year. Fourteen million men were unemployed in 1932, one out of every four American workers. Millions more had only part-time jobs to sustain them. People lost their homes, their farms, their businesses. Factories closed by the thousands, and bank failures were rampant. Beggars appeared on city streets, migrants on country roads. President Hoover continued to affirm the soundness of the economy, declaring that prosperity was "just around the corner." But anyone looking around the corner in 1932 was likely to see yet another breadline, yet another soup kitchen.

Jobina began working sixteen-hour days. She was the first to arrive at her office each morning and the last to leave, taking work home with her at night. She worked on weekends and holidays. Often she arose before dawn and spent hours at her desk before going to her office. It was not choice but necessity that drove her, for she was fighting to save her company and the jobs of her seven hundred employees. Sales had dropped ten percent in the first full year of the Depression and twenty percent in the second; as she had feared, production was running far ahead of demand.

In early 1933 Jobina and Emile created the Fantasies line. The lipsticks were deeper, richer reds and burgundies; the eye shadows, smokier blues and greens and violets. The colors were glamorous, meant to suggest the glamour of Thirties' movie stars. Jobina furthered the movie-star theme in all company advertising. She refused to abandon her trademark butterfly, but now they perched upon the bare shoulders of models who resembled such stars as Constance Bennett and Joan Crawford and Carole Lombard.

Fantasies was a tremendous success, one of the very few success stories of the Depression. Jobina Inc.'s offices were expanded; a fifth factory employing two hundred more workers was put into production. Jobina herself was still working long hours, though at least part of her week was spent organizing soup kitchens and clothing drives. She was relentless, soliciting both contributions and volunteers for beleaguered city charities. Her own contributions were huge. "And I expect you to match them," she said to George one rainy autumn afternoon. "Dollar for dollar."

"I'm doing my part and then some," he replied. "Good Lord, I'll be a pauper myself if this keeps up."

"The only pauper with a brand new Cadillac!"

"Am I supposed to apologize for buying a new car? I thought you would be pleased, Jobina. It's my way of helping the economy. New cars mean paychecks and paychecks mean families won't go hungry."

"But families *are* going hungry, and cold. Winter is coming. The Children's Aid wants to distribute sweaters and mittens. Irene, I promised you would head the committee. Of course George will make a generous contribution, won't you, George?"

"So it seems."

"He grumbles," Irene explained with a laugh, "but he's glad to do it."

"Within reason. Don't you think you are getting just a little mulish about your charities, Jobina?"

"Not at all. I see people lining up for food. I see the despair in their eyes, the fear. You've never been afraid, George. You don't know what it's like. I do. It wasn't so

342

many years ago that I've forgotten. The girls and I always had food on the table, thanks to Greevy's Pharmacy, but if that paycheck had stopped . . . Those people standing in breadlines could be me. They could be any one of us."

"You cannot take the whole burden on yourself."

"I wouldn't want to," Jobina replied, a smile brightening her amber eyes. "We are all doing our share. Even the girls are helping. Daisy works at the Westside Soup Kitchen three afternoons a week. And she brings her friends from Barnard. Caroline has her Junior League committee raising funds."

"Is that why we've seen so little of her?" Irene asked.

"Perhaps. Your guess is as good as mine. Caroline was a happy child, then a serious child. She was a shallow adolescent. Now she is back to being serious. She spends most of her time in that studio I rented for her." Jobina rose and walked across the living room to the fireplace. Three small, unframed watercolors were arranged atop the mantel and she selected one, taking it to Irene. "Caroline has started doing seascapes," she said proudly. "This is my favorite. Isn't it wonderful?"

"The colors are marvelous, Jobina. Simply marvelous! The *mood* is charming. George, have you seen this? It's the view from our dock. Though she's given it a mood."

"Yes," he agreed, peering over Irene's shoulder. "Caroline has found her own style. I may ask her to do a cover for *Gotham* one of these days. Or would that be making things too easy? I hear artists are supposed to struggle and suffer."

"I think they have no choice, George," Jobina said. "There isn't much money in art."

"It will be a fine hobby when she marries. Is Brad Whittaker still the young man of her dreams?"

"Well, he's around here quite a lot. They seem to have an understanding. I try not to pry. Caroline is grown. She's entitled to her privacy . . . I keep hoping she will *volunteer* information. Of course she doesn't. But that's Caroline. Daisy is another story," Jobina added with a laugh. "She comes into my room every night to talk about Jim Shelby."

"He's a lovely young man," Irene said. "I approve."

"And I. I'm urging Daisy to finish college, but I think she's hearing wedding bells. Where does the time go?"

"Speaking of time," George said, pointing to his watch, "we are due at the Boltons for cocktails. Shall we?"

"By all means. Isn't it nice to be drinking *legal* whiskey again?" Jobina replaced the watercolor on the mantel. She turned, smiling as she saw Rose hesitating in the doorway. "If you've come to remind us of the time—"

"No, mum. It's . . . something else."

"Oh? Heavens, Rose, you look awfully grim. What's wrong? The sink again? I told Mr. Pedan to fix—"

"No, mum. There's someone to see you." Rose took a step back, motioning to the hidden visitor. "This way, Officer Clark," she said. "Mrs. Grant, this is Officer Clark."

Sudden alarm stirred in Jobina. She clasped her hands tightly together. She drew a breath. "Yes, Officer? What is it?"

"You're Mrs. Jobina Grant, ma'am?"

"Yes, what is it?"

"I'm sorry to tell you there's been an accident, ma'am. It's your daughter. They sent me to get you. If you'll come with me, ma'am, I'll take you to the hospital."

George and Irene went to Jobina's side. "What sort of accident?" George asked.

"A traffic accident, sir. The young lady was riding her bicycle when a bus swerved. It was raining. The street was slick . . . I have a patrol car waiting downstairs. If you'll come—"

"It's Daisy," Jobina cried. She was ashen, her mouth twisted in pain. "Oh God, *Daisy.*"

"Miss Grant," Sergeant Dozier explained to George, "rode her bicycle out of Central Park into Fifth Avenue. She was riding with the light, sir, but it was raining and traffic was bad. Starting and stopping, starting and stopping. That's how it was. Well, sir, in the middle of all this, there was a car trying to pull to the outside. There was a bus behind and the bus swerved. Miss Grant was caught between . . . I don't think you want to hear the rest of it."

"Go on, Sergeant."

"Are you sure, sir?"

"Go on."

"Well, the car hit Miss Grant first, then the bus. The poor girl was thrown ten feet in the air. It was a terrible sight, sir. I came running. I could see the poor girl's legs were broken, and her arm where she landed. But the worst was the blood. Blood was pouring—"

"Yes, I understand."

"We got her here as quick as we could, sir. The ambulance and us. It was a short ride and I thank God for that. Six minutes from beginning to end. The poor girl was unconscious the whole time. But she was in a bad way, sir. A bad way . . . The doctors took over then. There were three of 'em. They did what they could downstairs, then they brought the poor girl up here to surgery."

"I see."

"It's not a story Mrs. Grant should know, sir. I've had some experience with situations like this and telling the details only makes it worse."

"Thank you, Sergeant," George said, glancing across the hospital corridor at Jobina, "but I doubt Mrs. Grant is interested in the details right now."

Jobina had been pacing the corridor for an hour. She had refused the tea Irene had offered; she had refused conversation, comfort. A hundred times her eyes had darted from the clock to a passageway at the rear of the corridor. Beyond the passageway were the operating rooms and in one of those rooms was Daisy—sweet, sunny Daisy, just nineteen years old.

It was another hour before the doctor appeared. He walked slowly toward Jobina, slowly meeting her anguished gaze. "I'm sorry," he said. "We tried. We couldn't stop the bleeding. I'm very sorry, Mrs. Grant."

"*No.*"

"I'm sorry."

"*No.*"

"Jobina," George began, taking her arm.

"*No.* He's *lying.*"

"Mrs. Grant, your daughter never regained consciousness. I realize it's small consolation, but she didn't suffer. She felt nothing . . . Please, Mrs. Grant, come and sit down. I will get you a sedative."

"I want to see Daisy."

"In a few moments. Come and sit down, Mrs. Grant."

Jobina pulled her arm away. Her eyes were wild and filled with grief, but her voice, when she spoke, was composed. "I want to see Daisy."

"The nurses need a moment, Mrs. Grant. I must warn you . . . Your daughter sustained multiple injuries. Her appearance is . . . changed."

"Please take me to Daisy."

"Very well, if you insist. Come this way, Mrs. Grant."

Jobina leaned on George's arm as she followed the doctors along the corridor. Irene walked behind, tears streaking her cheeks. "I want to be alone with Daisy," Jobina said when the sad procession halted. "Please."

"All right," George reluctantly agreed. "But we will be close by," he added, stopping in the doorway.

Jobina entered the room. The lights had been lowered, the curtains drawn. Daisy lay in a narrow white bed, a sheet pulled to her chin. She was hardly recognizable, for the left side of her face had been shattered, the flesh torn from the jagged bone. Traces of blood remained, darkening her scalp and her bruised, swollen temple. "Daisy," Jobina cried. "Daisy . . . It's Mama, darling."

Irene, watching, buried her head on George's shoulder. "Oh God," she murmured. "Oh God."

Jobina moved closer to the bed. She bent, touching Daisy's cold cheek. She screamed. Points of blackness

347

danced before her eyes and then a pit of blackness opened at her feet.

"Just as I expected," the doctor said, pushing past George and Irene. "She's fainted. Don't worry. It's quite a normal reaction. She will be fine."

But Jobina was not fine. She was slow to revive and when finally her eyes fluttered open she said nothing. She allowed herself to be taken home and there she was put to bed. Damp cloths were pressed to her feverish brow. Brandy was fed to her spoon by spoon. Dr. Porterfield was called, though his medicines proved useless. All through the night she lay mute, unseeing, oblivious to her friends and even to Caroline. "It should have been *me*, not Daisy," Caroline cried tearfully, running from the room. If Jobina heard, she gave no sign.

Once again George found himself making funeral arrangements. Irene urged a simple ceremony and he tried to comply. "It is easier said than done," he explained, shaking his dark head. "The newspapers want to send photographers to the cemetery. I gave out the wrong time. I hope they are fooled by it."

"Photographers!"

"Well, Jobina is an important woman now. And the accident was grisly enough. I suppose people are curious."

"You can't let this turn into a circus."

"I am doing the best I can, Irene. I confess I don't know what to do about Jobina. She doesn't seem in any condition to attend the funeral. Dr. Porterfield believes it would be unwise."

"I disagree. Jobina would never forgive herself if

she . . . Oh," Irene said as Caroline entered the living room. "I thought you were sleeping, dear."

"No."

"Have you eaten? Rose has lots of cold chicken and ham."

"I'm not hungry, Aunt Irene." Caroline walked to the terrace, staring out at the gathering twilight. She was pale and there were circles under her eyes. In profile, her face looked gaunt. "Mama is very sick," she said.

"She needs time. You mustn't worry, Caroline. Your mother is strong. I suspect she is stronger than all of us put together."

"Mama just lays in bed and stares at the ceiling. She won't talk. Emile spent hours with her. She didn't say a word."

"Time is the cure."

"Time? The funeral is tomorrow."

"I know, dear. We must wait and see what tomorrow brings."

Caroline sank down on the couch, putting her head in her hands. "Why wasn't it *me?*" she cried.

"Stop talking nonsense," George replied sharply. "You are feeling sorry for yourself. Perhaps it's natural at a time like this, but it accomplishes nothing. I'm serious, Caroline. What if your mother heard such talk? She loves you very much. She would be very hurt. She would be devastated."

"Mama's thinking it should have been me."

"Caroline!" Irene gasped, but Caroline had already risen. In the next moment she was rushing away, her long golden hair streaming out behind her as she disappeared into the hall. "Poor Caroline."

"It's a bloody mess, isn't it?" George sighed. "I'm glad Ian will be here tomorrow. I am going to place him in charge of Caroline."

"He won't mind."

George looked at Irene. He took her hand, smiling wanly. "I hate to think about tomorrow," he said. "I wonder if any of us will get through it."

"Starting with Jobina."

"Yes. Good Lord, yes."

To everyone's great surprise, Jobina left her bed on the morning of the funeral. She was shaking, her legs weak, but still she managed to bathe and dress and comb her hair. "Is it time?" she asked when Caroline came into her room.

"Mama—"

"Is it time?"

"Yes, Mama."

"Hold my hand, Caroline. Don't let go."

"I won't, Mama. I promise."

Daisy was buried at Good Shepherd Cemetery, not far from where William lay. It was a rainy morning and the freshly turned earth had a sweet, clean scent that reminded Jobina of spring. But Daisy won't see another springtime, she thought, bitter tears stinging her eyes. She fumbled for her handkerchief as she lifted her black veil. She saw the masses of flowers. She saw the minister open his Bible over the polished mahogany casket. *Daisy*, her heart cried. *Daisy*.

The minister concluded his readings with the twenty-third psalm. He nodded then and Daisy's college glee club rose to sing Ave Maria. Their young voices seemed to float on the misty air, offering each word as if to the heavens. George bent his head, brushing at his eyes. Irene began to weep. Caroline held fast to Jobina, but her other hand sought Ian's comforting grasp.

Several photographers were waiting near the cemetery gates. They chatted quietly amongst themselves, surging forward when the mourners approached the long line of parked cars. Jobina heard cameras click. Through her tears, she saw sudden flashes of light. She stumbled and George caught her arm. "Come, Jobina," he said. "Here is Claus with the car."

"Where's Caroline? I don't see her."

"She's a few steps behind. She's quite all right. Ian is with her. Here is the car, Jobina. In you go . . . Irene, you're next." George held the door for Caroline. "In you go. That's it . . . Ian, you and I will ride up front."

"Beekman Place, sir?" Claus asked.

"As quickly as possible."

The car sped away. No one spoke, though now and then a ragged sigh was heard. Caroline's eyes were downcast, her hands clasped stiffly in her lap. Irene was so still she did not appear to move at all. Jobina stared out the window, tearing her handkerchief to shreds.

A luncheon had been planned. The Sisks were there, the Boltons and the Claymores. Emile was there without Inge, for they had had another argument. Miss Pym was there, standing to one side. All of Daisy's friends were there, gathered together in somber little groups of twos and threes. Jobina spent a few moments with each of the guests. Shortly after noon she excused herself and went to her room. She remained in her room throughout the day, throughout the long night. Caroline came to her door twice, Irene five or six times, but Jobina refused to see them. She refused visitors and telephone calls and meals. She sat in a chair by the fire, staring vacantly into space.

"I think Mama is drinking," Caroline said to Ian the next week. "I heard Rose telling Aunt Irene that brandy is disappearing from the liquor cabinet."

Ian circled the living room and sat down opposite Caroline. At twenty, he bore a strong resemblance to his father, though his dark eyes held Irene's amused twinkle. Like her, he was inclined to speak his mind. "What are you doing to help?" he asked now.

"What *can* I do? Daisy was Mama's favorite."

"So you're still feeling sorry for yourself, are you? Poor, unloved Caroline."

"I didn't say I was unloved. I said Daisy was her favorite."

"Daisy was everybody's favorite," Ian replied with an amiable shrug. "She was always smiling, laughing about something or other. You were always off in a corner, sulking."

"I was not!"

"The truth hurts, eh?"

Caroline tossed her golden head. "You're terrible, Ian Thayer," she exclaimed. "You've done nothing but insult me today. When are you going back to Yale?"

"Do you really want me to go?"

"*Yes.*"

"Really?" Ian smiled. "Cross your heart?"

"Well . . . it *is* your last year. I assume you plan to graduate."

"Oh, I'll graduate. Don't worry about that. Right now, I think I'm needed here. You can't keep moping around, Caroline. Someone has to give you a push, or perhaps a swift kick. I'm the man to do it. Your Bradley Whittaker III isn't up to the job."

"Leave Brad out of this."

"He's a perfectly nice fellow. But you need a strong hand. You need someone who isn't afraid of you."

"That's the silliest thing I ever heard."

"Is it? We'll see. Tell me what you're doing to help your mother. Have you tried to talk to her?"

"Of course. She doesn't want to talk to me, Ian. She was the same way when Papa died. It was a long time ago, but I remember. I was so frightened. I didn't understand . . . I waited for Mama to come and explain. She didn't. All I had was Miss Pym. And then Mama sent Miss Pym away. I was alone."

"What a sad tale. Not quite in Dickens's class, though you're getting there." Ian leaned forward, staring into Caroline's deep blue eyes. "Listen to me," he said. "Your mother was very young when she lost your father. She had two children to support, no money, and no prospects. Okay, she made mistakes. We all make mistakes, Caroline. Just look at what else she did. She went to work behind a toiletries counter. Jobina Winslow Grant behind a toiletries counter, for God's sake. She built a company, an empire, from nothing. And she gave her daughters everything they wanted. Schools, clothes, lessons, fancy parties. That's not bad, kiddo. When you consider where she started . . . I'm sorry, Caroline. I didn't mean to make you cry."

"I'm not crying."

"Here, take my handkerchief for the tears you're *not* crying."

"Thank you," Caroline sniffled. "It's just a cold."

"You're allowed to cry, you know. You don't always have to be serious and perfect."

"Oh, I don't know anything anymore."

"I do. Have you told your mother you love her? Have you ever told her? She's the one who's feeling alone now, Caroline. Stop being a damned whiny baby and help her."

"It's hard for me to . . . say things."

"Try."

"If you come with me."

"No," Ian replied, shaking his head once and firmly. "You're not going into the lion's den, you know. You're going to see your mother."

Caroline wiped her eyes. She rose. "I'll try," she said. She left the living room and walked slowly through the hall. She paused at Daisy's door, then continued on. "Mama?" she called, opening the door to Jobina's room. "May I . . . May I talk to you?"

"I'm rather tired, Caroline."

"Please, Mama . . . Please. It's important."

Jobina turned, lifting her head. Her face was gray, her eyes hollow and red rimmed. "Come along then." She sighed, gesturing wearily to a chair. "Sit down. Don't make it a long story, darling. I can't concentrate on long stories. I can't listen."

"We're worried about you, Mama. I mean, I'm worried about you. I want you to know I . . . I love you."

Caroline spoke for more than an hour. She kept her eyes averted and occasionally she stammered, but she managed to express her feelings, her fears—the old fears that had colored her life. At the last, she spoke of seeing her father lying in a pool of his own blood. "Miss Pym tried to pull me away . . . It was too late. I saw. I saw the gun. It's very strange, but somehow I knew. I knew the truth, Mama. I didn't understand it. It was all jumbled in my head. But I swear I knew. It was a . . . a feeling. I just knew . . . I'm sorry, Mama. You didn't want to listen to a long story."

"I didn't think I did. I was wrong." Indeed Jobina had listened to Caroline's every word. She had been confused at first, then slowly, through the mists of secrets and misunderstandings, her confusion had cleared. She saw the past; in the past, she saw the daughter she had lost and now had found again. "I should be apologizing to you," she said, going to Caroline's side. "Your father's death was such a horrible tragedy. I was in such pain. I never considered *your* pain, darling. I thought you were too young to . . . I failed you, Caroline. You needed me and I wasn't there. I'm so sorry, so sorry."

"It's all right, Mama. Everything's all right now."

Jobina put her arms around Caroline. "We can *make* it right," she said. "We have a second chance . . . Do you remember when you were very little? Oh, perhaps three or four? We used to snuggle together and have wonderful conversations, just the two of us."

"It's just the two of us now, Mama."

"Yes, darling, it is. And we must go on from here. I think I know a good way to start. Some hot chocolate and a roaring fire and conversation. Mother and daughter conversation. How does that sound?"

"Fine," Caroline said, tears filling her eyes. "Fine."

"I imagine you have a few questions about . . . what happened to Papa."

"Yes."

"Well, you are old enough to have the answers. It's a start. We've spent a lot of years being strangers, Caroline . . . Now we can be mother and daughter."

Jobina returned to her office after Christmas. She was thinner, still pale, but she was rested and that was a blessing, for she returned to find her desk heaped with messages and correspondence and sales reports. There were new production schedules to approve, new budget figures to analyze. There were color samples from Emile's lab, sketches from the advertising department. It was a daunting accumulation, though not entirely unwelcome. Work calmed her frayed spirit, solaced her grieving heart. The pain of Daisy's death was no less, but with the passage of time came a gradual acceptance. She began to feel stronger, more able to cope. When asked, she replied that work had saved her; by the spring of 1934 she knew that work—its distractions and demands and challenges—had made her well again.

Certainly Jobina worked hard as 1934 progressed. The Depression had deepened and, with it, unemployment. Average factory pay, for those lucky enough to have jobs, hovered around fifteen dollars a week; national income was barely half of what it had been before the stock market crash. In Washington, President Roosevelt and his numerous "alphabet" agencies fought to turn the tide. The WPA created jobs, while the NRA boosted wages and shortened working hours. Other agencies were formed to stem the avalanche of foreclosures and to insure depositors against bank failures. Despite protests from board rooms and executive suites, the SEC was formed to regulate the dangerous excesses of Wall Street. It was a massive assault on complacency, aptly termed the New Deal.

But the reforms of the New Deal came too late for some. Huge companies had been destroyed. Huge fortunes had been lost, if not overnight, then in the aftermath. It was rumored that Jonas Winslow was amongst the group of once-powerful men now facing bankruptcy. Jobina dismissed the rumors at first, though she dispatched Philip Claymore to investigate. Much to her amazement, the rumors were confirmed. "Jonas mortgaged the timberlands to invest in the market," Philip explained. "Of course that was during the market's heyday. He made millions. His mistake was staying in the market too long. When it crashed, so did he. He's been holding on, or trying to. Now the lands are going to be foreclosed."

"There is nothing left?"

"Jonas owns some acreage in Vermont. It's not much.

Apart from that, there is his house in Palm Springs and the San Francisco estate. The estate is up for sale. He was asking a million dollars, cash. The current asking price is three hundred thousand."

"Buy it."

"I beg your pardon?"

"Buy it," Jobina repeated.

"But it's a white elephant. The upkeep alone is monstrous. What would you do with it?"

Jobina sat back in her chair, a wry smile playing at the corners of her mouth. "Oh, I will think of something," she replied. "Something . . . appropriate."

"But why would you *want* it?"

"Let's say I am settling an old score."

"An old score? I don't understand, Jobina."

"Father will understand. And that's the point."

It was autumn of 1935 when Jonas Winslow's estate became the William Grant Foundation, a charity established to assist needy widows and orphans. Jobina provided the endowment and hired the staff and formed a board of directors drawn from San Francisco society. Jonas was not invited to join the board, nor did he attend the opening ceremonies; he fled to Palm Springs, where he was reported to be in seclusion.

Seventeen years after William's death, Jobina put the past forever behind her. She looked ahead now, watching happily as Ian courted Caroline. It was a jaunty kind of courtship, high-spirited, and it seemed to lighten Caroline's serious nature. Laughter was heard often in the Beekman Place apartment. Flowers arrived at odd hours and for no particular reason. There were mysterious little notes and breathless midnight telephone conversations. "I think we are going to be inlaws," Jobina said to George one winter day. He did not disagree.

In the spring of 1936 Caroline walked down the aisle of St. James Episcopal Church on George's arm. Astonished gasps rose from the flower-bedecked pews, for she was an exquisite bride. Her gown was a billowing cloud of white *peau de soie*, with cascades of lace at the sleeves and hem. Her gossamer veil, meticulously hand sewn with hundreds of tiny seed pearls, floated about her radiant face. There were pearls in her upswept golden hair, and Jobina's pearl necklace graced her slender throat. She carried white roses, each little blossom tied with long satin ribbons. No one could recall a more beautiful bride; even the Reverend Withers, usually immune to brides, was moved by the sight of the vision gliding toward him. "My child," he whispered as Caroline reached the altar rail. She smiled shyly at him and then looked at Ian. Ian was staring at her, his eyes dark, ardent. "I love you," he murmured, taking her hand in his.

The reception was held in the grand ballroom of the Hotel Pierre. Five hundred guests drank champagne and dined on *noisettes de veau aux truffes*. The wedding cake was a magnificent creation, six tiers high and adorned with small, spun-sugar doves. Jobina made the first toast to the bride and groom. She was almost as radiant as Caroline. Wearing an elegant dress of lilac silk, and with diamonds and pearls encircling her neck, she seemed to sparkle. "How will I ever convince people that you are my mother-in-law?" Ian asked, only partially in jest. "You look too young."

"I'm glad Caroline married you," Jobina replied with a laugh. "You always say the right thing. It's a talent. A talent you will need, if I know my daughter."

"I promise to make her happy."

Jobina wrapped her arms about Ian. "There isn't the slightest doubt," she said. "You and Caroline were meant for each other. I thought so even when you were putting frogs in her pockets, even when she was throwing all your toys in the fire."

"It was *one* frog," Ian protested, amused. "And it was long ago."

"The years go quickly."

"What do I call you now? Are you still Aunt Jobina? Are you Mom? Aunt Mom? Mother Grant?"

"Mom sounds wonderful."

"Well, Mom, what's next for you? Your business is roaring along. Your daughter is married. What comes next?"

"I suppose I will have to wait and see. Life is full of surprises, isn't it?"

Chapter Sixteen

"Have you heard? Have you heard?" Emile cried, bursting into Jobina's office. "Only a crazy man does such things. He is a crazy man!"

"Who? What are you talking about?"

Emile tossed a newspaper onto Jobina's littered desk. "There is the whole story," he said.

Jobina looked at the stark black headline: "Hitler Invades Poland." She folded the paper and thrust it aside. "He won't stop with Poland. They say he wants all of Europe. And they say his armies—"

"The armies of a crazy man! When I go to the movies, I see the newsreels. Always Hitler is in the newsreels, strutting like a goose. I want to laugh. Then I see his eyes and my face is not laughing anymore. I can see in his eyes he's crazy."

"Do you see how the people cheer for him?"

"Because he puts the bread back in their mouths. Germany was starving, yes? The inflation, it made their money worthless. In Germany the people needed bushel baskets of money just to buy bread, to buy milk. So Hitler

361

is the savior. That's what they think. They don't know he is crazy. *I* know. There will be war, Jobina. President Roosevelt, he says no. But there will be war."

Indeed there had been talk of war, and the talk had grown increasingly dark as Hitler and his armies had gathered strength. Jobina had tried not to listen, turning her thoughts to other things. When forced to comment, she had flatly declared that another war was impossible. Now, on this chilly autumn afternoon in 1938, she was no longer certain. "The Great War was supposed to have been the *last* war," she said with a sigh. "That's what we were told."

"Always there is another one. People, they don't learn. Some people, they think . . ." Emile sat down. His eyes were quiet, without their usual twinkle. His hands were still. "Maybe you have heard of the *Bund*, Jobina?"

"Those clubs in Yorkville?"

"They are more than clubs," Emile replied. "My Johnny, he belongs to the German-American *Bund*. He tells me it is, how you say, cultural? He tells me lies. From other people, I learn the truth. The *Bund*, it is for Nazis."

"Nazis?" Jobina asked, horrified. "In America?"

"Sometimes I read little stories in the newspapers. I say no, no, no. But it is true . . . Last week, I am home all alone. I go to Johnny's room. There is one closet locked, but I am pushing and pulling and the door comes open. I find his uniform . . . black trousers, black cap, and a white shirt with the *swastika* armband."

"Oh, Emile."

"I rip it to pieces. I throw the pieces in the garbage.

That is the right place, yes? When Johnny comes home we argue all night."

"There . . . there must be some explanation."

"Hitler is the explanation! Johnny says Hitler is a great man. He brings me a book, *Mein Kampf.* I spit on it. Then I tell Johnny to get out of my house."

"Emile, I'm so sorry. I don't know what to say. How could he have been drawn into that group?"

"That is what I ask myself. How? When he was a boy he was a fancy-pants. Johnny wasn't a good enough name. He called himself Jacques. Always he was putting on airs, like his mother. Now he grows up to be a Nazi. I think maybe it is because he wants to be a big shot. Marching and wearing uniforms and giving orders. That is big shot, yes?"

"What are you going to do?"

Emile shrugged. "Johnny will not listen to me," he said. "From people in Yorkville I hear the truth about the Nazi swine. They are the people fighting the *Bund,* good people. They have articles, books. They have family in Germany. They know the truth. But Johnny, he will not listen. I tell him I will take him to hear the truth for himself. He laughs in my face. So I tell him get out."

"Can't Inge do something?" Jobina asked.

"She is on his side. Not about the Nazis. They are nothing to her. But Johnny is her angel. Always she is on his side. She is giving him money, how you say, under the chair."

"Table."

"Under the table. I know it, but what can I do? Inge and I, we are *finis.* It is all over. She goes her way, I go mine . . . There is no divorce in the church so we are together, but not together. I pay the bills. She runs the house. *Finis!*"

"Johnny may still come to his senses, Emile. He's young."

"He's twenty. A man now, not a boy. I don't make excuses for him. Maybe I make too many excuses before, yes? Inge, she says it's his life. Johnny says the same. If he wants to be swine, then I let him be swine. He is not my son anymore."

"Only in your heart."

"My heart, it breaks many times, Jobina. And your heart also. We think we will die, but we don't. Is that good or bad? I don't know." Emile sighed. "I have lost Inge, and now Johnny. Pierre is Pierre, a fancy-pants. He is his mother's son . . . I am putting all my hope in Billy. I am putting my faith."

"Billy is a wonderful boy."

"He is spoiled too, though not so much as the others. We will see, yes?"

"I see a man who needs to relax. Come with me to George and Irene's tonight. Their parties are always great fun. Your mind will be distracted. Really, Emile, it will do you good."

"I would like to, but I have made plans already."

"Bring her along."

Emile looked quickly at Jobina, surprise clear in his dark eyes. "You know about Helen?" he asked.

"Oh, I don't know who she is. I just know there *is* a she. It's hard to keep secrets around here. The switchboard operators talk. The messengers talk. There are two or three secretaries who seem to do nothing but talk. You happen to be the current topic of conversation. In a very nice way, of course. Everyone is very fond of you, Emile."

"Helen, she is a widow. I met her at the movies. Loretta Young and Tyrone Power in *Second Honeymoon*. She was lonely, like me. Now we are not lonely. We have happy times together."

"You deserve happy times."

"But I am a sinner," Emile replied with a sudden, brief smile. "Father Rossini warns me I will burn in Hell. Maybe he is right. Maybe not. I think there are some things the priests don't understand. To them a sin is a sin. The reasons don't matter. I wish I could be so holy as that."

"You're *fine* the way you are. You put up with Inge all these years. How, I don't know. I'm glad you found someone who makes you happy. You must bring her to the party tonight."

"We have plans already. The theater. It's good you are going to the party, Jobina. Enjoying life, yes?"

"I'm trying." She laughed. "I'm certainly trying."

The Thayers hosted several large cocktail parties a year. They were lively affairs, for Irene's ever-changing guest lists blended writers and politicians and Broadway producers and what she called "more ordinary folk"— lawyers and brokers and business people. Food and liquor were plentiful, the drinks mixed by barmen and served by waiters. Conversation was spirited as voices rose in laughter or in loud, yet good-natured, argument. "Well, you've done it again," Jobina said now, lifting her glass to Irene. "It's another marvelous party."

"Are you having fun?"

"I'm loving every moment," Jobina replied, her amber eyes sparkling. "So far I've talked to a chorus girl, to a Lord Ransall of something or other, and to John O'Hara, one of my favorite writers in the whole world. How do you get all these people together? Tell me your secret, Irene."

"George is my secret. It helps to have a husband who is a magazine publisher. He's been publishing John's stories for years. Most of the people here have some sort of connection to *Gotham*. Even General Campbell."

"General Campbell?"

Irene turned, glancing across the crowded room. "Goodness!" She laughed. "The poor man is surrounded, isn't he? I'm not surprised. He's *so* handsome and charming . . . Look there, Jobina. There he is. Mark Crossland Campbell. Isn't he handsome?"

Jobina followed Irene's glance. "Oh, I see," she said, her breath catching suddenly in her throat. She stared at the general, for he was indeed handsome, rugged and square jawed, with black hair and a quick, brilliant smile. He was tall, his lean frame clad in a uniform immaculately tailored and glittering with medals. There was an unmistakable air of authority about him. He was, she thought, a man accustomed to giving orders and to having those orders obeyed. "He . . . He is rather young to be a general," she managed to say.

"Mark is your age. *You're* rather young to be running

Jobina Inc."

"Why is he here, Irene?"

"Now don't look at me that fishy way. George invited Mark, not I. You obviously haven't seen this week's issue of *Gotham*. Mark's article is in it. An excellent article too. It's called 'A General's Diary.' So there!"

"A literary general. How nice."

"Mark is *everything*. He's handsome and charming and smart. And *rich*," Irene added happily. "His family tree has at least one old-time robber baron. Well, one and a half."

"Let me guess. General Campbell is single and available."

"I can't help that, Jobina. Mark's wife died years ago. It's not my fault he never remarried."

"But it's convenient."

"You are such a suspicious person. What am I going to do with you? You're impossible."

"And you're devious." Jobina laughed. "I've been in the middle of your devious matchmaking schemes before. Remember?"

"This is no scheme . . . But you *are* here, and Mark's here. Goodness, it wouldn't hurt you to talk to him. I am certain he doesn't bite. He's quite civilized. A West Pointer, in fact. He tells wonderful stories about his experiences there."

"You sound infatuated, Irene."

"I am, a little. Mark has that effect on women."

"Ah, a ladies' man. Thank you very much, but I will pass."

"Too late. Mark is coming over. You can't be rude.

Where is your patriotism?"

"For heaven's sake, Irene."

Irene was not listening. She turned, holding out her hand to Mark. "Jobina," she said, "may I present Brigadier General Mark Campbell. Mark, this is Jobina Grant."

"The famous Mrs. Grant. How do you do?"

"How do you do, General." Jobina looked up, looking into the bluest eyes she had ever seen. She flushed, though she continued to hold his gaze. "It's so nice to meet you," she said. "Irene has been singing your praises."

"Is that true, Irene? I'm delighted."

"Any time. Now if you will excuse me, I must see to my other guests. I leave you in good hands, Jobina."

"That *is* true," Mark said as Irene rushed off. "I can be a very entertaining fellow."

"Can you? I don't know that I want to be entertained, General."

"Please call me Mark. I am generaled and sirred almost to death."

"And you love it."

Mark laughed. His laugh was deep, rich, and brought a warm glow to his amused eyes. "Let's say I'm used to it," he replied. "But I prefer that beautiful women call me by name. You, Bean, are a beautiful woman."

"It's Jobina."

"Much too formal."

"We're supposed to be formal. We just met."

"But I've been hearing about you for years. My praises aren't the only ones Irene sings. I met Irene and George a long time ago, in Bermuda. She's been trying to get us together ever since. Or is that a surprise?"

"Irene is always trying to get me together with someone. She is a born matchmaker."

"You resist all her efforts?"

"Fervently."

"Don't you want to meet Prince Charming?"

"According to Irene, *you* are Prince Charming."

"I do my best."

"Yes, I have the feeling you do."

Mark took Jobina's arm, leading her away from the crush of guests, from the passing waiters, from the pianist playing a Gershwin medley. He found a quieter corner and there he sat her down. "A tactical retreat," he explained.

"Isn't the object of war to advance?"

"This isn't war. A duel perhaps. You're trying to keep me off balance."

"I'm not doing very well, am I?" Jobina smiled. Her face seemed to shine as she gazed into the incredible blue of Mark's eyes. Her heart beat faster, her head was light, and her thoughts skipped giddily in a kind of dance. "Of course you have more experience," she said.

"Experience?"

"I couldn't help noticing all your medals and decorations. Are you an honest-to-goodness hero?"

"My unit saw some combat. I was a lieutenant then."

Mark Campbell had been a newly commissioned lieutenant fresh out of West Point when he had sailed for France. In those last months of the war the demand for manpower had been urgent, and young, untested officers

had been rushed to the front. Mark himself had arrived at
headquarters only to be rushed into a truck twenty
minutes later. An hour later he had found himself
stumbling through the woods of Château-Thierry. His
trunk and bedroll had been left behind, as had his blanket
and pack; on the eve of battle, his equipment had
consisted of a web belt, a forty-five automatic, and a flat
tin hat. He had not known where he was going, nor had he
seen a map. His guide, a corporal even younger than he,
had led him to the company command post—an old shell
hole deep in the woods. By dawn he was in the middle of
an artillery battle, seventy-fives firing over him, shells
exploding.

The battle had raged all that first week, quieting a little
at night, resuming with the pale rays of dawn. The
tactical problem, as Mark had analyzed it, was to reach
the edge of the woods before his platoon was surrounded,
then to climb the nearby crest to the German emplacements. In the first command decision of his life, he had
ordered an advance. And he had led the advance.
Crawling on his belly, propelling himself with knees and
elbows, he had led his men through a zigzag course away
from the firing lines. The next day, with a small unit of
volunteers following behind, he had led the climb up the
crest. He had circled to the rear, pulling the pin on his
grenade and heaving it into the emplacements. He had
advanced again, knocking out the second emplacement,
and the third. When one of his men had become trapped
in cross fire, he had crawled across the open field and
dragged him back to safety.

Mark had been twenty-two when the war had ended,

the veteran of half a dozen bloody battles, one more horrifying than the other. He had been promoted to captain, awarded the bronze star, the silver star, and the purple heart; the French government had awarded him the *Croix de Guerre* with palm.

"Your unit saw some combat?" Jobina asked now. "I suspect there's more to it. That's the *Croix de Guerre,* isn't it?"

"Front line troops made up a little song during the war. 'The colonel got the *Croix de Guerre,* and the son of a bitch, he wasn't there.' Well, *this* son of a bitch was there." Mark laughed. "If you will pardon my language."

"What do you do between wars?"

"I'm at the Pentagon these days."

"Hatching diabolical schemes to set loose on the world?"

"Keeping the peace," Mark replied, his eyes twinkling. "For civilians like you, Bean."

"Then I should be grateful."

"You certainly should!"

"Why did you choose the army, Mark?"

"I wanted to feel I was doing something worthwhile. I spent a year at Harvard. Harvard is the family school. It was fun. We had great times. But then what? Business never appealed to me, nor the usual professions, law, medicine. I transferred to the Point the next year. Perhaps it's in my blood. The first Campbells in America fought at Valley Forge. Welcome to America and here's your musket."

"Any regrets?"

"None," Mark replied.

"But all that marching and saluting and giving orders," Jobina said, recalling Emile's words.

"Marching hurts the feet. Saluting is automatic after the first few months. And I've taken as many orders as I've given. That's all beside the point. It has to do with discipline, which in wartime can save a man's life. If a man stops to question an order at the front, he can have his *derriere* shot off. Not a pretty sight."

"You've kept your sense of humor."

"I manage, even at the Pentagon." Mark opened a slim silver cigarette case. Almost instantly, a serious-looking army colonel appeared at his side, lighter in hand. "You're always sneaking up on me, Frye," Mark said, smiling. "Jo, this is my aide, Colonel Gerald Frye. Mrs. Jobina Grant."

"How do you do, ma'am?"

"Colonel. It's nice to meet you."

"Well, what is it, Frye?" Mark asked. "I see your worried frown."

"Sir, the car is here."

"In a moment."

"Sir—"

"In a moment, Colonel."

Mark had not raised his voice, but his tone had changed and his expression also. Colonel Frye stepped back. "Yes, sir," he said.

Mark turned back to Jobina, smiling once again. "I'm making a speech at Columbia," he explained. "I can't be late. We'll continue our conversation tomorrow night."

"Tomorrow night?"

"You haven't seen the last of me, Bean. Not by a long

shot. I'll pick you up at seven."

"Just like that? Shall I salute?"

"Don't worry," Mark replied, a wicked gleam in his eye, "I'll tell you when. I'll even show you how."

Jobina had risen, but she said nothing, for Mark was striding away. She watched him go, her gaze following his progress through the crowded room. She took a step forward. She took another step and another. Soon she was hurrying toward the windows, oblivious to the party all around her, to the people who called her name. She parted the silken draperies. Parked at the curb beyond was an army staff car, a bored sergeant leaning against the hood. Moments later the sergeant snapped to attention, saluting. Mark returned the salute. He nodded and Colonel Frye opened the car door. Jobina continued to watch; she was still watching as the car drove off.

"Well?" Irene asked.

"Oh, you scared me to death!"

"I see our Mark made quite an impression."

"All right, I'll admit he's charming."

"You're smitten."

"I am not," Jobina protested, though she felt herself blush. "I'm not a schoolgirl, Irene."

"You're smitten! You're absolutely radiant and that is a sure sign . . . When are you going to see him again?"

"I don't know. Perhaps never."

"Come now, Jobina." Irene laughed. "There is something cooking and you have to tell me what. It's terrible to keep me in such suspense. It's mean. I've waited years to bring the two of you together."

"Mark said he would pick me up tomorrow night at

seven. I may or may not be there when he arrives. I don't know. I'm not thinking very clearly just now."

"Aha! Another sure sign!"

"You needn't gloat, Irene."

"But I'm so happy, Jobina. You and Mark . . . You've met your match in Mark. And he in you. Oh, I see *wonderful* times ahead. I'm so happy I could cry."

Jobina did not sleep that night. She lay in her bed, recalling over and over again her moments with Mark Campbell. She recalled his words, his smile, his laugh. She recalled the intensity of his blue eyes and, as she did, she felt her heart skip a beat. She sighed. In the darkness she hugged her pillow and whispered his name.

"Hasn't my black dress come back from the cleaners?" she asked Rose the next day. "I can't find it."

"Which black dress, mum?"

"You know the one I mean. The one with the lace collar."

Rose glanced around the room. She shook her head, for dresses and shoes were strewn everywhere. "I'm wondering how you could find anything in this mess," she said. "It's a shambles, it is. Did you turn your closets out, mum?"

"I can't decide what to wear," Jobina admitted sheepishly. "I thought the black, but now I can't find it. Help me, Rose. What should I wear?"

"There's no question about it. You should wear your new black velvet. You'll catch his eye in that, you will."

"I'm not trying to catch anyone's eye."

"You can't fool me," Rose replied with a smile. "I know how it is, mum. I'm the same way when I'm going to meet Albert. All fluttery like. Worrying is my hair right, is my dress right. You'd think I was going to meet Clark Gable! And that's how you're acting now. He's special, isn't he? If you don't mind my asking."

"No, I don't mind. But I hardly know him, Rose. It's too soon to know whether he's special or not."

"You're the kind who knows straight off. If you're going to all this trouble, you know what's what."

"They *why* don't I know what to wear?" Jobina sighed, throwing up her hands.

"Your new black velvet, mum."

"Help me find it, Rose. Heavens, look at the time. We must hurry . . . If I wear the velvet, I will need pearls. But which pearls? Oh, I'm so glad you're here. I couldn't manage otherwise. I feel like a chicken that lost its head. What's *wrong* with me?"

"I told you." Rose laughed. "It's the flutters. Here, sit down and drink your tea. I'll find your dress. I want you looking grand tonight, mum. Just leave it to me."

"Bless you, Rose."

"Ah, it's no trouble at all." Rose scurried back and forth, happily collecting clothes and jewelry. She snatched the pins from Jobina's nervous fingers, brushing her glistening chestnut hair atop her head. She retrieved fallen powder puffs, searched the dressing table for lipstick and mascara and exactly the right shade of rouge. "There!" she cried an hour later. "You're a vision, you are. You'll take his breath away or I'm Eleanor Roosevelt!"

"What time is it?"

"Five minutes to seven."

Jobina drew a breath. Her heart was pounding, her throat so dry it ached. "A drink would do nicely," she declared, rising. "Will you join me, Rose?"

"I'm still teetotal, mum. I promised Albert. You have your drink and I'll sit myself by the front door. I want a good look at the fella who's giving you flutters."

"Tell me if you approve."

"Oh, I will, mum. You can count on me to speak my mind, like always."

"You're a great comfort," Jobina replied, a smile lighting her face. She picked up her purse and gloves, then took a mink jacket from the closet. "Forward march," she said, walking into the hall.

"What's that, mum?"

"The man coming tonight is an army general, General Campbell."

"A general, mum! I never met a general."

"You will, and soon. He is likely to be prompt."

Indeed Mark arrived on the stroke of seven. Rose showed him to the living room. She lingered a while, then withdrew, casting a last reverent glance in his direction. "I believe Rose is impressed," Jobina said.

"The uniform."

"No doubt."

Mark sat down, accepting the drink Jobina gave him. His eyes swept over her radiant face, over her long, slender neck, over the deep curves of breast and waist and hip beneath the draped black velvet. He had known many beautiful women in his forty-two years; he had had many liaisons, none of them, save for his late wife, serious. But Jo is different, he thought now. Somehow she is different. "Am I staring?" he asked. "Sorry, of course it's your own fault. You're very alluring tonight. Deliberately, I hope."

"You must be up to your ears in *alluring* women."

"Not quite. Though it's a fine idea. I like your thinking, Bean."

"Don't be too sure."

"I'm always sure," Mark replied lightly. "So are you. That's a good beginning." He finished his drink. He stood. He plucked Jobina's jacket from a chair and held it for her. His hands touched her shoulders, the back of her neck. He hesitated then, but only for an instant. "Shall we go?" he asked. "I have a taxi downstairs."

Jobina nodded. She did not trust herself to speak, for Mark's touch, fleeting as it was, had thrilled her. She turned. She looked up, gazing into the depths of his blue eyes. She waited for his smile and when it came her heart soared. "Where . . . where are we going?" she murmured.

"On the town."

Mark took Jobina to a small, exquisite restaurant near Central Park. The banquettes were deep gray velvet, the linens and china pale ivory. Tall ivory candles shimmered softly, reflecting their glow in the smoked mirrors. There were violins playing and there were flowers, gardenias in fluted crystal bowls. "All right?" Mark asked when they had been seated.

"It's lovely, just lovely."

"Are you surprised?"

"Well," Jobina said, glancing around. "I suppose I am. It doesn't seem your sort of place, Mark."

"But it's yours. Candlelight becomes you . . . Especially when you blush." Mark moved closer to Jobina, stroking her cheek. His eyes darkened, flashed; in the next moment he dropped his hand, looking away. "You're a disturbing female, Bean," he said with a sigh.

"Disturbing?"

"I couldn't sleep last night. I was thinking of you. I couldn't wait for the day to be over. I was thinking of seeing you tonight. When I was dressing, I noticed a very foolish grin on my face, a certain thumping in my chest . . . That's not like me, Jo."

"If it's any consolation, I was awake all night too. I hadn't planned to tell you."

"I'm glad you did."

"Why?"

Mark smiled, his reply silenced by the sudden appearance of a waiter. The waiter greeted him as he would an old friend. The ensuing conversation was in rapid and perfect French. "I ordered champagne, and caviar to begin," Mark explained after the waiter had gone.

"Yes, I understood that much. I speak a little French . . . You speak a lot of French."

"Languages are useful in the military."

"And how many languages do you put to use?"

"French, German, a bit of Spanish," Mark replied. "I get by in Italian. I hope you're suitably impressed," he added with a laugh.

"Overcome."

Mark laughed again. "*You* are a challenge, Bean," he said, tilting her chin to him. "I love a challenge."

"You must be up to your ears in—"

"At the moment, I'm up to my ears in you."

Jobina met Mark's gaze and a thrill ran along her spine. She felt giddy, almost intoxicated. Her voice, when she spoke, was breathless. Her eyes shone. She hardly tasted her food, picking at course after sumptuous course until finally coffee was brought. "A delicious meal," she said now.

"How would you know?" Mark asked, amused. "You didn't eat enough to feed a bird."

"I was engrossed in your stories. What happened after the war? Did you stay in Europe?"

"For awhile. I was sent to Germany. Then I was ordered back to the States to direct an officers' training program. After that I spent two years in the Philippines. My wife, Lucy, died there, in childbirth. Our son died the next day."

"Mark, I'm sorry."

"It was many years ago. The army managed to keep me busy." In his more private thoughts, Mark credited the army with saving his sanity. He had been crushed by his wife's death, seized by a black and bitter despair. His fellow officers had rallied to him, but in vain, for everywhere on the base had been reminders of his beloved Lucy. He had requested leave; instead the army had sent him to the Command and General School at Leavenworth. There his days had been filled with lectures and seminars, his nights with study. His mind had been occupied and, slowly, his spirit had mended. A year later, as a major, he had been sent to the Army War College. A string of commands had followed—bases in Texas and Georgia and California; in 1934, as a full colonel, he had been sent to command a training base in England. His next promotion, to brigadier, had brought a transfer to the secret and elite Plans section of the Pentagon. "I've worn out three sets of luggage; *that's* how busy they've kept me."

"And now Washington is home."

"I still keep a bag packed. One never knows. What about you, Bean? Do you yearn for exotic places?"

"New York is pretty exotic, don't you think?"

"A very stimulating town," Mark replied, staring into Jobina's amber eyes. "Yes, very stimulating. The women are so beautiful."

"Are they?"

"Goddesses."

Jobina forced herself to look away. "And that from a connoisseur," she said.

"Have you been hearing tales about me?" Mark laughed. "Lies, all lies."

"Irene said you have an effect on women. I think she may be right."

"Do I have an *effect* on you?"

"I'll let you wonder about that," Jobina replied, lifting her eyes once more to Mark. "It's part of the challenge."

"Or the strategy. I warn you, I've been trained in strategy. You might find yourself outflanked."

"Then again, I might not."

"We'll see, won't we?" Mark was smiling as he paid the bill. He helped Jobina up, taking her arm when they emerged from the restaurant. A taxi was waiting. He held the door open, helping her inside. "Either way," he whispered, "it will be fun."

Mark and Jobina went dancing at the St. Regis Roof. It was a clear night and the lights of the city twinkled majestically all around them. They drank champagne; they talked, looking long into each other's eyes. "'S Wonderful" was playing when Mark led Jobina onto the dance floor—the same song that had been playing at Irene's party. Our song, thought Jobina, her last defenses melting in the warmth of Mark's arms.

She snuggled close to Mark during the ride home, her head on his shoulder. Every few moments she raised her head to look at him, to memorize anew the lines of his handsome profile. Several times her lips parted but no sound came. Her heart fluttered. Her eyes were dazed, dreamy, for she was a woman in love.

"I didn't want this evening to end, Jo," Mark said when they had reached her door. "I really didn't."

"It doesn't have to end yet. Come in and have a nightcap."

"No, I don't think so." Mark swept Jobina into his arms. He kissed her hair, her eyes, her neck. He pressed his mouth on hers, drawing her closer, ever closer. Moments later, he released her, stepping back. "If I come in, I'll stay," he said quietly. "And I'm not sure I should."

"I want you to stay, Mark."

"I know, because it's what I want. I want *you*, Jo. But you're a woman for a lifetime, not a night. I return to Washington the day after tomorrow. My life is there.

381

Next week, next month, it may be halfway around the world."

"I don't care."

"I do. I'm in love with you, Jo. I shouldn't be. I have no right to be, but I am. I think it happened the first moment we met . . . I heard a little voice telling me to run fast and far. I didn't, of course. Tonight, when we were dancing, when I held you in my arms . . ." Mark sighed. "I should have listened to the little voice," he said.

"I have a little voice too." Jobina unlocked the door. She turned, holding our her hand. "My voice has been calling your name. So has my heart."

Chapter Seventeen

Moonlight streamed through the windows of Jobina's bedroom. A fire blazed in the hearth. Little bouquets of jasmine were all about, their soft, luscious fragrance floating on the air. The brandy decanter had been filled and next to it were two crystal snifters. The bed had been turned down. Mark surveyed the romantic scene. He smiled. "'Come into my parlor,' said the spider to the fly."

"I didn't do any of this. It must have been Rose."

"A likely story."

"I *didn't*. It was—" Jobina said nothing more, for Mark was kissing her. He slipped the jacket from her shoulders, tossing it away. He took the pins from her hair. He undressed her, slowly brushing his lips against her naked flesh. "Mark," she whispered, utterly enraptured, utterly lost. "Mark."

He carried her to the bed. His own clothes fell to the floor and then he was beside her, caressing her breasts, her thighs, the sweet darkness between her long legs. "I love you, Jo," he murmured over and over again. They were murmuring to each other, their trembling bodies consumed by a passion both tender and savage. Ecstatic cries rose in the scented air and in that moment their love was one with the roaring of the fire and the passing of the moon.

Afterward, Jobina lay peacefully in the crook of Mark's arm. She was wide awake and smiling, savoring the joy she felt. She peeked at Mark and she saw that he, too, was awake. She raised herself on her elbow. "I love you," she said.

"I love you, Jo." He turned, stroking her bare shoulder. "Tonight we discovered magic. Do you believe in magic?"

"I do now. And I want it to go on forever."

Mark glanced away. His blue eyes were thoughtful, staring into the distance. "We'll find a way," he said quietly. "I don't know how. I only know we will."

"Washington isn't so far."

"Suddenly it seems far, *damned* far. I want you with me, Jo. I want to say the hell with everything but us." Mark smiled at Jobina, shaking his dark head. "Look what you've done to me. I'm reeling."

"Not you . . . I know you have a career. I understand that. I don't expect you to surrender your stripes."

"Stripes?" Mark cried in mock dismay. "Stripes are for sergeants. *I* have a gold star."

"My humble apologies." Jobina laughed. "Will you forgive me?"

"Better yet, I'll bring you an Army manual."

"An Army manual! Really? You're too kind."

"I try." Mark lighted a cigarette. He turned from

Jobina, watching the curls of gray smoke.

"What are you thinking about?"

"Life. Life in the military isn't always easy, Bean. It's hardest for the wives."

"General's wives?"

"They get all the ceremonial duty," Mark replied. "They christen battleships and cut ribbons and put wreaths around race horses. They give tea parties and bridge parties for the wives of junior officers. They smile until their jaws ache. They're not allowed a bad moon or an off day or a controversial opinion." He turned back to Jobina. "General's wives don't have careers of their own, much less businesses," he said.

"I see."

"It's not the life for you, Jo."

"But you're the man for me and that's enough. I don't care about the rest of it. We're not children, Mark. I love you. I'll go on loving you, with or without a wedding ring."

"Everything's happened very quickly, Jo. I'm afraid you'll be hurt."

"Things happen when they're supposed to happen. Irene wanted us to meet years ago. We didn't, and I'm so *glad* we didn't. I wasn't ready to love again. I was on guard. You would have scared me to death. This is the right time, Mark. I know my mind, my heart. I know I love you. What else is there?"

"You know very little about me."

"Do you have lots of annoying habits?" Jobina smiled. "Do you squeeze the toothpaste tube in the middle? Do you snore? Perhaps you read the newspaper at the breakfast table?"

"No, no, and yes."

"Well, that settles it. You're a terrible person."

Mark laughed, his eyes twinkling. His arms went around Jobina again and they clung together, two people with but one heart and soul. "Jo," he murmured. He threw the quilts back, kissing her, stroking her until she cried out. She pulled him closer and their bodies met in wave after wave of blissful pleasure. "Magic," he whispered, as dawn shadowed the room, and, for them, it was true.

Mark returned to Washington early on Monday morning. He and Jobina said their good-byes privately, for Colonel Frye was waiting in the car. It was a difficult moment. They embraced; they held each other and then he was gone, the elevator doors closing with a thud. Jobina went to the window. She stared at the street below and when she saw Mark she smiled. She watched the brisk exchange of salutes and her smile faded as the car drove away. So engrossed was she, she did not hear Rose enter the room.

"Breakfast, mum?" Rose asked. "You didn't touch your tray."

"Oh, you startled me. You never make any noise."

"It's my training, mum. It's the way I was taught. Will you have some breakfast now? You can't go 'round on an empty stomach. You'll get sick, you will."

"I'm not hungry, Rose."

"He's gone? The general?"

"As if you didn't know," Jobina replied, amusement clear in her eyes. "I will bet you were watching at the window also."

"I had a peek. No harm in that . . . Is there going to be a wedding, mum? My fingers are crossed tight."

Jobina lowered her gaze. She turned. "Perhaps someday," she said. "It's much too soon to think about weddings."

"That's what Albert's always telling me. I'm wondering what's wrong with the men in this country. You need a rope to get them to the altar. A good, sturdy rope."

"Have you seen my briefcase?"

"You've plenty of time. It isn't even eight o'clock yet."

"My briefcase?"

"On the hall table, mum. But you should have a bit of breakfast before you go. I'll fix a nice soft-boiled egg."

"I couldn't eat a thing. Stop worrying, Rose. I'll be fine."

Jobina's mind was on Mark as she traveled downtown to her office. A dozen times, a hundred times, she recalled his voice, his look, his touch. She sat at her desk and scribbled his name, a dreamy smile flickering about her mouth. She got through the day—through stacks of correspondence and reports, through endless meetings—returning home to find an enormous bouquet of jasmine sitting atop her bedside table. There was a card attached. *I love you,* read Mark's bold, black hand. "He loves me," she murmured, hugging herself.

Mark telephoned that night. They talked a long time, whispering to each other, sighing, teasing. Later that night, Jobina tucked a sprig of jasmine and the card under her .pillow. She closed her eyes. She slept. It was a wonderful sleep, for in her dreams she saw Mark. She was smiling when she awoke the following morning; she was smiling when she arrived at her office. "The stars, they are back in your eyes," Emile remarked. "And the moon I see also. *Voilà*, it's love!"

Everyone noticed the change in Jobina. She was absolutely radiant, her step so light she seemed to float. Her voice was eager, breathless; her eyes glittered. At odd moments she giggled to herself, as if savoring some private and intimate joke. Mark was never very far from her thoughts. "My darling," she would murmur as she rushed home each evening to await his call.

Jobina crossed off each day on her calendar, for each passing day brought her closer to the weekend and Mark. By Friday morning her bags were packed, her train tickets safely hidden in her purse. She was almost out the door when Mark called to say he was flying to North Carolina. "I have to inspect a base," he explained. "I just now got word." There was another base, another inspection, the next weekend, but the weekend after that an exultant Jobina boarded the southbound train. Her hands were trembling, her cheeks quite flushed. At last, she thought, sinking into her seat.

It was Jobina's first trip to Washington. She had heard of the city's many splendors. She had even thought to visit them, but by the time she departed Union Station, such thoughts had been forgotten. She hurried into a taxi and rode to the Mayflower Hotel. There, as arranged, she registered and was shown to her suite. She tipped the bellman lavishly, sending him on his way. A moment later, without so much as a glance at the suite, she hurried to the telephone and called Mark. "I'm here," she cried into the receiver. "I can't believe it! I'm here!"

"Pardon, ma'am, but would you be Mrs. Grant?"

"Yes." Jobina turned. She looked up to see a tall, middle-aged Negro in a dark suit and cap. "Yes, I'm Jobina Grant."

"I'm Noah Johnson, ma'am. The general's houseman? The general sent me to fetch you to Doe Hill."

"Doe Hill?"

"The general's house. It's not far, ma'am. Over the bridge in Virginia. I'll take your bag. The car's right here. Traffic's not so bad this time of day. It's a nice ride. Pretty country."

"Thank you, Mr. Johnson."

"Noah's good enough," he replied with a slight smile.

"Thank you, Noah." Jobina followed him to the dark Mercedes Benz. He helped her inside and then walked to the front, slipping behind the wheel. "Lovely," she said, leaning her head back. "But I confess I'm a little confused. I thought Mark . . . General Campbell lived in Georgetown."

"During the week it's Georgetown," Noah explained. "Weekends we move to Doe Hill. The general, me, and my wife, Ivy. Ivy's the housekeeper and cook. I hope you like southern cooking, ma'am. Ivy can cook just about anything. Southern style is her best. Fried chicken. Sweet potato pie. Pecan pie and cream."

"Heavens!" Jobina laughed. "*I* hope I don't gain ten pounds."

"Maybe one or two." Noah smiled again, glancing at Jobina in the rearview mirror. "Ivy likes folks to clean their plates. She fusses till they do."

Jobina listened as Noah chatted about his wife. She smiled, for he had a comfortable, pleasant manner and a pleasant voice, soft with the accents of the South. "Are we in Virginia now?" she asked some thirty minutes later.

"Yes, ma'am. It's pretty country."

To Jobina's eyes it was beautiful, all trees and birds and gentle blue sky. She glimpsed the wildflowers growing in patches near the side of the road. She rolled down the window and happily breathed the fresh air. There was a sudden wind and she leaned forward, peering through the rustling trees at the outlines of a large, stately white house. "Noah, I think I see Doe Hill," she cried.

"Not yet, ma'am. The next turn in the road."

Jobina found it hard to sit still. The road seemed to stretch out forever and she sighed, willing the car to go faster. She saw another large white house, and then a flash of lawn. "Are we almost there, Noah?"

"Soon, ma'am. See those willows up ahead? That's the start of Doe Hill." He steered the car around the turn onto a tree-shaded avenue. On either side of the avenue were wide, rolling green lawns enclosed by white board fences. "This used to be plantation land," he explained. "It used to be tobacco, far as the eye could see. That was in the old times . . . Look up ahead, ma'am. You can see the house now."

Jobina leaned forward once more. Past the centuries-old willows and oaks, past the dogwood bushes and the gardens, she saw a classic antebellum plantation house. She stared in wonder at the tall white columns, the graceful balconies, the deep, trellised verandas. "My God," she gasped. "Is it real?"

"It's real, ma'am." Noah chuckled. "Everybody knows Doe Hill, leastways all the folk around here." He stopped the car on a graveled path. A moment later he opened the door for Jobina, helping her out. "I reckon we're on time," he said, glancing in the direction of the splendid white house. "There's the general."

Jobina followed Noah's glance. Her pulse quickened as she saw Mark descend the steps. She had almost forgotten how handsome he was, how tall and erect. She watched him, her breath catching, then flew into the warm circle of his arms. "Mark," she sighed. "Oh, Mark, I missed you so much."

"I missed you, Jo. I've been counting the days, the minutes." He drew her closer, crushing his mouth on hers. "Darling Jo," he murmured. "Darling Jo."

"We're together now. That's all that matters."

"Yes." Mark smiled. He stepped back, gazing into Jobina's eyes. "You look wonderful," he said.

"You look wonderful too. But you look different. I'm seeing a new side of you." She laughed, playfully brushing at his tweed jacket, his cashmere sweater. "Very nice."

"My country clothes."

"And that reminds me. You've been keeping secrets. Secrets like Doe Hill. I'm overwhelmed."

Mark put his arm around Jobina's shoulder and led her toward the house. "I really thought we'd be stuck in Georgetown this weekend," he replied. "I was able to clear my schedule, but by then you were on the train . . . This is my hideaway. It's a special place, Bean. Apart from my sister, you're the only female I've allowed here."

"I'm honored." Jobina glanced about, shaking her head. "Though I feel a little like Scarlett O'Hara. I half expect to see the Confederate Army riding off to battle. Shall I call you Rhett? You're no Ashley Wilkes, thank heavens."

"Thank heavens."

"How long has this been your hideaway?"

"Not quite a year. The last member of the Cantrell family died last year and Doe Hill came on the market. It wasn't exactly a bargain, but it was what I wanted. I had to have a place within reasonable distance of Washington, yet far enough away. And I wanted a place where I could keep horses. Do you ride, Bean?"

"I used to."

"Were you any good?"

"Superb!"

"We'll see." Mark laughed. "We'll see." He took Jobina's arm as they walked up the steps to the house. He opened the broad double doors, then stood aside. "Welcome to Doe Hill," he said.

Jobina entered the vast center hall, gazing raptly at the hand-carved wood paneling, the burnished parquet floors. Her gaze moved to an exquisite crystal chandelier and then to a curved and inlaid staircase of dark oak.

"Mark, how lovely," she declared breathlessly.

"A bit frayed around the edges, if you look carefully. I bought the furniture along with the house. Laura tells me it's awful. She's probably right. I don't pay much attention."

"Laura?"

"My sister. She travels down from Boston every few months." Mark took Jobina's arm again, leading her across the hall into the living room. "You can change anything you don't like," he said. "Change it all, if you want. Except for the library. That's my office and it's off limits."

"Yes, *sir*."

Mark's eyes twinkled. He swept Jobina into his arms, holding her so tightly that he could feel the wild beating of her heart. He kissed her, his hands slipping beneath her jacket. Almost in the next instant he drew back. "I have to leave you for awhile, Jo," he said. "Frye's waiting in the library. We won't be long, twenty minutes at the most. We're finishing a report that must get to the Pentagon today. It's important. If it weren't, I would have met you at the hotel myself. I wanted to. I had to stay here and work."

"I wondered about that," Jobina admitted.

"Of course you did. I wanted to meet you, Jo. I couldn't. I want to be with you now . . . But there's Frye and there's a report."

"You mustn't worry, Mark. I understand." Indeed she was beginning to understand the complexities of life with Brigadier General Mark Campbell—the sudden changes in plans, the sudden conferences, the sudden trips. "You warned me about your work," she said. "I'm not complaining. Go along and do what you have to do."

"That's my Bean. I'll make it as fast as I can. Noah will show you upstairs and bring you something to eat." Mark was striding away. He looked back once, then continued on.

Jobina turned. With a resigned sigh, she tossed her jacket and purse aside. "Welcome to Doe Hill," she murmured. Her spirits rose as she gazed around the room, for it was an odd mixture of Louis Quinze and English Country and she thought it charming. On closer examination she saw that some of the dainty chests were scratched, some of the chintzes faded. The Aubusson carpet was magnificent but in need of cleaning; the draperies, heavy cream silk, were water stained. She began to picture the room as it might be with just a few changes. She smiled. Reverently, she ran her hand across the carved moldings, the pale marble fireplace. She walked to the French doors, staring out at the gardens and the lawns so green in the sunlight. I'm home, she thought.

"Pardon, ma'am. Would you like to go upstairs now? Ivy's fixing a tray for you. It's a while till dinner."

"Thank you, Noah. I'm not hungry. And I'm happy right here. The view is *lovely*. In the city, all I see are tall buildings."

"Would you like tea, ma'am?"

"Tea would be very nice. Thank you."

When Noah returned, moments later, he was carrying an oval tray upon which sat a beautiful Georgian tea service. It was at least two hundred years old and each of the matching pieces was elegantly sculpted and embossed. "I reckon today's a special day," he commented, chuckling. "Ivy dragged out the good silver."

"Good?" Jobina exclaimed. "It's an absolute treasure!" She bent, her finger tracing the ornate pattern. "Did all this come with the house too?" she asked.

"Sure did, ma'am. There's a whole closet full. Cantrell silver, from the old times." Noah arranged the tea things, deftly clearing space on the tray. "I'll leave you now," he said. "The general will be coming along any minute. Make yourself to home."

"Thank you, Noah."

Jobina wandered the length of the room, stopping to inspect a collection of miniature music boxes, a collection of Chinese porcelains. She shook her head, for everywhere she looked she saw something rare and precious. After awhile, she wandered back to the doors, staring outside once again. Mark came into view then. He walked briskly, speaking to Colonel Frye. His face was intent, his hand jabbing the air. The colonel did not appear to speak at all; he nodded agreement, nodding even as he climbed into his car and drove off.

Jobina opened the doors and slipped onto the veranda. "Mark," she called, running toward him. "I'm here, Mark."

He looked up. I'll always remember this moment, he thought, struck by Jobina's beauty. He could not take his eyes from her, from her hair shimmering with sunlight and her face rosy in the wind. "Jo," he whispered. He wrapped his arms around her. "I didn't mean to be so long," he said.

"It's all right. I had a grand time exploring your treasures. Do you know the treasures you have in there?"

"*You* are my treasure," Mark replied, catching Jobina's hand. "And I have you to myself. The weekend is ours, Bean."

"Will you show me Doe Hill now?"

"I think you and Doe Hill have been waiting for each other. Come, I'll give you the tour. There's a lot to see." There were kennels and stables and glass-walled conservatories in which bloomed exotic plants. There were summer houses and two charming, latticed gazebos shaded by willow trees. There was a pine grove, utterly still and crowned with light. At the far end of the property, past bridle paths, past rich green fields, there was a stream, its banks a sweet tangle of wild lilacs and forsythia. "This is really why I bought the place," Mark said. "I escape here when I've had enough of the world. Or the world's nonsense."

Jobina leaned her head on Mark's shoulder. "I wish we could stay here always," she murmured.

"You're a romantic. Admit it." Mark smiled, stroking her hair. "How do you manage to keep your romantic notions while running a company?"

"There are two of me."

"I wouldn't be surprised . . . Jobina Inc. is very important to you, isn't it?"

"It's been my life for a long time. I had my girls, but when children start school they start leading lives of their own. They start growing away. And Caroline was such a distant child . . . I needed something more, Mark. Work filled all the empty spaces. After Daisy died, work was my salvation. I can't imagine *not* working, but there are times when I wonder. I'm here now, close to you, and I wonder."

"Yes." Mark gazed up at the darkening sky. Birds swooped and soared in the twilight. Trees rustled, showering their leaves upon the stream. "Wouldn't it be nice if we could chuck everything and run away?"

"Even if I could, you couldn't."

"What makes you so sure?"

"It's a feeling. Perhaps it's more than that. I saw you with Colonel Frye before. You were completely absorbed, wearing your general's face. And loving every moment of it."

"I love you, Jo."

"You've loved the Army longer. I have quite a lot of catching up to do."

Mark smiled. "Let me help," he said, sweeping Jobina into his arms. "Let me be your ally."

Mark and Jobina sank to the dewy ground. Soon their clothes were cast aside, their anxious bodies pressed together. "Mark," Jobina murmured. "Oh, Mark." The stream rushed by, splashing the smooth and polished rocks. The moon rose. The night birds called, and the loveliness of their song hung in the air like a benediction.

The evening was warm, caressed by gentle breezes. Mark and Jobina dined on the veranda, gazing at each other through the flickering candlelight and speaking the words of lovers. Later, hand in hand, they strolled the shadowy grounds. It was midnight when they ascended the stairs. "I've put you in the rooms next to mine," he explained, "in case you want privacy."

"Privacy!" Jobina laughed. "I don't intend to let you out of my sight."

"You're a woman after my own heart, Bean."

"That's exactly right. I'm after your heart."

"You have it," Mark said. He opened the doors to a large sitting room. Beyond was the bedroom, with walls of pale blue silk and darker blue chairs and settees. There was an old-fashioned vanity table, its ruffled skirts slightly bedraggled. Between the arched balcony doors was a lacy canopy bed. "My rooms are rather plain," he commented. "Wood paneling and brass lamps and the like. This is more your style. Shall we stay here tonight?"

"I'll stay anywhere you want."

Mark looked away, his eyes suddenly troubled. "What I want and what I can have are sometimes two different things. I *want* you with me every day, every night. I *don't* want you living in the shadows."

"The shadows?"

"You know very well what I mean, Jo. You had to register at a damned hotel, just for the sake of appearances."

"But we agreed—"

"Of course we agreed. We had no choice. Washington gossip is quick and vicious. Not much would be said about me. Men are allowed their love affairs. Your reputation, however, would be destroyed. I've seen it happen, Jo. I won't let it happen to you . . . So we fall back on the old ploys. They don't fool anyone, but they seem to quiet the talk. Phony hotel registrations are only the beginning. You have no idea what you're in for."

"I don't care."

"*I* care."

Jobina smiled at Mark. "You're spoiled," she said. "You're too used to being in control of things. And why not? Your orders are instantly obeyed. Your needs are anticipated. Every time you turn around, somebody is saluting. Don't look now, but you lead a charmed life."

"What about your life, Jo?"

There were many answers to his question, several of them complicated. She chose the simplest one, and certainly the truest. "You make my life a joy," she said.

Mark wanted to believe that, for he could not bear the thought of hurting Jobina. She was in his heart now, in his mind, his blood. He had never expected to love so deeply again, but it had happened and, despite his concern, he was not sorry. "You're quite a woman, Bean," he said. "Quite a woman."

"You bring out the best in me."

"I'm flattered. Or do you say that to all your conquests?"

"Are you my conquest, Mark?"

"I surrendered the moment we met. I knew even then." It was true. He was not an impetuous man, much less a man to credit love at first sight, yet he had loved Jobina from the first. If he had looked for a logical explanation, he had looked in vain; love, he had decided, was a riddle, the eternal riddle of men and women.

"Speaking of surrender," he said, drawing Jobina close, "it's your turn."

"Gladly," she murmured. They fell to the wide feather bed. They undressed each other, caught once again by passion, by magic. "Mark," she murmured long into the night. "Mark."

The sun was bright when Jobina awoke the next morning. Somewhere birds were singing and she smiled. She stretched her arm to the pillow, reaching for Mark, but he was not there. There was no note, no answer to her call. Hurriedly she bathed and dressed, peeking into all the rooms along the hall before she rushed downstairs. "Ivy," she said, coming upon the housekeeper, "have you seen General Campbell?"

"He's gone to Washington, Miz Grant. Noah drove him early this morning." Ivy Johnson, like her husband, was tall and slender, her hair sprinkled with gray. She was a kindly woman and now she smiled at Jobina. "Don't go worrying," she said. "The general's always running back and forth."

"But it's Sunday."

Ivy shrugged. "Weekday or weekend, it's all the same," she replied. "Come have your breakfast, Miz Grant. The table's set on the veranda. You don't want to be indoors on a nice day like this . . . The veranda's a good place to watch for cars."

"Ivy, you read my mind."

"While you're watching, you can have your breakfast. It's warming in the oven."

"Juice and coffee will be fine."

"That's for city folk, Miz Grant. Doe Hill is country."

And five minutes later Ivy served a true country breakfast—grits, scrambled eggs, pancakes, sausages, hash brown potatoes, hot biscuits dripping honey. Jobina stared in astonishment at the bowls and platters heaped with food. Suddenly she felt ravenous; she filled her plate and finished every last crumb. "No more," she laughingly protested when Ivy brought peach cobbler. But she finished that as well, drinking yet another cup of rich, black coffee.

It was a beautiful morning, the air cooler now, crisper. Puffy white clouds drifted across the sky and in their shadows birds soared. Jobina watched the birds, her smile widening. She left the veranda and watched a squirrel scamper up a majestic oak to his nest. Every few moments she turned, looking past the lawns to the road. She heard the car before she saw it. She ran toward the sound, clapping her hands together as the Mercedes came into view. Now she ran back to the path. She was there, waiting, when Mark emerged. "I thought I'd been abandoned!" she cried.

"Never. Never in this world . . . Come with me."

"Where are we going?"

"It's a surprise. Do you like surprises, Bean?"

"*Some* surprises."

"I think you will like this one." Mark led Jobina to the gazebo, setting her down on a pretty latticed bench. "I suppose Ivy told you I went to Washington," he said. "I had an errand. A very important errand."

"Well?" Jobina laughed. "The suspense is terrible."

Mark sat down beside her, taking her hand. "There are many reasons why we can't be married now," he said. "There's no reason why we can't be engaged." He slipped a small velvet box from his pocket. He opened it, displaying a huge and perfect diamond solitaire. "I love you, Jo. I love you with all my heart. Someday, perhaps sooner than we know, we *will* be married." Tears misted Jobina's eyes. She held out her hand and he placed the ring on her finger. "In token and pledge of my love," he whispered.

"Oh." She sniffled. "Oh, Mark, I'm so happy. I'm . . ." She flung her arms about his neck, covering his face with kisses. "I'm not dreaming this, am I?"

"We're real, darling. We're here together and we're real . . . We're official too," Mark added, flashing his quick, brilliant smile.

"Official?"

"I had to get Mr. Wixted to open his jewelry store. If I know Wixted, he's been burning up the telephone wires ever since. He must have called half of Washington by now."

"That's the end of your little black book."

"What makes you think I have a little black book?"

"*Had.*" Jobina laughed again. "Past tense. And half of Washington, the female half, must be brokenhearted."

"I certainly hope so."

Jobina gazed at the diamond's fiery sparkle. Her face was luminous, and a single tear glistened on her cheek. "You've made me the happiest woman in the world, Mark," she said softly. "I'll need weights to keep from floating away . . . I can't wait to call Caroline. Oh, and I should call Irene. Dear, wonderful Irene. I will *never* stop being grateful to her."

"Yes, you'd better call Irene. I had Frye wire three dozen roses to her. She will be wondering what I'm up to."

"You're sweet."

"I know."

Jobina smiled. She stood, linking her arm in Mark's. "I want to shout the news," she said. "I want to be silly and giddy and ridiculous. Is that all right?"

"Sounds fine to me. You'll have your chance tonight. We're going to a dinner party. The usual pomp and ceremony in Georgetown . . . But the day is ours, Bean. All ours."

Mark and Jobina returned to the house. They telephoned Caroline first, and then Irene. Later they went riding, he in immaculately tailored jodhpers and polished boots, she in an outfit pieced together from Laura's closet. They picnicked on the banks of the stream and there they made love, witnessed only by the birds and the endless sky.

It was eight o'clock when they arrived at the elegant Georgetown row house. Their hosts, Senator and Mrs. Voss, greeted them warmly. "So you're the little lady who stole Mark's heart," the senator said.

"I'm the little lady," Jobina replied, amused. She was introduced to several other senators, to members of President Roosevelt's cabinet, and to members of the military—none of them lower in rank than colonel. "I will be on my very best behavior," she whispered to Mark as an admiral's wife led her away.

The dinner was long and formal. There were many toasts, many courses. Afterward the men adjourned to the library, to cigars and port; the women adjourned to the drawing room and *demitasse*. "I know we are all going to be great friends," Mrs. Voss said, offering Jobina a chair. "Mark is a great favorite of ours. And you're just the right girl for him. You have spirit. Imagine building that big company all by yourself."

"I have a partner, Emile Lanteau."

"To handle the business side of things, I imagine."

"Emile is the creative genius. I handle the business side."

"Why, how fascinating! You must tell us more, my dear."

Jobina noticed the other women edging closer. They formed a kind of loose circle around her, and from its midst came the first tentative question. Dozens of questions followed; there was rapt silence as she replied. "I'm afraid I've been monopolizing the conversation," she said twenty minutes later. But still the questions continued. If a few of them were subtly condescending, most were straightforward and tinged with approval. Grudging approval, she thought to herself, though she was willing to settle for that.

"How did it go?" Mark asked when finally they were in the car, driving away. "Were you very bored?"

"I was the center of attention. Elsie Voss and her friends were sizing me up."

"I hope it wasn't an inquisition, Jo."

"Not exactly. Oh, there were lots of questions. I can understand why. All the women I met tonight lead the same sort of life. The idea of a career is strange to them. The idea of running a company is positively bizarre. They were curious, Mark. Mrs. Burleigh kept looking at me as if I had horns."

"Good old Maud. Any minute now she will be calling the hotels to see if you're registered."

Jobina nestled her head on Mark's shoulder, lifting her eyes to his handsome profile. "Are the people here really so mean spirited?"

"Maud Burleigh is. There are others like her. They consider themselves social arbiters. *I* consider them a colossal pain in the ass."

"The admiral's wife was lovely."

"Anne is a nice woman. Unfortunately, she and John are leaving soon. John's been ordered to Pearl Harbor. They leave for Hawaii next month."

"Hawaii," Jobina murmured. "I hear it's a paradise. They must be thrilled."

"Anne's happy. John's awfully tired of Pacific commands. This will be his fourth . . . They bought a house in Maryland about eight years ago. They've lived in it a total of eight months, off and on."

"The Navy is as bad as the Army."

"Worse." Mark laughed. "Though the Navy has a glamorous reputation. The Navy and the Air Corps. I think it has something to do with the uniforms."

"Are you jealous?"

"Let them have their glamour. I have you, Bean." Mark leaned forward, speaking a few words to Noah. He leaned back again, smiling in the darkness at Jobina. "You didn't see much of Washington," he said. "But there are a couple of places you must see, if you're not too tired."

"I'm not tired at all, Proceed, *mon général.*"

The wide avenues of the city were quiet now, with only a soft breeze rustling through the trees. Slowly, the car drove past the domed splendor of Capitol Hill, past the simple and eloquent majesty of the White House. Noah stopped the car at the Lincoln Memorial. There Mark and Jobina got out. "I wanted you to see this in the moonlight," he explained.

Jobina's breath caught, for it was an extraordinary sight. The moon struck the white marble, and in Mr. Lincoln's sorrowful face she saw beauty, a true grandeur. She clung to Mark. "I'm so glad we came," she said, her voice hushed.

"I couldn't let you leave until we did."

"I don't want to think about leaving, Mark. I won't think about it, not yet."

"It's all right, darling. We still have tonight."

Chapter Eighteen

It was raining when Jobina arrived in New York. After the serenity of Doe Hill, she was startled by the noise—the honking horns, the shrilling whistles, the screeching brakes. She felt oddly out of place, staring at the maze of traffic, at the throngs of rushing people. She gazed at the tall buildings as if she had never seen them before. She strained to catch the rapidly spoken words of passersby. She bumped into a lamppost and only narrowly escaped the path of a speeding police car. "Taxi!" she shouted, waving her hand. "Taxi!" Wet, tired, she struggled into the back seat; it was several moments before she could remember her office address.

"Good morning, Mrs. Grant," Muriel greeted her brightly. "My, you're soaked to the skin!"

"Don't put any calls through just yet. I want to change clothes."

"Mr. Lanteau is in your office with some men."

"Some men?"

"I don't know who they are. If I may say so, Mr. Lanteau seemed upset."

Frowning, Jobina opened the door. "Emile?" Her glance went to the far end of the room. Emile sat slumped on the couch, his head in his hands. Standing over him were two men, strangers. "Emile, what's wrong?" she asked, her frown deepening.

"A terrible thing, Jobina. A terrible thing."

"Who are you, ma'am?"

"I'm Jobina Grant, the president of this company. Who are you?"

"Ed Walby," the taller of the two men replied, reaching into his pocket for identification. "FBI. This is Agent Boyd."

"FBI?" Jobina blinked, utterly confused. She threw her suitcase down and rushed to Emile. "What in the world is going on? Emile, what is it?" He said nothing, shaking his head from side to side. "Mr. Walby . . . Agent Walby, can *you* tell me what this is all about?"

"It concerns Mr. John Lanteau. Do you know him, Mrs. Grant?"

"Johnny? Of course I do. Has something happened to him?"

"Would you happen to know where he is?"

"No, I wouldn't." Jobina turned to Emile. Her alarm grew, for he was very pale, his hands trembling. "Emile," she said softly, "why are these men interested in Johnny?"

"It is a terrible thing, Jobina. These men, they say . . . they say Johnny is a traitor to America. They say he has been working at the Brooklyn Navy Yard and stealing secrets . . . secrets to give to the *Nazis*," Emile added with a broken cry.

"Oh, my God."

"A traitor, Jobina."

"But it can't be true. Surely there's some mistake," she said, looking at Agent Walby.

"There's no mistake. He's been under surveillance for two months now. We were ready to make an arrest when he disappeared. We have his accomplices in custody, but he's dropped out of sight. You understand how serious this is, Mrs. Grant."

"Yes . . . May I speak privately with Mr. Lanteau?"

The agents glanced at each other. "Five minutes," Agent Boyd replied.

"Thank you." Jobina waited until they left. She turned once more to Emile, taking his hand. "Do you know where Johnny is?" she asked. "You must tell me the truth, Emile."

"I'm not sure. At first I think no. Then I think again. At home I have seen receipts from the messenger company. Inge's name is on them . . . She has been sending money to Johnny. I think it is by mail, but maybe it is by messenger. Maybe Johnny is in a hurry, yes?"

"Did you ask her?"

"The FBI men, they have spoken to her already this morning. She tells them she knows nothing. That is a lie. Jobina . . . I remember the address on the messenger receipts."

She rose, pacing back and forth. She removed her dripping jacket and flung it away. "My God!" she cried. "I can't believe it! Would Johnny do such a thing, Emile? Is it *possible?*"

"He is a Nazi . . . He is born here. Here he has a good

life. But he joins the *Bund* and he is a Nazi."

"Would he actually steal government secrets?"

"The Nazis, they will do anything. They are swine, Jobina. Filthy swine. My friends in Yorkville, they know. They tell the truth."

"I'm afraid you will have to tell the truth too," she replied quietly. "Painful as it is."

"Johnny, he is my firstborn. When the FBI men come, when they say my firstborn is a traitor to America . . ." Emile could not continue. Sobs choked his throat; bitter tears splashed his cheeks. Again and again he pounded his fist on the couch.

Jobina rushed across the room. She sat down beside Emile, taking him into her arms. "I'm so sorry," she said, her tears mingling with his. "I'm so very sorry . . . I want to believe there's a mistake." The door opened then. The agents reentered the office. She looked up, hastily drying her eyes. "Mr. Lanteau has something to tell you."

"Mr. Lanteau?"

A sigh shook Emile's thin shoulders. "At home I have seen receipts from the messenger company," he began.

"Poor Emile," Irene said, her dark eyes filled with concern. "How is he taking it?"

"He was in a very bad way by the time the FBI left," Jobina replied. "I managed to get Helen's telephone number out of him. She came almost immediately. Emile resisted, but in the end she whisked him off to her country house."

"Where is Inge in all of this?"

"I don't know and I don't care. For years Inge's made Emile's life miserable. Now he has a woman who loves him. Not his money, *him*." Jobina went to the fireplace. She picked up the poker and began stirring the flames to golden fury. "Inge is a fool," she said.

"What happens next?" George asked. "Are you expecting more visits from the FBI?"

"There's no reason. Emile told them everything he knew, which wasn't much. He gave them some names he had overheard."

"It's really quite incredible. Nazis right here in America."

"We have the Ku Klux Klan in America," Irene said. "Why not Nazis too? Their philosophies are similar, if one can call such vile ideas philosophies."

"Perhaps it is time *Gotham* did a piece on the whole stinking mess. The trouble is that people aren't interested. They aren't, Irene. Hitler and his thugs are viewed as Europe's problem, not ours."

"Well, our problem or not, I think Jobina has heard enough about Nazis for today. Besides, *I* want to hear about Mark. I certainly want another look at that marvelous diamond. Mark doesn't do things halfway, does he?"

"No." Jobina smiled. "He has great style. And the most wonderful romantic streak, though he denies it."

George sipped his drink. After a moment he looked up at Jobina, a frown creasing his brow. "Does Mark know of today's events?" he asked.

"I called and told him," Jobina replied. "I was so worried that he might somehow be tarred by this,

411

even indirectly."

"What was his reaction?"

"He had a few choice words for Johnny, but otherwise he didn't seem concerned. He said it had nothing to do with me and therefore nothing to do with him . . . As a matter of fact, he was a good deal calmer than I was."

"That's our Mark!" Irene declared. "He always says the right thing and he always does the right thing. He's *perfect.*"

"In case you haven't guessed, Irene is the honorary president of the Mark Campbell fan club."

"Not anymore, love. The honor is Jobina's now. Come show me your ring again, Jobina. And you must tell us all about your weekend at Doe Hill. I'm dying to hear."

"I wouldn't know where to begin."

"With your engagement, of course. Were you surprised?"

"Astonished." Jobina smiled, sitting down next to Irene. "It was Sunday and we were in the gazebo."

"The gazebo! How charming! What happened then?"

"Mark took a little velvet box from his pocket. I don't remember what I thought. My head was spinning. Everything was a blur. Really, I felt faint."

"Sounds rather like flu," George said.

Irene glanced at him, her eyes twinkling. "Pay no attention, Jobina." She laughed. "George is in one of his droll moods tonight. It's the excitement . . . Tell me how Mark proposed."

"He didn't, not exactly. He said we would be married, perhaps sooner than we knew. He was sweet about it. He said lovely things. But there wasn't a formal proposal.

There couldn't be, Irene, considering the circumstances."

"You can change the circumtances," George suggested.

"I've thought about it. To be honest, I've thought about little else. There are problems, George. I could sell my half of the company easily enough. Heaven knows I've had offers. Where would that leave me? Mark is *so* busy. His time isn't his own. If he isn't at the Pentagon, he's flying around the country inspecting bases and gathering statistics for reports. Where would I fit in? What would I *do?*"

"Other women must be in similar situations, Jobina."

"Yes. They're used to it. It is all they have ever done . . . I had a long talk with an admiral's wife, Anne Meacham. Anne told me there are two kinds of officers' wives . . . those who make a career of promoting their husbands' careers, and those who nag their husbands to resign."

"I have no doubt you could be very helpful to Mark's career."

"In the first place, Mark doesn't want that sort of help. He's done quite well all by himself. In the second place, I'm not sure I'm up to it. Mark has explained what's expected of officers' wives. Getting past the dinner parties and the tea parties and the bridge parties, there are the ceremonial events. Ribbon cuttings and tree plantings and such. Getting past all that, there is the matter of always having to be on guard."

"On guard?"

"Well, on one's best behavior. In Washington, the

wrong word is more than a gaffe. It's a disaster."

"You are exaggerating."

"Not by much, George. Officers' wives aren't so different from politicians' wives. Public comments on any subject other than home and hearth are discouraged. Public comments on controversial subjects are all but forbidden."

"You're forgetting about Mrs. Roosevelt," Irene said.

"Mrs. Roosevelt is showing the world that a woman can love her husband and still have her own interests, her own opinions. That is a genuine achievement. An amazing achievement, when you think about it. But then she's an amazing woman. The rest of us are still expected to walk two paces behind and keep our mouths closed."

"The old ways are the best ways," George replied with a smile.

"More drollery?" Jobina asked. "It's hard to tell."

"I am merely trying to hold up my end of the conversation."

"Trying and failing."

"All right," Irene said. "Enough of that. We are straying from the subject. I want to know how long I shall have to wait for a wedding? Problems and conflicts aside, how long? Our Mark isn't a man to let things drift."

"Certain things are beyond even Mark's control. You're shaking your head, Irene, but it's true. You mustn't worry so. Mark and I *will* be married. I just can't say when. I wish I could. Believe it or not," Jobina laughed, "I'm as anxious for that day to come as you are."

"Oh, I believe it. I have never seen you looking more

radiant. You're actually glowing!"

"Mark deserves all the credit." Jobina touched her ring, turning her hand toward the light. She thought of Mark and a lovely shiver tickled her spine, the back of her neck. "I miss him already," she said softly. "I started missing him the moment I stepped on the train. Does that sound silly?"

"Not a bit. Though I wonder how you will stand these separations."

"Good Lord, Irene," George declared with an exaggerated sigh, "Washington is hardly on the moon. It's only hours away. And it happens to be a very pleasant ride."

"As if that mattered!"

"It helps," Jobina said, shrugging. "I will be *living* on trains, Irene. Mark plans to come to New York whenever he can, but most of the time I will be going there. Washington is a beautiful city and Doe Hill is enchanting. Things could be worse."

"A sensible attitude, Jobina."

"Did I hear correctly? Did you call me sensible? George, I'm overwhelmed."

"Your behavior has taken a sensible turn. Mark's influence, no doubt."

"No doubt." Jobina rose. Smiling, she plucked the glass from George's hand and carried it to the bar. "If the children don't get here soon," she said, "we will all be quite drunk. I wonder what's keeping them."

"Caroline has a poor sense of time. It's rubbed off on Ian. He used to be punctual to the minute."

"But Caroline is an artist," Irene replied. "We can't

expect her to watch the clock. Her thoughts are of an . . . ethereal nature."

"Bah! Even artists have to eat. I suppose dinner will be burned again."

"Don't let Rose hear you say that," Jobina warned, giving George his drink. "You are liable to wind up with pot roast in your lap."

They all laughed and the conversation resumed. More drinks were poured, the last of the canapes devoured. Several times Rose peeked into the living room, her brow wrinkling as she swept back to the kitchen. Jobina glanced often at the clock. When finally the doorbell rang, she jumped to her feet. "I'll get it, Rose," she called, rushing to the hall. Her own frown became a smile when she saw Caroline and Ian holding hands, beaming at each other. "We were beginning to worry," she said.

"I'm sorry, Mama. It's my fault we're late. Is dinner ruined?"

"Let me take your things and then we'll see . . . Caroline, you look different tonight. You too, Ian." Jobina paused, studying their flushed and happy faces, their eyes brimming with excitement. "Heavens, you're both shining like Christmas trees!"

"It isn't every day you get engaged, Mom," Ian said, kissing her cheek. "We're celebrating."

"You're certainly celebrating something. Well, come inside. We'll figure it out together . . . You have time for only a very quick drink. If Rose has to hold dinner any longer, she'll be wild."

"Is she grumbling?"

"You know Rose . . . Look who's here at last," Jobina said, returning to the living room. "I suspect they have an excellent excuse."

"Is that true?" George asked. He stood, glancing from his son to his daughter-in-law. "I must say you make the wait worthwhile, Caroline. You're lovely tonight, my dear."

"Thank you, Uncle George. I have a new dress."

His reply was interrupted by Rose. She strode briskly into the room, stopping halfway between the bar and the couch. "Two hours late," she announced, her hands on her hips. "Do you know what two hours late does to a roast? Turns it to shoe leather, that's what."

"Tasty shoe leather, I'm sure." Ian smiled. "Does everyone have a drink? Everyone but Rose."

"I'm teetotal, Mr. Ian."

"Not tonight." He poured sherry into a small glass and gave it to her. "I insist," he said. "This is a special occasion. Albert will forgive you."

"Albert's stubborn, he is. And my roast's shriveling up in the kitchen."

"I will buy you a whole cow, Rose. I promise." Ian joined Caroline, taking her hand in his. "Tell them, honey," he urged.

"This really should be Mama's night," Caroline began. She looked at Ian. A moment passed and still she looked at him, clinging to his arm. "But . . . But we have a surprise too. It's the most wonderful surprise . . . We're going to have a *baby*," she cried. "A *baby*."

Caroline said nothing more, for suddenly she was surrounded. She was kissed and patted and hugged, encircled by one pair of arms after another. She was led to a chair, a pillow slipped behind her back, a stool beneath her feet. She was the blushing, smiling center of attention and her radiance seemed to fill the room. "I think you're forgetting Ian," she said some moments later, shyly lifting her eyes to her husband.

Now Ian, too, was kissed and hugged, his back pounded. "Congratulations, son," George said. "You don't know how long we have been looking forward to this day."

"Are you ready to be a grandfather?"

"Ready and eager." George drew Irene to his side, draping his arm about her shoulder. "You've made us very happy," he said. "When your mother stops crying, she will tell you so herself. Women and their tears," he added, though his own eyes were misty.

"Are you happy, Mama?" Caroline asked.

"Happy isn't the word, darling. I'm in the clouds . . . Do I see a tiny frown? You aren't frightened, are you?"

"Oh no, Mama. Well, I was, sort of. But I had a wonderful talk with Dr. Porterfield. I'm not frightened anymore."

"What then?"

"I was wondering about something. Did you really keep all my old toys?"

"Not all. There were so many . . . I know what you want!" Jobina cried, her head bobbing up and down. "When you were a little girl you had an enormous teddy bear. You two were inseparable. And now you want him for your baby."

"Ian was talking about the nursery. I remembered Ralph."

"Ralph? Was his name Ralph? I never knew."

"It was a secret."

Caroline and her secrets, thought Jobina. She turned, looking at Rose. "We still have Ralph," she said. "I'm certain we do."

"Yes, mum," Rose replied. "The big stuffed bear with the falling off arm. The storage closet was getting full, so I moved him to Miss Caroline's old closet. He's still there, he is. And wrapped in that tablecloth you told me to throw away. It keeps the dust from settling in."

"Shall we go see?" Jobina asked, holding out her hand to Caroline. "We'll have a reunion!"

"Mama, I just wanted to say . . ."

"What, darling?"

"I just wanted to say I love you, Mama. My baby will be so lucky to have you."

Tears glittered in Jobina's eyes. "Come, darling," she said. "We'll go see Ralph."

Once again time seemed to pass very quickly and Jobina often thought there were not enough hours in the day. She rushed everywhere—to her office, to the stores to shop for baby clothes, to holiday gatherings, to Grand Central Terminal and the southbound train. She explored Washington with Mark; on his arm she attended endless rounds of receptions and dinner parties, laughing about them afterward as the car drove back to

Doe Hill. Mark planned to come to New York for Thanksgiving, but those plans were canceled at the last minute. "Orders," he said. "I promise I will make it up to you."

Jobina hid her disappointment, joking about the Army and its uncertainties. Her real thoughts she kept to herself and, cheerfully, she looked ahead to Christmas. Each day she brought armloads of presents home; each night, after Mark's phone call, she wrapped them, placing the beribboned packages under the tree. "You've bought out the stores!" Rose exclaimed, observing the growing accumulation, and it was almost true. As Christmas drew nearer, presents were heaped high around the tree, around the hearth, atop the mantel strewn with holly. There were wreaths in all the windows and poinsettia plants on all the sills. Tiny silver bells were strung through branches of white birch. Mistletoe was strung in the doorway and crowned by a flowing red velvet bow.

Family and friends began arriving early on Christmas Eve. Jobina was at the door to welcome them, her smile widening as she called holiday greetings. Last to arrive was Mark. She heard his voice, saw his eyes sparkling above the mountain of presents he carried, and she rushed to him. "Darling, you're here," she cried. "You *are* here? I'm not dreaming?"

"I'm here somewhere," he laughed, dropping his packages to the floor. "Does Santa get a kiss?"

Jobina flew into his arms. "Oh, Mark," she murmured. "Oh, Mark."

"Merry Christmas, Jo."

"Our first Christmas together."

"With so many more to come . . . I love you."

"I love you, my darling."

Jobina clasped his hand, guiding him through the sea of guests. Introductions were made, congratulations offered. George offered a formal toast to their engagement and Caroline added a few words of her own. Dinner was served then, a traditional dinner of roast goose and chestnut dressing. At midnight the presents were opened. Amongst her presents Jobina found matching gold wedding bands; the card read: *Sooner than we know.* "We'll find a way," Mark whispered into her ear. "I promise we will."

Mark and Jobina celebrated New Year's alone at Doe Hill. They spent the afternoon riding through the woods, the evening curled in each other's arms before a roaring fire. Later they took champagne and glasses to the stream, toasting 1939 as all around them stars shone and night birds sang. The moon dipped low. The wind ruffled the trees. "Mark," Jobina murmured. "My darling."

It was difficult for Jobina to leave Doe Hill, more difficult than it had been in the past. She cried during the trip to Union Station. She had to force herself to board the train and, once settled in her seat, she cried all the way home. I'm tired, she thought, trying to make sense of tears that would not stop. "I'm tired," she said to Emile when he questioned her red-rimmed eyes.

"I know why," he replied. "You are doing too much. Running here and there. Worrying all the time. It is too much."

"I don't see any choice, Emile. I want to be with Mark. That means I must travel back and forth."

"But *here* you could make things easier. I watch how things are, Jobina. Always you are reading every report, every letter. Our company, it is big now. So many important decisions you figure out. The other decisions, not so important, other people could figure out instead. We have executives, yes? Fancy-pants titles they have. And fancy-pants salaries they are not earning because you are doing their work."

"I enjoy the work I do."

"It is too much," Emile said again. He glanced at the stacks of papers crowding Jobina's desk. Sadly, he shook his head. "Today you will be here very late. Tomorrow also. Tomorrow and tomorrow until it is time to run for the train."

"Heavens!" Jobina laughed. "Am I really that busy?"

"You are joking, but I am serious."

"I'm sorry, Emile. I appreciate your concern. It's just that I'm used to working hard."

"From your hard work comes our whole company. But life changes, yes? Now there is Mark in your life. You need more time for yourself."

Jobina looked down at her desk. She saw the stacks of file folders, the waiting correspondence, the lists of telephone calls that had to be returned. Her appointment calendar was full, meetings scheduled every thirty minutes. Her memo pad was covered with hastily scribbled notations. "Yes." She sighed. "You may be right."

"You will think about what I said, Jobina?"

"I promise. A little more time for myself sounds awfully nice. It sounds *luxurious*."

"That is the least you deserve."

Jobina smiled, leaning back in her chair. "I'm glad we had this talk," she said. "I was starting to feel pressured. So many things to do and never enough time. I'm afraid my concentration isn't what it used to be. *I'm* here, but all too often my *mind* is at Doe Hill. Not a very efficient way to run a company."

"You don't have to run it alone, Jobina. Let our fancy-pants executives earn their pay. I see them in their offices. I see how they are. A few calls, a few reports, and *voilà*, their day is done. It is different for you. Always you are staying late. Your briefcase, it is bulging with work you take home afterward. That's wrong. You agree that's wrong?"

"I must give some thought to reorganizing things around here."

"When?"

"Soon, Emile."

"When is soon?"

"Tonight," Jobina replied. "Tonight I will give the matter serious thought."

"Thought is good, but then you must spread out the work. Fred Warner, he is an example. All day he sits and sits, doing nothing. For this he gets a fat paycheck. Also a fat *derriere*."

"Poor Fred. He has been dieting for years."

"Work is the best diet. Give him work to do. Give them all work, Staley and Bateson and the rest. We will see if they can, how you say, cut the ketchup."

"Mustard." She smiled. "Cut the mustard. And I'm certain they can. But first they must have the chance."

Jobina had never doubted the ability of her department heads, for they were a talented group, a mixture of eager young men who had worked their way up and older, more seasoned men who had been lured from other companies. She had encouraged their ideas, though not their independence. "I've guarded my position too carefully," she explained. "Perhaps it's time to let the barriers fall."

"When?"

"Soon. I promise."

A staff meeting was called late in February. The heads of all eleven departments filed into the conference room, casting nervous glances at one another as they took their places around the table. Chairs scraped and papers rustled. Curls of gray smoke rose from the ashtrays, wreathing the charts that had been turned to the wall. It was exactly nine o'clock when Jobina entered the room. "Please sit down," she said. "I see a lot of worried faces. There's no need. I have a few announcements . . . I believe you will be pleased," she added, looking at her notes. "The first announcement concerns our perfumes. In the spring we plan to introduce two new fragrance lines, Jasmine and Wild Lilac. At the same time we plan to create a separate perfume division within the company. This division will be Lanteau Inc. and will be headed by our new executive vice president, Fred Warner." Jobina paused, for there were several startled gasps. She smiled, waiting until the room quieted. "Congratulations, Fred. It's a challenge, but I know you're up to it."

"I asked for you, Fred," Emile said. "With me, you will have your hands full. No more long lunches at fancy-pants restaurants. Hard work, yes?"

"Yes, sir," Fred Warner replied amidst much laughter. "I'm ready."

"We all have hard work ahead of us," Jobina went on. "Our company has grown very quickly. The time has come to reorganize. With that in mind, we plan a total of three new divisions and three new executive vice presidents. Fred, of course, will head Perfume. Skin Care will be headed by Paul Bateson. Cosmetics will be headed by Hank Staley. Congratulations, gentlemen." Once again she waited for the room to quiet. She looked at Emile, smiling. "Well, it's done," she said.

"You will be glad."

"I hope so." Jobina turned back to the table. "If I may have your attention . . . Thank you. Muriel has prepared charts to illustrate the new system, but before we see them, I would like to say that things are going to change for all of us. In the past, Emile and I made virtually every decision affecting the company, whether those decisions were large or small. We will continue to make policy decisions, but each of you is going to have far more latitude within your departments and far more authority. There are guidelines. During the next two weeks, Jack Sisk will be visiting your departments to explain. As always, your ideas will be welcomed."

"You aren't leaving the company, Jobina?" Hank Staley asked.

"Heavens, no! Whatever rumors you might hear, I am *not* leaving the company and the company is *not* going public. This reorganization is an efficiency measure. Emile will continue to oversee the lab and the creative process. I will continue to oversee the business end, which includes long-range planning. I will be thinking less about day-to-day details and more about where we go from here. At least that is the way it's supposed to work out. Time will tell, won't it?"

"Maybe we should show the charts," Emile suggested.

"Yes, by all means. Muriel? We're ready for the unveiling now . . . Everybody have a look. It's really quite a simple system. Go on," Jobina laughed "have a look. There are no nasty surprises." There were questions however, scores of questions. The meeting lasted through the morning and when finally it ended, the three new vice presidents stayed to discuss their new roles in the company. "I think that's enough for today," she said an hour later. "I'm just about talked out."

"I feel the same," Emile agreed. He stood, walking swiftly across the room and opening the door. "So now it is back to work. Working is better than talking. You want to get a good start."

"It's been a good—"

"That is more talking, Fred," Emile interrupted. "Working is better than talking."

"Yes, sir. We're going."

"Emile!" Jobina cried when the three had gone. "You practically threw them out!"

"I was watching. This meeting, it was hard on you."

"Oh, I suppose it was. Giving away bits and pieces of the company is like giving away bits and pieces of myself."

"But it is not giving away. It is to help you, Jobina. What helps you helps the company."

"I wish I could say I did it for the company . . . I did

426

it so I could take Fridays off without feeling guilty. So I could have my weekends free and clear . . . I did it for Mark."

"That is the best reason. Love, yes? Love is always the best reason."

"*Love* is very complicated, Emile."

"You are not sorry?"

"Not at all. Look at me. My face is smiling."

Emile followed Jobina into the corridor. He walked slowly, glancing at the long line of offices, at the vaulted reception room emblazoned with scarlet butterflies. "All this we built from Mr. Greevy's basement," he said. "Every day I am grateful. But there is more to life, yes?"

"What's troubling you, Emile? Why isn't your face smiling."

"I am remembering our beginning. Such excitement I had. The first day I come here to peek into the offices . . . They are empty, but I can see my sons sitting at the desks. In my head, I can see them. Father and sons working here together. That was my dream."

"Emile, you've heard something about Johnny. What's happened?"

"The FBI men, they call me. They say Johnny is gone. They say he goes to Lisbon and from there to Germany. To his Nazi swine."

"Oh, Emile." Jobina sighed, reaching for his hand. "How terrible. I'm very sorry."

"My dream, it is over. Your dream you must make come true. Love, Jobina. With love you will find the way."

Chapter Nineteen

"Jo is an extraordinary woman," Mark said to George one warm spring evening at Doe Hill. "She never complains."

"Complains?"

"We're in a difficult situation. She's had to make sacrifices. Christ, she's turned her life upside down. She deserves more than the weekends we manage to steal. A lot more."

"I agree the situation is far from ideal, but Jobina has obviously accepted it. Why, she seems to radiate happiness."

Mark finished his drink. He strode to the edge of the veranda, gazing past the lush flower beds to the wide, green lawns. "She seems to, most of the time. There are other times, George. When she's packing to return to New York ... When she's overheard some spiteful comment about the *length* of our engagement. I've seen the pain in her eyes. She tries to hide it, but I know her too well."

"You both knew there would be problems."

"I'm used to solving problems, not causing them. I've drawn Jo into a kind of limbo. We're together, yet apart. Even when we are together there are complications. Jo arrived here last weekend just as the Pentagon was calling. An hour later I was in a meeting, a meeting that took the whole day . . . Sometimes I think about throwing it all over."

"Not you, Mark. This is the life for you."

"It's not the life for Jo."

"Perhaps you underestimate her."

"Meaning?"

"She is adaptable. She has had to be. Once, long ago, I thought her life was ruined. Certainly it was in pieces. I held out very little hope. I was wrong. She picked up all the pieces and went on. Look what she accomplished. Good Lord, it's a bloody miracle!"

"I can't ask her to walk away from that miracle."

"You can. And I believe she would do it, if you asked. But why should you?"

"Certain things are expected of generals' wives. There are certain unofficial duties."

George smiled. "You military men tend to think in absolutes," he said. "The rest of us have learned the value of an occasional compromise. I'm not saying Jobina would be a model wife. I'm saying she would do her part and somehow make time to run her company also. She is capable of that."

"I know."

"Well then?"

"There's more to it, George. I don't know where I'll be a year from now, a month from now. You're a publisher.

You're aware of what's going on in Europe."

"I am. So is Jobina, though it is a subject she refuses to discuss. We're all aware, Mark. I grant you the possibilities are ugly. We find comfort where we can. I have noticed that women often find comfort in marriage."

"An interesting observation."

"I'm afraid it's only an observation. I don't pretend to understand women, least of all Jobina. Still, I feel she would be happiest as your wife, no matter the circumstances. You wanted my opinion and there it is."

Mark turned, an amused twinkle lighting his eyes. "Did I want your opinion, George?"

"I'm on to you, my friend. All your roundabout musings had a purpose. It is true I'm not half the chess player you are, but I'm not bad."

"Am I losing my touch?" Mark asked with a laugh. "You used to be easy pickings."

"Well, I have to admit I was expecting something like this. I know that the situation, as you put it, has been on your mind."

"Day and night. I don't want Jo hurt."

"She doesn't need your protection, Mark. She needs you."

"Who needs Mark now?" Jobina called, gliding onto the veranda. "It must be exhausting to be so much in demand. Is it, darling?"

"I manage to bear up under the strain."

"How brave." Jobina smiled. "And how handsome you look tonight." She felt his arms wrap around her, his lips brush the top of her head. Very softly she murmured a few words. He nodded and then they were silent, staring at each other through the deepening twilight.

"Aren't they adorable, George?" Irene whispered.

"Adorable. But it's getting late."

"No, you mustn't disturb them."

George turned quickly, following Irene's gaze to Mark and Jobina. They were indeed a splendid sight—he in his dress uniform, medals glittering on his chest, she in pale blue silk and pearls. The breeze lifted her hair, blowing it about her luminous face. Her eyes were pools of shimmering amber. "I see what you mean, Irene . . . But it *is* getting late. We can't be late to the White House."

"Oh, I suppose not."

"Mark," George said. "It's past six."

"Past six?"

"I should have brought a bugle." George sighed, throwing up his hands. "Past six *o'clock,* Mark. Eighteen-hundred hours, or however you tell time in the Army."

"We have to be going, Bean."

"I'm ready . . . As a matter of fact, I can't wait! My first visit to the White House! I hope I don't disgrace you."

"Never."

"Come along, you two. This reception is for the Society of Magazine Publishers and *I* don't intend to disgrace my colleagues by arriving late."

"All right, George, we're coming." Mark glanced over his shoulder toward the driveway. "Noah's brought the car around. We'll get the show on the road."

"At last."

"Is he always so jumpy, Irene?"

"I confess I'm a little jumpy myself." She laughed. "It is the *White House* after all."

Jobina's heart was pounding as the car passed through the White House gates. "I can't believe I'm here," she cried, clutching Mark's arm. "Of course you've been here before."

"When they need an extra man. Be glad this isn't a State dinner. You would be sitting through twelve courses . . . Publishers," he added, nodding at George, "rate only cocktails and *hors d'oeuvres*."

"What do generals rate?"

"We're a humble lot. We settle for anything."

"Humble!" George exclaimed. "That will be the day!"

There was laughter but nothing more was said, for ushers were rushing forward to open car doors. The guests were whisked inside; almost in the next moment, or so it seemed, they found themselves in the elegant, historic Red Room. "It's beautiful," Jobina whispered. "Irene, isn't it beautiful?"

"I'm quite overwhelmed."

"Yes, that's the word."

Jobina gazed around the room. There were perhaps seventy guests—publishers and their wives, senators, a few Washington hostesses, a few of the Pentagon elite. Ushers stood by, ready to answer questions, to provide assistance of any kind. Gloved stewards served drinks and canapes on gleaming silver trays. Conversation was hushed at first, though after a while voices began to rise and laughter was heard. "It's just another party," Mark said. "Have a good time."

Much to Jobina's surprise, she had a wonderful time. She wandered about, memorizing every tiny detail of the room. She mingled easily with the other guests, listening to their stories and to harmless bits of gossip. Beaming, she chatted with Mrs. Roosevelt. "What a nice woman," she said when the President's wife had moved on.

"She's lovely," Irene agreed. "Simply lovely. So gracious too. I was . . . What's wrong?" she asked, seeing Jobina's sudden frown.

"We're in for it now."

"In for it?"

"The woman coming toward us isn't nice at *all*. That's Maud Burleigh. She's a witch . . . And it's too late. She's seen us . . . Hello, Maud. Maud Burleigh, Irene Thayer."

"How do you do, Mrs. Thayer? You're new to Washington."

"My husband and I are visiting from New York."

"New York! You must think us awfully provincial here. Perhaps I can change your mind. Where are you staying?"

"General Campbell is an old friend. He has—"

"Then you're staying at Doe Hill with Mark and Jobina. I rather imagined you and Jobina were friends. You had that chummy look. We worry about Jobina, you know. The perpetual fiancée and all that. Fun is fun, but really we must think what's best for the dear girl."

Irene's lips parted. She glanced at Jobina, then turned her eyes back to Maud. "I don't know who you are, Mrs. Burleigh," she said, her voice icy, "but it's obvious you have had too much to drink. If you will excuse us."

"I beg your pardon?" Maud cried so loudly that heads turned. "Too much to drink?"

"If you will excuse us—"

"I most certainly will *not* excuse you."

"Irene," Jobina murmured, "please let's walk away. Right now. Please." She was starting away when she felt a hand on her arm. Warily, she looked up. "Mark. Mark, I'm very sorry. Maud isn't feeling well."

"Maud is drunk."

"How dare . . ." Maud's protest was silenced by the look in Mark's eyes. She flinched, as if from a blow. She fumbled for her handkerchief, then pressed it to her pale mouth. "I skipped lunch today," she said. "Silly of me."

"Your car is waiting, Maud."

"Yes, that's how it's done."

"Shall I ask Robert to show you out?"

"I'll find my way. Give me a moment, Mark. I don't want to leave while people are looking."

"I'm sure you can stay, if you behave yourself, though no one is going to speak to you. You've put your foot in it this time, Maudie. I can hear the doors slamming all over town."

"Boyd will be home in two days. He'll set things straight. He always does."

"Not this time. Mrs. Roosevelt wasn't amused."

"I see."

"Come ladies," Mark said, taking Jobina's arm and then Irene's. "There is a very funny congressman from Ohio I want you to meet. He hasn't been in Washington too long. He still has his sense of humor."

"You wouldn't leave me standing here alone?"

Mark bowed slightly. "Good evening, Maud." He smiled. "Ladies, shall we?"

They had walked halfway across the room when Jobina stopped. For one terrible instant she thought she was going to cry. The room blurred and she put her hand to her head. She felt tired, utterly drained. "All the excitement has caught up with me," she said.

"Do you want to go home, darling? I think you do. Irene, will you look after Jo while I say our good-byes? Where's George?"

"Making his way through the crowd. Don't worry, we will be right here when you're ready." Irene plucked a glass from the tray of a passing steward. "Have a sip, Jobina," she urged. "It will kill the taste of that dreadful woman. Look at her slinking off."

"I've seen enough."

"Yes. I must say you handled the situation well. Such restraint! You kept your wits and your dignity. Really, I give you credit."

"Stop trying so hard, Irene. There is no bright side to this. I don't like being insulted, but what I like even less—what I *hate*—is that Mark had to be involved. I hate to put him in that position. I can just imagine the talk at the Pentagon tomorrow."

"Mark is a big boy. He can take care of himself. And I'm certain the fellows at the Pentagon have more important things to talk about."

"You don't know Washington. The time I've spent here has taught me that *every*body talks about *every*thing. Appearances count for a lot in this city."

"In New York also."

"It isn't the same . . . I'm the newcomer here, Irene. I'm trying to prove myself, to fit in. If I'm a liability to Mark—"

"Liability! But that's nonsense, Jobina. I am beginning to see the problem. You worry too much and so does Mark. You are both so busy worrying about each other that you make matters worse. It's the truth, absurd as it may be. I'm surprised at you. Both of you. Two strong, successful people acting like broody adolescents."

"We're not that bad," Jobina replied, a small smile edging her mouth. "Are we?"

"You must stop this worrying, this *agonizing*. Mark will always prevail. It is his nature. And yours. Neither of you would be where you are otherwise."

Jobina's smile widened, for she had begun to feel better. "What would I do without you, Irene? You have a way of putting my problems in perspective. You have the gift."

"The gift?" George asked, joining them.

"I was paying your wife a compliment. I needed a pep talk and she obliged."

"I see. Tell me, what was all that shouting a while ago?"

"Cocktail party foolishness," Irene said. "It will be forgotten by morning."

"Hardly the place for foolishness."

"Don't be stuffy, love. These things happen, even at the White House. I'm sure they happen even at Buckingham Palace."

"Remind me not to take you to Buckingham Palace."

"Oh, George, you're grumbling because you're

hungry. It's all right. Here is Mark now. We can drive back to Doe Hill and have one of Ivy's marvelous dinners. My mouth is watering already . . . Are we on our way, Mark?"

"On our way. Mrs. Roosevelt thought you were charming, Bean. She told me so before she left. I agreed, of course."

"Did you?"

"With great enthusiasm."

"You two are getting that look again," George said. "That look means we will be standing here forever. And *that* means we will be stuck with Greg Marley and his wife. I have been avoiding Marley all night. Good Lord, he's the biggest bore in the Society. Let's go while we can."

"We might as well. Cars will be lining up for blocks. Ready, Bean?" Mark asked, offering his arm.

"Ready."

The Maud Burleigh incident was not mentioned during the ride home. Mark steered the conversation in other directions, regaling them all with anecdotes about the White House aides they had met. His voice was light and if once or twice he peered anxiously at Jobina, no one seemed to notice. Jobina herself said very little. She was relieved when the car reached Doe Hill, and she turned her head to the comforting sounds of crickets and tree toads and birds. Home, she thought. Home at last.

"There's a message for you, Miz Grant," Ivy said at the door. "You're supposed to call New York. I have the number here."

"Who is it, Bean?"

She shrugged, studying the paper Ivy had given her. "I don't know. I had better find out. Why don't you open the wine, darling? I won't be long."

"Promise?"

"Word of honor."

"For goodness sake, Mark," Irene said with a laugh, "you needn't look so glum. She's gone to the library, not the moon."

"Glum? I'm never glum."

"I told Jobina to stop worrying about you. Now I'm telling *you* to stop worrying about her. Stop treating each other as if you were made of cake. *Steel* is more like it. Cheer up! That's an order!" Irene said, laughing again.

"Yes, ma'am."

"Come, we will open the wine and then we will have our dinner."

"I have a nice Bordeaux. A '32. You're the wine expert, George. You can tell me if it's something special or if . . . Jo, what's the matter?" Mark called, for Jobina was running through the hall, her pearls swinging back and forth, her hair flying about her flushed face. "What's happened?"

"It's wonderful!" she cried. "It's wonderful!" She threw her arms around Mark, whirling away to throw her arms around Irene. "We're grandmothers! *Grandmothers*. And you haven't heard the best part. Caroline had twins, a boy and a girl. *Twins*," she repeated, seeing the astonishment in Irene's eyes. "Caroline is fine. The babies are fine. Ian is ecstatic . . . Oh, I almost forgot. Ian is on the telephone. He wants to talk to you. And to you, George. George, you're a *grandfather*."

They all rushed to the library. There, amidst the cozy scents of wood and lemon oil and leather, they savored the happy news. Irene and George put the phone between them, listening to the excited burst of words from the other end. Tears splashed Irene's cheeks. George, though dry eyed, had to clear his throat again and again. "Yes, son," he said. "Yes . . . Mother and I are delighted . . . We will . . . That's right. The first train tomorrow. Don't hang up yet. Jobina wants to say something else. Jobina?"

"Are you there, Ian? Tell Caroline I love her. Mark and I send our love to you both . . . Yes . . . Yes, the first train. Good night, dear." Jobina replaced the receiver. She turned, running into Mark's outstretched arms. "Isn't it wonderful?"

"Congratulations, darling."

"I can't wait to see them. What is the earliest train in the morning?"

"The train is too slow. A friend of mine owns an air service. I'll have a plane fueled and ready for takeoff at seven A.M. All right?"

"Perfect."

"You're perfect, Bean. Or should I say Grandma Bean?"

"Say it again. I love the sound."

Caroline was sitting up in bed, her long golden hair spilling over the pillows propped behind her back. She looked tired but quite lovely, for her face glowed and her wide blue eyes danced with light. She wore a lacy bed jacket with blue satin ribbons tracing the ruffled sleeves. On her hand she wore a dazzling sapphire surrounded by diamonds, a gift from Ian. Flowers were everywhere— roses and daffodils and purple iris and great baskets of camellias. Presents had begun to arrive. Boxes from Tiffany and Cartier sat upon the sills; the chairs were heaped with teddy bears and dolls and two large, lop-eared plush rabbits. "Emile sent the rabbits, Mama," Caroline said now. "He sent an absolutely *huge* check too."

"That's Emile."

"We're raking in the cash." Ian laughed. "I've never seen anything like it."

"Well, twins don't come along every day. And such beautiful twins! I had to be dragged away from the nursery window. All the babies are sweet, but yours are *beautiful*."

"You wouldn't be prejudiced, Mom?"

"Of course I would. It's my right as a grandmother."

"They cry a lot."

"They're supposed to, darling. You will get used to it."

"Aunt Irene said the same thing. I'm glad we'll have Miss Cullen. She's the baby nurse we hired. I hope one nurse will be enough."

Ian shook his dark head, beaming at Caroline. "I work for a living, kiddo." He laughed again. "Until I become a full partner at Brown & Company, one nurse will be *more* than enough. Anyway, we have only so much room. If we got a second nurse, we'd have to hang her from the ceiling."

"Perhaps we should move."

"What a chore that would be! Move with two babies, two cats, a dog, and all your thousands of dresses? We'd need a caravan. Tell her, Mom."

"Oh no," Jobina replied, smiling. "Leave me out of it."

Ian bent over the bed, gently kissing Caroline's cheek. "I want a few words with Mother and Dad," he said. "If I can unglue them from the nursery. Okay?"

"You won't be too long?"

"Not a chance."

Caroline clung to Ian's hand. They whispered to each other and she blushed. She was still blushing as Ian strode into the corridor. "He's so happy, Mama."

"Are you happy, darling? How do you feel?"

"I'm fine now . . . But it wasn't easy. I understand why it's called labor. I screamed and screamed. I even cursed."

Jobina hid her smile behind her hand. "Did you?"

"The pain was horrible. It went on for hours. Finally Dr. Porterfield put a kind of mask over my nose and I went to sleep. When I woke up the nurses brought the babies. Everything was all right then. They *are* beautiful, aren't they, Mama?"

"Exquisite."

"I couldn't believe there were *two*. They were so little. I was afraid. But when I held them, I wasn't afraid anymore . . . It was the strangest feeling. It was as if my heart just filled with love. Ian felt that way also . . . I want us to be good parents, Mama. *Perfect* parents."

"There's no such thing, darling. You will make your share of mistakes. We all do. Love is what counts. And

442

patience," Jobina added, clasping Caroline's hand.

"You were very patient with me."

"Not always. There were times you drove me crazy. At times your little ones will drive *you* crazy. That's how it works. Headaches, heartaches. Worries. But it's worth it. It's worth anything, because there's such joy. You felt it the first time you held your babies. You will feel it every day of your life . . . Darling, you mustn't cry."

"Happy tears," Caroline said, brushing at her eyes. "My life could have been different. It could have been . . . Have you seen the newspaper, Mama?"

"Did your babies make the headlines?"

"We should put an announcement in the *Times*, but that's not what I'm talking about."

"What then?"

Caroline reached across the bed to the nightstand. She picked up the newspaper and gave it to her mother. "This."

Jobina read the headline aloud: "'Beverly Hills Realtor Slain By Movie Star's Husband.' I don't understand," she said.

"The realtor is . . . was Teddy Hamilton. Do you remember him?"

"No, I don't think I . . . My God, Teddy Hamilton!" Now Jobina opened the paper, scanning the lurid story, the photographs of Teddy and his lover, the movie star Polly Mitchell. The last photograph brought a gasp, for it showed Teddy lying dead in the parking lot of Romanoff's, shot by Polly Mitchell's enraged husband. "My God! Emile always said . . ."

"What did Emile say, Mama?"

"It isn't important. Emile didn't care much for Teddy."

"You didn't either."

"Oh, it was so long ago." Jobina returned the paper to the nightstand. She sighed. "I didn't think Teddy was a very nice person. He certainly didn't come to a very nice end."

"A predictable end, Mama? I've heard things about Teddy over the years. I've heard that when he was living in New York he was a . . . a kind of gigolo. That his family had disowned him . . . No one seemed to know where he got the money to go to California. He must have had a stake. When his movie career flopped, he had enough money to start buying real estate."

"The Depression was on. Real estate was cheap."

"Did you give him the money?"

"Caroline, he couldn't possibly matter to you anymore."

"He doesn't. I don't think he ever did."

"Then why all these questions?"

"For months and months," she replied slowly, "I've been wondering about what it means to be a parent. The responsibilities, Mama. Today, after I saw the newspaper, I remembered a lot of things. Did you give him the money? If you did, you saved me and I want to say thank you."

Relief was clear in Jobina's eyes. She laughed, shaking her head from side to side. "You are full of surprises," she said. "I never know what to expect . . . Yes, I gave Teddy some money. I honestly can't recall the amount. I was convinced he was wrong for you, darling. So profoundly wrong that I gave him the money to go away." She paused. There was more to the story, of course, but nothing more she intended to reveal, now or in the future. "You were a young sixteen. I did what I thought was best."

"You were right, Mama. I hope I'll know the right things to do for my children. Will I?"

"I haven't the slightest doubt. It gets harder as children get older, but you and Ian will sense what's right. You're worrying too much, Caroline. Just enjoy your children. Love them, and let them love you."

Caroline was smiling, her gaze fast on Jobina. "You think I'm standoffish, don't you, Mama?"

"Well, perhaps a bit reserved. Ian is changing that. You're a happier person now, darling. You're able to share your love."

"Did I tell you we've chosen names for the babies? Sam, after Ian's grandfather, and Daisy."

"Another Daisy," Jobina said quietly. "It will be wonderful having another Daisy."

"Are you pleased, Mama?"

"Very pleased. I'm touched." Jobina turned as the door opened. "I hope you haven't come to chase me out," she said to the nurse. "Not so soon."

"It's nursery hour, Mrs. Grant. We're showing the babies. You'll have to hurry if you want a good spot."

"Go ahead, Mama. I don't mind."

A crowd had already gathered around the nursery window—proud parents and grandparents cooing over the tiny bundles in the nurses' arms. Jobina found Irene and George at the center of the crowd, their noses pressed to the glass. "Am I in time?" she asked.

"We should be next," Irene replied. "There are so many babies."

"Where's Ian?"

"He wanted to see the doctor."

"Nothing wrong, Irene?"

"No. You know how new fathers are . . . Oh, here are our babies now. Aren't they *precious?* Look at those tiny little ears. And look at Daisy. She has more hair than Sam. A louder voice too," Irene said laughingly, for Daisy had begun to howl. "That's good. Sam won't be bossing her around . . . Aren't they *precious?*"

Jobina gazed upon the faces of her grandchildren, her heart swelling with love. "Precious," she agreed. "Sam has the Thayer chin, but I think he has your eyes. Daisy is the picture of Caroline."

"I see the resemblance," George said, tapping the glass.

"Won't it be fun, Jobina? We can spoil our grandchildren rotten!"

"I'm looking forward to that. All the fun and none of the responsibility." She leaned closer to the window as the babies were returned to their bassinets. "Sleep well, darlings," she murmured, waving at their tiny forms. "Do you suppose babies have dreams? Probably not."

"Come, let's congratulate the new mother again. She must be in the clouds."

"Yes. I know *I* am."

"More tears, Jobina?" George asked when they had reached the door. "I keep waiting for you to run dry."

Irene frowned. "Hush," she said. "These tears are

different. What's wrong, Jobina?"

"Pay no attention to me. It's just . . . It's just that I wish Mark were here."

"But he's—"

"I know, I know. He's busy. I should be used to it by now. He's *always* busy."

Jobina stood at her bedroom window, watching the sun lighten the sky. It was a cool October morning and she drew her robe close, hunching her shoulders as she crossed the room to the hall. "Rose, you startled me! What are you doing creeping around in the dark?"

"I wasn't creeping, mum. I was coming to get you. You said you wanted an early start."

"You didn't have to get up."

"Coffee's all ready. I'll put the eggs on. Hurry now or you'll catch a chill. Mr. Pedan's being stingy with the heat again. He'll get a piece of my mind, he will. You should have seen me falling over myself, trying to light the fire in the hearth. Half asleep I was. Mr. Pedan will hear from me and that's the truth . . . Sit down, mum. Drink your coffee while it's hot."

"You set two places, Rose."

"For you and the general. He'll be arriving any time."

"I wouldn't count on it."

"He told me seven on the dot. I have corn muffins in the oven. Corn muffins are his favorite."

"I hope they don't go to waste."

"The general will be here, mum. Don't you worry. He wouldn't miss the twins' christening day. He's the godfather, isn't he?"

"One of them. I warned Caroline she might wind up one godfather short."

"Ah, you're in a mood today. You're nervous things won't go right. It's only natural, a christening and all. But the general told me seven on the dot and seven it will be. He'll be walking through the door at any time, mark my words."

Jobina sipped her coffee. She turned her head to the fire, staring at the crackling reds and golds and oranges. "I hope so," she said quietly. "You know how busy he is."

"Not too busy for a christening, mum."

"We shall see."

With a sigh, Rose disappeared into the kitchen. Jobina put her cup down and bowed her head over her hands. She thought: The phone is going to ring and it will be Mark saying he can't come after all. He'll have a good reason, but the result will be the same. It's always the same. Oh Mark, not this time. Please not this time.

"Jo?"

She looked up. *"Mark!"* she cried.

"Surprised?"

"I was just . . . Mark, you're really *here*." Jobina sprang from her chair, toppling cups and glasses and bowls as she rushed to him. "Darling, I'm so happy," she said. "I'm ashamed of myself. I was thinking awful thoughts. I was sure the telephone was going to ring."

"Poor Bean. You must hate the telephone."

"I do." She laughed, flinging her arms about Mark's

neck. "But I love you."

"How much?"

"Very, very, *very* much."

"Enough to marry me?"

Jobina's arms fell away. She took a step and then another. Quite suddenly she stopped, gazing at Mark. "Don't tease, darling," she murmured. "I can't joke about—"

"I'm not joking."

"But—"

"I love you, Jobina Grant. I want you to marry me. Today, this morning. I've made all the arrangements. We can drive to Connecticut and be back in time for the christening. I plan to make an honest woman of Grandma, if Grandma is willing."

"*If?*"

"I haven't heard the magic word. I haven't heard a yes."

Jobina's smile was radiant, her face glowing with color and light. "Yes. *Yes,*" she cried, running into Mark's open arms. She felt his lips on hers and it was many moments before she could speak. "Is it real, darling? Is this really happening?"

"It's our wedding day, Jo." Mark turned, hearing a loud cheer from the direction of the kitchen. "That makes it official," he said with a hearty laugh.

"But all the problems."

"To hell with all the problems. We'll do our best and if the Army doesn't like it, to hell with the Army."

"Mark, I'm going to cry."

"No time for that. I have a car downstairs. George and Irene are in it. I woke them at the crack of dawn. They'll be our witnesses. It seemed fitting."

"You're so sweet."

"No time for that either. Unless you want to be married in your bathrobe. Hurry and dress, Bean. Everything else has been taken care of . . . Hurry. And remember to bring the rings."

"Yes, *mon général.*"

Mark and Jobina were married in a small country church near Weston. They gazed at each other throughout the ceremony, hardly hearing the ancient words, making their responses in dazed whispers. When the Reverend Perkins, a former Army chaplain, pronounced them husband and wife, they fell into each other's arms. "I love you," they murmured together, their voices caressing the deep and perfect stillness.

Tears streaked Irene's face, continuing even as the beaming newlyweds left the church. She showered them with rice while George held his camera high, snapping picture after picture. "This way," he called. "Look over here."

But they were not listening. Mark clasped Jobina's hand, leading her along the path. He led her to a bench beneath a cluster of golden oaks and there he stopped. "I have something for you," he said, reaching into his pocket. He removed a small box and opened it to reveal two glittering diamond butterflies. "A matched pair." He smiled. "Like us."

"Oh, they're *beautiful*."

"Turn them around."

Gently, Jobina lifted the brooches. Her eyes misted as she read the engravings: *No sooner had they met but they looked;* and on the other, *No sooner had they looked but they loved.* "Oh, Mark." She sniffled. "Oh, Mark."

"Happy wedding day, Bean."

Chapter Twenty

"When are you going to have your honeymoon?" Emile asked as 1941 drew to a close. "It is two years already."

"Our honeymoon is whenever Mark and I are together. We *steal* time. It's really very romantic."

"All this romance is agreeing with you. I see the stars in your eyes and the roses blooming in your cheeks. Happiness, yes?"

Jobina smiled. She smiled often now, for despite the strains of her new life, she felt blessed. Certainly her life had changed. She spent just three days a week in New York, dividing the rest of her time between Washington and Doe Hill. In Washington she played hostess at teas and luncheons and elegant dinner parties. She served on the correct charity committees and cut her share of ceremonial ribbons. She was a judge at the flower show, a special guest at the horse show, a spectator at countless fashion shows. These were the wifely duties of which Mark had warned. They were expected, and if she found them exhausting and more than a little inane, she was careful to keep her complaints to herself.

"There are rewards," Jobina pointed out time and time again, and it was no secret, even in cynical Washington, that when she spoke of rewards she meant Mark. They had four nights a week together, nights they treasured above all else; once or twice a month they had whole weekends together at Doe Hill. Wherever they were, they reveled in each other. They seemed always to be touching and whispering and gazing into each other's eyes, two people utterly in love. It was said that the Campbells lived in a world of their own. The Campbells themselves were quick to agree.

There was but one shadow clouding Jobina's happiness, the long and ominous shadow of war. If war had seemed a distant threat in 1938, it seemed, in this winter of 1941, an ever more likely possibility. Poland had already fallen to Hitler's armies, as had Holland and Belgium. France had fallen to the collaborationist government at Vichy. England, isolated, virtually alone, had survived the *Luftwaffe* bombings during the Battle of Britain and continued to fight on, a gallant nation under siege.

The war reports were never far from Jobina's mind, though still she refused any discussion of the subject. Mark's hours at the Pentagon grew longer and longer. His fellow officers gathered more often in the library of the Georgetown house. She said nothing, for the reasons were obvious, too terrible to speak aloud. "No, Ellen," she said now, "it's no use. War talk is *forbidden* here. I simply won't allow it."

"I wasn't talking about the war, not exactly."

"The war, the Nazis, it's the same thing. Years ago we should have sent someone to shoot Hitler. One nice clean shot right between his beady eyes."

"I was just wondering what you thought, Jobina. That newspaper article said the Nazis have death camps. It said—"

"Yes, I read the article. I don't know what to think anymore. Emile won't say how, but he's managed to make contact with the Resistance. He's trying to get money to them . . . From what he's heard, he believes the stories are true."

"It must be awful for Emile."

"Well, he feels he has to atone for the traitors at Vichy. And most of all, for Johnny. It's so incredible, Ellen. Johnny was such a sweet child." Jobina sighed. She looked away, her gaze sweeping over the lawns of Doe Hill. The trees were almost bare, their leaves forming pillows of bronze and brown and umber upon the darkening earth. The rose bushes, too, were bare, and some of the birds had flown off to warmer climes. "I wonder if we will have snow this year," she said quietly. "Doe Hill is something to see in the snow."

"I'll bet the snow stays clean. Not like in the city."

"Not at all like the city. Mark bought a sleigh last Christmas. He dressed it with bells and then *he* dressed up as Santa Claus. The twins were absolutely thrilled."

"I can imagine." Ellen laughed, her blue eyes twinkling. She had changed very little in the twenty-odd years she had known Jobina, though through Jobina her fortunes had changed, and in her open, unpretentious way, she was grateful. "Do you ever think back to the old days?" she asked. "Our old building on Lexington Avenue is still there."

"And Greevy's, but it has another name now . . . I remember the day I got my first raise. What a glorious feeling that was . . . We've come quite a distance since the *old* days."

"You have. Thank God you dragged us with you, Jack and me."

"As Emile would say, Jack earns his pay. Especially now. I'm always on the run. I have to depend on a few key people. Jack, Fred Warner, Hank Staley. They are all good men, but Jack was there from the beginning. He's learned to anticipate me. You have no idea how helpful that is, Ellen. Sometimes I have to leave in the middle of a meeting. At least I know Jack can take over."

"Oh, he loves his work."

"There's a lot of it. I do as much as I can, but time is a problem. I'm at the mercy of train schedules and Pentagon schedules."

"It sure hasn't done you any harm. Look at you, Jobina! You're glowing! That doesn't come from a jar either. If you could put it in a jar, you'd make another ten million."

"All compliments happily received," she replied with a laugh. She bent, gathering a handful of leaves. "A nice shade of brown, don't you think? I must save it for Emile."

"A new eyeshadow is born."

"Could be." Jobina smiled, tucking the leaf in her pocket. "I've found inspiration here before. Doe Hill is . . . Oh, there's Mark." She shaded her eyes against the bright afternoon sun and now her smile fled. "He's wearing his uniform. He's wearing his general's face too . . . Mark," she called, running toward him. "Mark?"

"I haven't much time, Jo."

"Something is wrong. I can feel it. Tell me what's wrong."

Mark put his arm around her shoulder. "I wish there were a way to make this easy," he said. "There isn't. The Japanese have attacked our naval bases at Pearl Harbor. Casualties are heavy. The first reports are very bad."

Jobina was ashen. Her hands had begun to shake and she hid them behind her back. "Our naval bases?" she asked. "The Japanese?"

"It was an aerial attack. The bastards hit us hard."

"Then we're at war."

"Jo, I have to get to Washington. I want you to stay here for awhile. The roads will be jammed. Noah will drive you in later . . . Can you stay over tonight? I don't know when I'll be home, but—"

"Of course I'll stay, darling. I'll be waiting."

"You may have a long wait."

Jobina gazed at Mark. His face was impassive, but in his eyes she saw both anger and pain. "I'll be waiting when you get home," she said. "Don't worry about me." She watched him stride away to the car. She heard the soft purr of the motor, the sharp crunch of gravel as the car sped off. "Mark," she murmured.

Ellen came up beside her. "What was that all about? You're so pale, Jobina. What is it?"

"War," she replied, tears slipping down her cheeks. "*War*."

It was after three when Jobina and the Sisks left Doe Hill. They drove to Georgetown in silence, each desperately hoping that the news would somehow improve. But as hours passed the news grew worse. Radio commentators spoke of bombs raining from the skies over Pearl Harbor, of battleships going down in flames, their crews trapped aboard. All hope vanished and shock turned to grief, for later reports confirmed thousands of deaths.

"I can't listen anymore," Jobina said now, switching off the radio. "It's too horrible. Those poor men. My God, those poor men."

"I guess we know what happens next," Ellen replied. She dried her eyes, looking sadly at Jobina. "We don't have to wait for the President's speech. We know."

"I wish Mark would call."

"He will."

Jobina paced the library, her head bent, her hands clasped tightly behind her back. Many thoughts rushed through her mind, terrifying thoughts. She stopped, staring down at Mark's desk, and tears came once again to her eyes. Impatiently, she brushed them away. "I feel so helpless," she said. "Scared and angry and *helpless* . . . It won't be a short war."

"We'll win it, Jobina. We'll give it to 'em good."

Yes, and at what cost? she wondered. She knew the young would suffer, for it was always the young who suffered in wars. Young men would lose their lives, young women their husbands and sweethearts. Children would lose their fathers. Her heart sank when she remembered the untold European children already orphaned by war; there would be others, many others. "Jack," she said quietly, turning as he entered the room, "were you able to make your calls?"

"I got through, finally. I spoke to New York, Chicago, and California. Walt Morris says there's a lot of panic in California. It seems some people are expecting a second Japanese attack. He's put extra guards on the factory, just in case the panic gets out of hand."

"Good."

"Anyway, I told them all we're open for business tomorrow . . . I hate to talk about business at a time like this, Jobina, but we're going to be facing some problems."

"It's all right. Our employees will need their paychecks, war or no war. Whatever employees we have left after enlistments and the draft."

As Jack sat down, the light from the fire cast a rosy glow on his drawn face. "That's what I was thinking," he replied. "Some of our men will enlist immediately. Others will be drafted. Still others will leave to work in defense plants. We need contingency plans."

"Women."

"I beg your pardon, Jobina?"

"Quite a few women went to work during the last war. They had to. They had to earn a living. Women worked during the Depression too, women who could *find* work. Do you see the pattern?" she asked with a slight smile.

"It's acceptable for women to work during a crisis. Well, we have another crisis. I suggest you start opening our factories to women now. You may hear some grumbling. I don't care about that."

"We have women in our factories."

"Clerks and switchboard operators and the like. We can do better. Under the circumstances, we will have to."

"I told Hank to set up a meeting for tomorrow morning. We'll get estimates, department by department." Jack glanced at his notes, absently brushing his dark mustache. "Most of our workers are young," he said. "Don't hold me to it, but I'd guess we could lose fifty percent of them."

"Fifty percent would put us out of business. Let's make certain it doesn't come to that. We can, if we broaden hiring policies."

"Understood." Jack closed his notebook. He stood. "Ellen, we'd better be on our way. Traffic is bad and God only knows what the trains will be like."

"Noah will take you to the station. Where are your bags?"

"We left them in the hall," Ellen said. She went to Jobina, looking into her eyes. "Try not to worry too much," she urged gently. "Mark's been in this spot before. He knows the ins and outs. He has the medals to prove it."

"He certainly has. I'll be fine, Ellen. It would be very selfish of me to put my worries first, wouldn't it? There's a war to win. We will all do our part."

"That's the spirit!"

"Come on, Ellen," Jack said. "We really have to be going."

Jobina walked them to the door, waiting until Noah brought the car. "Safe home," she called. She returned to the library, forcing a smile when she saw Ivy. "I'm afraid we didn't touch your sandwiches," she said. "We were busy talking."

"They'll keep. I have fresh coffee here. It'll do you good, Miz Campbell. Likely to be a long night."

For Jobina the night was endless. She wandered from room to room, but always her steps took her back to the library, to the comfort of Mark's things—his books and maps and two old leather chairs he refused to discard. Every half hour or so she turned on the radio, listening briefly and then turning it off again. She began a crossword puzzle and moments later tossed it aside. She paced up and down. She watered the plants and stirred the fire. Sighing, she went to the window and stared out at the tree-lined street. "Oh, Mark," she whispered. "Oh, Mark."

It was dawn when she heard his step in the hall. She rushed to him, her eyes suddenly eager and filled with relief. "Darling, you're home," she cried. "Are you all right? Are you hungry? You must be starved. Let me get you some breakfast. Unless you're too tired. Sleep, that's what you need now."

"Am I allowed to say anything?" Mark asked, amused. "I appreciate all the fuss, Bean. I love it, but it isn't necessary. I've already eaten and I even managed a quick nap between meetings. Come, let's sit down. We have to have a little discussion."

Jobina's heart was pounding, for she knew what he wanted to discuss. She took a breath. "You're going overseas," she said, sinking onto the couch. "The only question is when."

"That's not a question I can answer yet. There are more immediate problems. We have a lot of work to do and damned little time. It's make or break, Jo. From now on I won't have a minute to myself. I mean not a minute. I'll be at the Pentagon. I'll be at the White House. I won't be *here* . . . It would be best if you returned to New York today. I want you to stay in New York until things are clearer."

"I can't leave you, Mark. You can't ask it. We don't know how much time we'll have before . . . No, you can't ask it." Jobina felt tears sting her eyes. She took another breath, trying to calm herself. "Please, you can't."

Mark gathered her into his arms. He kissed her, tenderly stroking her hair, her cheek. "I *am* asking," he said. "I love you, Jo. I love you . . . But you married a soldier. A soldier whose life isn't his anymore. I have responsibilities, darling. Men are going to be sent to fight a war. Many of them will die."

"But *you* will be fighting a war too."

"Generals don't die in war, Jo. The troops do all the fighting. Young, scared, inexperienced troops. It's my responsibility now to make sure they'll have all the support they'll need . . . Victory is the first goal of war. The other goal is to protect our troops."

"I'm sorry." Jobina sniffled. "I don't mean to be selfish. It's just that I'm frightened."

"Everybody is frightened."

"Not you. Oh, you're angry about all this. You're sad. But you're not frightened."

A smile edged Mark's handsome mouth. "Within

twenty miles of the front," he replied, *"everybody* is
frightened. I remember one particular general during the
last war. His division had been through hell. They fought
like bastards and they held their ground, despite heavy
casualties. A visit from their commander would have
meant a great deal. It was his duty, but he never
appeared. He spent his tour safe and warm at HQ."

"Will you have a division?"

"Yes." Mark smiled again. "And my men will know
I'm there. Beyond duty, it's a matter of honor."

"You and your honor."

"A poor thing, but mine own."

Jobina rose. She walked to the fireplace, staring into
the flames. After a moment she turned. "All right,
darling," she said. "I'll go back to New York. I'll leave
today. I suppose it's time I started behaving like a
soldier's wife . . . Well?" She laughed. "Don't I get a
reward?"

"Will you settle for a kiss?"

"Happily."

Mark went to Jobina, pulling her to him. "I love you,
Mrs. Campbell," he murmured.

"When will I see you? I *will* see you before you go
away, won't I?"

"I promise we'll have a few days to ourselves. We'll
make them very special days." Mark stepped back, tilting
Jobina's face to him. "I don't want us to be apart," he
said. "Not for a day, not for an hour. I wish to God there
were a choice. As it is, you'll be better off in New York.
You'll have your family and your friends and your work.
If you stayed here, you would be rattling around an

empty house. You would be alone, Jo. I couldn't bear the thought of that."

"I'm beginning to understand why you never asked me to give up the company. You never even hinted about it. Now I understand why. You were afraid I'd be at loose ends if you had to go away. What a clever fellow!"

"Clever enough to know you need your work. You're not the kind of woman to be content rolling bandages and knitting socks. There are other ways to help the war effort."

"I intend to help, Mark. The cosmetics business suddenly seems quite frivolous . . . I see a naughty gleam in your eyes. What are you thinking?"

"Only that frivolity has its uses. Morale, for one. Morale on the homefront and overseas."

"Overseas?"

"Soldiers get leave," Mark replied with a laugh. "They don't spend it in church, no matter what they tell their mothers. They go looking for girls. And they take little gifts, a pair of stockings, a lipstick. I can guarantee you will be doing big business at our post exchanges. Raising morale all *over* the place."

"Oh?" Jobina laughed too, snuggling in Mark's arms. "I hope you don't plan to go looking for girls."

"You're my girl, Bean. Forever and ever."

It was a brisk February afternoon and Jobina paced her office, glancing from Emile to Hank Staley to Meg Lowe, the head of public relations. "We are agreed that we want to support the war effort," she said. "The question is how. I've studied everyone's suggestions. Emile and I have discussed them. We've decided to introduce a new cosmetics line. The line will be called Victory, and all profits, every cent, will be donated to the war bond drive. An outright donation, no strings attached. We want the idea promoted, Meg. It may encourage other companies to follow suit."

"I'll need the details."

"Muriel is typing a memo now. I've already spoken to advertising. They've promised rough drafts by the end of the week. We plan to give Victory the best possible start, though obviously we can't neglect our other lines. We still have factories to run and a payroll to meet. You will have to do some careful balancing, Hank."

"The trick is not to compete with ourselves," he replied. "If we're giving the Victory profits away, we have to make damn sure the line doesn't overlap the others. Can I work along with your chemists, Emile? These are special circumstances. I have to have access."

"You will work with me. *I* will work with my chemists."

"Fair enough."

"The colors, they are going to be bright and very clear. Not so much shading. Clear tones. They will be good for younger women. That is a big market, yes? They will sell like pancakes."

"Hotcakes, Emile," Jobina said, smiling. "And that reminds me . . . We want the line *priced* for younger women too. Low end, Hank. Drug stores, variety stores, and so forth."

"I don't know. That might not sit well with our customers."

"Well, as you said, these are special circumstances. It's for a good cause, after all. We're making it easier for people to contribute their money to the war effort."

"Some people may think we're taking advantage of the war to line our pockets."

"No, they won't," Meg declared, "because each month we will announce the Victory profits and turn over a check. There are lots of things we can do, Hank. We can have charts printed for the stores to show how much their customers have contributed. We can put enclosures in our packages. The point we're trying to make here is that everybody should buy war bonds and we're doing our part."

"Exactly! We're all in this war together. We all want to help any way we can."

"I admire your spirit, Jobina. Not to mention your optimism. You're risking a lot of money. The start-up costs alone—"

"I've taken risks before. And survived to tell the tale. Someday Emile and I will tell you how the company began. Talk about risks!" She laughed, glancing at her watch. "I'll leave this project in your hands," she said. "Remember, our other lines aren't to be neglected. That means extra work for you, Hank."

"A small sacrifice, everything considered. When do I see the memo?"

"It will be on your desk tomorrow morning," Jobina replied. "Emile, are you ready? We should be going . . .

My housekeeper is getting married," she explained. "Emile is giving the bride away."

Hank stood, watching as his bosses snatched up their hats and coats and hurried from the office. "They're quite a pair," he said. "I never know what to expect next."

"But they have the touch."

"What touch?"

"The *golden* touch."

Neither Jobina nor Emile heard these comments, for they were dashing through the hall to the elevator. "I hope we are not late," Emile said. "Such an exciting day. Rose, she finally got her Albert. It is persistence, yes? That is the word?"

"In this case, *war* may be the word. Rose claims the war has brought out Albert's sentimental side."

"She is happy?"

"Floating on air. It's a shame she doesn't have any family here," Jobina remarked as she stepped out of the elevator. "Though I suppose we're her family. Heaven knows we've shared good times and bad . . . Is Billy coming to the wedding?"

"I asked him. I think he will have other plans. Every day he finishes teaching his class and then poof, he rushes home to his wife. They are the lovebirds. I see them together and my face is smiling." Emile held the door open for Jobina. He walked to the curb, waving his arm until a taxi screeched to a halt. "Beekman Place," he said to the driver. "Maybe you could hurry? We are late."

"Sure, pal."

"I'm glad Billy is doing so well," Jobina said as the taxi drove off. "Even if he did choose teaching over our company," she added, her eyes twinkling with light.

"Now he is choosing the Army. My son, he is ready to enlist. He has decided."

"Oh? How do you feel about that?"

"Proud. He will be fighting for America, yes?"

Jobina patted Emile's hand. She turned, gazing silently to the long lines of traffic, at the people scurrying from place to place. There are more soldiers these days, she thought, for it seemed that everywhere she looked she saw young men in uniform. She knew they would soon be going overseas and she knew that many of them would never come back. Quickly, she lowered her eyes. She twisted her wedding ring around and around, thinking about Mark.

"Something is wrong, Jobina?"

"No, nothing."

Caroline was waiting at the door when Emile and Jobina arrived. "Mama, I've been frantic," she cried. "The minister is here, and the photographer. Albert is pacing like a lion in a cage . . . Rose has been dressed and ready for *hours*."

"Hours? We're only twenty minutes late."

"Can we get started, Mama? I'm *so* nervous."

"Of course, darling. And thank you for holding the fort. I'm sure it's been chaos. Where is Rose?"

"In her room. If she hasn't fainted by now."

Jobina smiled. She threw her things on a chair and linked arms with Emile. "We will go see to her," she said. "Give us a moment and then start the music."

"Yes, Mama."

They found Rose perched at the edge of the bed, her bridal bouquet resting in her lap. She wore a short dress of ivory silk and a matching hat, its raised crown trimmed with tulle. She was smiling—smiling serenely, thought Jobina. "Caroline was afraid you'd fainted."

"Fainted, mum? I'm raring to go, I am. It's true I wish there was a priest to do the marrying . . . but like I told Father Coyne, a minister is what Albert wants. I'll be working on him though. We can always have a priest say the words another time."

Jobina heard the wedding march begin. "That's our cue, Rose. We mustn't keep the groom waiting. I will go first. You follow on Emile's arm."

"Don't forget your flowers, mum. A bridesmaid has to have flowers."

It was a lovely ceremony. Candles had been placed all about, bathing the living room in soft golden light. The mantel had been dressed with columbine and white azaleas and long, white satin ribbons. Rose scarcely seemed to notice, so intent was she on Albert. Her voice was firm as she spoke her vows and her eyes never left his face; Albert, though more subdued in his responses, could not stop grinning. "Well, the knot is tied," he said when the minister pronounced them husband and wife.

"It'll stay tied, it will," Rose replied.

George and Irene came forward to offer congratulations, followed by Caroline and Ian and Emile's companion, Helen Westcot. The wedding presents were opened then; afterward, there was an elegant buffet of cold lobster and veal. "Now you must cut the cake,"

Jobina said, leading the newlyweds to a luscious three-tiered confection of spun sugar and cream. "Stand closer, Albert," she said with a laugh. "We want you in the pictures too!"

The reception ended at eight o'clock, for Rose and Albert were taking the evening train to Niagara Falls. "Don't give my job away," Rose said before they left. "We're saving up to buy a house, Albert and me. You know what houses cost, mum."

"Your job will be here when you get back. How would I manage without you?" She walked with them to the door, ducking to avoid the shower of rice. "Albert, you take good care of our Rose." She smiled, lightly kissing his cheek. "Promise?"

"That I do, Mrs. Campbell . . . Mrs. Campbell, I just want to say we're grateful. The wedding party and all. It was grand."

"Have a wonderful honeymoon."

"Good-bye, mum," Rose sniffled. She hugged Jobina, then hugged her again. "You won't forget to eat? I know how you—"

"Have a wonderful honeymoon, Rose. *Scoot.* There's a car waiting downstairs. Hurry or you'll miss your train." Jobina waved as they stepped into the elevator. She closed the door, then leaned against it. After several moments she returned to the living room. "Mr. and Mrs. Cutler are on their way," she announced.

"*Now* can we have something decent to drink?" George asked. "That fruit punch was vile."

"We could all use a drink. You do the honors."

"Not for us," Ian said. "We have to get home."

"So soon?"

"This is Miss Pym's night off," he explained. "She's very good about switching nights. Very agreeable, but we don't want to take any chances. That woman is worth her weight in gold. She's actually civilizing our little monsters. Isn't she, honey?"

"I wish you wouldn't call them little monsters."

"I calls 'em as I sees 'em," Ian replied with a laugh. "Come on, get your things."

Emile stood. "Helen and I must be going also," he said. "Theater tickets," he added, shrugging. "If we hurry, we can catch the curtain." He went to Helen's side, clasping her hand. "You are ready?"

"Ready."

Jobina watched them. She smiled, for they looked so good together—Emile small and dark, Helen small and red haired. Their gestures were similar, and their attitudes. Certainly they shared the same sweet, easy disposition. "We don't see enough of you, Helen. Next time we must have a long visit."

"I'd enjoy that."

"But now there is the theater, yes? There is Mr. Cole Porter."

"I have my car, Emile," Ian said. "We can make a detour across town. Mom, you stay here and relax. We'll find our way to the door."

"Yes," Caroline agreed, kissing Jobina. "You've been running yourself ragged."

"No lectures now. Get going."

They all said their good-byes, then Ian led the way into the hall. Their footsteps faded. The closet door opened and closed, and then the front door. "Peace!" Irene exclaimed. "At last! Shall I help you with this mess, Jobina?"

"I have a cleaning woman coming in the morning." She sat down, taking the drink George held out. "Thank you. Just what the doctor ordered."

"I hope he has ordered sleep. You look tired."

"I am, a little. Now that you mention it, you and Irene look a little droopy yourselves. Is anything wrong?"

"Not wrong," George replied. "I wouldn't say wrong . . . We had a few moments alone with Ian tonight. He's decided to join up. The Navy. Caroline doesn't know yet."

Jobina was very still. She felt the sudden throbbing of her heart, the throbbing at her temples. "He could wait to be called," she said in a small voice. "The war isn't going to end tomorrow. He could wait for his notice."

"Ian's made his decision, Jobina. It wasn't entirely unexpected. His feelings on the subject are quite strong. He wants to serve. He feels it's his duty. He has agreed to wait until spring, no longer."

"Until the twins' third birthday."

"Yes."

Jobina turned to Irene, taking her hand. "Did you try to talk him out of it?" she asked.

"Tried and failed. I'm proud of him for wanting to go, but at the same time . . . Well, no mother wants to see her son go off to war. I reminded him of his duty to his own children. Of course he didn't need reminding. He feels he will be fighting for his children's future. I didn't know what to say to that. I ran into the bathroom and cried . . . I imagine women are crying in bathrooms all over America these days. Have you see the lines at the enlistment centers? The faces are so young and eager." Irene paused, brushing her handkerchief to her eyes. "We can be proud of our young men."

"Why has Ian chosen the Navy?"

"He wants the Pacific," George explained. "He wants a crack at the Japanese. Then there is the matter of influence. He said if he joined the Army, you might ask Mark to pull strings. To find him some cushy desk job in Washington."

"Oh, I'd ask, all right. I suspect the answer would be no."

"What do you hear from Mark?"

"Very little," Jobina replied quietly. She glanced away, twisting her wedding ring once again. "He's been working almost around the clock. But time is getting short now. I expect the announcement any day."

"The announcement?"

"That he's going overseas. I've been steeling myself. I'm determined not to cry or fuss or make a scene. Whatever time we have together . . ." Jobina could not finish her sentence. Whatever time we have together, she thought, and the words were like stones pressing on her heart.

Mark and Jobina were to have a week together, but in the end they had two days and two nights. They cherished each moment, never once speaking of war, of the uncertainties that lay ahead. The Thayers gave a cocktail party in their honor and Mark insisted they attend. "'S Wonderful" was playing when they arrived. Later they danced to their song at the Stork Club; later still, they made love in their jasmine-scented bedroom.

The next day they strolled hand in hand about the city, seeing it as if for the first time. Laughing, they had their pictures taken in a booth at the penny arcade. They had lunch at the zoo and drinks at the Plaza. Amidst the lengthening shadows of twilight, they rode a hansom cab through Central Park. That night they dined alone by the fire. They murmured to each other; they undressed each other, knowing one last time the wondrous passion of their love.

The morning was gray and rainy. Jobina drew the curtains, a sigh falling from her lips. "All ready, darling?" she asked, turning.

"Frye is downstairs. We're off."

"Won't you let me see you off? Won't you change your mind?"

"It's best this way, Jo."

"Yes, I suppose it is."

"A kiss?"

Jobina flew into Mark's arms. She pressed close to him, lifting her gaze to his blue eyes. "I love you," she said.

"I love you . . . I'll write when I can."

"I'll write every day. Take care of yourself, darling, will you?"

Mark smiled, stroking Jobina's cheek. "I will if you will. Do we have a bargain?"

"Mark—"

"No, don't say good-bye. It's not good-bye."

"*Au revoir, mon général.*"

They kissed, and then suddenly Mark was striding away. "Remember you're my girl, Bean," he called. "My one and only."

"Oh, I'll remember . . . I'll remember," she whispered as the door closed. She rushed to the window, flinging the curtains aside. She saw a staff car parked at the curb below. Moments later she saw the sergeant and Colonel Frye snap to attention, saluting. Mark returned their salutes. He was almost in the car when he stopped. He looked up, his eyes scanning the penthouse windows. She waved. "*Au revoir,* darling," she murmured. "I love you."

Chapter Twenty-One

There were other farewells. Billy Lanteau enlisted at the end of March. Ian, after long and sometimes emotional discussions with Caroline, enlisted the following week. They were assigned to Officer's Training School, and ninety days later they were on their way to war—Billy as an Army captain headed for Europe, Ian as a Navy ensign headed for the Pacific.

Jobina saw the pride in Emile's eyes when his son's troop ship left the dock. She understood, just as she understood the fear in Caroline's eyes when Ian's train left Grand Central. "I think you and the twins ought to come live with me," she said. "I have plenty of room. And there's Rose to help. Really, it would be fun."

"No, Mama," Caroline replied. "I'm not a brave person, but I must try to manage on my own. Ian and I talked about it. He said this war is a kind of test. He's right. He'll be testing himself every day . . . over there. The least I can do is—what is the expression? Keep the home fires burning?"

"That's the expression." Jobina smiled. "I'm proud of

you, darling."

"I want Ian to be proud of me. I love him so *much.*"

"I know."

"We all have to do what we can, don't we, Mama?"

"You might start by doing some volunteer work. The Red Cross, the USO. You could be very useful, Caroline. To yourself also. Work is such a marvelous distraction!"

To Jobina work provided both distraction and solace. She was busy all the time, for the war meant shortages of labor and supplies and even fuel to keep factories and trucks running. The labor shortage was critical as employees were lost to the draft and to defense plants, which seemed to spring up everywhere, almost overnight. Women were actively sought to replace departing workers, but this solution was not without problems. "Our women have children to worry about," she explained to Jack Sisk. "They are dependent on babysitters who may or may not be reliable. The only answer is a nursery school. Here and in each of our factories."

It was a radical idea, discouraged, scorned, by every one but Emile. "We are having nursery schools," he declared to their glowering executives. "That is that."

The matter settled, Jobina turned her mind to other concerns. She began visiting her factories, establishing incentives for old and new employees alike. She saw to their morale too—financing company bowling teams, picnics, contests, scrap drives, and rallies at which war bonds were sold. She arranged for each factory to have its own victory garden, its own collection center for packages going to servicemen overseas.

"Our fancy-pants executives," Emile said in the spring of 1944, "they agree now you are right. All these things you are doing. There use to be jokes. Not anymore. They see the production figures soaring to the sky and they agree you are right."

"The figures are excellent," Jobina replied. "But I have much better figures here. Come look, Emile. The Chicago factory contributed two tons of scrap during the last drive. Two tons! The North Carolina factory wasn't far behind. And look, New York and California are leading in war bonds. Do we have wonderful employees or do we have wonderful employees?"

"You put the fire under them."

"We must keep the fire going."

Emile laughed, his dark brows moving up and down. "With you to light the match, there is no doubt."

Indeed Jobina's support of the war effort was unceasing. She continued her travels. She raised money for the Red Cross and for veterans' hospitals. She collected clothing to send to Europe and she served as a hostess at the USO; she made the Georgetown house available to the USO, providing overnight shelter to military personnel stranded between trains. It was a hectic pace, eased by occasional weekends at Doe Hill. There she walked the paths she and Mark had walked together. She visited the gazebo, the stream, the woods blooming with wildflowers. Some of these visits she shared with her grandchildren, laughing while they chased after butterflies and squirrels and Noah's ill-tempered pet peacock.

I can get through the days, Jobina often thought; the

nights are harder. She chose to spend her nights alone. Invitations to dinner parties and to the theater were declined, for she felt closer to Mark when she was home. She pored over the newspapers, matching each dispatch to the huge map she had posted in her study. She listened to all the evening news broadcasts on the radio, tuning in the BBC on the shortwave. Again and again she re-read Mark's letters—funny, loving letters that referred once or twice to Italy but never to specific locations.

Like millions of other Americans, she knew moments of optimism and moments of despair. She cheered major American victories at Midway and the Coral Sea, mourned major defeats at Corregidor and Bataan. She mourned the casualties, including Philip Claymore's only son, killed at Guadalcanal, and the Sisks' son-in-law, killed at Anzio in 1944.

It was a time of grief, a time of fear. Jobina slept poorly, her dreams filled with bizarre and bloody images that jolted her awake. The ringing of the telephone late at night, the arrival of a telegram at any hour, struck terror in her heart. "I'm always expecting the worst," she admitted to Irene. "I can't seem to help it."

Certainly she was expecting the worst when a Western Union delivery boy appeared at her door one autumn morning. There was a great chill through her body, a terrible sickening. *Mark*, she thought, tearing open the envelope. The telegram was brief: "Jonas Winslow died heart attack Friday. No services. Signed Jordy Winslow." She wept then, not in sorrow but in relief.

Emile received a telegram the next month. He wept

too, for his telegram read: "We regret to inform you Captain William Lanteau reported missing in action and presumed dead."

"I'm worried about Emile," Hank Staley said, pacing Jobina's office. "One of the secretaries offered her condolences last week and he practically bit her head off. There have been similar incidents, all very unlike Emile. What's going on?"

"He believes Billy is still alive."

"I gathered as much. But the Army—"

"The Army can't *prove* otherwise."

"It's been two months, Jobina."

She sighed, leaning back in her chair. "Two months, two years," she said. "Emile believes Billy is alive. Wouldn't you, if it were your son? *I* would."

"It's just that we're concerned. You know how everybody feels about Emile. We don't know what to say, what to do."

"There's nothing to do, Hank. Let Emile deal with this in his own way. Allow him his hope . . . I've noticed that people grow quiet when Emile passes by. They hang their heads and look gloomy. They shouldn't. Beyond allowing him his hope, we must share it."

"Well, you're probably right. We can try. Poor devil, I wish there were something more we could do for him." Hank turned, walking to the door. "I'll have the regional sales figures on your desk first thing in the morning. Okay?"

"Fine." Jobina heard the door close. She reached her

hand to Mark's photograph. This damned war, she thought, sighing again. Sometimes I wonder if it will ever end.

"Mrs. Campbell?"

"Yes." She glanced up. "Yes, Muriel, what it is?"

"There's a man here to see you. He won't say what he wants, but his name is Winslow."

"Winslow?"

Muriel nodded. "You have twenty minutes before your meeting with advertising."

"Very well. Send Mr. Winslow in." Jobina clasped her hands atop the desk. She was frowning, her gaze fixed on the door. "Mr. Winslow?" she asked as a man of perhaps twenty-five or so entered. His hair was a light shade of chestnut, his eyes a clear brown. He was an attractive young man, tall and quick, though he walked with a cane. "I'm Jobina Campbell."

"You're not what I expected."

"Oh?"

"The name is Jordy Winslow. I'm your half brother."

Jobina's frown deepened. She took a breath. "I'm . . . I'm afraid you've caught me by surprise. I don't know quite what to say."

"It's all my fault. I wanted to call, but I didn't think you would see me. An awkward situation, isn't it?"

"Please sit down, Jordy. Make yourself comfortable. Can I offer you coffee? Perhaps a drink?"

"I had a drink before I came here. A shot of courage. I'm not much of a drinker, but under the circumstances . . . As I said, it's an awkward situation. I know how you feel about the Winslows and I sympathize. I lived in Father's shadow for twenty-seven years."

"Were the two of you close?"

"Close!" Jordy exclaimed, his laugh dry, bitter. "Father couldn't stand the sight of me. He valued perfection. I was born with a club foot and a withered leg. He was repulsed. Mother did what she could to soothe things. She died when I was fourteen."

"I'm sorry," Jobina said. "It must have been difficult for you."

"I don't mean to sound like a character out of Dickens. On the contrary. Father sent me to the best schools, even to the best tailors. He gave me everything I needed. He just didn't want me anywhere near him. After college I went my own way."

"What brings you to New York?"

Jordy was quiet, shifting his cane from hand to hand. "That's a long story," he said finally. "I'm sure you're aware Father lost most of his money in '29. Most, but not all. He took what was left and started buying up land in Palm Springs. He always had a keen eye for land. At the time of his death, he was worth some three million dollars. And the Winslow name is still important out West. So when I was disinherited—"

"Disinherited?"

"Father had a poor opinion of me. His will read—and I quote: 'I specifically make no provision for my son, because he must prove himself to be a man.' The newspapers had a lot of fun with that line."

"Jordy, how awful."

"To make a long story short, my wife and I decided to start over in the East . . . I've come to ask you for a job. Any job at all. I have references. I was a junior executive at Tyson & Company in Los Angeles. Tyson manufactures office supplies. Second largest company in its field, though not as large as yours."

"What do you know about the cosmetics business?"

"Nothing," Jordy replied honestly. "My wife uses your lipsticks. I see them all over the dresser. And she uses your Wild Lilac perfume. That is the extent of my knowledge. But I learn fast. I'm not afraid to take responsibility . . . Please don't misunderstand. I'm not asking for a handout. I promise you will get your money's worth and more. I'm asking for a chance. Call it a trial. If you're not satisfied with my work, I'll show myself the door."

Jobina stared at her half brother. She was smiling, remembering a similar offer she had made to Mr. Greevy so long ago. "We are always looking for eager young men," she said. "Welcome to the company. There won't be any special privileges, of course."

"I wouldn't want any."

"Then we are agreed. I'll schedule an appointment for you to see Jack Sisk. He will put you in our training program. After that, it's up to you. Can you be here tomorrow morning at nine?"

"Nine sharp."

"Where are you staying, Jordy?"

He shrugged, once again shifting his cane back and forth. "We found a little hotel across town, a fleabag.

Clair and I haven't been able to sell our house in Los Angeles yet. We're counting our pennies."

"I have a guest room. It's quite comfortable."

"Thank you, but we couldn't impose. The hotel isn't all that bad. Clair says it's different. She's being a wonderful sport about everything."

"I'll see you get an advance on your salary. Don't argue, Jordy. New York isn't the city for empty pockets."

"Yes, I've noticed."

"One more thing. We've never taken family members into the company before. I don't want you to hide the fact that you're family, but I don't want you to make a point of it either. All right?"

"I understand. I'm not here to ruffle anyone's feathers." Jordy stood, reaching for his coat. "What do I call you?" he asked with a grin. "I can't call you Sis, not after all these years."

"Jobina will be fine."

"In the office?"

"We're a rather informal group." She stood too, walking around the side of her desk. "You and Clair must come to dinner," she said, clasping Jordy's hand. "Are you free this evening?"

"Every evening. We don't know a soul in New York."

"Come about eight. It's the Stockard, on Beekman Place. You have some other relatives to meet. My daughter, Caroline, and her twins."

"You're a *grand*mother?"

"I certainly am!"

"It's been an interesting day. I was expecting you to

be . . . well, over the hill. I was also expecting to be thrown out on my ear. Instead you're a looker and I have a new job. Life is strange."

"To say the least . . . Jordy, if you don't mind my asking, who inherited Father's three million? I'm curious."

"A man named Martin Chadway. That's the strangest thing of all. Chadway's almost ninety, a recluse who hasn't left his estate in years. The lawyer said he and Father were business associates once upon a time. Personally, I think Father just picked a name out of a hat. He had to leave his money to someone. He didn't believe in charities and he disliked his friends. I think it was some sort of joke. He enjoyed his little jokes."

"He enjoyed having the last laugh. The crueler the laugh the better. I doubt he's laughing where he is now." She turned as Emile entered the office. "Emile," she said, "I'd like you to meet my brother, Jordy Winslow. My long-lost brother," she added, smiling. "Jordy's moved here from California and he's going to work for us."

"Surprises." Emile laughed, holding out his hand. "Always in this office there are surprises. I hope you are ready to earn your pay, Jordy. We are busy all the time. Your sister, she cracks the whip."

"I'm ready, sir . . . Jobina, I won't keep you. Thank you for giving me the chance."

"See you at eight."

"Good-bye. Good-bye, sir."

"A nice young man," Emile declared when Jordy had

gone. "He is the one who sent the telegram about your father?"

"He's the one."

"So now the family is together."

Jobina sat down, glancing toward the door. "Perhaps," she said. "I plan to watch him for awhile. He does seem very nice, but he's a Winslow and I want to be certain he's not up to something."

"You are a Winslow also. All the Winslows, they have success. It's in the blood, yes?"

"Perhaps . . . Emile, you look tired."

"Today I sign the separation papers with Inge. Such carrying on there was! She wants this, she wants that. She wants everything. I tell her to take what I offer and be glad."

"Did she?"

"After tears and more carrying on. Two million dollars."

"Two million!"

"A cheap price, Jobina. Now I don't have to see her again. We are *finis*. And it is official."

"I suppose it's a relief, no matter the price."

"For me and for Helen. I wish I could be signing divorce papers, but there is no divorce in the church."

"If the priests knew Inge, they would make an exception."

"They are not allowed, Jobina. Also they don't understand. They are, how you say, above such things. Not me. It's good I am not a priest, yes?" Emile bent his head over the desk, glancing through a stack of layouts.

"I like these new ads," he said. "I like how the butterflies shine . . . What about the radio ads?"

"We'll soon find out. Advertising has prepared six or seven jingles for us to hear. Are you in the mood to listen?"

"Something is wrong with my mood?"

"Well, you had a rough morning with Inge. And you have so much on your mind . . . Emile, have you had any news of Billy?"

"Billy will come home. This I know. They will all come home, Billy and Ian and your Mark."

"Of course they will."

"Normandy, it was the end for the Germans. Now there is only the finishing off. The *coup de grace*. You must not worry, Jobina. I know what I know. To make sure, I am praying every day to St. Jude."

"I've been praying quite a lot myself."

"They will come home, Jobina. It is settled."

"Grandmama! Grandmama!" Daisy squealed, bounding into Jobina's lap. "Sam is being *bad*. He took all my crayons away. He won't give them back. And he pulled my *hair* too. Shouldn't he have a spanking?"

"Oh, I don't know about that. First you must tell me what you did to Sam." Jobina laughed, wrapping her arms around the pouting six-year-old. "Did you hide his turtle again?"

"No."

"The truth, miss."

"It's just a smelly old turtle."

"Sam is very fond of that smelly old turtle. Now you rescue him from his hiding place and put him back in his box . . . Go on, scoot. And stay out of the kitchen. Rose is trying to fix lunch. We're having your favorite meal."

"Hot dogs!" Daisy cried, clapping her hands together. "We never have hot dogs at home."

"*Scoot.*"

Daisy slid off Jobina's lap, her long golden braids bobbing up and down as she skipped across the living room. "Hi, Mommy," she said, rushing past Caroline. "First I have to put the turtle back and then we're having hot dogs."

"Only if you behave yourself."

"I will."

Caroline watched Daisy disappear into the hall. "At least twice a day she promises to behave. The next minute she's playing another trick on Sam."

"I wouldn't worry, darling. Sam's begun playing a few tricks of his own, turning the tables, so to speak. It's all in fun . . . Did you find what you wanted in the trunk?"

"You really are a pack rat, Mama. And I'm glad. Some of my old skirts are good as new. With a little tailoring, Daisy can wear them to school in the fall. That will stretch our clothing coupons. Clothing coupons! Shoe coupons! Food rationing! I'm so *tired* of it. Look at me, wearing leg makeup to save my nylons for special occasions."

"The war can't last much longer."

Caroline walked to the window and stared at the calm

May sky. She thought of Ian, picturing him on his cargo ship somewhere in the South Pacific. "He won't recognize the twins," she murmured. "He's missing their childhood."

"Come away from there, darling," Jobina said. "It does no good to brood . . . We're all tired, but I know we're coming to the end. I feel it."

"Do you, Mama?" Caroline turned. "Are you still mooning over that magazine?" She laughed. "You must have memorized every word by now."

Jobina laughed too, holding up the service magazine *Yank*. "'Brigadier General Mark Campbell,'" she quoted, "'often called the GI's general because of the interest he takes in his troops.' Isn't that a lovely compliment? I wish the photograph were more recent. I keep trying to imagine how he looks now. If he's changed any."

"He's three years older, Mama. So are we."

"*We* haven't gone through a war."

"Sometimes I feel as if we have. Oh, it's not the rationing, the shortages. It's not the silly things. It's the waiting." Caroline sank down beside Jobina. She sighed. "I can't stand the waiting. I jump when the phone rings. When the doorbell rings, I want to run and hide."

"But you don't. You've managed very well, Caroline. I'm proud of you. Ian is going to find his wife all grown up."

"It took long enough, didn't it, Mama?"

"Some of us are late bloomers. I was."

Caroline smiled and the light returned to her beautiful blue eyes. She opened her arms as the twins ran back into the room, Daisy leading the way, Sam following. "Have you two settled your argument?" she asked, ruffling Sam's short, curly hair. "Are you friends again?"

"Yes, Mommy," they chorused.

"Did you wash? Let me see your hands . . . Both sides . . . All right, now let's see if you can stay clean until lunch."

Jobina stood, carefully placing her magazine atop the mantel. "I'll have a peek in the kitchen," she said. "Perhaps I can hurry things along."

Lunch was served fifteen minutes later, a lunch of hot dogs and french fries and Rose's own homemade tomato relish. "Mind your manners," she chided when Daisy aimed a spoonful of relish at Sam. "It's a sin to waste food. Don't you know children are starving in Europe? And don't look at me so innocent, Miss Daisy. You're a scamp, you are."

"Yes," Caroline agreed. "What would Miss Pym say?"

"She'd say, 'Stop it at once.'" Sam giggled. "She'd say, 'No dessert for you, Daisy Thayer.'"

"Oh, pooh!"

"Daisy, behave yourself or leave the table."

"Yes, Mommy . . . But can't I have dessert?"

"Eat your lunch *nicely* and then we'll see." Caroline leaned her head toward Jobina, trying not to smile. "I remember being sent from the table once or twice," she said.

"Your weapon was oatmeal. How I hated breakfast time."

"I remember."

Memories, thought Jobina, her gaze settling on the twins. She watched them all through lunch, taking great pleasure in their sudden exclamations, their sudden bursts of laughter. "Let them enjoy themselves, darling," she said when Sam mashed his ice cream into his peach pie. "The years go so quickly."

"Miss Pym would have a fit."

"This is Miss Pym's day off. What she doesn't know won't hurt her."

"You spoil them, Mama."

"Of course I do. But not all the time and not that much. Aunt Irene is worse than I am. Admit it."

"I'd call it even."

"Well, there were times when I spoiled you too, darling. You're fine."

Caroline looked at her children. Her expression softened and amusement twinkled in her eyes. "All finished?" she asked. "How about a nap?"

"We're too *old* for naps, Mommy," Sam protested.

"Too *old*," Daisy agreed.

Jobina left her chair, holding out her hands to the twins. "Perhaps just a little nap," she suggested. "A cat nap." She paused as a loud cry came from the kitchen. "Good heavens, what now? Rose?" she called, rushing through the door. "Rose, what's the matter?"

"On the radio, mum. The war . . . The war is over!"

"Mama—"

"Hush, darling. Let's listen." They bent their heads to the radio. An instant later they heard the news bulletin announcing the unconditional surrender of Germany.

"Thank God," Jobina murmured. "Thank God."

"Did we win, Grandmama?" Sam asked, jumping around the kitchen. "Is Daddy coming home now?"

Jobina gathered the twins into her arms. "Soon," she said. "Your daddy is still fighting in the Pacific, but he will be home soon." She went to Caroline then, gently clasping her daughter's hand. "Soon," she repeated.

"Oh, Mama, why couldn't it all be over?"

"It will be."

"When? Dear God, *when?*"

"When it's time," Rose said, pouring champagne into long-stemmed crystal glasses. "Meanwhile there's a victory to celebrate. Drink up, Miss Caroline. You too, mum. A victory is a victory."

V-E Day was celebrated all across the nation, in towns and cities and tiny rural villages. In New York huge crowds thronged the streets, shouting and cheering. Strangers embraced strangers, tears streaming down their faces. Children sat atop their parents' shoulders, waving flags and tossing confetti. Church bells rang out, the glad sound a message of hope to a war-weary people.

There was another celebration three months later, a celebration more joyous than the first, for it marked the unconditional surrender of Japan. General MacArthur, accepting the surrender aboard the battleship *Missouri*, offered the hope "that peace be now restored to the world, and that God will preserve it always."

"I don't understand," George said. "Is Mark expecting

you in Berlin?"

"Certainly not," Jobina replied. "He doesn't know a thing about it. I plan to surprise him. Oh, I'll have a cable sent," she added, laughing, "but *after* my plane has taken off. Don't look so gloomy, George. I'm not breaking any laws. I have all the proper papers and clearances."

"Berlin is in ruins."

"I know. That's why Mark wants me to stay away. But he's apparently going to be there a while longer, and I am determined to be with him. I don't care if Berlin is in *flames*. We've been apart four years. It seems a lifetime."

"Does anyone want my opinion?" Irene asked. "From the look on George's face, I suppose not."

"You are going to say it's very romantic. You forget that Mark has a job to do over there. A wholly *un*romantic job. He has responsibilities."

"He has a wife also."

"A wife who would be far better off where she is."

Jobina rose, drawing the curtains against the gray winter sky. "Let's not argue." She laughed again. "It's decided. Next week I will be in Berlin. I would have been there three months ago, but I wanted to wait until Ian was home, and until we had some word of Billy. Thank heavens he's all right."

"All right? He's skin and bones, poor thing."

"Well, two years in a German prison camp. He *will* be all right, Irene. That's what matters. Emile can relax now. I can leave with a clear mind."

George sipped his drink, staring thoughtfully at

Jobina. "Can you?" he asked. "What about the company?"

"It's in good hands. I trust Jack and Hank to run the day-to-day operation. Of course I'll be in touch. There is a business side to my trip, you know. The government is considering various plans to help rebuild Europe. Whatever plan they choose, it must start with putting people back to work. That means rebuilding factories from the ground up. American investment will be needed. Quite a few companies have already sent representatives over to look around."

"Are you going international, Jobina?"

"Could be. Jordy submitted an interesting proposal. A bit ambitious perhaps, but interesting nonetheless. It won't hurt to explore the possibilities."

George shook his head. He laughed suddenly. "So now it's Jobina International. What happened to the dithery female who couldn't add two and two without using her fingers?"

"The *real* world happened. I still remember your lectures, George. They spurred me on. It was a question of pride. Pride and poverty. They are wonderful incentives!"

"They were. Are there any incentives left?"

Jobina was silent, her gaze sweeping over the living room. "Goals change," she said after several moments. "But the challenge remains. When Emile and I started, we didn't have a lot of competition. Today it's quite a different story. A company like ours has to grow or it dies. That's where the challenge is . . . And there is a certain pleasure in knowing we're building something that will continue long after we're gone . . . Something for our grandchildren and their grandchildren. Years ago we could have taken the company public. We didn't, because we had an idea about family. Jordy is a part of that now as well. Come spring, he will have a child of his own."

"The word is dynasty."

"A rather grand word, George," Jobina replied with a smile. "I prefer the word family. When I step aside, I want it to be to family."

"Step aside? You?"

"Emile will be going to his lab when he's ninety. And that's fine, for him. Not for me. I don't want a long-distance marriage. The war cleared up what few doubts I might have had. Four years out of our lives. Four years lost. I won't go through that again."

"I'm sure you won't have to," Irene said. "Mark expects to be sent back to the Pentagon sooner or later. It is the logical place, after all."

"The Army isn't always logical. Ask any GI."

"Mark isn't *any* GI. He's a brand new major general! A two-star! It's terribly exciting, Jobina. Sam is very proud of his grandpapa. Caroline says he's been lording it over his classmates."

"Mark sent him all those war souvenirs. I wish he hadn't. Sam is too young, too impressionable for such things. I wouldn't want him to get the wrong idea about war."

496

"Nonsense," George replied. "At Sam's age, war is merely another version of cowboys and Indians."

"You mean it's a game."

"To children, everything is a game. But he is genuinely proud of Mark. Aren't you?"

Jobina smiled. "His line of work scares me to death," she said. "The uncertainties of his schedule drive me crazy. The demands on his time make me jealous. With all that, *yes*, I'm proud. And I plan to tell him so."

"In Berlin?"

"Berlin, here I come!"

Chapter Twenty-Two

Mark shaded his eyes, scanning the sky over the Berlin airfield. His heart quickened as the faint outlines of a plane appeared. He took a step forward, watching the plane until it touched down, engines roaring, wheels screeching. "Jo," he murmured. It seemed an eternity before the plane taxied to a halt, another eternity before the doors were opened and the stairs lowered into place. He pushed through a side gate, striding across the field. Now his heart soared, for amongst the tangle of passengers he saw Jobina. "Jo," he called. "Jo, over here."

She looked up, smiling, utterly radiant in a dress and coat of vivid scarlet. "Mark," she cried. She ran toward him, her chestnut hair blowing about her flushed face, her arms flung wide. "Mark."

They embraced, gazing at each other through eyes moist with tears. "I should wring your pretty little neck," Mark said when he was able to speak. "I should put you on the next plane back to the States . . . but I won't."

"I won't let you."

"I've missed you, Bean. *God,* how I've missed you." Mark gazed once again into her eyes. He took her hand, almost reluctantly leading her to the gate. "I had a different kind of reunion planned," he said. "Away from here. Away from war and destruction."

"We're together, darling. That's all I care about."

"Together in the ruins. Berlin is a scrap heap, Jo. There's nothing left." Mark held the gate open. He saw Colonel Frye waiting a few steps beyond and he nodded. "Everything taken care of?" he asked.

"Yes, sir."

"Hello, Colonel. How are you? It's been a long time."

"Yes, ma'am, it has. Welcome to Berlin. If you'll give me your passport and luggage tags, I'll make it official."

"Of course," Jobina said, reaching into her purse. "Thank you, Colonel . . . Such an efficient fellow." She smiled, turning to Mark. Her smile dimmed when she saw the weariness in his eyes, the two deep lines etched at the sides of his mouth; despite the perfect cut of his uniform, she saw he was thinner. "Are you all right, darling? You need a holiday. How do we arrange that? Shall I kidnap you?"

"Be careful, Bean," he warned with a laugh. "I'm armed."

"So I noticed. Must you really wear a gun?"

"Orders. The uniform of the day, at least for the time being. I promise not to shoot you."

"You're too kind."

Mark lifted Jobina's hand to his lips. "I'm in love," he replied. "A lonely soldier far from home, and in love.

Have I told you I love you, Mrs. Campbell?"

"Tell me again."

He bent his head, whispering something, then slowly drew away. "Well, Frye," he said as the colonel returned, "are we all set?"

"All set, sir. The luggage is in the car. And here's your passport, ma'am. It's best to keep it with you."

"Thank you. I will."

"I'll leave you now, sir. I'll take the jeep."

"Fine. Remind General Cordis that I expect the sector reports finished by the time I get back. I'm damned tired of his excuses."

"Yes, sir." Colonel Frye saluted. "Good trip, sir," he added, walking off toward the jeep.

"Good trip?" Jobina asked. "Are we going on a trip?"

"I believe you mentioned a holiday. I thought you might, so I wangled some time. We have four days."

"Oh, Mark, how wonderful! Where are we going?"

"Away from this godforsaken place. There's a little picture-book village near Salzburg—"

"The Alps!" Jobina cried, clapping her hands together. "What a wonderful surprise!"

"Do you mind a long drive?"

"Not at all."

Mark led Jobina to a staff car. He opened the door, helping her inside. A moment later he slid behind the wheel. "I hope you brought warm clothes," he said. "It's hard to buy anything over here. Most of the stores are gone, destroyed. The few still standing have empty shelves."

"Are things that bad, Mark?"

"You'll see for yourself. I warn you, it's grim."

The Berlin Jobina saw was grim indeed, a city of rubble, of bombed out buildings and cavernous holes. Entire blocks had been leveled, reduced to huge piles of bricks and glass and jagged stones. On other blocks, houses and stores had been charred black, their windows shattered, their roofs blown off. Power lines had been downed, lampposts flattened to the crumbling sidewalks. Trees had been uprooted, the dead branches coated with soot and ashes that even now seemed to smolder. "My God," she said when at last the city was behind them. "It's worse . . . much worse than I had imagined."

"I wanted to spare you."

"Why is the air so gray?"

"We dropped a lot of bombs, Jo. After the bombs, there were fires. The whole damned city is the color of ashes."

"My God."

"Let's forget about the war during these next four days. Let's try. This is our time, darling."

Jobina rested her head on Mark's shoulder. "Four days all to ourselves," she murmured. "A honeymoon."

It was night when they arrived in the charming Alpine village of Zinbruck. Here the air was clear and crisp, the sky a brilliant pattern of stars. Lights glowed at the windows of immaculate little cottages and timbered inns. Smoke curled from the chimneys, drifting over a landscape fragrant with edelweiss. "Mark, how lovely," Jobina said. "I feel as if we've wandered into a fairy tale.

Look at the gingerbread houses."

"I'm too busy looking at you." He smiled, helping her out of the car. "I like what I see."

"So do I."

Gazing at each other, they walked hand in hand to the inn. They were greeted by the innkeeper, a small, white-haired man named Schmidt. *"Willkommen, Herr* General Campbell," he said, bowing. *"Frau* Campbell," he added, bowing again.

Mark replied in German, standing quietly while *Herr* Schmidt made a brief, impassioned speech and then hurried away. "He'll have his son bring our bags, Jo."

"What else did he say? What was that all about?"

"He wanted to assure me he had nothing to do with the Nazis. In his case, it's true. We wouldn't be here otherwise . . . There are a great many people trying to distance themselves from the Nazis now. Of course there are still those who would just as soon spit in your eye, forever loyal to *Der Fuhrer.*"

"You can't mean that."

"Fascism is as insidious as Communism. For my money, they run neck and neck." Mark smiled suddenly, leaning close to Jobina. "Though the only neck I care about now is yours. It leads to such interesting places."

"What a naughty smile."

"You bet it is."

Mark and Jobina were shown to a room on the second floor. It was a cozy room, scrubbed and spotless, with a large feather bed, flower-sprigged feather quilts, and ruffled white curtains. Edelweiss filled a white porcelain bowl atop the dresser. A fire crackled in the hearth, its golden flames leaping and dancing on the stones. The curtains had been opened to a breathtaking view of sky and stars and mountains pure white in the moonlight. "Mark, you must see this."

He closed the door and crossed the room to Jobina. "All I want to see is you," he said. He drew the coat from her shoulders. He began unbuttoning her dress, kissing her hair, her eyes, her mouth. "Jo," he murmured as her dress and then her slip dropped to the floor. "Jo." His hands caressed her swelling breasts. His lips caressed her eager body.

In the next moment she was pulling at his clothes, tossing them aside. She pulled him to her, pressing against him, moving against him until they both cried out. They fell upon the bed, their cries at one with their seeking hands. "Darling, my darling," she murmured, swept by wave after wave of sweet ecstasy. All through the night Mark and Jobina clung together, joined in body and in soul. Their passion raged and quieted and raged again, for it was without end—the glorious, eternal passion of love.

Sunshine was bright in the room when Jobina awoke. She stretched her arms above her head. She smiled. "Aren't you the early bird," she said when Mark brought her a cup of coffee. "Or did I oversleep?"

"No. I've picked up some nasty habits, Bean. Like rising at the crack of dawn. Don't mind me. You can sleep all day if you want. It's your honeymoon too."

"Sleep! I want to go play in the snow!"

Frau Schmidt lent Jobina a warm jacket and boots. From her own suitcase she took slacks, two heavy sweaters, and fur-lined gloves. From Mark's suitcase she took a woolen muffler. Mark said she looked wonderful and certainly she felt wonderful. The fears with which she had lived for four years were gone, as was the terrible loneliness, the sense of being somehow incomplete. The worst is behind us now, she thought, rushing into the brisk Alpine morning. Silently, she thanked God.

"Here comes the snow," Mark called, aiming a snowball just past her shoulder. "That was a warning shot. Here comes the real thing."

They threw snowballs at each other, their laughter carrying on the wind. They made angels in the snow and then they built a snowman, a crooked little fellow slanting precariously to the right. It was afternoon when they reached the ski lodge. They lunched there, devouring sausages and potato pancakes and dark bread thick with sweet, fresh butter. They lingered over brandy, holding hands while the fire rose in the hearth. "Tomorrow we'll try the slopes," Mark said. "I used to be pretty good, though I'm going back a while."

"Is there anything you're not good at?"

"I prefer to think there isn't." Mark laughed. "All modesty aside."

"I love you."

"I love you, my darling." He brushed her hand to his lips. "Forever and ever . . . Do I see tears in your eyes?"

"It's because I'm so happy. *So* happy."

"To happy times," Mark replied, raising his glass.

Indeed it was an idyllic time, their days filled with long

505

walks and skiing and sledding and twilight drives to Salzburg, their nights filled with love. It was a honeymoon, though all too brief. "We'll come back," Mark said on the morning of their departure. "I promise we will."

"I'll hold you to that promise." Jobina sighed, gazing for a moment at the peaceful countryside, at the mountains soaring pure white in the sun. She went to the car, opening the door. "But now it's on to Berlin."

"You're a good soldier, Bean."

"A soldier's wife. A soldier's wife who knows when to get the show on the road!"

"Are you ever going to talk about the war?" Jobina asked as the car neared Berlin. "You haven't said a word."

"There isn't much to say. We won. I'm sorry Roosevelt didn't live to see it . . . I'm sorry so many of our boys didn't live to go home. I don't like war stories, Jo. I never did. It's bad enough sending kids to die . . . And they *were* kids. They seemed younger this time around. Perhaps because *I* was older this time around."

Jobina studied Mark's handsome profile. The strain was gone from his face now, and the weariness, but his eyes were still troubled. "*Yank* called you the GI's general," she said quietly. "I was so proud of you, darling. I knew the troops were in good hands."

"Not always. We lost our share."

"You were in the thick of things, weren't you? Don't shake your head. When I was packing your uniform I saw a new decoration. It's a combat decoration. Another Silver Star. Why didn't you tell me?"

"I happened to be in the wrong place at the right time."

"What does that mean?"

"It was chaos at the Bulge, Jo," Mark explained, his eyes fast on the road. "Utter chaos. Replacement troops had been rushed in after Normandy. They were green kids. Some of them literally green with fear . . . To make a long story short, I happened to find an advance patrol trapped behind the lines. I got them untrapped. That's all there was to it."

Jobina moved closer to Mark. "You could have been killed," she said, a chill prickling her spine.

"I wasn't. That same night I was eating cold beans and rereading your letters. I have them memorized," he added, for her letters had gone everywhere with him—to Anzio and Normandy and the Bulge and, later, to the unspeakable horrors of Dachau when his division had joined others in freeing the survivors of Hitler's camps. "Shall I quote the best parts?"

"I believe you." Jobina smiled. "I memorized your letters too. I kept them under my pillow . . . Mark, were you able to find out anything about Johnny Lanteau?"

"He called himself Johan Lanz. *Herr* Lanz is listed as a spy *and* a war criminal. Beyond that, it's hazy. There was so much confusion. It's possible he's escaped to South America. A lot of the bastards slipped through. Rats deserting the sinking ship . . . If he's still in Europe, he'll be found and tried. Execution is what he deserves. People don't always get what they deserve." Mark pulled the car over to the side of the road and turned off the engine. "I'm going to be in Berlin for at least six months," he said, taking Jobina's hand. "It may be longer. You've seen something of the city, or what's left of it. It's a terrible place. I'm living in a small house on a block that's half rubble, half MP station. You see what I'm getting at, darling. There's no life here, no happiness. You would be better off in the States."

"No, I won't leave without you, Mark."

"Listen to me—"

"*No*, I won't leave without you. I knew how things were. I had an idea anyway. I made my decision. I'm here and I'm staying here. I don't care if we live in a tent, as long as it's *our* tent."

"I'll be busy most of the time, Jo."

"Surprise, surprise."

"It's a city full of ghosts."

"I'm staying."

Mark saw the quickening golden fire in Jobina's eyes. He saw the stubborn set of her chin and he laughed. "You're impossible," he said. "What am I going to do with you, Bean?"

"Take me home."

"To the rubble and the MPs?"

"I'll manage."

"We could have used you at the Bulge." Mark laughed again. "Such determination. Such spirit. I wish I could put you in uniform."

"*Home*, General."

"All right. Don't say you weren't warned." He started the engine, glancing at Jobina. "We have a housekeeper,

508

a nice old woman from Daheim. Her name is Frau Brandt . . . She lost her whole family during the war. They were hiding a young Jewish couple when the Nazis came. They were all shot. Her wounds were minor, but she pretended to be dead . . . and the bastards left her for dead."

"My God."

"There are worse stories, Jo. Stories from the concentration camps. The world still doesn't fully grasp what happened in those camps. Here we know the truth. We've seen it. To look into the eyes of survivors is to see the tortures of hell."

"I think the world wants to forget."

"Yes," Mark agreed. "I wonder if the survivors will forget. I wonder if Frau Brandt will forget . . . You'll like her, though she's used to running the house by herself. Her own house was lost in a bombing raid."

"Don't worry, darling. I won't interfere. Does she speak English?"

"Some. When I called to say you were coming, she said she would practice. She's anxious to please. Over-anxious. She has no other place to go."

"Poor woman." Jobina turned, staring at the shadowy Berlin streets, at the blackened debris. There were a few people about, somber figures bundled against the cold. There were a few lights visible in sooty, undraped windows. On one block there was a little girl walking a dog. "Signs of life," she said with a wan smile. "We must be getting closer to home."

"Two kilometers past this checkpoint," Mark replied. He slowed the car as they drove past, returning the salutes of the soldiers on guard duty. "I'll arrange a pass for you, Jo. You'll need a pass to go from sector to sector . . . The Russian sector is off limits. Period."

"Why? Are we mad at the Russians again? Or are they mad at us?"

"Sometimes it seems everybody is mad at everybody over here. But special care is required with the Russians. They suffered staggering losses during the war, upwards of ten million people. They're going to be *very* protective of their borders from now on. Protective to the point of paranoia. Stay away, Bean. We don't want an international incident, do we?"

"I will be on my best behavior. If I even *glimpse* a Russian, I'll run the other way."

Mark was smiling as he brought the car to a halt. "Here we are," he announced. "Home sweet home. What do you think?"

Jobina looked around to see a narrow, three-story house, its brickwork charred, its upper windows covered with boards. The small front yard was an oval of mud and ashes and shattered flower pots. The steps were cracked, the railings bent and twisted. "Well," she said after a moment, "the roof is still on."

"Rather handy in the rain."

"A roof and four walls. That's where we start. It's a challenge, Mark."

"A challenge! More like a lost cause!"

"Perhaps not. Give me some time. There are . . . possibilities. Yes, there are definite possibilities . . . I can make a list of what I'll need and have Irene send it over."

"Can she send a bulldozer?" Mark laughed, helping

Jobina from the car. *"That's* where we start."

"O ye of little faith."

"Good evening, Corporal," Mark said to the young soldier patrolling outside the house. "My wife is going to be living here now. You keep a sharp eye."

"Yes, sir. I will, sir."

"Come along, Jo. Your dream house awaits."

The door was opened by a short, plump woman of sixty or so. Her gray hair was wrapped in a neat bun at the back of her head. Her dress was old but freshly laundered; her white apron sparkled. "Frau Brandt," she said, thumping her hand to her bosom. "I make clean for you, missus. *Kommen sie, bitte."*

"Thank you. I mean *danke."* Jobina followed Frau Brandt through the dim hall to the parlor. She smiled suddenly, for the room was immaculate, the bare wood floors scrubbed almost white, the furniture polished, the hearthstone swept. A fire blazed in the hearth, and on a nearby table sat a steaming coffeepot and a tray of thick ham sandwiches. "It's wonderful," she cried. *"Wunderbar,* Frau Brandt . . . Mark, it really is. I was expecting more rubble, just bits and pieces of things. Frau Brandt has worked wonders!"

Mark spoke to the housekeeper in German. She listened carefully, her face lighting up; with a shy bow to Jobina, she scurried away. "I told her what you said," he explained. "I told her to relax, all is well."

Jobina walked about the room, stopping here and there to inspect the table and chairs, the rocker, the overstuffed sofa. "It's homey," she declared. "Is the rest of the house like this?"

"We have a kitchen and a small dining room down here. Upstairs are three bedrooms. The top floor is closed off . . . Here's the bad news," Mark added, his blue eyes twinkling. "The plumbing is in terrible shape. The lights flicker. Until the coal burner is fixed, there's no central heating . . . It isn't Doe Hill, Bean."

"Oh, it's fine. It's *ours*. And you will see the difference when Irene sends a few things. Some curtains for the windows. Perhaps a rug. If I take measurements, she can send slipcovers. It will be charming!"

Mark took Jobina into his arms. "You're quite a woman," he murmured, pressing his lips to hers. His hands slid over her breasts, over the deep curve of her hips. Sighing, he stepped back. "I'd better not start what I can't finish," he said. "I have to check in at HQ. My desk will be piled high by now."

"I'll be awake when you get home. *Home*. How I love the sound."

Jobina made it a home. She enlisted Frau Brandt's help in tracing down workmen—a long-retired painter who plastered the cracks and colored the walls a soft yellow, an ancient plumber who repaired the pipes, a stonemason and his son who labored around the clock to reface the bricks and replace the crumbling steps, a young sergeant who happily spent his off-duty hours building shelves and rebuilding the staircase. With Frau Brandt she set to work in the ruined yard, mucking out ashes and litter and mud. She spread fresh topsoil and planted flower seeds, watering her tiny garden every day. Noah would be proud of me, she often thought, recalling the gardens at Doe Hill.

As weeks and then months passed, bright chintz bloomed at the spotless windows, scatter rugs decorated the gleaming floors. *Potpourri* scented the bedrooms and the parlor; candles glowed atop the mantel. "Our home," Jobina said to Mark one evening in July. "For the first time in years I *feel* married."

"How does it feel?"

"How can you ask?" she replied, falling into his waiting arms.

There was no doubt that Jobina loved her new role. She disliked Berlin, with its reminders, its ghosts, but inside her little house she knew only happiness. She was there when Mark came home from headquarters each night; she was there to see him off each morning. She was his hostess, entertaining his fellow officers from the base and officers from the British sector at informal dinner parties. She was his wife, fussing over his diet, his busy schedule. Always she was his lover.

Jobina Inc. was less and less in her thoughts. She telephoned the offices three times a week, speaking with Emile and Jack and Hank and Jordy. She read the memos and reports they sent, dictating more lengthy replies to the secretary she had hired. At least once a week she visited the site of a proposed factory, rechecking estimated costs. She did all these things, though with a certain reluctance. When she realized that a trip to New York could no longer be postponed, she found herself in tears. "I don't want to go, darling," she said, clinging to Mark's hand. "It's the factory. If we're to have a factory here, we must decide now. All of us. I considered bringing everyone to Berlin, but that isn't practical."

"Of course it isn't. Besides, a couple of weeks in New York will do you good. I wish I could go with you."

"Well, I suppose the time will go quickly. I've missed Caroline and the twins . . . I have so much to tell Irene. Letters aren't the same . . . And I can pick up some things for the house."

"Don't raid the stores, Bean. We won't be here forever. Another few months and then who knows?"

"Yes. We could be in *Alaska* next, couldn't we?"

"Would you really follow me to Alaska?"

"To the ends of the earth, *mon général*. You're stuck with me."

It was a brilliant autumn morning when Jobina arrived in New York. She went first to see Caroline and Ian and the twins, savoring their hugs, their cries of surprise. She too was surprised, for Caroline was pregnant again and the parents-to-be were planning a new house in Connecticut. "A house with lots of bedrooms," Caroline said. "With lots of closets," Ian added.

That afternoon she went to her office. She felt as if she had never been away, easily settling into the routine of meetings and reports. She studied charts showing rising sales, rising profits. She studied the results of the latest advertising campaign, declaring it a success. Amidst such rosy news, the European expansion was unanimously approved. "Who will be in charge?" Emile asked when the others had gone. "You will stay in Europe?"

"I don't know where I will be," Jobina replied, shrugging. "But I have no desire to run the European operation. It means starting from the beginning. It means long hours, seven days a week. I'm past that now . . . I think Jordy might be the right person, if he and Clair are willing. If they are, I'll make it official. We haven't much time, Emile. I want our plans finalized before I return to Berlin."

"Two weeks, yes?"

"At the outside."

"I'm glad you are deciding to trust Jordy. He has earned it. Such a hard worker he is. But always his face is smiling. Not sly smiling, like some of them. It is from the heart."

"I agree. And he has quite a talent for business. He has just enough Winslow in him to keep the wheels turning, but not enough to throw him off balance."

"Maybe he will be the boss one day."

"Oh, it's too soon to speculate. Jordy needs seasoning. Europe will give him plenty of that."

Emile gazed thoughtfully at Jobina. She was fifty now, though so radiant was her complexion, so bright the shine of her chestnut hair, she looked years younger. "Europe, it has been good for you," he said. "You have the glow. Me, I have the sagging face and the dark circles. Tell me your secret."

"I use our cosmetics, Emile. In ever greater quantities as time goes by."

"It is more than cosmetics. It is Mark."

"I love being with him. Believe it or not, I'm still on my honeymoon . . . But the truth is I wish we could be here. The twins are getting older and there's a new baby on the way. I'd like to watch my grandchildren grow up. You can understand that, Emile. You're going to be a grandfather soon yourself. It's difficult being thousands of miles from home. It's very difficult not knowing where we will be next."

"Do you say this to Mark?"

"Heavens, no!" Jobina laughed. "I knew what I was getting into. I was warned. The Army isn't going to change its ways for me. And Mark is Army. The best I can do is hope his next post is Stateside. It's funny. I never really cared much for Washington. Now I would give anything to have him reassigned there."

"I will pray to St. Jude."

"Pray hard, Emile." Jobina rose, wandering the length of her office. On the walls were many framed sketches of their trademark butterflies, some from the 1930s, others more recent. She stared at each one, absently touching the diamond butterflies pinned to her suit. "Time goes so fast," she said, as if to herself.

Colonel Frye was waiting at the airfield when Jobina arrived back in Berlin. "The general is in a meeting, ma'am," he explained, once again tending to her passport, her luggage. The ride home was quiet, for she was remembering the first ride through the grim and ravaged city. The task of rebuilding had seemed impossible then, but now, brick by brick, stone by stone, the city was slowly being restored to life. "Things improve every day, don't they, Colonel?"

"Yes, ma'am. We still have a long way to go, but we're getting there. In the Western sectors, that is. The Russians haven't done much yet . . . Five years from now you won't recognize Berlin."

Five years, thought Jobina. Where will we be five years from now? "I hope your surveyors and engineers leave our little house alone." She sighed. "It's such a dear little house."

"I can't say for sure, ma'am. It's possible. That block is in pretty good shape, everything considered. We're saving what we can."

Jobina opened her traveling case, removing a Dunhill box and placing it next to Colonel Frye. "A present," she said. "Those Cuban cigars you like so much."

"Why, thank you, ma'am," he replied, a small, surprised smile edging his mouth. "You're kind to remember me. I'll have to put them under guard. We don't get many luxuries in Berlin."

"Yes, I've noticed." The car passed through the first checkpoint, and the second. Jobina leaned forward, smiling when she saw her street. "Home sweet home."

"I'll bring your bags, ma'am."

Jobina hurried from the car, calling a greeting to the corporal on duty. She found the house empty, for Mark was still at his meeting and Frau Brandt at the new butcher shop several blocks away. "Well, it's just you and me, Colonel," she said, disappointed. "Will you stay for coffee?"

"I'd like to, ma'am, but I have to get back to the base.

I'm sorry it isn't more of a homecoming."

"That's all right. At least it *is* a homecoming. Oh, don't bother about my bags. You can leave them here in the parlor . . . When you see the general, will you tell him I'm back?"

"He knows, ma'am. They telephoned from the checkpoint. The general's orders."

"Of course." She laughed. "Like the Shadow, he knows all things." She walked Colonel Frye to the door, waving while the car drove off. She turned. "Welcome home, Bean," she murmured in the silence. With a sigh, she took her bags upstairs. She set out dozens of presents for Mark. She bathed and dressed, dabbing her own Jasmine perfume behind her ears. She was brushing her hair when Mark came into the room. "Darling," she cried, the brush falling from her hands. She rushed to him. "Darling, you're here!"

"I'm sorry I wasn't here earlier," he said, holding her close. "It couldn't be helped. Let me look at you . . . You look wonderful, Jo. I missed you. I'm used to having you around now."

"Did you really miss me?"

"You know the expression, absence makes the heart grow fonder. I'll show you *how* fond in a moment, after I tell you my news."

"News?" Jobina asked, her eyes suddenly anxious.

"We're leaving Berlin after the first of the year. The exact date hasn't been set."

"Leaving? Oh, Mark . . . Where are we going?"

"Would you be very disappointed if I said Guam? Yes, I can see you would. I won't say it. I'll say Washington instead. I'm being sent back to the Pentagon, Bean."

"Oh, Mark, thank God . . . I must sit down before I faint. Washington," she murmured, laughing and crying at the same time. "St. Jude's done it again!"

"What's that? St. Jude?"

"Never mind, darling. Don't expect me to make sense. I'm too happy. I'm in the clouds."

Mark sat beside Jobina, clasping her hand. "I hope they aren't rain clouds," he said. "Remember, Washington comes with a full social schedule. I'll be back at the Pentagon and you'll be back giving teas and cutting ribbons."

"Gladly . . . What will happen to our little house?"

"Frau Brandt will be allowed to stay on. It took some doing, but it got done. She will be given title." Mark smiled, stroking Jobina's cheek. "Our little house is safe," he said. "Feel better?"

"I feel blessed. Can we go to Zinbruck before we leave?"

"Not this time, Bean. Another time. We'll visit Zinbruck again. I promise we will. For now all I can offer is Doe Hill."

"Doe Hill. Oh, Mark, I hope I'm not dreaming."

"Shall I wake you with a kiss?"

Jobina smiled. "And so they lived happily ever after," she said.

Chapter Twenty-Three

Mark and Jobina returned to America in the winter of 1947. They were lavishly welcomed, the guests of honor at parties in New York and then in Washington. At Doe Hill the Thayers surprised them with a dinner dance, a glittering affair that continued until dawn. But when all the parties ended, their lives settled into the patterns they had known before the war. Mark was busy at the Pentagon. Jobina, commuting once again, juggled a schedule that included work and family and the social obligations of a general's wife. She became a grandmother for the third time, doting on the tiny baby boy named Matthew. Her last grandchild was born the next year, a sweet, dark-haired girl named Jill.

The whole family gathered together to celebrate the new year of 1950. Indeed there was much to celebrate, for with peace had come prosperity. All across the nation homes were being purchased in record numbers, the dreams of young couples made possible by expanded credit and GI loans. Car sales boomed. Television was a new and wonderful toy. Shiny appliances from pop-up toasters to electric refrigerators filled millions of kitchens. Such extraordinary economic growth brought extraordinary rewards to business. Jobina Inc. was a huge corporation now, as typically American as drive-in movies and backyard barbecues and *I Love Lucy*.

Jobina herself was happier than she had ever been, though she knew that this decade, like others, had its darker side. The Cold War had begun, and the Communist witch hunts that would destroy so many innocent lives. There were ominous stirrings in the Pacific; more and more, Korea was in the news. It was June when Korea burst into the headlines, for in that month the armies of North Korea invaded South Korea.

Now Mark tossed his briefcase on his desk, gazing across the study at Jobina. "We're going in," he said. "Technically, we will be just one of eighteen countries under the UN banner. The truth is that American forces will make up the largest contingent."

"Combat forces?"

"Yes."

Jobina sank into a chair. She was pale, her hands trembling, but she was not surprised. She had sensed Mark's preoccupation during the last two months; certainly she had noticed the increasing demands on his time. "You knew this was going to happen, didn't you?"

"We play war games at the Pentagon, Jo. We play 'what if.' But what I know and what I can say, without breaching security, are different things."

"Can you say why we're facing yet another war? Is there a reason? Or has war become a habit?"

Mark sighed. "The reason," he said, "as you're well

aware, is Communism. The North Koreans have to be stopped. Stopped cold. South Korea is strategically important. The Rhee government is our ally."

"Syngman Rhee is a dictator."

"A dictator friendly to American interests."

"If Hitler had been friendly to American interests, would we—"

"Don't, Jo. We're not talking about Hitler." Mark went to Jobina. He stared down at her, his hand caressing her hair. "There was a time," he said, "when war was a simple matter. The good guys against the bad guys. It isn't simple anymore. It isn't always easy to tell the good guys from the bad guys anymore. But in Korea we have no choice."

"No. No, I suppose not . . . When do you leave?"

"Ten days."

"Ten days," Jobina repeated, the words chilling her very soul. She gazed up at Mark. She rose, sighing as his arms wrapped around her. "I'm going with you," she said.

"What?"

"I don't mean to Korea. I'll rent a house in Tokyo. When you can steal a day or two, I'll be there."

"That's all we'll have, Jo, a few stolen days now and then. If you stayed here—"

"I can't stay here. I can't go through that again. Jumping every time the phone rings, every time a telegram arrives. I want to be as close to you as I can, darling."

"You were so happy to come home."

"Because we were *together*," Jobina said. "Home is

where we're together."

Mark took her hand and led her to the French doors. Outside the twins played on the sunny lawn. Daisy skipped rope as Sam chased after a small white terrier named Alfie and a smaller golden terrier named Cornelius. "Can you really leave all this behind?" he asked. "All the weekends with the kids? All the birthdays and report cards and pranks? I have to, Jo. You don't."

"We won't be gone forever."

"Kids grow up quickly."

Too quickly, thought Jobina as tears misted her eyes. The twins were eleven now, that sweet age between childhood and adolescence. Her youngest grandchild was fourteen months old, just starting to talk. "I admit it will be hard," she said. She looked into Mark's handsome face, tracing the line of his mouth, his chin. "But I'm a soldier's wife and I'm going to Tokyo."

"Are you sure?"

"Absolutely."

Mark smiled and a swift gleam lit his eyes. "Then I can tell you how glad I am," he said. "If I could put you in my pocket and keep you there, I would. Tokyo's the next best thing."

"Perhaps it will be a short war. Do you think so, darling?"

"We can hope, Bean. We can hope."

"I'm your welcoming committee, Jobina," Elizabeth Frye said on a warm and lovely afternoon in July. "My colonel is off with your general, so it's just the two of us. I hope you don't mind."

"Mind? I'm delighted! This is my first time in Japan. I don't know anything about the country. I don't know a soul here. You're a godsend!"

"The blind leading the blind," Elizabeth replied with a smile. "I've only been here a month myself. But you must be anxious to see your house. Come in. Koh will bring your bags while I show you through . . . It's quite a place."

"It certainly is," Jobina agreed, glancing around. "Is it all mine?"

"For the duration, as they say. It's one of those houses that belonged to the Mitsuis . . . You know, part European and part Japanese. Before the war, many wealthy Japanese built homes combining East and West. In a way, it's a shame. I've seen some traditional Japanese houses and they're exquisite. But the advantage here is modern plumbing. It's a nice thing to have."

"The house is very large, Elizabeth."

"Well, it's sort of in two sections. Come, I'll show you."

Jobina followed her through rooms filled with antique carpets and velvet draperies and ornately carved furniture of several different periods. "I assume this is the European section," she said.

"Yes. Nothing's been changed. But here's something special," Elizabeth added, opening another door.

"Oh, how charming," Jobina cried, for now she found herself in a traditional Japanese setting—all delicate scrolls and matting and *shoji* screens and rice paper windows. The rooms were small, in perfect proportion, the furnishings graceful and chaste. "I wonder if I will get the hang of this," she said, easing herself onto one of the pale silk cushions beside the low dining table. "What fun! Have we seen everything?"

"There's the . . . I don't know what it's called. It's not a bathroom exactly. The only thing in it is a tub, an enormous tub raised on a platform. The Japanese bathe together, you know. Whole families. I'll tell you, Jobina, I've never seen cleaner people than the Japanese . . . Can I help you up?"

"I'm fine. It's good exercise. What is that heavenly scent?"

"The gardens," Elizabeth replied. She slid open a partition, and led Jobina to the rear of the house. "You'll love the gardens."

The women stepped out into the bright sunlight. Jobina's breath caught as she saw the flowering cherry trees, the profusion of azaleas, the tiny and perfect dwarf pines. She studied the intricate patterns of the rock garden, the serenity of the reflecting pool. "How did such beauty survive the war?" she asked.

"Some areas around Tokyo fared better than others. The city itself is still bad in certain spots, though not for long. The Japanese are amazing."

"You sound won over."

"I am. I hated the Japanese during the war. *Hated* them. I didn't want to come here. But since I've been here . . . I don't know how to explain it, Jobina . . . There was grumbling in Germany after the war, maybe not a lot, but enough. You won't hear any grumbling in Japan. The Japanese have accepted their defeat. They've put it behind them. They're just as gracious as can be. They're not friendly in the American sense. You won't find any backslappers. But they're . . . nice."

"I was little concerned about coming here too. I didn't know how I would feel. I still remember the day I heard about Pearl Harbor. Then again the Japanese must remember the day they heard about Hiroshima and Nagasaki. It's complicated. Mark says it's important to turn an old enemy into a new friend, and of course that's true." Jobina bent, sniffing the azaleas. "If we all stayed angry forever, the world would be a terrible place. It would be even more dangerous than it is now." She stood, allowing her gaze to roam over the trees, over the gentle landscape. "Looking around, I can hardly believe there *was* a war."

"That was my reaction."

"What's next, Elizabeth? Is there anything I'm supposed to do? Anyone I'm supposed to see?"

"Nothing official. Not yet. Koh will have lunch ready by now. I can give you an idea of what's expected while we eat. Unless you want to rest for awhile. You had a long flight."

"I slept most of the way. I am learning to sleep on planes." Jobina started back toward the house. "Do all Americans live so splendidly here?" she asked as they went inside.

"The Army takes good care of its generals. Its colonels too," Elizabeth added an instant later. "I didn't mean to suggest—"

"Oh, it's all right." Jobina laughed. "Our husbands have to be formal with each other. Military courtesy and all that. *We* can be ourselves."

"I was hoping we could." Elizabeth smiled. She was a pleasant, fair-haired woman in her late forties, less reserved than her husband and far more humorous. The daughter of a retired Army major, she was accustomed to the strictures of Army life, to the protocols. "I was hoping we could relax."

"Is your house near here?"

"About ten minutes away. I'm still shaky on directions, and naturally all the road signs are in Japanese. You have a car assigned to you, Jobina. Koh will drive you where you want to go. He speaks English. Just don't talk too fast . . . Oh, there you are, Koh," she said as the houseman appeared in the hall. "Jobina, this is Koh. He'll look after things for you . . . This is Mrs. Campbell, the general's wife."

"Mrs. Campbell," Koh replied with a bow. "Miko serves lunch now."

"Miko?"

"His wife," Elizabeth explained. "You have two in help, and the gardener comes every Friday. The idea is to keep up the property so we can return it to the Japanese in good order. That's what the Pentagon briefing book says. I have a copy for you."

"I thought you might. What would we do without our briefing books?"

"Make a lot of mistakes."

"Officers' wives?" Jobina laughed again. "Never! Do the books have a language section? I don't know a single word of Japanese."

"You'll pick up what you need. I have an extra phrase book."

"Elizabeth, you are a gem!"

Indeed Jobina was grateful to have Elizabeth's advice. She was grateful to have companionship too, for as time passed, she felt the isolation, the loneliness of a post so far from home. She had her official duties—entertaining and often counseling the wives of junior officers, visiting wounded soldiers at the military hospital in Tokyo, visiting clinics and craft centers and schools. She had her own work—studying the scores of company reports sent from America and Europe, dictating lengthy replies to the Nisei secretary she had hired. She had occasional excursions with Elizabeth—to the Ginza, to the ancient temples of Kyoto and Nagoya, to the Kabuki. But no matter how busy her schedule, she was lonely.

She tried to arrange her schedule around the daily mail delivery, for she treasured any word of home. Irene wrote every week, long chatty letters that made her smile. Caroline's letters were briefer, though they always included notes from Daisy and Sam, and sometimes included snapshots of Matthew and Jill. Emile's letters were filled with cheer, with happy news of his infant grandson. George's letters were filled with business news and passing accounts of recent events; amongst them, the death of Martin Chadway.

These letters meant a great deal to Jobina, but Mark's letters, few as they were, meant everything. She followed the progress of the war and all her old fears returned. Once more there was a sick, hollow feeling in her heart;

once more her dreams were nightmares of blood-soaked battlefields and death. "*Mark,*" she would call from the depths of her tortured sleep, waking to find her pillow wet with tears.

It was November before she saw him again. They had a week together, a week of quiet dinners and moonlit strolls in the gardens and love. They had two days between Christmas and New Year's, the last days they would have together for some time. "I could move to Seoul," Jobina said now, putting a heavy sweater in Mark's traveling bag. "I would be closer."

"Seoul is nothing more than GIs and bar girls and street kids old before their time. It's no place for you."

"I would be closer."

"Distance isn't the problem, Jo. Time is. I told you there's a big push coming. I won't be making any side trips for awhile, not to Tokyo or Seoul."

"I've heard rumors of a truce."

"That's all they are, rumors. They circulate in every war. Don't get your hopes up. The Chinese are pouring troops into the North . . . Don't believe anything you hear unless you hear it from Armed Forces Radio."

Jobina went to the dresser and opened a drawer. "Irene sent you those warm socks hunters wear," she said. "I'll put them in your bag, if I can find room. You need a bigger bag."

"I need to pay attention when I'm packing. I was in a hurry, Bean. I threw all my stuff in without looking."

"Yes, I . . ." She paused, lifting a pair of field glasses to the light. Her heart began to thump, for she saw a bullet embedded in the shattered frame. "Mark . . .

530

Mark, what's this?"

"What's what?" He stood. He strode across the room, peering over Jobina's shoulder. "It's the damndest story," he said with a laugh. "We were driving back from a MASH unit. We had a flat. While the sergeant was changing the tire, I was scanning the terrain. I heard the shot. I didn't see the bullet until I picked myself up off the ground. Sniper fire. The woods around there are perfect cover for snipers."

"You might have been killed," Jobina said, shock and anger mingling in her amber eyes. "How can you laugh about a thing like that?"

"I'm sorry, Jo," Mark replied quietly. "I was thoughtless. In my view it was just a damned peculiar incident. I know in your view it's much more. I'm sorry."

"A damned peculiar incident! My God!"

"Jo, that sniper was hopelessly inept. He hit the jeep. He hit the flag. He hit every tree along the road. He didn't come close to me."

"Didn't come close?" she asked, holding up the glasses, then flinging them away. "My God!"

"Jo . . . Jo, where are you going?" Mark followed after her, catching her at the door in two long strides. "Jo, I said I was sorry and I am. You must understand that when a man is regular Army, when he's been through combat, he sees things differently. I don't like being shot at, for Christ's sake, but it happens. And when it happens this way, it's not even worth thinking about."

"I *hate* the Army."

"I know, darling."

Jobina glanced up, searching Mark's face. "You do?"

"Of course I do. But we have our place in the scheme of things. Without the military, we might all be speaking German now, or Japanese. When there is a genuine threat, the military responds."

"What is the genuine threat in Korea? Why can't we give them arms and money and let them fight it out themselves? Why do we have to *be* here?"

"I don't make those decisions, Jo. I don't always agree with the decisions that are made . . . I was at that MASH unit to visit some of the men from my division. One of them was a nineteen-year-old private who had lost his leg. I was too late to visit the private's best buddy. He had already died. Another nineteen-year-old. It wasn't my first visit to a MASH. It wasn't my last. That's what war is, Jo. Should we be in this war? I honestly don't know. But we *are* in it and we're in it to win. A failed sniper attack is the least of my concerns. I have to think about the kids who are doing all the fighting and dying."

Jobina put her arms around Mark and gazed into his eyes. "It's my turn to apologize," she said. "I don't mean to be selfish. Fear brings out the worst in me."

"There is no worst in you, Jo. Except perhaps that you worry too much. I'll be all right. I'm pretty good at what I do, you know."

"Oh, you're good at everything."

"More, tell me more," Mark replied with a broad smile.

"I can't. You have a plane to catch. I'll finish packing your bag. Rose sent a tin of chocolate chip cookies. If they've gone stale, you can throw them at snipers."

"That's the spirit!" Mark laughed. "That's my Bean."

* * *

Another Christmas passed, another New Year's, and still the war dragged on. Jobina called it the war of the hills, for there was Pork Chop Hill and Christmas Hill and Dagmar, named after a curvaceous American television personality. There were hills named simply by numbers, endless hills that were taken and then lost and then retaken again. Casualties were heavy on both sides. Bombing raids destroyed cities and peasant villages alike, sending vast streams of displaced Koreans to makeshift shelters in fields and woodland clearings. Aid Stations and MASH units were inundated with the wounded. At the military hospital in Tokyo, almost every bed was filled. "We have a USO show coming next week," Jobina said to Elizabeth one sunny day in 1953. "Notices were distributed around the hospital this morning. The men were so happy. You should have seen their smiles. Some of them are blind, some of them are crippled, and they were smiling. It made me cry."

"There are rumors of progress in the peace talks. Have you heard?"

"Peace talks! It took them six months to decide on the shape of the conference table . . . My hopes have been raised too many times, Elizabeth. I just wish there were some clue in Mark's letters. His letters are always the same. Always bright and funny no matter how the war is going. They must teach letter writing at West Point."

"Could be. Gerald is that way also. I get more information from *Stars & Stripes* than I get from him. That reminds me. Do you want to do that interview with them? They'd like a general's wife."

"Not this general's wife," Jobina replied. "I worry about saying the wrong thing. Lofty ideals aside, I'm no fan of this war, or this police action, or whatever it is. I'll do anything I can for the men, but the rest of it . . ." She turned suddenly, walking over to the radio. "They're playing ''S Wonderful.'" She smiled. "That's our song. Imagine hearing our song in Japan . . . I wonder where Mark is now."

"It's best not to wonder," Elizabeth said when the song ended. "Come look at the gorgeous silk I bought. I bought ten yards. God knows what I'm going to do with it, but I couldn't resist."

"The color is lovely. Here, let me see . . . Oh, it *is* gorgeous, Elizabeth. It is from that tiny shop on the Ginza? I bought the kimonos there. I bought kimonos for *every*one. I'll need an extra trunk to hold all the things I bought over here. The porcelains and the jade. The *pearls*. I hate to think what I've spent on pearls. But my daughter told me not to come back without them."

"That's the advantage of having a son. The only thing Chip wants from Japan is a Samurai sword. Of course he would, being in military school. The Army tradition continues."

"Are you pleased?"

"I'm resigned, Jobina. There's still time for him to change his mind. I doubt he will. Chip is already looking ahead to the Point. And with Gerald's enthusiastic approval."

Jobina was about to reply when her attention was once again drawn to the radio. "They're reporting from Panmunjom," she said.

"Panmunjom. The peace talks."

"If this is another false alarm, I'll scream." The two

women were silent then, listening as the Armed Forces announcer came on the air. A moment later they were hugging, jumping around like schoolgirls, for the cease-fire was official. The war was over at last. "It's over!" Jobina cried, tears filling her eyes. "It's over!"

"Is that the plane, Mom?" Fourteen-year-old Sam asked, pressing his nose to the wide terminal window. "Is that it? Gosh, it's big. Look how big it is, Daisy."

"Oh, it's just a plane. A silly old plane."

"What's silly about it?"

"You make such a fuss. That's what."

"That's enough, you two," Caroline said. She reached her hand out, smoothing Daisy's long golden hair. "Can't you two ever agree on anything?" She smiled. "You were squabbling the day Grandmama left and you're still at it."

"Because he's silly, Mommy."

"Am not."

"Are so."

"The plane is landing, kids."

Sam and Daisy watched, moving closer together as the plane roared to a stop. They whispered to each other, one of them beginning a sentence, the other finishing it. "Grandmama!" they chorused when the first passengers began disembarking from the plane.

Caroline bent to her children, her hands resting lightly on their shoulders. "Behave yourselves now," she said. "Mind your manners."

"We will," they chorused again.

It was some moments before Caroline glimpsed Mark

and Jobina. "Don't they look wonderful," she murmured, for she had almost forgotten what a beautiful couple they were. Hand in hand they walked across the tarmac—Jobina wearing a coat and hat of sparkling yellow, Mark wearing his dress uniform emblazoned with medals and decorations. They were utterly radiant, so radiant that light seemed to fall from them. "Over here, Mama," Caroline called.

An airline attendant came forward. He opened the gate and the twins burst through. "Grandmama!" they shouted, racing ahead. "Grandpapa!"

Jobina flung her arms wide, gathering the twins to her. "My darlings are so grown up," she sniffled. "I missed you so much . . . Oh, it's a lovely homecoming."

"What about me?" Mark laughed. "Where are my hugs and kisses?"

"Grandpapa!" Daisy raced into his arms. "Grandpapa, did you miss me?"

"I certainly did. You and Sam. Are you too old for hugs, Sam? How about a handshake instead?"

Sam, with all the dignity of his fourteen years, clasped Mark's hand. "Did you get more medals?" he asked. "Did you kill any Reds?"

"There will be no talk of killing, young man," Jobina said.

"But Grandpapa is a *hero.*"

"Of course he is. We're all very proud of Grandpapa." Jobina looked up to see Caroline standing a few steps off to the side. "Darling," she said, embracing her daughter. "I missed you. I can't tell you how much . . . You've cut your hair. A pageboy, is it?"

"Do you like it, Mama? Ian was furious."

"It's charming. You're lovelier than ever, Caroline." Jobina glanced around. "Where are Matthew and Jill?"

"Oh, Matthew has a cold and Jill is a little sniffly. Nothing serious, but Miss Pym wanted to keep them indoors. Mark," she smiled, kissing his cheek, "welcome home. I hope you're home to stay."

"If the fates are kind."

"Never mind the fates," Jobina said. She linked her arm in his, gazing into his brilliant blue eyes. "We're home to stay."

Chapter Twenty-Four

"Twenty years," Jobina said on a cool autumn evening in 1959. "I can't believe Mark and I have been married for twenty years. Do you remember that sweet little church in Connecticut, Irene?"

"I remember everything. What a joyous wedding day it was."

"It was the twins' christening day also."

"Where does the time go, Jobina? Nowhere near you, I see. You look better each year. And younger. I'm positively green with envy."

"You are not." She took Irene's hand, leading her to the dressing table. "Look in the mirror," she said. "Look at us side by side. Not bad, for a couple of old broads."

"*Old broads?* Oh, you got that from Sam. He was going through his Frank Sinatra ring-a-ding-ding phase, wasn't he? Every female under thirty was 'baby,' every female over thirty was 'a sweet old broad.' Thank goodness Ian had a talk with him!"

"I thought it was funny."

"Well"—Irene laughed—"to be truthful, so did I.

George was horrified, of course. Poor George, he finds this younger generation quite baffling. The swingers. Is that what they're called? And then the Beats in those dark Greenwich Village coffeehouses. I confess I am sometimes baffled myself."

"Each generation has its own twist, Irene. Flappers, bobby-soxers, Beats. I can hardly wait to see what the Sixties bring."

"At the moment, I'm more interested in tonight. You haven't told me who is coming."

"Everyone. Emile and Helen. Billy and his family. The Sisks and the Boltons and the Claymores. Jordy and Clair are in from Europe with their children. They'll be here. The Fryes will be here. The Warners. Rose and Albert are coming from Staten Island. And there's our whole brood, Caroline and Ian and the grandchildren. And Miss Pym . . . Have I left anyone out? We planned a family party, Irene."

"I am dying to know what you got Mark. No more secrets. Tell me."

"It's a surprise," Jobina said, her eyes twinkling. "Actually I have two surprises for tonight. I'm saving them for just the right moment. But I'll show you my gown," she added, disappearing into her dressing room. "Ready?"

"Ready."

"What do you think?" she asked, draping her new gown across the bed. It was an elegant creation, the Empire style bodice of rich black velvet, the skirt voluminous black taffeta. "Isn't it wonderful! It's a

Givenchy. It cost the moon, but I don't care. I'm going to wear my diamond butterflies and diamond drop earrings. What do you think?"

"I'm speechless. It's absolutely *marvelous*, Jobina. Such a deep black. So perfect for your skin. Mark will be *dazzled*."

"That's the idea. Come help me dress. It's getting late."

"First tell me what you got Mark."

"It's a surprise, Irene."

"I promise not to breathe a word."

"Well . . . all right, but not a word . . . Later this evening a shiny new Jaguar is going to appear in the driveway. A shiny new black Jaguar with a giant bow."

"A Jaguar! How exciting, Jobina! I want to be there to see Mark's face. He'll be thrilled."

"That isn't the real present. The *real* present is two tickets to Zinbruck. We always said we would go back. Somehow we never did. Now is the time. A second honeymoon. I'm so happy I could cry."

"Have you told Jobina yet?" George asked.

"No, I haven't," Mark replied. "And be careful you don't let anything slip. I've had to make some difficult decisions in my life, but this . . . I frankly haven't found the right words. There are no right words. You know how Jo feels."

"You don't seem very pleased yourself."

"I'm not. I think it's a terrible mistake. Let's drop the

subject, George. Nothing must interfere with Jo's party. Nothing."

"I understand."

Mark crossed the hall and knocked on the door. "Jo," he called, "our guests are here."

She threw open the door and smiled as she gazed upon her husband. He was so handsome in his dinner jacket and black tie, and the silver streaking his temples only added to his good looks. "Happy anniversary, darling," she said.

"Happy anniversary, Jo." He stroked her glowing cheek, the soft curve of her chin. "You're impossibly beautiful tonight. You know that, don't you? I look at you and see a young girl."

"Flattery will get you everywhere."

"No, it's true." And to Mark it was indeed true. He looked at her and saw chestnut hair still shining and luxuriant. He saw the light that still danced in her lovely amber eyes. He saw the smile that still melted his heart. In twenty years he had not tired of her touch or her scent or the feel of her bare skin against his. "I love you, Bean."

"I love you."

"Shall we greet our guests?"

Jobina picked up her skirts. "Irene? We're going downstairs now."

The Thayers and the Campbells descended the stairs together. Jobina clung to Mark's arm, and on his arm she entered the glittering Doe Hill ballroom. There, amidst the candlelight and jasmine, amidst the sparkle of old silver and crystal and gold-traced china, she greeted her guests. "It's your night, Bean," Mark said as they circled the room.

"Our night, darling. They're even playing our song."

Mark and Jobina danced and drank champagne and nibbled caviar. They whispered to each other all through dinner. They held hands, listening in rapt silence while a succession of family and friends rose to offer toasts. Mark slipped a ring on Jobina's finger—a scalloped gold band inlaid with twenty small, perfect diamonds. There was a matching bracelet, the clasp a huge diamond solitaire.

At midnight Jobina took Mark outside to see his new car. "For you, darling," she said. "You like? Yes," she declared with a laugh, watching him rush toward the gleaming black Jaguar, "I see you do."

"Come on, Jo," he called. "Let's take a spin."

"We have guests."

"A quick spin then. Come on, Bean. How can you resist?"

"All right, a quick spin . . . Thank you, Noah," she said as he held the door open. "Has the other matter been taken care of?"

"In the glove compartment, ma'am."

"You're terrific!" Jobina turned, watching Mark fiddle with the many gauges and dials of the dashboard. "A boy and his Jaguar." She laughed again. "I suppose all men are boys when it comes to cars."

"This isn't just a *car*. It's a work of art. Listen to the purr," he said, starting the engine. "Hear it?"

"It's very nice."

"Nice? *Nice?* You have no appreciation for the finer things in life. Let me educate you, my child."

"Ready when you are, *mon général.*"

The car shot off into the moonlight night, gliding over the paths, responding instantly as Mark shifted gears. "A work of art," he said once more. "She's a beauty."

"She? Do I have a rival?"

"Never. Never in this world."

"Darling, we really can't drive too far."

"I know." Mark turned the car back toward the house. "Did you see that?" He laughed. "She turns on a dime. Wait until you see what she does on the open road . . . In case you haven't noticed, I'm crazy about your present. You're full of surprises, Bean."

"I have another surprise."

"Oh?" Mark slowed the car, parking it at the end of the driveway. "Am I supposed to guess?"

"Open the glove compartment . . . That's right. Now open the envelope . . . Well?" Jobina asked with a bright smile. "Are you surprised?"

"Zinbruck," Mark replied quietly, staring at the airline tickets, at the letter from Herr Schmidt's inn. "Jo, I had no idea."

"Isn't it wonderful? A second honeymoon! All the arrangements are made. Next month we'll be in the Alps, playing in . . ." Her voice trailed away, for she saw Mark's troubled expression. "What's wrong, darling? I thought you would be happy."

"Jo, I have something to tell you. I didn't want to tell

you tonight. I hoped—"

"Tell me what?"

Mark gazed at Jobina. He gazed into her wide, anxious eyes and it was a moment before he could speak. "There's no way to make this easy," he said. "I'm sorry, Jo, but I won't be here next month. Nor will I be in Zinbruck. I'm being sent to Vietnam."

"You're teasing me."

"I wish to God I were. It's official now. I leave in three weeks. Orders."

Slowly, the color drained from Jobina's face. Her lips parted. Over and over again she shook her head. "I don't believe it," she cried. "I refuse to believe it. Are you telling me you're going off to another war?"

"Not to war. We'll be serving as military advisors to the Diem government. Advisors, Jo. There are no American combat troops in Vietnam."

"*Yet.* It's only a matter of time, isn't it?"

"I can't predict the future and neither can you."

A cry escaped Jobina's throat. She hurried out of the car, her skirts flying about her ankles as she ran along the path to the house. She felt Mark's restraining hand; in icy silence, she pushed it away. Oblivious now to the party swirling all around, she ran to the stairs.

Mark followed his wife up the curving rise of the staircase, past the grandfather clock gently striking the late hour, past the family portraits adorning the walls. There was a rustling of taffeta when Jobina reached the landing, but still she did not speak. He opened the bedroom door, stepping aside to let her enter. "Jo, we have to discuss this," he said, closing the door.

"There is nothing to discuss."

"There is *everything* to discuss."

"No."

Mark stopped, swinging on his heel, and from across the room he stared at her. His eyes flickered briefly, though his expression was impassive. "I understand how you feel, Jo."

"I doubt that very much."

"Can we sit down and talk like reasonable people?"

"How? *Your* idea of reason is three wars in less than twenty years. I understood World War II. I understood we had no choice. I didn't understand Korea. I certainly don't understand this. Once again we're going halfway around the world to fight Communism. That thousands of young men will die—that *you* might die—is irrelevant. We have our principles, after all."

"I told you there are no combat troops in Vietnam."

"*Yet.* I'm not a fool, Mark. I read the newspapers. I have even learned to read between the lines. Vietnam isn't so different from Korea. The Communist North against the South. Another civil war. I suppose it will be called a police action, just as Korea was. My God, America is becoming the world's policeman."

"We will be serving as advisors."

"Advisors! That's the way it starts. The way it ends is war. Haven't you had your fill of war by now?"

"As a matter of fact, I have," Mark replied.

"Well then?"

"I'm an Army officer, Jo. I go where I'm sent. It's

my duty."

"You've done your duty. What more do they want?"

"They want me to advise the Diem government."

"Diem! Another prince amongst dictators! It seems to me that if people had decent leaders, Communism would die a quick death."

"You know very well it isn't that simple."

"All right, it isn't that simple." Jobina turned. She parted the silken draperies, staring out at the moonlit grounds of Doe Hill. She watched the shadows deepen on the grass, on the winding paths to the stream. She heard the sound of laughter drifting up from the ballroom and she slammed the window shut. "Life isn't simple either, Mark," she said. "We're given only so much time, only so much luck. Whatever we have left, belongs to us . . . not to another war."

Mark went to Jobina and clasped her hand in his. "I didn't ask for this assignment," he said quietly. "I didn't want it. But I have my orders."

"And you're not sorry."

"Jo, how can you think that?"

"I don't know what to think anymore. I keep deluding myself. I should have seen this coming when you got your promotion."

"One thing has nothing to do with the other."

"They seduce you with stars."

"No one's seduced me, Jo," Mark replied, a brief, amused smile lighting his eyes. "For the record, I happen to believe that American involvement over there will fuel the fires. I believe it's a mistake. I said so at every opportunity. Eisenhower happens to believe otherwise. It's his decision. Whether I agree with his decision or not, he's still the President. That means I go to Vietnam."

"If you go, you'll go alone."

"Jo—"

"I'm serious, Mark."

"You once said you would follow me to the ends of the earth. Do you remember?"

"To the ends of the earth, but *not* into another war. If they send you to Timbuktu, if they send you to the moon, I'll be there. I won't be in Vietnam. I've had enough of nightmares and trembling and field glasses with bullets in them. I won't be a part of it, Mark. I can't."

"You're asking me to make a choice."

Jobina was silent. She felt the pounding of her heart, the sick churning of her stomach. She put her hand to her head, for suddenly the room seemed to darken. After a moment she walked away, sinking into a chair. "I can't go through another war," she said, her voice hardly more than a whisper. "I can't. We have a life together, Mark. A wonderful life. I cherish every moment. I won't help you risk what we have for some abstract principle, no matter how noble it might be."

Mark paced the room, his head bent, his hands clasped loosely behind his back. All the light was gone from his eyes now; now there was only pain. He went to the hearth, taking up the poker and stirring the flames to a fury of orange and gold. "We have a problem, Jo," he said at last.

"Yes."

He flung the poker away and turned, fixing his gaze upon Jobina. "How do we solve it?"

She did not reply. She saw his pain and she knew it was as real, as deep, as her own. Wearily, she lifted her hand and let it fall. Tears glistened in her eyes and stung her dry, aching throat. "I'm sorry," she murmured.

Mark started toward her, stopping abruptly when a knock came at the door. "Yes?" he called, opening the door. "What is it, Irene?"

"I came to remind you that there's a party . . ." Irene saw Mark's stricken face. "What's happened?" she asked. "Jobina?" She rushed to her friend. "Jobina, what's happened?"

But Jobina could not speak. She put her head in her hands and wept.

"Won't you at least tell us where you're going, Grandmama?" Daisy asked. "We're all very worried. It's not like you to run off. And just a week before Christmas too. Mom and Dad have planned a lovely Christmas."

"I'm sure they have, darling," Jobina replied, snapping her suitcase shut. "You must forgive me. I don't feel very Christmasy this year."

"That's exactly why you should be with your family."

"My family here or my family in Vietnam?"

"Grandmama," Daisy said, turning Jobina toward her, "Grandpapa Mark did what he thought was right. He has all those ideas about duty and honor. They're more than

ideas. They're . . . beliefs. You wouldn't want him to go
against his beliefs?"

"Wouldn't I?"

"You know he loves you."

"Yes, I know. But don't forget his other love, the
Army." Jobina sighed. She sat at the edge of the bed,
shaking her head. "You're too young to understand,
Daisy," she said. "You haven't watched all the years slip
by, as I have. I kept telling myself the time would come
when I wouldn't have to share Mark with his other love.
And the time did come, tantalizing little snatches of time
between wars."

"Even if there's war again, it doesn't mean he'll be in
it."

"*You* don't know your grandpapa Mark. He'll be in it.
He won't leave a job unfinished. He never has and he
never will."

"What are you going to do?"

"I'm not thinking very clearly, darling. I have to get
away. I have to think whether to go to Vietnam after
all . . . or whether to try to make a life for myself here."

"*Without* Grandpapa?"

"I don't want to talk about it."

"Okay, but *where* are you going to do this thinking?"

Jobina smiled. "You're a persistent young woman,
aren't you?"

"Mom says I'm just like you. I'm so glad."

"You are the picture of your mother when she was
your age," Jobina said, and it was true. Daisy was twenty
now, her long golden hair spilling over her shoulders, her

wide blue eyes the color of the night sky. Her features, like Caroline's, were perfect, her gestures utterly graceful. "The resemblance is extraordinary."

"The physical resemblance. Mom says she was a gloomy gus when she was young."

"Well, she was a bit . . . distant. Your father changed all that."

"Daddy's sweet. Sam's like Daddy, only sillier. And now he's in love." Daisy laughed, wrinkling her nose. "He's always falling in love."

"Of course he is. You've had your share of romances too, as I recall. Whit Rawlings comes to mind."

"He was okay. Kind of stuffy though. I'm waiting for a man like Grandpapa Mark. He's so dashing and funny and dear."

"Finish college first."

"I plan to, Grandmama. After college, I plan to work at Jobina Inc. I want a career before I settle down. Or maybe I'll have a career and a family both. You did."

"It wasn't easy, darling. It wasn't easy being pulled in two different directions. Sometimes the .choices were painful."

"I know."

Jobina rose. "Help me finish packing," she said.

"Won't you tell me where you're going?"

"I'm not entirely sure myself. I'm going to the airport. I'll decide when I'm there."

"It just breaks my heart to have you and Grandpapa upset with each other."

"I don't want to talk about it, Daisy."

"But I can see how sad you are. Your eyes are still red from crying. And you're much too thin."

"Stop fussing, Daisy. I'm fine. Can you bring that large suitcase over here?"

"You're taking a lot of luggage, Grandmama."

"I don't know how long I will be gone. A week, a month, a year."

"You wouldn't stay away *that* long?"

"No, probably not. I don't know, darling. I told you I wasn't thinking very clearly."

Daisy gazed at Jobina and stroked her short chestnut hair. "Poor Grandmama," she murmured. "It's so sad."

"The suitcase?"

"Yes, coming."

Jobina was quiet as she finished packing her bags. She packed winter things and summer things, and at the last minute went to her closet for her sable coat. She peered into the wall safe and looked through her jewelry. With a sigh, she touched the diamond butterflies pinned to her beige wool dress. She reached into the safe then, removing the ring and bracelet that Mark had given her on their anniversary. She closed the safe and spun the lock. "I hope I haven't forgotten anything," she said.

"Mama?"

Jobina turned suddenly. "Caroline, what a nice surprise! I wasn't expecting you. What are you doing in New York?"

"Really, Mama, I couldn't let you go off to God knows where without saying good-bye. Or do we know where now?" Caroline asked, glancing at Daisy. "We don't."

She sighed. "Mama, this isn't like you."

"Daisy has already said that."

"Daisy was my last hope. She's usually quite expert at prying information out of people."

"There isn't any information, darling."

"We're very worried, Mama. Can't you at least stay with us through the holidays? Jill is playing Mary in the school Christmas pageant. Matthew is going to be a shepherd."

"I'm not up to Christmas this year. Try to understand."

"Oh, I do and I don't. Mostly I'm worried. How can you just leave? What about the company? Emile must be frantic."

"Heavens, Caroline, you know that Jordy is all but running things now. And doing an excellent job too. I can keep in touch by telephone. If that's your best argument—"

"It isn't, Mama. Mark is terribly upset. I don't blame him. Why won't you take his calls?"

Jobina's eyes darkened. She looked away, twisting her wedding band around. "I know you mean well," she replied quietly, "but I'd rather you didn't interfere."

"Well, he's been calling us. He's been calling Aunt Irene and the Sisks and *every*one. He even called *Rose*. The poor man is thousands and thousands of miles from home. He has to depend on us for information. Only we don't *have* information."

"That's enough, Caroline."

"I'm sorry, Mama. I wish . . . Is there *anything* I can

tell Mark?"

"No. I need to clear my mind, to think. When there is something to say, I'll say it myself . . . Darling, I really must be going."

"Wait," Caroline said, catching Jobina's hand. "I asked Molly to put tea on. You have time for tea, Mama. I drove in from Connecticut. I can drive you to the airport whenever you want . . . Please, Mama. We won't see you during Christmas. Let's make this sort of a Christmas tea, just the three of us."

Tears misted Jobina's eyes. "I'd like that," she said, linking arms with her daughter and granddaughter. "I'd like that very much."

The Alpine morning was clear and crisp, though lacy snowflakes danced on the wind. Christmas wreaths decorated little gingerbread cottages and rustic inns. Church bells rang, their joyous sound echoing over the hills, over the mountains that rose in pure white splendor against a sky of endless blue. Jobina gazed upon the landscape, calmed by its serene beauty, but not comforted. There is no comfort, she thought, no comfort without Mark.

Mark filled her thoughts as she walked the snowy paths of Zinbruck. Alone with her memories, she found her mind wandering back twenty-one years to the day she had met him. She recalled that day and all the days that had followed—days spent in New York and Washington and Germany and Japan. She recalled their days at Doe Hill and the silent, angry day when he had flown off to Vietnam. She walked for hours, trying to make sense of what had happened, trying to decide what to do. In her mind she heard his words from long ago: *You married a soldier, Bean.* She heard her own pledge: *To the ends of the earth, mon général.* She heard the words of so many years, words that wrote the story of their love. She sighed, lifting her eyes to the whitened treetops. *Mark,* her heart cried. *Oh, Mark.*

It was afternoon when she started back toward Herr Schmidt's inn. The snow was heavier now, and from somewhere in the distance came the voices of carolers. She brushed a tear away, sighing again. Her eyes blurry with tears, with snow, she did not see the tall figure coming closer. She jumped as a hand touched her shoulder. She spun around. "Mark!"

"Merry Christmas, Jo."

Her breath caught. Her heart began to pound, to race. She felt giddy, and for an instant she thought she was going to faint. "Mark, I don't understand," she gasped. "What are you . . . How did you know I would be here?"

"Where else would you be?"

"I almost went to London."

"We have no memories in London. Not yet."

"I don't know what to say."

"Are you glad to see me?"

"Of course I'm glad . . . but I'm still angry."

"Jo, I've flown halfway around the world to see you. Don't I get points for that?"

"Why did you come?"

"*Why?*" Mark laughed. "What an impossible female you are! What a beautiful, wonderful, impossible female!" He paused as his hand caressed Jobina's cheek, her mouth. "I missed you, darling," he said. "I want to be with you . . . today and tomorrow and all our tomorrows."

"That's what I want," she sniffled, melting into his arms. "I'll go to Vietnam, Mark. I'll go anywhere."

"Will you go to Doe Hill? I brought you a Christmas present, Jo. My retirement papers."

"Don't tease me."

"I'm not teasing," Mark replied quietly. "It's official. In sixty days I will be a *retired* lieutenant general. I may do some writing. I may do some teaching. Or I may take you on the longest honeymoon in the history of the world. Would you like that?"

Jobina's face was luminous. She was crying and laughing, shaking her head from side to side. "I can't believe it. Is it true? Really true?"

"The papers are in my pocket."

"But . . . But will you be happy, darling?"

Mark took Jobina's hand and strolled with her toward the inn. "I did a lot of thinking in Vietnam," he said. "There's no doubt war is coming, a war I can't support. Under the circumstances, I can't and won't send more kids off to die . . . But war or not, my decision would have been the same. I did a lot of thinking about us, Jo. About all the time we've lost, all the years. That's over now. I want us to be together always. You're my happiness, darling."

"Oh, Mark, I love you so much."

They stopped, looking long into each other's eyes. They touched. Snowflakes whirling and leaping around them, they kissed. "Tell me," Mark said when he was able to speak, "did you get our old room at the inn?"

"Our old room. It's just as I remembered it. Edelweiss and scrubbed cedar and a big feather bed."

"A big feather bed, eh?" Mark smiled, drawing Jobina's furs close about her. "I like the sound of that."

"I thought you might."

"Are you ready for a second honeymoon, Bean?"

"Ready when you are, *mon général.*"

THIS CHERISHED DREAM BY BARBARA HARRISON

'It's a man's world,' young Mary Kilburne had been told, 'and a woman could only find a place in it.' And find a place in it she did! Making her way to America's golden shores with nothing except a few pennies and her pride, the ambitious, chestnut-haired beauty was unwilling to give in to despair or concede to defeat. She was determined to work hard, to become rich, to rise above the Lower East Side squalor – even to give up a once-in-a-lifetime passion if it meant that she would succeed.

From the black mists of the moors to the elegance and grandeur of Sutton Place, from an insecure scullery maid to a poised, prominent empire builder, through two world wars and the Great Depression, Mary Kilburne sacrificed happiness, betrayed her own heart, but always fought for *This Cherished Dream*.

0 553 171852

PASSION'S PRICE by Barbara Harrison

Katie Gallagher was a survivor. Raised in the stifling poverty of New York's Hell's Kitchen, the golden-haired beauty quickly learned the value of money, the power of wealth, and the secrets of passion. Someday, she would have it all.

And as the nation recovered from the horrors of war, Katie struggled to make her fortune, to build an empire. In her ruthless search for success, there was little time for love – until she met millionaire Josh Thurston.

Suddenly her days were filled with dazzling triumphs, her nights with glorious rapture. But even the strong arms of her beloved could not protect Katie from the dark side of desire. For even the rich and beautiful must always pay . . . *Passion's Price*.

0 553 17208 5

A SELECTED LIST OF FINE TITLES AVAILABLE FROM BANTAM BOOKS

THE PRICES SHOWN BELOW WERE CORRECT AT THE TIME OF GOING TO PRESS. HOWEVER TRANSWORLD PUBLISHERS RESERVE THE RIGHT TO SHOW NEW RETAIL PRICES ON COVERS WHICH MAY DIFFER FROM THOSE PREVIOUSLY ADVERTISED IN THE TEXT OR ELSEWHERE.

☐	17172 0	Wild Swan	Celeste de Blasis	£3.95
☐	17255 2	Swan's Chance	Celeste de Blasis	£2.95
☐	17189 5	The Two Mrs Grenvilles	Domick Dunne	£2.95
☐	17240 9	The Alchemist	Kenneth Goddard	£2.95
☐	17354 5	Balefire	Kenneth Goddard	£2.50
☐	17205 0	Jealousies	Justine Harlowe	£2.95
☐	17185 2	This Cherished Dream	Barbara Harrison	£2.95
☐	17208 5	Passion's Price	Barbara Harrison	£2.95
☐	17165 8	Promises and Lies	Susanne Jaffe	£1.95
☐	17151 8	Scents	Johanna Kingsley	£2.95
☐	17207 7	Faces	Johanna Kingsley	£2.95
☐	17174 7	Mistral's Daughter	Judith Krantz	£2.95
☐	17242 5	I'll Take Manhattan	Judith Krantz	£3.95
☐	17389 8	Princess Daisy	Judith Krantz	£3.50
☐	17204 2	The Sicilian	Mario Puzo	£2.95
☐	17209 3	The Class	Erich Segal	£2.95
☐	17285 9	The Riding Officer	Richard Stuart Wood	£2.95
☐	17192 5	The Enchantress	Han Suyin	£2.95
☐	17150 X	Till Morning Comes	Han Suyin	£3.50

All these books are available at your bookshop or newsagent, or can be ordered direct from the publisher. Just tick the titles you want and fill in the form below.

TRANSWORLD READERS' SERVICE, 61–63 Uxbridge Road, Ealing, London, W5 5SA

Please send a cheque or postal order, not cash. All cheques and postal orders must be in £ sterling and made payable to Transworld Publishers Ltd.
Please allow cost of book(s) plus the following for postage and packing:

U.K./Republic of Ireland Customers:
Orders in excess of £5; no charge
Orders under £5; add 50p

Overseas Customers:
All orders; add £1.50

NAME (Block Letters) ....

ADDRESS ....

....